Dear Romance Reader:

This year Avon Books is celebrating the sixth anniversary of "The Avon Romance"—six years of historical romances of the highest quality by both new and established writers. Thanks to our terrific authors, our "ribbon books" are stronger and more exciting than ever before. And thanks to you, our loyal readers, our books continue to be a spectacular success!

"The Avon Romances" are just some of the fabulous novels in Avon Books' dazzling *Year of Romance*, bringing you month after month of top-notch romantic entertainment. How wonderful it is to escape for a few hours with romances by your favorite "leading ladies"—Shirlee Busbee, Karen Robards, and Johanna Lindsey. And how satisfying it is to discover in a new writer the talent that will make her a rising star.

Every month in 1988, Avon Books' *Year of Romance*, will be special because Avon Books believes that romance—the readers, the writers, and the books—deserves it!

Sweet Reading,

Susanne Jaffe
Editor-in-Chief

Ellen Edwards
Senior Editor

Other Books in
THE AVON ROMANCE Series

BELOVED ROGUE *by Penelope Williamson*
BOLD SURRENDER *by Judith E. French*
CHASE THE DAWN *by Jane Feather*
DARK DESIRES *by Nancy Moulton*
DEFIANT ANGEL *by Lisann St. Pierre*
PASSION FIRE *by Mallory Burgess*
UNTAMED GLORY *by Suzannah Davis*

Coming Soon

INNOCENT FIRE *by Brenda Joyce*
PRIMROSE *by Deborah Camp*

Avon Books are available at special quantity discounts for bulk purchases for sales promotions, premiums, fund raising or educational use. Special books, or book excerpts, can also be created to fit specific needs.

For details write or telephone the office of the Director of Special Markets, Avon Books, Dept. FP, 105 Madison Avenue, New York, New York 10016, 212-481-5653.

MAYO LUCAS

AVON BOOKS • NEW YORK

MATTERS OF THE HEART is an original publication of Avon Books.
This work has never before appeared in book form. This work is a novel.
Any similarity to actual persons or events is purely coincidental.

AVON BOOKS
A division of
The Hearst Corporation
105 Madison Avenue
New York, New York 10016

Copyright © 1988 by Mayo M. Lucas
Published by arrangement with the author
Library of Congress Catalog Card Number: 87-91451
ISBN: 0-380-75537-8

All rights reserved, which includes the right to reproduce this book or
portions thereof in any form whatsoever except as provided by the U.S.
Copyright Law. For information address Collier Associates, 2000 Flat
Run Road, Seaman, Ohio 45679.

First Avon Books Printing: May 1988

AVON TRADEMARK REG. U.S. PAT. OFF. AND IN OTHER COUNTRIES, MARCA
REGISTRADA, HECHO EN U.S.A.

Printed in the U.S.A.

K-R 10 9 8 7 6 5 4 3 2 1

Chapter 1

Baltimore, 1894

Loaded drays filled the narrow street, their drivers fighting for space with legs braced, neck veins straining, as they lashed their horses with leather and tongue. The occasional closed carriage picked its way among these heavily laden beasts with daintiness and care. This part of town was the working man's domain.

It was raining steadily now, the drops pocking the muddied cobbles. The sharp clatter of iron-rimmed wheels and hooves was drowned briefly beneath the nearby screech of a train whistle. Dark blooms of umbrellas had appeared, leaving only the drivers and shopboys visible as they rushed from errand to errand, aprons or caps marking their trade. They were too busy to be concerned that spring, a brash youth like themselves, was hurrying across the city.

Looking down on this scene from his third floor window of the Rushton Building was Nat Rushton himself. Worrying his small, gray mustache, he lifted blue eyes to focus on the plumes of smoke feathering the skyline. He began to count, as he always did, the number of buildings he either owned or had built, or both. Rushton Enterprises had come a long way from the tiny development company he had started just after the war. One of the biggest now, his was still only one of many rising conglomerates. Everywhere and with everyone there was a sense of urgency, the need to get it done today, yesterday. . . . The child that was Baltimore was growing, and all its fathers of industry labored to keep her clothed, fed, and happy.

A sudden explosion of curses drew his gaze back down to one of the daily collisions in the intersection, but his attention soon drifted, and he was no longer seeing the struggles on the street below. Instead, he was seeing a more private one—his own.

Power and time. He'd used them both over the years to get where he was, but things had changed. What a man started out doing for himself, he ended up doing for the future, for his sons, and his sons' sons. All those years of work couldn't have been for nothing. It had to be perpetuated. Power and time. . . . He still had the one, but the other was running out. At fifty-eight he could finally admit he wasn't going to live forever. His mouth twisted. Not unless those fancy doctors in Europe knew something he didn't.

He resumed his pacing, the blood-colored carpet muffling his steady tread. The dull patina of etched gold flashed briefly as he opened his watch again . . . three minutes until ten. Almost time.

Moving to sit behind his immense slab-of-mahogany desk, he rubbed thick knuckles up and down over cold metal vest buttons, his eyes bright beneath their shelf of bushy gray. It was always the same, this exhilaration when he was about to match wits with someone. The fact that it was his son in this case didn't matter at all. Nathan's tenacity pitted against his own carefully laid plans should prove an interesting contest—and knowing he was going to win only added to the fun of it.

He knew some would call him cruel for what he was about to do, but what other solution was there? Nathan was his one hope, always had been. That boy knew as much about the business as he did. He knew the markets, the people; he knew when and where to expand, and had built the construction arm of Rushton Enterprises into one of the biggest in the state. Nathan could have it all—if he didn't destroy himself first.

And there was the girl to think of, a girl who could have been his own if only he and Emily . . . Ah, well. That was a long time ago. And if he hadn't married for love, at least he'd married money. The love had come later, almost too late.

Just then, the sound of Nathan's voice penetrated the heavy oak door as he exchanged greetings with Henry, Nat's secretary. This is it, he thought, rising as the door opened to frame his son's tall, dark-haired figure. *Except for the blue eyes, he looks more like his mother all the time.* That sharp nose and full underlip were Meg's—God rest her soul—all over again.

The two men nodded to each other and shook hands. Without a word, the younger one reached into his dark suit jacket and produced a bank draft. Taking it with equal lack of comment, the father pointed to a chair, then sat down again himself.

Pretending not to see the gesture, Nathan went to lean casually against a windowsill. He was doing his best to look relaxed, but his collar felt too tight and his head felt too big. He knew he looked like hell. The fact that his father hadn't said as much disappointed him. Knowing how it irritated was what he liked best about drinking—and not having it brought up only cemented his feeling that something new was in the wind today.

He waved a hand to indicate the office in general. "Why such a formal meeting?"

"This is business and this is where I like to discuss business. Besides, I thought it might do you good to see the inside of a place where people actually work for a living."

Nathan took the barb about his three-day absence with a rueful smile. "That's a new policy, isn't it?" he asked, pointing to the bank draft being tucked into a drawer. "Replacing company losses out of personal funds?"

"In my day, there was no such thing as 'company losses.' They were called personal mistakes—" Nat stopped, biting off the rest of his lecture with obvious effort. "Let's just call this a sort of insurance against it ever happening again. I must admit though, this is the kind of thing I'd've expected from your brother, not you."

"The MacGruder project was mine, remember? Besides, I don't see where Teddy's done so badly."

Nat tucked in his chin with a snort. "You know as well as I do Teddy has no head for this business—nor for any other that I can see. Chasing skirts seems to be his only talent in life."

Nathan studied the toes of his boots to hide a sudden smile—he couldn't deny his brother had an abundance of charm when it came to the ladies. Indeed, he seemed to go through women like some went through eggs at breakfast. "Well, in that case," he said with a sigh, "I'd better go downstairs and see what I can do about getting things back on schedule."

"I'm glad to see you so eager to work for a change, but please—" he indicated the chair again, "sit down for a minute. There's something else I want to discuss with you."

By this time, Nathan's instincts for self-preservation were setting up a regular hum inside his head. *Careful*, they warned. *Be very, very careful.*

Accepting the invitation to sit, he did so only after he'd moved the chair around the corner of the desk.

Conversing across that empty expanse of mahogany always made him feel like a recalcitrant schoolboy in the headmaster's office. It was a disadvantage he didn't need, not with this man.

Nat reached for the teakwood case of cigars and placed it on the desk between them. The ritual of lighting up took several minutes as each man chose his cigar with all the care of one choosing his weapon on the field of honor, then sucked it rhythmically to fill the air with a blue haze of smoke he could squint through.

The noises filtering up from the street magnified the growing silence in the office.

Nathan knew this waiting game well. He'd had to play it often over the years, but today it stretched his frazzled nerves perilously thin. His latest attempt to wash away the world had left a nasty taste in his mouth, and the blood was still pounding behind his eyes. All he wanted was to go home and go to bed.

"Well?" he finally snapped.

"Fred Alton died."

"I'd heard. I'm sorry." When his father just nodded, he knew it was up to him to keep things moving. "How's his daughter?"

"Amanda? Oh, she's fine, just fine. A real trooper that one—and prettier than ever. Freddie made me her guardian, you know."

Nathan didn't know, but from the smile his question got, it was obvious he'd asked the right one. *Maybe now we'll get to the point.*

"Let's see . . . you'll be twenty-eight soon, won't you? You're not getting any younger, you know, and I've been waiting a long time for grandsons. A man my age likes to see his family growing up around him."

Letting out a pent-up breath, Nathan felt the knots

in his stomach begin to uncoil. So this was it. It was a familiar lecture—one that was almost overdue, in fact. Settling in for the siege, he told himself to remain calm. He wouldn't let this end up in a shouting match as it had so many other times. "There's always Teddy for that."

"That one'll only get me bastards."

Nathan frowned. The animosity between those two always made him uncomfortable. Not that he didn't understand it. . . .

"No, what you need is a wife," his father counseled.

"Maybe." The word was belied by its very tone.

"I'm serious. Ever since you've come home from the army it's been one bit of fluff after another. It's time you were married and settled down—and the day you say 'I do' this place becomes yours."

"That's not what you said when I wanted to marry Suzanne."

His father's face folded into lines of distaste. "She wasn't the one for you and you know it."

"And you certainly went out of your way to prove it, didn't you?" A muscle in his cheek twitched and the smile he offered was deliberately facetious. "But I'll shop around while you're gone this summer and see what else I can find."

"That won't be necessary."

"Oh?" A dark eyebrow arched. "And why not?"

"Yesterday evening I told Amanda that you and she would be getting married."

Nathan stared at him. "You told her *what?*"

"I told her," Nat repeated evenly, "the two of you would be getting married before I left for Europe on Saturday."

Nathan could only gape at the baldness of such a statement. What gall! What incredible gall—even for a man known for the trait. "Well, you can just *un*tell her! I don't need a wife picked out for me like I was some half-wit from the last century! I have no intention of marrying her—nor anyone else for that matter." Good God! Would he never be free to live his own life?

Father and son glared at each other for a long moment in a silent clash of wills.

"I'm not going to marry her."

"I'm afraid you have no choice."

So push was now coming to shove, was it? "One . . . always . . . has a choice."

Nat shifted the cigar to the other corner of his mouth and spoke around it. "Then let me put it this way: You won't like the alternatives."

Ready to get up and walk out at this point, Nathan reluctantly decided against it. If the old man thought he held a pat hand, he wanted to stay and see the cards. "And they are?" he asked quietly.

"You either marry the girl or I sell this place. You lose it all—your inheritance from me—everything."

"Sell it! To whom?"

"Wagner. Lock, stock, and barrel. He's been after me to sell for years—as well you know."

"I don't believe it. I don't believe you. You'd at least turn it over to Teddy, and we both know it."

"Bah! If I did that, this place would be reduced to rubble in less time than either of us would care to think about."

Despite his unwillingness to believe, Nathan was beginning to feel the first prick of alarm. "But why? Why marriage?"

"Because alone you're ruining your life."

"That's my business, isn't it?"

Nat's face puckered with emotion. "Only until it affects Rushton Enterprises! Then it's my business!"

He shook two meaty fists in the air. "I built her with *these* and I'll not see her destroyed by the only man capable of giving her a future when he's not throwing himself into a bottle! My God, what's happened to you, boy? You were the one I trusted, the one I depended on, and you're letting me down now when I need—" He banged a fist on the desk. "*Damn* that DuBell woman! Is she worth your future? That's what you're ruining. If you're so determined to become a drunkard, then give me a grandson to hand it all down to. This place deserves to have a future, by God! If I can't count on that from my own flesh and blood, I'll give it a new direction before I'm through!" He glared at his son a moment longer, then turned away, jamming his cigar into his mouth, and puffing away furiously.

Left staring at his father's immutable profile, Nathan unconsciously did the same with his own cigar. Dammit to hell! This couldn't be the end of it. He would not be backed into a corner like this. There had to be another way, if only he could think fast enough. If only . . . Suddenly, he was struck with so obvious a solution it was hard to hide the triumph he felt. "Then if selling out is what you're so determined to do," he said, "I'll buy it."

"I won't sell it to you."

The words were light and airy, without substance, yet they hit him with all the force of a sledge hammer and drove the air from his lungs. With a silent snarl, he erupted from his seat. Three strides took him to the window. Ripping up the sash, he flung his cigar into the street, and thrust his head out to gulp in great lungfuls of air.

Behind him, his father went on speaking almost as if to himself. "Best cure for a man's sorrow is to throw himself into his work, not a bottle. I should know, shouldn't I? How do you think I built all this in the first place?"

But Nathan wasn't listening. Something else had just occurred to him. Stiff-arming himself away from the sill, he whirled around. "Tell me this: How does Miss Alton feel about all these plans of yours?"

"She's a little unsure of her feelings right now, but she'll come around."

"Oh, come now. You mean to tell me she didn't jump at the chance for a husband and a fortune all trussed up and handed to her like a Christmas turkey?"

"She's not like that."

Nathan came over and leaned down, his face on a level with his father's. "They're *all* like that," he sneered. Spinning on his heel, he stalked to the door only to whip back and glare down the length of a finger he jabbed in his father's direction. "I promise you one thing: If you succeed in forcing this marriage—and I say *if*—I'll make that girl's life such hell you'll both be sorry."

Nat chewed the corner of his mustache as he contemplated the unexpected cruelty he saw in his son's face. This was the one thing he couldn't control and they both knew it. "She's had nothing to do with this," he assured his son quietly. "And I know you better than you think. You won't treat her badly because of me." Fervently, he hoped he wasn't wrong.

Throwing his arms wide, Nathan let them fall limp at his sides. "You're worse than I thought. If what you say is true, then you're ruthlessly throwing a lamb to a lion, expecting the lion to be 'decent' enough not to maul it!" Without another word, he wrenched open the door and slammed it behind him.

When the last crashing echo died away, Nat carefully placed his cigar aside and sat back, relaxed. So . . . the "lion" had roared just as expected. But then lions, he mused as a smile spread itself across his features, have been known to be tamed.

Amanda Alton looked up at the darkening sky and decided it was time she headed for home before Sophie started to worry and sent Joe out to find her. She was already going to get lectured for muddying her shoes and skirt in the tall grasses. No sense adding to it by being late.

All afternoon she'd stood by the window, fidgeting, watching the steady rain streak to the ground in cold gray needles. By the time it had slacked off to nothing more than a heavy mist, it was all she could do to call out her intention before grabbing a cloak and flying out the door. With no particular destination in mind, she'd absently let her feet follow the fence rows that separated the fields, her guardian's words repeating themselves like an internal metronome with each step: *married by Friday . . . married by Friday . . .*

The whole thing was preposterous. He couldn't possibly be serious, yet he certainly wasn't joking when he'd hung a fist from each lapel and said, "I like to think of myself as a good judge of character, and I think you and Nathan are ideally suited. You're just the sort he needs."

Flattering, of course, but she hadn't seen Nathan in years.

"But you do remember him, don't you?" he'd asked.

Remember him? Of course, she remembered him. Who could forget that crooked smile, or the way those dark brows of his seemed quirked in perpetual amusement? Yes, she remembered him—and felt the blush stain her cheeks as she'd answered. But what made him think Nathan wanted to marry her? And if he did, why didn't he ask her himself?

MATTERS OF THE HEART 11

Her guardian's smile had been knowing (either because of her blush or his own confidence; she couldn't tell which) when he assured her Nathan would marry her—and within the week.

She was horrified. Her father was hardly cold in his grave! Why couldn't it wait?

Making her feel like a rebellious child, Nat Rushton had admonished her with another smile. "I regret the rush, certainly, but be sensible, girl. You can't stay here. Your father left half a dozen liens against the place—one of which I hold myself. At eighteen, you're too old for a finishing school, so as your guardian, it's my job to find you a husband—which I have. Besides," he'd added with a sly wink, "Nathan's a very wealthy man in his own right. You'll want for nothing."

As if that made the difference!

"Since I'm leaving Saturday to join Penelope, my sister, in Europe," he went on, "I need this matter settled before I go. That's why I want the two of you married by Friday" . . . *married by Friday* . . . *married by Friday* . . .

Preposterous.

It was nearly dark when she rounded the corner of the old farmhouse and crossed its sagging, paint-bare porch.

Inside, she hurried to unbutton her soggy boots and toss them aside, wrinkling her nose at the way the wet, heavy hem of her blue wool skirt clung coldly to her ankles. The yellow glow from the kitchen and the smell of fat hanging in the air told her Sophie was busy with supper. If she hurried and changed, it was just possible she could avoid a lecture—or worse—one of Sophie's mustard plasters.

Heading for the stairs, she paused in front of the mirrored hall tree long enough to try and smooth some of the unruliness out of her damp hair. She was finally past the age of wishing it any color other than its fiery red, but could still find it in her heart to pray for a little less wayward activity.

Suddenly, Sophie's round, black face appeared behind her in the glass, startling her. For a big woman, Amanda thought, she could move as silently as a cat.

"You're jes' like your mama was at this age, always disappearin'. Where you been, child? There's company waitin' to see you, and jes' look at you! If you ain't a sight!" she scolded. "An' here that nice Mr. Rushton's come to see you."

"Again?" The sitting room was dark and there'd been no carriage out front. "Where?"

"No, no. Not that'n. This here's the young'n. I told him you was out, but he said he'd wait jes' the same." A gnarled finger pointed toward the study door. "Said he'd wait in there."

Amanda stared at the closed door across the hall and absently patted the woman's arm. "Thank you, Sophie . . . thank you." She should have expected this, so why did she feel so unprepared?

As the woman waddled away, Amanda turned back to the mirror. Her chignon was still frizzy and slightly askew, and her once-crisp collar was limp, the white cotton streaked with dark fuzz from her cloak. It was then she remembered her bare feet. Looking down, she wriggled her toes in dismay. Well, if he insisted on calling without notice, she thought with an emphatic nod at her reflection, he'd just have to take her as she was. Smoothing clammy palms down the sides of her skirt, she took a deep breath, and crossed the hall.

"Good evening, Mr. Rushton. I—" she stopped, her hand still on the knob.

Except for the red glow from the embers in the grate, the room was dark. Seconds later there was the

MATTERS OF THE HEART 13

sound of a lucifer being struck, and the shadows retreated to the corners of the room to reveal a stranger lighting the lamp on her father's desk.

Amanda stared. It was Nathan, and yet it wasn't—at least not the one she remembered. His dark, vested suit was finely made, but it fit him badly, as if he'd lost weight. The dark hair, the lean planes from cheekbone to jaw, and the square, clean-shaven chin were all unchanged, yet the face was different somehow. Gone was the laughter from those deep blue eyes, and so was the well-shaped mouth that once smiled so easily. In its place was a thin white line etched on either side by tiny little marks. As she watched, one heavy dark brow lifted in sardonic question.

"Shall I disrobe?"

Her eyes widened to dish-size. "I—I beg your pardon?"

"I asked if I should disrobe. You seemed so interested, I thought you might require a closer look."

Amanda could feel the heat in her cheeks spread all the way to the roots of her hair at the same time her already cold fingertips were turning to ice. "I'm sorry if I seemed rude, but you don't look—what I mean is, you seem so different from the last time I saw you, that's all."

When he merely lifted his other eyebrow, there was an awkward moment of silence. I was right, she thought, he doesn't want to marry me. *Then why is he here?*

"Yes, well . . ." She glanced with a brief spate of longing toward her favorite retreat, a deep, curtainless window seat between the two bookcases, but decided against it. Something told her this was no time for retreat. Quickly, hoping to hide her bare feet, she scooted past him to the other side of the desk and perched on the edge of the green leather chair. "I hadn't expected to walk into a darkened room, either," she added with a defensive lift of her chin.

Still standing, he made a brief apology, then resumed his seat. Suffering the beginning stages of a hangover, the light stabbed his eyes with prickly fingers, and he rubbed them tiredly. "I didn't realize it had grown dark," he lied. "I was thinking about something."

Contriving to look more casual than he felt, he slouched in the small, comb-back chair and rested an ankle across the other knee. Purposely, he said nothing while he studied her as closely as she had him.

He took a certain villainous pleasure in watching the girl's primness turn to uneasiness. So this is what stands between me and my inheritance, he thought, a little disappointed she wasn't the cheap-looking, hard-bitten type. He remembered she'd been a pretty child and full of promise, of course, but who would have expected her to ripen into womanhood so well?

Her auburn hair was a cloud of tiny curls that clung in damp tendrils to her forehead and cheeks, framing the square-jawed little face and setting off the deep green of her eyes. Everything about her, from the imperious arch of brow to the tilt of her nose, marked the Irish in her. He couldn't help wondering if she had a temper to match.

"So you're the one," he began without preamble. "Tell me, Miss Alton, how does it feel to be the means to an end?"

She looked startled. "Excuse me?"

"How does it feel," he repeated evenly, "to stand between a man and his future?" When she continued to stare at him without so much as a flicker of understanding, he leaned forward with a frown. "Come now, Miss Alton. Didn't my father explain this marriage was the price I'd have to pay for Rushton Enterprises?"

"No . . . no, he didn't," she whispered.

He nodded, his lips stretched thin. "Yes. It seems I've been remiss in supplying him with a string of grandchildren to bounce on his doting knee. Apparently, he's decided you're the perfect one to remedy this oversight on my part." He waited for the blush to finish with her cheeks before continuing. "But then, I suppose you wouldn't know anything about that, would you? I'll wager you're going to tell me you're just a poor innocent pawn in all this."

"Surely"—she paused to wet her lips with a tiny triangle of pink tongue—"surely you're not suggesting any of this was my idea?"

"Let's dispense with all the coyness, shall we?" His eyes were flinty hard. "Frankly, I don't care whose idea it was. I just want the matter finished and out of the way. Now, how much do you want?"

She stared at him stupidly. "How much?"

"Pay attention, Miss Alton. We're talking money. How much money do you want to drop your part in all this?"

"What are you talking about?" she bristled at last. "I don't want your money! You and your father seem to think your money solves everything!" She paused and squeezed her eyes shut in an obvious effort to control her rising temper. "Listen, Mr. Rushton. I don't know what you've been told, but so far, no one has even bothered to ask me what it is I'd like to do. My father wasn't even an hour in his grave before your father was telling me—Oh, never mind!" she finished with a weary sigh. "Just believe me, I do not want your money."

"Bravo, Miss Alton! Have you ever considered making a career of the stage? A very impressive act, but considering what I know of your situation here," he gave the cluttered room a disdainful once-over, then swept her with a look that was only slightly less insulting, "well . . ." He shrugged, and let the rest of his sentence trail off.

Her mouth pinched angrily. "My 'situation here,' as you call it, is no concern of yours, and regardless of what you or your father think, I am not, I repeat, *not* interested in your money!"

"I've never met a woman yet who wasn't."

"Then perhaps, sir," she said, fixing him with a small, superior smile, "you've been keeping the wrong kind of company."

The dark brows shot upwards. Just who was baiting whom?

They measured each other in silence for a full minute before he finally rose to his feet. It made the room seem smaller, and smaller still when he placed the flat of both palms on the desk and leaned his face down close to hers.

"And what would you know of the company I keep?" he asked with deceptive gentleness.

She swallowed convulsively. This was not the Nathan she remembered. This one frightened her into saying things she wouldn't ordinarily have dared just to cover that fear. "Well, I, uh—I don't actually . . . but then, I don't have to, do I, Mr. Rushton? The papers are full of your activities, so it's not hard to imagine the kind of company a—a 'jaded libertine' keeps," she added quickly, the term applied to him coming to mind and mouth before she had time to reconsider.

His eyes widened. "Well, well . . ." he breathed, a wolfish grin spreading across his face. "Jaded libertine, is it? What would an innocent child like you know of jaded libertines?"

MATTERS OF THE HEART

With a shaky little shrug, she came to her feet, disliking the advantage he had in towering over her. "Believe me, I'm not as innocent as I look." Good Lord! What on earth possessed her to say that?

His grin widened as he stepped around the desk, unconcerned that she skittered backwards to avoid him. "Maybe not," he conceded agreeably. "Why don't we find out?" He made a sudden grab for her, but like quicksilver, she avoided his outstretched arm and sidestepped him neatly to put the big leather chair between them.

Her heart pounding so hard she felt faint, she wrinkled her nose at the sudden fumes. "You're drunk!"

He made a lazy gesture with one hand. "I confess to having had a few libations before coming here—in celebration of our coming nuptials, of course—but that was hours ago and certainly not enough to affect a jaded libertine like me." Slowly, with each word, he had moved closer.

Retreating another step, Amanda was unnerved to feel the wall at her back. In one last attempt to control the situation, she pointed a none too steady finger at the door. "I think you—you'd better leave."

"What?" he exclaimed in mock horror. "Before we've even discussed the wedding plans?"

"Believe me, Mr. Rushton, there isn't going to be any wedding! I wouldn't marry you if—if being drawn and quartered was my only other option!"

Deliberately, he stretched out an arm and placed his hand on the wall behind her head. "Promise?" he asked softly.

A second earlier, her heart had hammered so violently she was sure the sound echoed off the walls. Now, it was as if everything—heart, breath, the flow of blood—was stilled. She watched, like a bird transfixed by the cobra's eye, as Nathan's lecherous grin was slowly replaced by an even more disturbing stare, a gaze so heated it carried with it a physical weight wherever his eyes touched her. He was so close her senses were filled with the combination of his cologne, sweat, and something indefinably male.

At the last moment, she tried to shy away, but his hands came down on her shoulders, pulling her roughly to him, crushing her against his chest. With one hand, he grabbed a handful of her hair and dragged her head backwards, his mouth coming down on hers, hot and demanding. She couldn't breathe, she couldn't think past each new sensation, and her mind splintered to keep up with them all. His hand stroked the length of her back, pressing her impossibly closer. When she felt the unexpected electricity of his tongue touching hers, her thoughts stuttered close to the edge of pure panic.

Nathan told himself he hadn't meant to kiss her, not really. But seeing her mouth so close beneath his own, the innocent lips so pink and trembling, it all happened before he could stop himself. Now, his own game was backfiring on him as he kissed her hungrily. Only the salty taste of tears brought him out of his headlong rush, and he pulled back, his hold on her relaxing.

It was the only opening she needed. With a shove just hard enough to knock him off balance, she ducked under his arm and bolted for the door. Just as she reached it, and gave the knob a desperate twist, Nathan's hand shot over her shoulder to hold it shut.

She whirled to do battle, but blinded by her own tears, she couldn't even defend herself from the hard hands that clamped both her wrists. "Take your hands off me, you—you—you have no right! *No right!*" she spat, trying to wrench herself free from the iron grip. "Let me go!"

Even as he struggled to protect himself, Nathan

regretted his heavy-handed tactics and wanted to let her go, but was afraid she'd bring the house down around his ears before he could explain. Staring down the barrel of a gun wouldn't exactly strengthen his position. He tried to apologize, but his words went unheard as she continued to heap a mountain of coals upon his head.

Finally, exhausted and out of epithets to hurl, she fell silent, her chest heaving.

"I'm sorry," he said again, at last releasing her wrists to give her shoulders a small, emphatic shake.

It was then they both became aware of someone knocking at the door. "'Manda?" Sophie called for the second time. "'Manda, you all right?"

Quickly, Nathan pulled Amanda over to the combback chair and pushed her into it just as the door opened and the woman's head poked into view.

Frowning at Amanda's tear-stained face, she shoved the door wide and planted her sizable bulk firmly inside the room, hands on her calicoed hips. "You all right, Missy?"

"She's fine, fine," Nathan spoke up quickly. "She just . . . misunderstood something I . . . something I said. That's all. Very minor." His smile didn't even feel right to him. *But don't stop now, old boy.* "Why don't you bring in some tea or something? That'll fix her up." He clapped his hands together and rubbed them heartily. "I know I could sure use some. How about you, Amanda?"

Amanda glared up at him, and Sophie tilted her head suspiciously.

"Is that what you want, Miss Amanda? You want I should bring in the 'freshments now?" She was asking the girl, but she never removed her cold stare from Nathan's face. It was a look that, had he been many years younger, would have made the sweat pop out on his brow.

Amanda sniffed, childlike, and rubbed the heels of both hands across her eyes. "I—I suppose so," she grumbled.

Sophie nodded, adding to no one in particular, "My husband, Joe, he's in the barn mendin' harness . . . old shotgun across his knees. Guess I'll call him in for supper now." Before she left the room she stopped to push the door as wide open as it would go.

The minute she was out of sight, Amanda shot to her feet and prodded his chest with a forefinger. "I want you out of here!" she hissed.

In an effort to calm her down, Nathan made the mistake of putting his hands on her shoulders again. Furiously, she shook him off.

"Out!"

Agitated, he ran a hand through his hair and reached over for the brandy decanter on the desk. Pouring a small amount in one of the glasses beside it, he handed it to her with the command "Drink!"

She shook her head, blurring its fiery aura.

"Drink it."

"I don't want any."

"I said drink it!"

"No!" she screeched, and grabbing the glass, flung it against the wall above the fireplace, where it smashed into a thousand silvery pieces. Both of them stared at the amber rivulets running down the wall onto the mantle, then she dropped back into her chair with a fresh sob.

He was exasperated. "Look! I said I was sorry, and I realize—"

"Sorry!" Her voice was shrill. "Is that all you can say? *Sorry?*"

"No, that isn't all I can say, but you keep interrupting me before I can explain!"

"There's nothing to explain." She sniffed. "You're a bully."

Heaving a sigh, Nathan leaned tiredly against the corner of the desk. "I'm sorry," he repeated again, offering her his handkerchief, an offer she pointedly refused by producing one of her own from inside a sleeve. He couldn't blame her for being upset. He'd treated her badly with no better excuse than his own frustration—he certainly hadn't meant to keep the threat he'd made to his father.

"Believe me, I'm not usually so boorish, Amanda. It's just that I didn't know what else to do. I thought, maybe, if you disliked me enough—"

"Well, you certainly succeeded there!"

"I thought if you disliked me *enough*, you'd refuse to marry me and that would be the end of it."

Wiping her eyes one last time, she began to refold the neatly embroidered square. "So you tried to buy me."

"Buy you *off*," he corrected with a smile. "If I were to 'buy' you, it would be for an entirely different purpose than to have you leave town." By her suspicious stare, he could tell she wasn't sure if she'd been insulted or not. Gad! he thought. What an innocent.

She finally waved away his words. "Yes, well . . . you forget one thing, though. As your father's ward, and dependent upon him, I'm hardly in a position to refuse much of anything."

"But that's just it! If you—Oh, never mind." Jamming his hands deep in his pockets, he leaned his head back and stared up at the ceiling. "God! but this has been one of the worst weeks of my life!"

"Mine, too."

Nathan dropped his chin to his chest. Those simple

words did more to make him feel the cad than all the ranting accusations in the world. Here the girl's father had just died, and he was making noises about how difficult his week had been. It was a sobering thought to realize he could behave just like his father at times.

The rattle of china signaled the approach of Sophie, and Nathan surprised both women by meeting her at the door and relieving her of the tray. With a charming smile, he closed the door firmly in her face and strode back to the desk with the tray. Setting the cups in their saucers, he began to pour the steaming brew.

Amanda had risen, but now sank back into her chair, captivated by the alien sight of a man's large, tanned fingers adroitly handling the fragile china.

Looking down at her, he raised a brow with each thing he offered as he prepared her cup. Sugar? Cream? Lemon slice? She shook her head to all but the cream, and only after he'd handed her the cup did he speak. "Amanda . . . I am sorry about your father."

She acknowledged him with a nod but didn't say anything. It was not something she wanted to talk about, and certainly not with this man. For the moment, she would much rather watch as he continued to drop lump after lump of sugar into his own cup. When he looked up and saw her watching him, he hastily began to stir the stuff, and finally, with a great air of satisfaction, brought the cup to his lips. When he made the expected face, she couldn't help giggling. "You don't drink tea, do you, Mr. Rushton?"

Embarrassed, he put the cup down. "No," he admitted, easing some of the tension between them with an answering smile, "but don't you think you should make it 'Nathan' again?"

She felt the pleasure warm her face. "I was beginning to think you'd forgotten we'd ever met before."

"What an ungentlemanly thing to do." He threw up

his hands. "I know, I know. I'm no gentleman—at least not tonight." Folding his arms, he grew serious again. "I hope you don't think there's anything personal in it when I say I don't want to get married."

Amanda told herself the plummeting feeling in the pit of her stomach was just the tea going down. "No, of course not."

"I don't want to marry anyone right now."

"Oh, me either."

"No?" He seemed surprised. "Well, it's too bad you weren't after my money. It could have made things a whole lot easier."

"How?"

"It would have proven my father wrong about you. Maybe then he wouldn't insist I marry you."

She made a great show of indifference, but the china rattled in her hand. "Is he insisting?"

"He says he'll sell Rushton Enterprises lock, stock, and barrel if I don't."

Studying him, she was still trying to reconcile this grim-faced stranger with the happy, smiling man she had once known. "Would he really do something like that?"

"That's just it, I don't know. But it's certainly not a gamble I'm prepared to take."

The china rattled louder and she had to set the cup down before she spilled tea all over the place. Standing up, she went to sit in the carpet-cushioned window seat. Carefully tucking her feet beneath the still damp hem of her skirt, she pulled her knees up and rested her chin. "So what will you do?"

Abruptly, he got to his feet. "I don't know! I've been asking myself that question all day." Pacing about the small room, he began touching this, poking that. "Don't you have any family at all? Somewhere?"

"No."

"Well"—he threw his hands wide and let them drop—"what do you want to do?"

"Me?" Oddly content in his company now that he was no longer the stalking predator, the question took her by surprise. She could hardly tell him she'd never wanted much beyond a home and a family. There was no way of knowing how he'd take it.

"Don't turn spineless on me now," he snapped. "You said nobody had bothered to ask you what you wanted. Well, now I'm asking. What is it you want to do?"

She rubbed her forehead. Suddenly, she was so tired, so weary of this whole situation. "I don't know. To have things back the way they were, I suppose."

"Yes . . . I can see why you would. But things change, Amanda."

The quiet sympathy in his voice surprised her and she had to look away, the tears in her eyes having nothing to do with anger this time. It was so unfair, she thought, all of it. "Perhaps . . . perhaps if I talked to your father."

He had been playing with a small globe on one of the bookshelves, spinning it faster and faster, but when she looked up, his fingers had brought the whirling sphere to a halt and he was grinning at her.

Her chin came off her knees. "What's so funny?"

"You. Or more precisely"—he pointed—"your toes."

"Oh!" Her bare feet were, indeed, poking out from beneath the hem of her skirt. Hastily, she tucked them out of sight again.

"You'd really do that?"

She frowned, flustered. "Do what?"

"Talk to my father?"

"Yes, of course. If you think it might do some good."

MATTERS OF THE HEART 25

His shrug was expressive. "One can never tell with him, but it's worth a try, I suppose."

Now that there was nothing more to be accomplished, he seemed ill at ease. "Well . . ." He leaned over and scooped his brown felt derby off the desk.

Unfolding herself from the window seat, she returned the uncertain smile. "Yes, well . . . Until tomorrow, then? After I talk to your father?"

He nodded. "Until tomorrow. I'll be in my office."

Together they walked to the front door in silence.

When he was halfway across the threshold, he looked back over his shoulder at her with a one-eyed squint. "Drawn and quartered, eh?"

Piqued by the mockery she suspected behind those dark lashes, she gave him a smile of utter coolness. "What's the matter, Mr. Rushton? Is it so hard to believe there exists a female who can resist you?"

After a thoughtful pursing of the lips, his only answer was a ghost of his old crooked grin. "Good luck tomorrow."

"Thanks. Keep your fingers crossed."

He held them up.

"'Bye."

"'Bye."

Pushing the door closed behind him, Amanda leaned against it, aware suddenly that she was trembling from head to foot. How could the world have gone so crazy in just a few short weeks? "Well, child?" It was Sophie. "Did he ask you?"

Chapter 2

She rocked her forehead against the cool wood. "No, he didn't ask me. He says he doesn't want to get married." When she turned around, it was to find herself the object of Sophie's concerned eyes.

"You all right, child?"

"I don't know, Sophie. I just don't know."

Seconds later she was being cradled in the woman's ample-armed embrace.

"You'll feel better on a full belly. Why don't you come eat some supper, and you can tell ol' Sophie all about it."

Amanda sighed into the warm, lilac-scented bosom that had been her heart's ease since childhood. "I'm not hungry."

"Well, you gotta eat something."

Shaking her head, she took up the lamp and headed up the stairs. "I'm not hungry," she repeated. *Maybe I'll never be hungry again.*

In her room, she set the lamp down on the mirrored bureau and found herself face to face with her own reflection for the second time that night. She looked different. Wild, wilder even than the hair now tumbling down her back, her eyes glowed, there was a flush in her cheeks, and the lines of her lips were softly indistinct—like a sketch blurred by the artist's thumb. Or a

MATTERS OF THE HEART

man's kiss. Abruptly, she turned away and began preparing for an early bed.

She removed each item of clothing, washed, brushed, and braided her hair with the total absorption and concentration of one determined to have no room left over for thought. The more the urge pressed, the more exacting she became in each detail: the placing of her combs just so, the folding of her washcloth thus. But the struggle to keep her mind from straying grew harder.

Laying out her blue flannel nightgown, she was annoyed by the heavy, functional feel of the fabric. She found herself wishing it were of fine lawn, something as smooth and soft as a whisper. With a grimace of infinite distaste, she jerked it over her head, punched her arms through the long sleeves, and proceeded to kick the pile of clothing she'd just removed into a heap by the door. She felt mildly better.

Impatiently, she returned to the bed and flung back the covers. But sleep was the farthest thing from her mind, and she rebelled at the thought of going calmly to bed. She was anything but calm. She felt wrung out, empty, ready to soak up new things. She felt exhilarated. It was like she'd glimpsed something wondrous yet tantalizingly beyond her reach. Oh, how she wanted . . . wanted—she blinked and shook her head. Maybe she was tired, yet the longer she stood there, putting it off, the more repugnant became the prospect of placidly climbing into the same narrow little bed she'd been climbing into since early childhood. It lacked something all of a sudden. But what? Nathan? She clapped a hand to her mouth as if to stop the thought, but it was too late; she'd lost the battle.

Returning to the bureau, she dug in the bottom drawer beneath layers of clothing until she found what she was looking for and brought it up into the weak light. It was a small diary covered in pink watered silk with little embroidered leaves trailing down the front and a small gold key dangling from a satin ribbon. Stiff with age, the spine crackled as she opened it to reveal a pressed flower that little resembled the yellow and white daisy it once had been. Hunched down, toes curled against the chilled floor, she stared at the crumbling blossom, seeing Nathan's face as he had presented it to her years before.

It had been the Saturday after her fourteenth birthday and her father was having a card party for several of his friends. Wearing a pale yellow muslin that boasted her first bustle, she'd felt so grown up greeting the men as they arrived. When Nathan came through the door in his finely tailored suit, he'd swept a jaunty derby from his head in a solemn bow.

"Miss Alton," he began with a smile in his voice, "I've been told by my father here that I've had the misfortune of missing the most auspicious of occasions." Then from behind his back, he produced a daisy, which had obviously just come from her own beds by the front steps. He presented it with a flourish. "A belated happy birthday," he said.

Thanking him shyly, she accepted it just as Sophie reached over to tug on her skirt and remind her it was time to step back and let the gentlemen enter. Flustered at her own lack of polish, she did, indeed, step back— and promptly tripped on her own hem. With lightning reflex, Nathan grabbed her to keep her from falling, but crushed his little gift in the process. Before she'd even had time to be disappointed, he grabbed it, dashed back outside, and returned with what was obviously a newly picked blossom. "Here," he said, "I fixed it." They both laughed, his a warm, rich sound that reverberated deep in her own chest. Then he stepped closer, pinched off the stem, and tucked the flower behind her ear, murmuring, "Flowers are even lovelier in a lady's hair."

That night she had lovingly laid the precious gift between the pages of her diary, carefully quoting Nathan as that day's only entry.

She smiled at it now, but shook her head. Foolish, foolish, foolish, she thought. Suddenly, she closed the book with a snap and shoved it back in the drawer. There was little use in denying it. She had adored Nathan Rushton from the first, and because of that, she'd let herself hope where common sense had told her not to. She had believed his father's assurances that Nathan would want to marry her because she had wanted to believe it. Now she had no one but herself to blame. No one.

Nat Rushton sat at his desk and waved his cigar irritably in the air. "No, I do not want to see that pimply-faced Foley now!"

Henry Byrnes looked pained. "This is the third day in a row he's been here to see you."

"I don't care. He's an ingratiating little twit! What's he selling this time? Pins and needles?" Byrnes started to answer, but Nat waved him quiet. "No, no. I don't want to know. Just stall him a while longer. Maybe he'll get tired and go away."

Byrnes sighed. "Or *I* will from having to listen to his insipid chatter," he muttered.

"What's that, Byrnes?"

"Nothing, sir," he said tonelessly, closing the door. A moment later, he opened it again and peered over his spectacles at his employer. "There's a Miss Alton out here to see you. Shall I tell her to wait, too?"

Nat looked up in surprise. "Heavens, no! Send the girl in."

Stepping aside, the little secretary waved Amanda in, then faded back into his own office.

Nat rose and went to take her small hand in his, genuinely pleased to see her. "Well, well!" he greeted with a smile, leading her to a chair. "What brings you into town? I was planning on coming out today to see how you're getting along." He leaned back against the edge of his desk, noting the shabbiness of her blue wool suit and the ridiculously out-of-fashion straw hat on her head, its single flower dangling sadly. Freddie should have been shot, he thought disgustedly. "So how are you getting along?"

"I'm fine, sir. Thank you."

He looked her over intently as if in study, but the delicately cut features and gleaming auburn hair were long since committed to memory. *Ah, Emily*. . . . Sometimes it all seemed as close as yesterday. His reverie ended unexpectedly, though, when she turned her eyes up toward his. That color! That wild, green color she could have gotten only from Freddie. Nat found himself hoping it was the only trait she'd inherited from her wastrel father.

"You're looking well rested," he observed abruptly. "I know your father's death was a shock, but you held up very well. I'm proud of you."

Amanda nodded and swallowed, trying to still some of the butterflies bent on beating a path right through her ribs. This was going to be more difficult than she'd thought. She'd been on the street corner since nine o'clock that morning, and wasted half an hour looking up at the Rushton Building, trying to think of just the right way to approach the man. Perhaps it was the result of an overanxious state of mind, but it seemed the structure itself bore an uncanny resemblance to her guardian in its solid squareness and the imposing way

MATTERS OF THE HEART 31

it appeared to preside over the other, smaller buildings around it.

It had taken all her powers of persuasion to get Sophie to allow her to come here today with Joe on his weekly trip to market. She succeeded at the last minute purely by wearing the woman down. It was doubtful the same tactic would work here.

She took a deep breath. "Nathan came to see me last night."

"I figured he would. How did it go?"

"Not very well"—she leaned forward, speaking quickly lest she lose her nerve—"and that's what I have to talk to you about. Sir."

He waved a placating hand. "Of course. I understand how this is all very sudden, but surely you see the wisdom of my decision?"

"No, I'm afraid I don't."

"Eh? What was that?"

"I said 'no'," she repeated clearly. "I do not see the wisdom of it. As a matter of fact, I—I think it's detestable."

His geniality paled noticeably. "Oh? Just what is it about marrying Nathan you find so detestable? I thought you liked him."

"I do. That's not the point." She wet her lips. She couldn't stop now. "The point is I think it's detestable the way you're blackmailing him with"—she waved a hand vaguely about—"with all this."

"So . . . he told you, did he?"

"Yes, he did, and I think it's horrible. How can you do such a thing to your own son?"

His face lost some of its stony reserve. "I know you won't believe this," he said with unexpected gentleness, "but I'm really doing it for his own good—and for yours, as well. You need someone to take care of you, and frankly, I'm too old. Too old and too tired."

"But don't you realize how much he'll hate me if you do this?"

Nat puffed thoughtfully on his cigar and went back behind his desk. "You don't give yourself much credit, my dear. With your beauty and charm, I'm sure you can prevent that. Providing you use it right."

"'Use' it? You mean . . . *entice* him?"

He chuckled. "Feminine guile is as old as history, child. Why, without it, the world's oldest profession wouldn't . . . ahem, well, anyway, it's hardly deceitful for a wife to charm her husband, now is it? Some might even say it was her duty."

She hadn't looked at it quite that way, but still . . . "Couldn't you at least give us some more time? Maybe just until you return from Europe?"

"How would that help?"

"Maybe with more time," she began hopefully, taking it as a good sign he was even willing to listen, "we could get to know one another better, and perhaps . . ." she sighed, feeling her own argument wash out from under her, "perhaps he wouldn't feel so forced into this marriage."

"And perhaps, given more time, it would be even more against his will."

"According to you," she reminded him archly, "my beauty and charm would make that impossible."

Nat smiled. "True. Very true, however, I can't do that."

Amanda heard the expected answer, but had hoped it wouldn't come to this. Steeling herself, she fixed her eyes on a point just above his head and spoke without inflection. "Very well, then. I refuse to marry Nathan."

Nat didn't blink, he didn't move a muscle. Even the constantly moving cigar was still, clamped tightly in the corner of his mouth. He squinted at her through the smoke. "You do, do you?"

"Yes. I'll marry whomever else you choose, but not Nathan."

Nat raised an eyebrow at that and regarded her speculatively. "Anyone else I choose?"

"Yes."

"Well . . . it just so happens there is a young man who's been pestering me for your hand ever since it became known I was your guardian."

Her eyes left the wall above his head and met his in surprise. "There is?"

He nodded. "It seems he saw you in town a time or two, became infatuated with you, and only recently learned of your identity. He's been here three times already."

"Oh."

"As a matter of fact, he was here again today. Perhaps you saw him when you came in."

She searched her memory of the outer office, but she had been so intent on her own purpose she barely remembered seeing Nat's secretary, much less anyone else. She shook her head.

"Byrnes!" he called out so suddenly she flinched.

The secretary poked his head around the door. "Yes, sir?"

"Is that young man, Arnold Foley, still out there?"

Henry rolled his eyes. "Yes, sir."

"Good! Send him in, will you?"

Henry blinked. "Yes, sir!"

Nat met the young man as he entered the room and pumped his hand with vigor. "Why, Arnold, my boy! It's good to see you again!"

The young salesman looked startled by the greeting, then beamed with pleasure. "Thank you, sir. I've been trying for days to—"

"I know, I know," Nat broke in, "and your patience has finally been rewarded." He held out a hand toward Amanda. "May I present my ward, Miss Amanda Alton?"

When Arnold's eyes lit upon Amanda, his smile became impossibly wider, almost to the point where she felt she could count every tooth in his head. Her smile of greeting remained fixed as he rushed over to bow deeply over the hand courtesy demanded she extend.

"This is indeed an honor, Miss Alton."

"Why, thank you, Mr. Foley," she responded, gently extracting her hand from his moist hold.

He admonished her with a wag of his dusty brown head and glanced quickly in Nat's direction. "Please, you must call me Arnold, also."

As the man continued to gush flowery sentiments all over her, she looked over his shoulder to see her guardian raise his eyebrows and lift a hand, palm up, as if asking for her opinion. She turned her attention back to Arnold, who seemed about ready to wind down, and felt sick to her stomach. Nathan was right. She *was* spineless. A lifetime of being despised by him was infinitely more attractive than spending five minutes being worshipped by this simpering idiot.

From the expression on her face, Nat read her thoughts almost to the letter. When Arnold turned around to speak to him, he clapped a hand to his shoulder and started steering him back toward the door. "Well, son, we have a lot to talk about, and I know you're anxious for an answer. I'll let you know something as soon as I can."

The young salesman blinked in confusion, but found himself pulled along in an iron grip. "But I haven't even—"

"No, no. There's no need for you to prove anything

to me. I can tell you'll be rising to the top of your profession before long."

Arnold Foley seemed inordinately pleased by this. "Do you really think so, sir?"

"Oh, I do. I do," Nat reassured as he all but shoved him out the door.

Just before he disappeared from sight, Arnold bade Amanda good-bye over his shoulder, a farewell she acknowledged with a wan little smile.

Quickly, before she could suspect anything amiss, Nat signaled for Byrnes. "Buy a dozen of whatever he's selling and get him out of here," he hissed at the bewildered man before shutting the door in his face. When he turned around, Amanda was sitting in a sad little slump, staring dejectedly at the floor. Only when he went to stand directly in front of her did she look up. Expecting to see misery and defeat on her face, it surprised him when her small chin came up to an even more determined tilt.

"I've decided," she said. "I'm not going to marry at all. Not anyone."

"No?" He stroked the corners of his mustache with a thumb and forefinger. He knew as well as she did that he couldn't carry her to the altar kicking and screaming, but perhaps there was an easier, more effective way to settle this. "Well," he made a gesture of concession, "I guess there's only one other alternative."

"Yes?" Hope flared visibly in that one, small word.

"I guess you'll just have to support yourself."

"Sup—port myself? Oh. Well, yes. Of course I could."

"You do have some marketable skills, don't you?"

"I—uh, I don't know."

"Well, not to worry. In this modern age of emancipation, you find women in all sorts of positions."

"You do?"

"Oh, yes. Take the job of secretary, for example. I hear women are even beginning to try their hand at that." He snapped his fingers with sudden inspiration, and before she had time to think, he had her in the outer office ready to prove her worth.

"Byrnes," he addressed the man behind the cluttered desk, "why don't you go to lunch a little early today?"

"Lunch? But it's only ten o'clock, sir."

"So? Go eat breakfast, then eat lunch."

"But sir, there's an awful lot of work—"

"Don't worry, Byrnes. Don't worry. Miss Alton here will be filling in for you, won't you, dear?"

"Y—yes. That is, if you don't mind, Mr. Byrnes."

The harried little man adjusted his spectacles to include Amanda in his baleful stare. "Not at all," he said tightly. After shuffling the papers before him into a neat, tidy little stack and setting them aside, he rose and left without another word.

Nat indicated the chair, and Amanda gingerly seated herself in the strange, roller-footed thing. He smiled benignly. "Don't worry. You'll do fine. This is called a typewriter. You just put the paper in so . . . and type up these figures over here"—he grabbed a piece of paper from one of the stacks—"so it looks like this. Over there is the pencil sharpener, and that thing behind you on the wall"—her head swiveled—"is a telephone. We had them installed last month. Two rings is for you, three is downstairs. Any questions? No? Well, good luck, then. I'll check on you later." She didn't move a muscle as he went back into his own office and closed the door with a twitching grin.

Very slowly, Amanda lifted her fingers to the edge of the desk and let her eyes move from one thing to another across its yellow oak surface. The typewriter was an ugly, spidery-looking contraption that appeared more like it ate paper than wrote on it. The papers were filled with columns and columns of figures and symbols, some written on the machine, some not. God only knew what she was supposed to do with them all. And she didn't even want to think about that telephone thing.

Picking up a clean piece of paper, she lifted her shoulders on a deep breath. "Here goes. . . ."

Downstairs, Nathan pushed open the front door and stopped. He'd been coming here almost every day of his life. His first memories were of this place. More than a second home—the place with his bed and his mother had been that—it was a way of life, his life.

A deep breath pulled the familiar smell of ink, paper, and well-oiled tools into his bloodstream, and he almost smiled. Down here, instead of that rarefied, power-saturated air his father breathed, there was light and air and chatter and movement. Life. The *clackety-clack* of the new typing machines, muddy workmen arguing around chart-strewn tables, errand boys darting about—somehow these were all oddly soothing to his agitated spirit.

It was ironic, he thought. He'd never been asked if he wanted to carry on in his father's footsteps, he'd been told. Still, he'd come to love it, and over the years, the promise of ownership had become both the carrot and the bludgeon to keep him in line with whatever his father wanted. But this time it wouldn't work. This time he'd find a way around him.

Exchanging monosyllabic greetings with the employees, he threaded his way toward the back and the privacy of his own office. He was looking forward to a few minutes alone so he could think. However, when he opened the door, there was Teddy—coatless, sleeves rolled up, feet propped on the desk, and feeding himself peanuts by way of energetic but not very accurate tosses into the air.

He looked up with a lazy grin. "So . . . the prodigal son returns. Again."

"And I see you're hard at work, as usual."

"God, no! That's one bad habit I've tried hard never to cultivate."

Nathan regarded the younger version of himself in stony silence, then pushed himself away from the door and shut it behind him. Shrugging out of his jacket, he hung it up on the brass rack nailed to the wall.

"How'd it go up on Mount Olympus yesterday?" Teddy asked.

"How did you know where I was?"

Teddy stuck a finger in his ear and wiggled it. "The thunder could be heard all the way down here. Was the old man in a real steam over that MacGruder thing?"

It was casually put, but Nathan knew his brother better, and he wondered again why he was always protecting him. "You can bet he wasn't too happy about it, but that wasn't what all the shouting was about," he answered, settling into a chair on the other side of the desk the two of them shared.

"Did you tell him it was my fault?"

"No."

Teddy missed another nut and it joined those already on the floor around his chair. "Why not? If it'd been me, I would have."

Nathan made a face. One never knew quite how to take Teddy at times. "Yes, you probably would've, but since it was my contract, it really was my fault—for not checking behind you. Count on it, though," he warned as he stretched his legs out in front of him, "I will from now on."

Teddy shrugged and continued munching. "Well, I

went back over the figures again, anyway. I just made a few minor miscalculations, that's all."

Thinking of how much those "minor miscalculations" had cost him, Nathan had to fight the urge to strangle his brother. An error was one thing, but this had been pure sloppiness. After begging to be left in charge, it was nothing short of gross irresponsibility to go off on a picnic without a word to anyone. A damned picnic! His blood boiled just thinking about it. Still, it was pointless to explain how he'd had to dangerously deplete his account in order to cover the losses. Teddy wouldn't be in any position to help. Living at home and on a small allowance from their father, he rarely hung on to more than the cost of an evening's entertainment. Nathan shuddered to think what would happen once Teddy came into his half of their mother's inheritance.

Sighing heavily, he held out a hand. "Let's see them."

Teddy leaned over, pulled a sheaf of papers from a drawer, and tossed them onto the desk.

Nathan gave them a cursory glance, then put them aside. He suddenly wasn't in the mood. Reaching into a bottom drawer, he pulled out a glass and a bottle, poured himself a shot, then thunked the bottle down on the desk. He grimaced at the early-morning bite of whiskey and scowled into space.

"Aren't you going to 'check behind me'?"

"Later."

"Hey," Teddy said, "what did go on up there?"

Nathan's eyes focused on the room's sparse contents. It sure didn't take much to run a construction company, he thought, even one as big as this. Some maps and charts occupied the pale green walls, while others were rolled and stacked on the floor, the windowsill, wherever there was a flat surface. A yellow oak desk, a couple of matching chairs, and a black iron coal stove were the room's only furnishings. The bare wood floor was none too clean, and the one curtainless window was gray with soot. Here and there, an idle thumb had rubbed a small circled view of the side street, but inside or out, the place wasn't much to look at. It unnerved him to realize he'd do almost anything to keep it.

"Well?" his brother prompted.

Nathan's scowl deepened. "It seems if this place is ever to be mine, I have to dance to a whole new tune."

Teddy grimaced as he missed another nut and it rolled off the desk onto Nathan's side of the floor. "Oh? Who's he want you to murder?"

"My bachelorhood."

Lips forming a silent whistle, Teddy brought his feet down with a thump. "He wants you to get married?"

"He's even picked out the bride."

"*Whoo-eee!* Who is she? Do I know her?"

"Her name is Amanda Alton—and she's hardly more than a child." The memory of some very unchildlike lips rushed heat to the surface of his own. He cooled them with a quick swig.

"Alton . . . Alton. . . . Nope. The only Alton I know of is that crazy Irish drunk you and the old man used to play cards with."

Nathan nodded. "That's her father. Or was. He died."

"Really? I didn't even know he had a daughter."

"Neither did he, judging by the way he left her out on that desolate old farm of his. Sometime before he died, though, he thought about her long enough to make our father her guardian."

Teddy snapped his fingers. "That's right! They were chums from the cradle or something, weren't they?"

MATTERS OF THE HEART 41

In an effort to squelch his younger brother's high spirits, Nathan glared darkly at him. He hardly expected him to be sympathetic about his predicament, but by the same token, he could do without all the cheeriness.

The youngest Rushton, however, didn't seem to notice. "You know," he mumbled, mouth full, "I'd heard old Alton spent his last penny supporting some fellow who claimed he was inventing a horseless carriage." He dug around for another nut among the shells, then tossed the bag over to Nathan. "Did I ever tell you about this chap I knew at the university? Said he was working on a machine that would fly. Fly, mind you! Boy, if he could've gotten hooked up with Alton, he'd've been set for life!"

The forbidding look on Nathan's face dissolved into a reluctant grin, then like kids again, they were both laughing, the tension between them forgotten for the moment.

Rubbing his eyes with the heels of his hands, Nathan sobered first. Absolutely nothing had changed, yet he felt better somehow—Teddy had always been able to make him laugh. Still smiling, he reached into the grease-stained sack for a peanut, but there was none left. How typical, he thought, tossing the bag back with a snort of disgust. Teddy never offered anything until he was finished with it.

"So what's supposed to happen to this place when you don't go along with his plans?" Teddy suddenly wanted to know.

Nathan's sigh was weary. "He says he'll sell it to Wagner—'lock, stock, and barrel.' "

He hadn't given any thought to how Teddy would take the news, but the last thing in the world he expected was the look of shock that suddenly bleached his brother's face. "He never thought you cared about the place," he scrambled to appease. "That's why he sent you to the university."

Teddy's laugh was mirthless and bitter. "He sent me there because he didn't know what else to do with me, and you and I both know it. But that didn't work out either, did it?" he smirked.

"You have to admit that thing with the caretaker's daughter was pretty stupid."

"I was drunk." He shrugged, his Rushton blue eyes sliding around to meet his brother's pointedly. "And at least I didn't have to marry the girl."

"Well, the deed isn't done yet, little brother."

"What are you planning to do?"

"I've already done it. Last night I had a little chat with the young Miss Alton, and she's agreed to try her hand at reasoning with the old man."

"The height of desperation, huh?"

Nathan's eyes locked with his brother's. "What's that supposed to mean?"

"You said yourself she's hardly more than a child."

Nathan scowled down at his boots stretched out in front of him. Teddy was right. What could she possibly accomplish that he hadn't?

The picture of her huddled in that window seat, bare toes peeking out from beneath her skirt, kept coming back to him. She was such an engaging little waif, and so . . . vulnerable. It was one of the things making him feel guilty; that and sending her up against his father. *I just hope she wants out of this as badly as I do.* He downed another swallow. *Or keeps it to herself if she doesn't.* He grinned suddenly, thinking of her temper. Who knows? Maybe he'll make her mad. . . .

The glass in the door rattled as one of Nathan's foremen opened it and stuck his bearded head through.

MATTERS OF THE HEART 43

"Hey, Mr. Rushton"—he was grinning—"seen your father's new secretary?"

Nathan looked up with a frown. "Byrnes? He isn't new."

"Nope. They say Byrnes stomped out of here about an hour ago. Seems some little redhead's taken his place. Everybody's been taking turns going up and peeking in." He motioned an invitation with his head, then shut the door.

"Redhead?" Redhead! "No . . . it can't be," Nathan murmured.

"What can't be?" Teddy asked.

"Amanda." Nathan's glass hit the desk top and he was on his feet. "It can't be, but it is. Somehow I just know it."

Teddy arched an eyebrow in the family habit. "A replacement for Byrnes *and* your wife? The old man has plans bigger than I thought. Good luck," he added as his brother opened the door—then he started to hum the wedding march.

Nathan threw him a less than kind look and jabbed a finger at him. "I want you gone and out to the work site by the time I get back, understand?" Grimacing as a nutshell crunched underfoot, he tossed over his shoulder, "And clean that mess up before you leave."

Teddy swallowed and smiled. "Sure—and don't worry. If she's pretty enough, maybe I'll take her off your hands," he called. But as the door closed, his smile vanished. Crushing the empty bag, he gave it a vicious twist and hurled it across the room. "Whatever you want, big brother. It's always whatever you want."

Upstairs, Nathan eased open the door to his father's suite and looked in. There she was—straw hat dangling, fingertips blackened, smudges on her chin, her eyes pink-rimmed with tears. She was sitting at the desk in the middle of what looked like a white paper hurricane. "Oh, dear," she was saying, "oh, dear. . . ."

The door hinge squeaked and her head snapped around, leaving the hat to catch up. "If you people don't quit this awful spying on me, I'm going to—oh, it's you!" The tears welled afresh as she leaped up, forgotten papers in her lap sliding to the floor. "Oh, Nathan, I'm sorry—"

"Amanda, what's going on here?"

"It's just awful. I'm awful. When I told your father"—they both glanced over at Nat's closed door—"that I wouldn't marry you, and I wouldn't marry somebody named Arnold Something-or-other, he said . . . he said I had to support myself, so I—"

He grabbed her wrist. "Come on."

"But what about all this mess?"

"Leave it," he snapped, angry at something he couldn't name. "We'll talk in my office."

Leading her downstairs and through an office full of curious people, he slammed the door behind them.

Teddy was gone, but the peanut shells weren't. Brushing one chair free of litter, he moved it next to the other one and pointed to it. "Here. Fix your hat and blow your nose." This time when he offered the handkerchief she didn't refuse.

While she repaired herself, he went to lean a shoulder against the window frame and rub a new view of the street. When he glanced back, she was refolding his handkerchief, the hat back atop her curls.

She looked around her with polite interest. "This is your office? It's nice."

"Are you all right now?"

"Yes, I'm fine." She sighed. "This has been such

an awful, awful week." Restlessly, she was on her feet again.

Staying where he was, he watched her begin to wander and pretend interest in the things she stopped to finger.

"Sometimes I think it's all a terrible dream and I'll wake up soon. It's hard to believe I'll never see Papa again, never hear him roll up the long drive in a clatter of wheels and hooves." She met his eyes, her smile tremulous. "He never stayed more than a few days, but now I don't even have that to look forward to."

Nathan looked away from the pain on her face—and down to his glass and whiskey bottle.

"It's strange," she was saying. "He was never around long enough for me to feel I ever truly knew him, but his existence was the tenuous thread holding all our lives together. Snap that thread and everything's begun to shred apart. It's scary to think about, but what's to become of me? Of Sophie and Joe?"

Nathan was beside her. He'd already put the glass out of sight, but just as he reached for the bottle, she picked it up. His hand clenched and dropped as she stood, reading the label.

"Oh. For a minute, I thought it was Jim Beam. That's what Papa used to drink." She smiled. "A lot. Of course, he wasn't cross or anything like that when he drank. A little hard to talk to, perhaps, like when I'd be trying to tell him about the leak in the roof or something and he'd be telling jokes and singing. He always sang. Joe would finally have to carry him off to bed, and he'd still be singing—right up to the time he'd pass out."

She was staring off into space as she talked, the forgotten bottle cradled in her hands. Seeing it there gave him an odd feeling in the pit of his stomach. It was like watching a child pick up a murder weapon.

Lifting it out of her unresisting hands, he put it in with the glass and closed the drawer. "I don't sing," he said.

There was some tone, some pain in the words that made her look up. For the first time, she noticed his hair wasn't combed, his collar and tie were gone, and his clothes looked slept in. His eyes, always so dark a blue they seemed black, were bloodshot and ringed with tired-looking smudges.

He didn't flinch under her steady gaze, but she had a sixth-sense impression he was holding his breath. "That's all right." She smiled at him. "I don't dance."

He smiled back. "Now, tell me: What's all this about you supporting yourself?"

She sank into her chair again. "There's not much to tell. When I told your father I refused to marry you, he brought in this awful Arnold Somebody. When I refused to marry him, he said I'd just have to support myself. He took me out into that other office—I'm afraid Mr. Byrnes was not very happy—and told me to try being a secretary."

Nathan found his usual perch on the corner of the desk, and shook his head, snorting, "And he was worried *I* would treat you cruelly. Being your guardian and telling you to support yourself—"

She watched disgust give way to hope in the blink of an eye.

"By Jove!" he said, smacking a fist into his other hand. "You know, it might work at that! It just might—that is, if you're willing to give it a try."

"I already did, remember? I wasn't very good at it."

"As he intended, no doubt. But there are other jobs out there, and if we can find you one, we can beat him at his own game—and with his own words, at that!" He dropped into the chair beside her, scooted it closer, and leaned forward attentively. "Now we just have to find what you're best suited for. What can you do?"

Knowing she couldn't back down now, she tried to sound hopeful as she informed him she could sew a little, "and I know some Koine Greek," she added at his look of disappointment.

He stared at her blankly for several seconds, then burst out laughing—a warm, familiar sound she found pleasant despite the fact she could see no reason for all the hilarity.

"I don't know," he said, still laughing, "that there's much demand for young ladies who sew 'a little' and know ancient languages, not unless they want to be . . ." He sobered suddenly. "A governess! Of course! A governess doesn't need to know much more than the children in her charge!"

"How kind of you to say so," she retorted acidly, but he wasn't even listening. He was busy nodding and muttering, "It might work . . . it just might work! What do you say, Irish? Are you willing to give it a try?"

She wrinkled her nose at the nickname, and found herself wishing he wasn't so very relieved at the prospect of being free of her. "I don't know. It all seems so—so underhanded somehow."

"So is blackmail, my dear, so is blackmail."

"You're right, of course, but . . . No, you're right."

"Good. Good!" He got to his feet.

"But there's one condition to all this."

Instantly, his expression became guarded. "What's that?"

Before answering, she stood up to look him as directly in the eye as her five-feet-four-inches would allow. "That you find positions for Sophie and Joe as well. They're both old and they can't do too much, but I'll not see them suffer because of this."

He looked relieved. "Don't worry. I'll find them something if I have to hire them myself." With a sudden bark of laughter, he threw back his head. "Ha! He thought he had me over a barrel, but he's outsmarted himself this time. Now, thanks to you, he's not going to win after all!" he crowed. "You know something, Miss Alton? You're wonderful!" Suddenly, he took her face in both his hands and kissed her hard on the mouth.

She went rigid—but then a curious thing happened. Instead of being afraid or angry this time, she felt suspended by the warm pressure of his lips on hers. She leaned toward him, a small sound escaping her throat.

Abruptly, he dropped his hands and stepped away. "Sorry." He cleared his throat. "I—I'll need to arrange for the interviews. How about if I pick you up Wednesday at, say, one o'clock? We don't have much time, do we?" He was talking fast, almost too fast.

Not willing to trust her own voice, she just nodded and returned his smile, determined not to seem any less happy than he.

They were back to the same discomfort of the night before, both of them awkward and uncertain how to end the meeting.

With a pivot that made her skirt swirl, Amanda headed for the door. She was surprised when he stopped her with a hand on her arm.

"How will you get back home?"

"The same way I came: with Joe."

"Ah. Joe. The one with the shotgun."

She fought the smile tugging at her mouth. "I'd better be going. He'll be waiting."

He stopped her again. "Someday you'll have to tell me how a young lady comes to learn Koine Greek."

The smile won. "Someday."

Gripping the door frame with one hand, the edge of the door with the other, Nathan watched her thread her way through the outer office and out the front entrance. "At last," he said softly. "I win."

Chapter 3

With the promise that warmer weather was finally here to stay, Wednesday morning dawned to find Amanda already bathed and dressed. She ate early, pleasing Sophie by devouring enough for two her size, then proceeded to drive the poor woman to distraction as she went from exuberance to anxiety and back again.

"I can hardly believe it, Sophie. I'm going to be one of those bluestocking girls. Do they call a governess a bluestocking? Oh, but what if I'm no good at it? What if I'm as bad at that as I was at being a secretary? What if I can't support myself? No, forget I said that. I'll do fine. Nathan said so. What time is it, anyway?"

It was always just five minutes later than the last time she'd asked, so when Nathan's carriage was finally spotted wheeling toward the house, Sophie was only too glad to shoo her back up the stairs.

"And don't come down for fifteen minutes," she admonished.

"But why?"

"'Cause a proper lady don't want to look too eager, that's why. She always keep a gentleman waitin'."

"But it isn't like he's courting me, Sophie."

"If these crazy plans of yours don't work out, this jes' might be the only courtin' you ever get, child. Now off with ya!" She watched with hands on her hips as Amanda scurried obediently up the steps, petticoats flying. Then, like an actress waiting off-stage for her cue, she listened for the knock at the door. When it came, she moved to answer it as one solid mass of dignity.

"Mornin', Mr. Rushton. Come on in. Take your hat?"

He removed the dark blue derby, but shook his head. "No, thank you, Sophie. I'm only here to pick up Miss Amanda."

"Yessir. She be down soon. Why don't ya sit yourself down in the parlor there while you're waitin'?"

A slight movement at the top of the stairs caught his eye and he looked up. But the landing was empty. After a moment's hesitation, he followed the solemnly efficient Sophie into the front room.

Sitting on the unyielding edge of a horsehide sofa, he declined the offer of tea with a suppressed smile. Later, when it looked like that was the only way to get a respite from the woman's continuous pillow plumping and knickknack dusting, he changed his mind.

When she was gone, he looked around him, feeling the sadness of gentility gone to seed. The place was worse than he remembered. The flowered wallpaper was faded and stained, the furniture mismatched and threadbare. *Take it as a warning, Nathan, old boy. It's what all drunkards leave behind.*

He ran a tanned finger around the inside of his stiff new collar, then reached for his watch. He frowned at the time. What was keeping her?

Seeing Sophie return with the tea tray, he watched her stop, look up the stairway, and shake her head vigorously. It finally occurred to him what was happening. Amanda was playing some coy, virginal game with him. It both irritated and endeared somehow—and only added to his doubts about her maturity to fend for herself.

Shushing Sophie with a wave of his hand, he went to lean a shoulder in the doorway. "Amanda?" he called loudly enough to carry up the stairs.

No answer.

"Amanda?"

"Y—yes, Nathan?" came an answer from the top of the steps.

"We really have to be going," he said. Casually twirling his hat in his hand, he grinned at the hurried *tap-tap-tapping* of Amanda's heels on the steps before she rounded the corner in a swirl of dark green velvet. It looked like an old-fashioned riding habit that had belonged to someone else, someone slightly less endowed, he judged, seeing the strain on the buttons down the front. The ribbons on the matching bonnet were rust stained with age, but tied pertly beneath her ear.

"Hello," she greeted him breathlessly.

"Hello yourself."

"I'm sorry to have kept you waiting," she said with a sidelong glance at Sophie and her sternly puckered mouth.

His expression was businesslike and detached as he answered with a small bow, but Amanda searched his face to see if he'd been drinking. Years of living with a drinker had taught her even the subtlest signs. Nathan was cold sober. And oh, but he was handsome in his dark blue, pin-striped suit. His white collar contrasted sharply with the deep tan of his neck, managing somehow to make his eyes a darker blue than ever. Draped across his vest front was a simple gold watch chain, and she liked the fact that it was the only jewelry he wore. He was definitely not a dandy.

He lifted an eyebrow at her close scrutiny, grinning roguishly when she blushed. "You're staring again."

"I am not, you conceited—"

"Amanda Paulin' Alton!" Sophie gasped.

He chuckled and indicated the door. "It's all right. Shall we go now?" He watched Amanda give the old servant an affectionate hug, and realized how few people the girl had left in the world. "Wish me luck!" he heard her say, but as the woman glared over Amanda's shoulder at him, her only answer was a short, "Hmph!"

Following Amanda to the door, Nathan was surprised when a hand on his arm held him back for a moment.

"Don't expect too much from her, Mr. Rushton. She been gently born and raised, y'know."

He patted the hand and nodded. "I know."

Outside, he helped Amanda up into the carriage seat and saw her settled against the red, button-tufted leather without a word. As if by mutual agreement, neither spoke until they'd turned off the long, rutted drive onto the road.

"What was that all about?" he finally asked.

She giggled. "Wasn't it awful? I'm afraid Sophie doesn't understand any of this."

He liked it that she didn't pretend to misunderstand him. "Is it that she doesn't understand, or she doesn't approve?"

"A little of both, I suppose. In her mind, young ladies go calling, go to strawberry festivals, or go courting, but never, never," she explained, "do they go seeking employment."

"What about you? How do you feel about being a woman of independence?" He watched her lift her chin and reply like a child reciting a lesson well learned.

"You gotta do what you gotta do, and if you're

lucky, you learn to like it." She shrugged at the bemused look he threw her. "At least that's what Pidgie always said about helping her father clean out the barn."

He made a face. "Who—or what—is a Pidgie?"

"Pidgie was a girl I knew in school," she explained with a laugh. "It's short for Pigeon—which wasn't her real name, either."

"Thank God for that! Did she learn Koine Greek, too?"

"No. I learned that from a man named Galen Waters, a friend of Papa's. Galen was an old chemist who lived with us for a time while he did some experiments trying to get gold from sea water."

He studied her carefully for long seconds, then shook his head. "You're a most unusual girl, Amanda Alton."

She shrugged. "Papa always said it was good to be different."

"Understandably. What I meant," he added quickly, seeing her neck stretch defensively, "was that he certainly didn't mind being different himself."

"I liked him," she sniffed.

"I'm glad. Everybody should like their father."

"Really? I didn't get the impression you much like yours."

He clicked his tongue at the horse, and frowned, irritated with the direction the conversation had taken. "It isn't that so much as wanting to live my life my way, and him wanting me to live it his way. He can get stubborn about the strangest things."

"Like this?"

"Like this."

After a moment, she reached out and laid a hand on his sleeve. "I'm sorry. I didn't mean to criticize."

He looked over, felt himself soothed by the lush green of her eyes, and smiled. "You didn't."

The warm rush of camaraderie they both felt at her answering smile was gone as suddenly as it came. Like two strangers colliding on the street, they each retreated from the unexpected contact to a safer distance of silence.

Finally, it was Amanda's curiosity that broke the uncomfortable stretch. "What kind of position did you find for me?"

Nathan let out a long breath. The closer it came, the more this all seemed ridiculous and futile. He'd been grasping at straws that day in his office. In the two days since then, he'd come up with at least a hundred different reasons why this strategy of theirs wouldn't work. Nonetheless, he tried to sound optimistic. "I found you two, actually. The first, arranged through a mutual acquaintance, is for the position of governess to the two children of an Edward Mills."

"And the second?"

"The second is for an elderly lady in poor health who needs a young companion—a Miss Edna Crittendon." He waited for some sort of reaction, but beyond a nod of acknowledgment, there was none. If she had any misgivings, she was keeping them to herself.

Amanda sighed a silent sigh of relief as she pretended great interest in the roadside greenery. She'd been dreading the sweatshop work she'd read about in such terms as "vile," "evil," and "exploitative," and she couldn't help feeling a tender wave of gratitude for the man beside her. Despite his desperation, he wasn't willing to give her over to that.

The Millses lived on the outskirts of the city, in a large Georgian-style place of red brick, and as Nathan halted the carriage opposite the double front doors,

Amanda viewed the place with a mixture of trepidation and excitement. Would this end up being her new home?

Nathan's hands felt comfortingly warm as he helped her down, but without meeting his eyes, she pointed her chin up the walk and marched to the front door. Together they waited in silence for a response to her knock.

Mrs. Blankenship, the Millses' housekeeper, greeted them with a perfunctory nod of her large gray head. Not being one to waste words, she beckoned them to follow as she stumped her way down the main hall toward one of the many darkly stained doors. Mr. Mills, she informed them briskly, would join them presently. Until that time, they were to please "remain" in the library. With that, she closed the door firmly in their faces.

"What a bizarre creature!" Nathan murmured, exchanging a look with her. Suddenly, they were both smothering their amusement.

It was a small thing, but the shared humor served to put her more at ease, and while she settled herself on the cordovan leather couch opposite a large, marble fireplace, Nathan ambled over to stare out one of the long windows.

Looking around, she could find little reason for this room to be called a library. The dark paneled walls were bare of shelves, and the few books in evidence were contained in a small, glass-fronted cabinet by the door. The only thing that relieved the studied Victorian gloom was a patch of sunlight painting the floor in front of each window.

Despite her interest in the room, she was still very much aware of Nathan's every move as he began to pace restlessly, a vague frown on his face. Probably impatient to get back to his precious business, she thought with a faint pout. Knowing she had no right to come out and ask what was on his mind made her feel more alone and lonely than ever before, so she turned her attention back to the door. Perhaps she could will the slow Mr. Mills into making his appearance.

It would have greatly surprised her to learn it was she and not business on Nathan's mind just then. Oh, not that he hadn't tried to concentrate on his own affairs, but with each effort, his thoughts had been disturbed, fragmented by the faint smell of lavender that clung to his hands. It was the same scent he remembered from the other night when he'd pulled her into his arms. He found himself breathing deeply. It occurred to him that if today's venture succeeded, she would have little further use for the extravagance of fragrance—governesses and companions could ill afford such things. Somehow, this disturbed him more than ever.

Look at her! he thought. Sitting there so damned prim and proper, totally unconcerned at the prospect of a life of service with that beastly housekeeper. In later years, would she end up just as sour and dictatorial? It was not a pleasant thought, but it wasn't his concern, he reminded himself. If anyone was to blame, it was his father.

Pulling out his watch, he was about to remark that they'd been waiting for almost a quarter of an hour when the door swung open and they were greeted by a florid-faced Edward Mills.

He looked to be in his late thirties or early forties, but was already well on his way to becoming the heavily jowled and portly man he would be in old age. His thin, sandy hair was parted precisely down the middle and his high, winged collar was so stiff and tight it had rubbed a visible ring around his neck.

Nathan stepped forward to perform the introductions, but Mills barely spared the time to shake his hand and bid him be seated before turning back to Amanda, openly appraising her from head to foot.

Swallowing nervously, she braced herself for a barrage of questions.

"A bit young," he pronounced doubtfully.

"I assumed Allen Forrest had informed you of the young lady's age when he arranged for this interview," came Nathan's voice from one of the chairs flanking the fireplace.

Mills waved a dismissing hand. "Yes, yes, of course." He paused, beaming. "But he neglected to tell me how lovely she was."

Amanda blushed at the unexpected compliment and glanced over at Nathan to see him stroking his chin and staring blandly at Mills's back.

"Stand up, girl. Stand up," Mills suddenly directed. "Let's have a look at you."

Obediently, she came to her feet, and was surprised when the man dropped an arm around her shoulders and drew her closer.

He wagged a finger under her nose. "I demand unquestioning loyalty from all my employees, my dear. But I'm always fair." He raised his invisible eyebrows. "And generous. So what do you say? Would you like to come work for me?"

She looked up into the face only inches from her own and hesitated. She felt uneasy, but whether it was due to the familiar embrace or her own feelings trying to betray her at the last moment she wasn't sure. She looked over at Nathan for one final boost of courage, but the chair was empty. His back to them, he was staring out one of the windows again. She was on her own. Looking back up into Mills's pale blue eyes, she stretched her lips into a smile and nodded her consent.

MATTERS OF THE HEART 59

"Fine, fine!" he said. "It's all settled then. You can start tomorrow."

"You mean that's all there is to it? Aren't there any questions you want to ask me? Things you want to know about me?"

"I know all I need to know," was the enigmatic reply.

It was Nathan who finally turned around and asked the one question she feared would be impertinent coming from her.

"What about the children, Mr. Mills? You've made no mention of them. Shouldn't they meet their prospective governess?"

Mills looked over at him as if surprised to find him still there. "They're not here right now. Miss Alton will meet them tomorrow when she starts her duties. Besides," he added, "their opinions are not required."

"It wasn't their opinion I was thinking of, sir, but rather Miss Alton's."

There was nothing threatening in Nathan's attitude that Amanda could see, but Mills hastily dropped his arm and backed away a step when Nathan came to stand beside her and take her elbow.

"Perhaps you were right, after all," Nathan said smoothly. "Perhaps Miss Alton is a bit young for the work you have in mind."

Amanda gaped up at him in astonishment. She must have missed something somewhere. There were definite undercurrents here she didn't understand. Mills, whose face was about four shades redder than before, was blinking rapidly and opening and closing his mouth like a fish.

"But—now see here!" he began to protest, but Nathan cut him off with a gesture.

"Oh, I understand, sir, and I'm sorry to have taken up so much of your time." His smile was tight as he propelled her to the door. "And don't trouble yourself. We know the way out."

Too stunned for speech, Amanda let herself be pulled along and out to the waiting carriage, where she was practically tossed into the seat. "Why did you do that?" she demanded, finding her tongue at last. "You heard what he said—I was hired!"

A grimace turned down the corners of his mouth. "You really are an innocent, aren't you?" Wheeling the rig around, he took them down the drive with unnecessary speed. "You were hired all right, but not as any governess."

"What do you mean? You were the one who said—well, even he said . . ."

"You still don't understand, do you?"

"No," she answered flatly. "I don't."

"While our Mr. Mills was busy with you, I got a look at one of his 'children' out the window as he chased a little serving girl around in a rather questionable game of tag. He was in need of a keeper perhaps, but hardly a governess."

"Did it ever occur to you that it might not have been one of his children? Or, if so, the others might have been younger ones?"

"From his reluctance to bring them out, I doubt it."

"He said they weren't home, remember?"

"Without a governess, where could they be?"

"Oh, for goodness sake! You're making no sense at all! Who knows? Who cares where they are or who they're with? They could be with their mother for all we know!"

His face darkened and their wheels sang a higher pitch. "I doubt that, too!"

If the top hadn't been up, she might have shot to her feet right there in the moving carriage, so incensed was she at this insanity of his. "You are the most stubborn, unreasonable—then tell me this, if you're so smart: why on earth would he agree to interview me if he didn't want a governess?"

"Because," he shouted, "he wanted you for himself—to warm his *bed*, you infant!"

When the carriage lurched and skidded she had to grab for the canopy brace, but it didn't stop her from shouting back, "That's absurd! And don't you dare shout at me, Mr. Rushton! This whole thing was your idea."

"Yes," he growled, slowing the rig to a more sedate pace, "and it's beginning to make me feel like a white slaver!"

"Well, no one's forcing you to do any of this."

"Yes, someone is, Miss Alton. My father."

"Oh, why must you continually blame everything on him?"

"Because—" His mouth snapped shut and he riveted his attention back to the road.

"Oh, no you don't! What were you going to say? Because what?"

"Nothing, I—" He glanced her way, then back to the road again, his anger suddenly dissipated. "I was just thinking that you may be a child, but sometimes you remind me of my Aunt Pen."

Not knowing the woman, Amanda had no idea if she'd just been insulted or not. Probably. "I keep telling you I'm not a child," she grumbled, yanking on the cords of her reticule as if strangling someone.

Lifting her chin, she stared straight ahead. Assured her silence would properly chastise him, she ignored him for the rest of the drive, contenting herself with watching the houses get closer together while she listed all the things she didn't understand about the man beside her.

Miss Crittendon's place was in a quiet, dignified

section of town, the kind that lent social credential by virtue of address alone. Hers was an imposing, three-story brick townhouse complete with solariums on each level. As they drew close to the curb, Amanda craned her neck to try to see all of it at once.

When Nathan came around to help her down, he ignored the hands she held out, and reached up to grasp her around the waist. When he continued to hold her just inches off the ground, she looked into his face to find him scrutinizing her with mock intensity.

"Ah, you do have green eyes," he said, setting her down at last. "It's been so long since I've seen them I wasn't sure I'd remembered correctly."

His sudden, lopsided grin made her regret her childish silence and she tendered him a small, penitent smile in return. The outbursts of a quick temper are seldom long-lived, and her good humor had already been restored by the tantalizing sights, sounds, and smells of the city.

They stood for a moment on the brick walk, Nathan looking up at the house with its round, turretlike corner, Amanda smoothing the creases from her skirt and listening to the pleasant sounds of the neighborhood. Having lived so far from people all her life, she was fascinated with the idea of so many living in one place with only the barrier of shared walls for privacy. It would, she decided, be a nice place to live.

"Ready?" he asked.

"Ready." With a brisk nod and a last tug on the bottom of her jacket, she marched up the steeply pitched steps with Nathan beside her.

A small, dark-haired maid admitted them, but in a matter of minutes they were back out on the steps again, Amanda's elbow once more in Nathan's firm grasp. This time, however, she had no trouble finding

MATTERS OF THE HEART 63

words as she jerked her arm free and whirled on him furiously. "Are you insane? How dare you!"

"How dare I what?" he drawled. "How dare I save you from being bullied by that old crone? I'd think you'd thank me."

Her mouth flew open, her squeal of indignation running off the scale. "Thank you? You told the woman my 'clumsiness' would probably 'annoy' her!"

He shrugged. "It was the most graceful exit I could think of."

With a splutter of pure outrage, she shook a finger under his nose. "Without your constant interference, I would've found work today!" She flung out an arm, pointing back up the steps. "That 'old crone' was my last—no, our last chance!"

He opened his mouth to retort, then clamped off whatever he was going to say when they both caught sight of some gaping passersby. Folding his arms tightly across his chest, he leaned back against the stone balustrade and examined the toes of his boots with undue concentration.

Amanda, too, was embarrassed by the public notice and began making a great to-do over smoothing the front of her jacket and skirt again. When she finally dared to look back up, there was still a grimness about his mouth, but the angry flush around the rim of his ears had begun to cool. As if feeling her scrutiny, he lifted his eyes.

"There was no reason for her to pinch you like that," he said quietly, reaching out a finger to touch the cheek still bearing the red mark of Edna Crittendon's misplaced temper. "You wouldn't have been happy there. She'd've run you ragged."

Amanda ducked her head away and put her own hand to her still burning cheek. She was touched by his concern, but couldn't afford to be mollified by it.

Not yet. There was still too much at stake here, and time was running out. She shook her head, bewildered. "You sure pick an odd time to be so chivalrous. I thought you wanted to avoid this marriage."

"I do. I guess I just let compassion get in the way of better judgment, that's all."

She glanced up and down the street quickly to see if they were still being observed before pushing her face close to his. "Well, now what, Sir Knight?"

He returned her glare with an equal thrust of jaw. "I guess we get married and live happily ever after!"

Recoiling from the sarcasm, she stared at him coldly, then stomped down the steps and headed for the carriage. "Never! I prefer the original plan, thank you."

"That was the original plan," he pointed out, falling into step beside her.

"I meant about my finding employment."

He stopped and threw up his hands. "All right! Fine! Which do you prefer? Would you rather be pawed or bullied?"

"Neither!" she snapped, skirts churning around her boot tops.

Staring after her retreating figure, Nathan blew his cheeks out in exasperation. Suddenly, he grinned. Not only had she passed right by his carriage, but her angry strides were so long they made her head bob up and down like an agitated channel buoy. He caught up to her with an easy jog. "Where we going?" he asked pleasantly, matching his pace to hers.

She stopped so abruptly he had to back up a step. "For a man so eager to remain a bachelor, you surprise me by overlooking the obvious."

"Oh? And what might that be?"

"The canneries."

All traces of humor vanished and he regarded her

seriously now. "You mean to say you'd actually rather work in some factory than marry me?"

She was surprised by the question. "I'd rather work anywhere than marry where I'm not wanted."

"You may not have a choice."

That hurt. "Now you sound just like your father," she retorted, feeling revenged when he winced, his nostrils flaring. She had returned sting for sting. "From what I've heard, they're always in need of labor at the canneries."

"And have you also heard what it's like in one of those places?"

Inwardly, she quailed as the words *evil*, *vile*, and *exploitative* flashed through her head, but pushed them away determinedly, literally waving a hand to brush his question away. "It doesn't matter. If you'll let me do the talking this time, both of us stand a good chance of ending this day with our lives in our own hands," she told him with a confidence she didn't feel.

Fists on hips, his coat spread open, he searched her face doubtfully. Just when she thought he was going to refuse to take her, he shrugged and took her by the arm. "As you wish."

She had won. She only hoped the prize was worth it.

The canneries were down near the harbor's southern shore in great open-ended sheds that squatted as close to their private railway extensions as they could get. During the half hour ride it took them to get there, Nathan never spoke, never looked in her direction. It appeared he was concentrating on the things involved in moving them through the city. Indeed, it did require a close eye to avoid collisions in the clogged intersections and to keep from running down the pedestrians who crossed the streets wherever they chose, but Amanda knew his silence was due mostly to his annoyance with her. She realized his pride had been pricked by her decision, but not to have made it would have left her own pride an open wound. No, she had to find work this time. If she failed . . . well, she didn't want to think about that.

Leaning forward in the boot, Nathan gripped the reins tightly. He hadn't felt this exasperated with a woman in a long time. Why couldn't she be like all the others he knew instead of this . . . kitten, complete with claws and hiss, who inspired such an urge to protect her? It was not an urge likely to rid him of her any time soon. He couldn't tell who was fooling himself more with this venture today, he or she. She was no more equipped to take care of herself than the man in the moon, he thought.

The streets had become narrower, the houses smaller. Even the cooking smells had changed from block to block as they passed from Italian neighborhoods to Polish to German—immigrants, the labor backbone of the city.

When the last block of houses was passed, the land suddenly opened out into scrub grass fields that ran right down to the oily, lapping waters of the harbor. Muddy, rutted roads crisscrossed this way and that before converging upon one long, low building. *McGann & Sons Canning Co.*, a sign said. *We Can Baltimore's Finest*, proclaimed another.

Some seventy feet back from the building stood a lone poplar on a slight rise. Parking the rig in its shade, Nathan wound the reins loosely around the brake handle and sat back. Silent, they watched the activity below them for a moment, each for his own reasons trying to squelch the urge to turn around and leave the dismal place behind.

Afraid she'd lose her nerve if she sat there any longer, Amanda climbed down. She didn't even look to see if he was coming with her, deciding the less she was aware of his presence the better.

At one end of the shed was a huge man in a sweaty, red flannel shirt stacking wooden crates. Begging his pardon, she asked whom she might see concerning employment, but he ignored her and continued to pile up the monstrous crates with ease. When she stubbornly repeated her question, he stopped, eyed her with a heavy-browed squint, and uttered exactly one word.

"Waxter."

"I beg your pardon?"

"Waxter," he repeated, jerking a thumb over his shoulder at a group of men just inside the shed.

"Hey, Bert!" he boomed, making her wince. "S'lady here ta see ya."

One of the men looked up, eyed her, and with an aside to his companions that made them roar with laughter, swaggered over to her with the cuffs of his dirty plaid trousers dragging the ground. Wiping the palms of both hands down his shirt front, he touched the brim of his stained bowler in greeting. "How do, li'l lady. Name's Bert Waxter. What can I do for ya?"

Amanda swallowed hard—and nearly jumped out of her skin when Nathan spoke up behind her.

"The 'little lady' here is seeking employment in your fair establishment. Do you think you can find something for her?"

Waxter looked blank for a moment, then a sly expression crossed his face as he glanced from her to Nathan. He gave Nathan a broad wink before shifting the slimy stub of a cigar from one corner of his mouth to the other. "So," he said, hooking thumbs behind his suspenders, "your friend needs a job, does she? Well, I guess I can find something to help out a gentleman such as yourself."

She didn't quite understand the suggestiveness in his tone, but decided to ignore it, praying Nathan would do the same. A glance in his direction showed that his eyelids barely flickered as he suggested Waxter take her on a brief tour of the place, and she relaxed.

"Sure thing," the man agreed, waving her ahead of him with his own version of a gentlemanly bow.

She walked in, determined to form no opinion, no impression of sight or sound until her job was secured, but it was a difficult vow to keep. The constant grinding, screeching, and clicking from the machinery made her wince and want to cover her ears. On top of that, the afternoon had turned unexpectedly warm, and the heat was oppressive even under the shade of the roof. She could already feel the moisture forming on her upper lip.

Running along one side of the building was a long row of tables where dozens of women, from the very young to the very old, sat shelling mounds of peas into baskets at their feet. Some of them were laughing and talking with their neighbors, but most just worked with a preoccupied frown on their faces. They all seemed oblivious to the fearful racket of machinery, but the perspiration stains under each arm denied the same attitude toward the heat.

As they moved farther into the shade-dimmed shed, Amanda glanced back to find that Nathan had remained behind to loll in the entranceway, a long stalk of grass dangling from his lips. Catching her eye, he grinned and waved. She turned back to Waxter without returning the gesture.

In two rows down the center were the machines that cut the tin, formed and soldered the cans, filled them, and even made the labels. After the cans were filled and packed into crates, they were taken outside and stacked on the platform next to the train tracks.

MATTERS OF THE HEART 69

Each step Waxter explained, his breath nearly overwhelming her as he pushed his face down near hers so his words would carry over the noise. About halfway down the aisle, he casually dropped a hand to her back. Forcing herself to keep up a steady stream of questions, she fought the urge to shake him off. Remember why you're here! she told herself firmly.

About every twenty feet or so along their path, burly armed guards hulked ominously, and when she asked about them, Waxter's eyes narrowed.

"Unions!" he snarled. Obviously a favorite subject, he dropped the offending arm to wave it about as he launched into a tirade about the can-making unions and how they resented the use of machinery to do the work once belonging to can-smiths. It seemed they'd done their best lately to try to sabotage his equipment in order to discourage other canneries from installing the same.

Lost in his own troubles for the moment, he scowled into space. But his attention wasn't diverted for long. As soon as his eye came back to her, his expression changed abruptly, and he grinned. "Fixin' to drop ya, is he?"

"What?"

"Him." He jerked his head back at Nathan, who was still lounging in the doorway. "Got tired of ya."

Finally understanding, she shook her head, but declined to offer any explanations that would correct his impression. Let him think what he would as long as he gave her employment.

When she started to continue down the aisle, he half turned and blocked her way. He leaned so close she was forced to support her weight on the metal railing between the rows of machinery in order to avoid bodily contact. Well aware that offending this man would quash any chance of a job, she prayed the distaste she felt didn't show on her face. She placed her hand lightly against the man's dirty shirt, hoping the subtle gesture would speak for her and he would back off.

"How much are the wages, Mr. Waxter?" she asked, glancing nervously in Nathan's direction. He wasn't even looking her way.

Waxter took the cigar out of his mouth, and she couldn't help wondering how many days he'd been sucking on the obnoxious thing. "That depends," he answered with a calculating flicker in his eyes.

"On what?" she asked, having to apply more pressure to the restraining hand. Another, more desperate, glance in Nathan's direction and she was nonplussed to see him twiddling his fingers at her in a perfectly asinine wave, a smug I-told-you-so smile on his face.

Fury matched her face to her hair. Oh, to slap that ridiculous smirk off his face!

"On how pretty your smile is," Waxter was saying as he rubbed a dirty, tobacco-stained finger down her arm, "and how nice you can be to ol' Bert."

"Look, Mr. Waxter, all I want is work. Maybe shelling peas back there, or loading crates—wherever you need some extra help." She was trying hard to sound reasonable and pleasant when what she really wanted to do was scream *Get your filthy hands off me!* "Whatever you can pay is fine with me."

His face got uglier. "You think since ya been with the likes of him, you're too good for me?" He grabbed her roughly and she was afraid he was going to shake her when an arm suddenly shot between them. It was Nathan's. At last.

Letting her go, Waxter stepped back far enough for her to straighten up, but essentially stood his ground as he gave Nathan a surly look. "You're gonna have a hard time findin' work for this one, Mister. She don't put herself out none to be very friendly."

Nathan pulled her beside him, turned her around, and gave her a small shove in the direction of the doorway. "I always did suspect her of having good taste," he said. His smile was so disarming it took the man half a beat to feel the insult.

"Hey! I was only trying to help ya out!" he cried, but Nathan was already following Amanda out of sight around the corner of the building.

As Nathan quickened his pace to catch up to her, he watched her scuff at the taller spikes of grass, yank off her bonnet, and let the ribbons drag the ground. She looked about ready to blow, and he was just deciding to hang back, not wanting to be the spark that set her off, when she broke into a run. Startled, he started running, too, catching her just as she was about to fling herself into the buggy. He spun her around just as tears splashed over her lashes.

"What's this?" he demanded. "He didn't hurt you, did he?"

She dashed a hand across her eyes. "N—no, but no thanks to you!"

He dropped her arm like a hot coal. "You made it perfectly clear you wanted no interference from me. I was to stay out of it and you were to gain both our freedoms, as I recall."

"Well . . ." she gulped back the tears, "I'm glad you didn't listen . . . completely."

Hands jammed in his pockets, he looked all around, everywhere but at her. "You're welcome."

Suddenly, she stamped her foot. "This is all so humiliating!" Her face crumpled and she broke into real tears this time.

Having always felt the usual male panic when faced with a woman's tears, he was momentarily flustered when she leaned weakly against him and sobbed into his shirt front. Other than to pat the back awkwardly and murmur, "There, there," over and over, he could never think of any way to comfort a weeping female. After a few false starts, he finally put an arm around her shoulders. "Come on now. Hush!" he said, beginning the awkward pat. "Marrying me can't be that bad!"

Angrily, she pushed away from him. "Oh, will you quit saying that! There's got to be something else we can do. This can't be the only cannery around here," she sniffed, accepting the handkerchief he handed her.

"No, but it won't be any different at the others."

"Why not?"

"It just won't."

"But why?"

He dragged a hand across tired eyes and down over a jaw beginning to show the stubble of late afternoon. "Because ladies of your background just don't seek work in places like these, that's why."

"That's just plain silly."

"Perhaps," he answered, helping her up into the seat, "but that's how it is and I doubt it'll ever be any different."

"What happens now?" she asked him when he'd climbed in and picked up the reins.

He slanted her a rueful look. "It looks like my father gets his way after all, doesn't it?" Hearing his own words, the reality of defeat settled like cold lead in the pit of his stomach, and he slumped back in the seat.

Amanda stared at him, her heart doing a queer flip-flop. What a twist of fate that her greatest fear would also be her greatest desire.

The longer he stared into space, the blacker his expression became, and she longed to say something, anything that would make a difference. Even if words had come, though, she doubted their ability to break through the almost physical barrier that had come crashing down between them. The sense of shared conspiracy was gone, and they were strangers once again.

Suddenly, from inside the canning shed below them there was an explosive clash of metal upon metal, then silence followed by an eruption of shouting and cursing.

"What was that?" she cried.

"The spring of a trap," he muttered without looking up.

The bitter monotone of defeat along with the vicious kick he gave the brake handle made her cringe into the corner as he turned the rig around and drove them, lurching, back onto the roadway.

The ride home was outwardly quiet with dark rumblings just beneath the surface. She could see him turning their situation over and over in his mind, and she wondered what contortion he was planning to put her through next.

"Exactly how old are you?" he finally asked, a faint curl to his lip.

"I'll be nineteen on the ninth of July," she answered, watching those hated white lines etch themselves deeper on either side of his mouth. It was the last straw.

"Well, for goodness sake!" she snapped. "What is it you want from me? My sympathies? Or should I just jump into the harbor and be done with it?"

"Now who's being ridiculous?"

"Not I! You're the one acting like the only person affected by any of this!"

"Oh, believe me," he assured her with heavy-lidded sarcasm, "I hadn't forgotten for a minute that you'd prefer anything, even sweatshop labor, to marrying me.''

She sighed heavily. So they were back to that, were they? It was one thing for him not to want her, but apparently the reverse was quite another matter.

Her fingers drummed the edge of the seat as she waited for the first sight of home. When it came at last, it was only the greatest exertion of self-control (and a glimpse of Sophie's face at one of the windows) that kept her from jumping down and running the rest of the way on foot. When Nathan pulled them close to the porch steps, she even managed to wait with ladylike patience for his assistance.

She had fully intended to reward his disgruntled behavior with bare civility in bidding him a good evening, but when he set her on her feet, something in his face caught at her heart, and her annoyance evaporated. He looked tired, but more than that, the weariness of a beleaguered soul showed in his eyes. She wanted to touch his cheek gently and offer comfort. Instead, she invited him to stay for supper.

He shook his head.

So after a subdued exchange of good nights, she forgot all about the waiting Sophie as she stood and watched the buggy roll down the lane and out of sight, leaving behind it a cloud of dust, all glittery gold in the dying light of day.

Nathan opened first one eye, then the other, but couldn't identify what had awakened him until he lifted his head from his arms and saw his brother in the doorway.

"Good morning, Sleeping Beauty," Teddy repeated, closing the office door behind him and coming over to sit on the corner of the desk.

Nathan sat up and rubbed a hand over his face, yawning hugely. "Hullo," he mumbled.

"Since when do you sleep in the office?"

"I don't. I just came here last night to do some thinking. Somewhere along the way I must've fallen asleep," he said, coming to his feet in a bone-creaking stretch. "What time is it?"

"Nearly nine. The whole world's been up for hours. Don't you hear all that racket out there?" He jerked a thumb toward the door separating the two offices. "Those are all your faithful menials with their noses to the proverbial grindstone. Been that way for hours, no doubt."

Walking over to rub a clean spot on the window and peer out, Nathan didn't say anything for a moment, then glanced back over his shoulder. "What are you doing up so early—and dressed fit to kill?"

Teddy hopped off the edge of the desk and struck a dramatic pose, thumbs behind his lapels. "Like it? Very natty, wouldn't you say?"

"Very, but—"

"And what do you think of this?" Teddy asked, tossing him the ebony walking stick he'd been twirling since he'd come in. "It's the latest addition to the Theodore Rushton image."

Reflex let Nathan catch it, and he looked it over a bit dubiously. The handle was carved into the likeness of a frog, its abnormally long tongue hanging out and down so far as to disappear into the stick itself. It was a grotesque piece of whimsy, but he could see how it would appeal to his brother's sense of the ridiculous. "Mmmm," was the most generous comment he could make before tossing it back. "You still haven't told me why you're up so early. I know mornings are your least favorite time of the day."

Teddy draped himself easily over a chair and

pretended to be absorbed in removing lint from his immaculate lapels. "True, mornings have never been my favorite time of the day. The few I've seen haven't overly impressed me, but"—he paused to beat out a tattoo with the tip of his stick—"I suppose I'll have to get used to them."

Long acquainted with his brother's love of the dramatic, Nathan played his part patiently. "Oh? And why is that?"

"Well, from what I've heard, the army has a nasty habit of rising early."

"The army?"

"Mmm-hmm. The cavalry would be nice, don't you think?"

"You're joining the cavalry?" Nathan couldn't imagine anyone less suited to the discipline of military life. "Why, for God's sake?"

"It was good enough for you," came the flippant reply.

His insides still churning over his own problems, Nathan was determined not to let his brother rankle him. Calmly and deliberately, he sat back down behind his desk and looked across at his younger brother. "Exactly what the hell does that mean?"

Teddy dismissed his own words with a shrug. "Who knows? Maybe I'll come back a hero like you did. Maybe then the old man will finally be satisfied with me."

"I did not come back a hero, and if you'd buckle down and do some honest-to-God work around here"—Nathan's jaw muscles ached from the effort to speak slowly and distinctly—"I'm sure he'd be more than satisfied with you."

Teddy was staring sullenly at the floor, but now he brightened, confirming Nathan's suspicions he'd been only half listening. "Have you ever noticed how we only refer to our father as 'he,' or 'him,' or 'old man'? Never 'Father,' or—God forbid—'Papa.' " He smiled to himself, shaking his head over his own private irony.

Nathan sighed wearily. It seemed his brother hid a tremendous amount behind that perpetually cheerful exterior. It made it hard to know what to expect from him next. "Your decision is made then?" he asked. "You're really going?"

"Let's just say I'm facing facts, okay?" All nonchalance was gone now. "If you don't marry the girl, this place gets sold, and I lose. If you do marry her, you get it all, and I still lose." He shrugged again. "At least now I know where I stand. I guess I always knew you'd get the lion's share, I just never thought he'd leave me with . . . nothing."

"Well, I wouldn't call inheriting the big house one day 'nothing,' but don't give up just yet, little brother. The game's not finished."

"Oh? You got a last ace up your sleeve I don't know about?"

"No." Nathan tapped his thumbs together in a steeple over his chest. "The old man's holding the last ace, but this particular time, the one who folds gets the pot—and can divvy it up any way he chooses." He watched the light dawn slowly in his brother's eyes.

"You—you mean you're actually going through with it? You're going to marry the girl? Hey, you didn't go and fall in love, did you?"

"Hell, no. This is just the easiest way to keep what's mine, that's all."

Teddy cocked his head to one side. "I take it she doesn't exactly look like a mud fence, either."

Green eyes and a soft pink mouth teased Nathan's memory. "No, she doesn't—but that doesn't have anything to do with it."

Very slowly, Teddy began to nod. "And there's nothing to say it has to be a . . . permanent arrangement. Once the company changes hands and becomes ours, you can send her away with a writ of divorce."

Lacing his fingers behind his head, Nathan propped his feet on the desk and considered his brother's sly but none-too-subtle suggestion almost against his will. Finally, reluctantly, he shook his head. "Her only crime was to lose her father. Divorcing her would hardly be an honorable thing to do."

"No, I suppose it wouldn't," Teddy conceded, unconcerned by the judgment. "So . . . have you announced your defeat to him yet?"

Nathan ground his teeth together. Sometimes his brother's choice of words could be as abrasive to the soul as Carborundum was to the skin. "I put a note on his desk last night. How about you? Told him of your plans yet?"

"No. When I tried to earlier, Byrnes informed me the old man was busy—seeing your Miss Alton, as a matter of fact," he said, studying the rump of his frog.

Slowly, Nathan's feet came off the desk. "Oh?"

"Mmm-hmm. I assumed you knew . . . but I can see you didn't. Wonder what she wants now?"

Staring at the door as if hoping to divine the answer from somewhere in its frosted glass surface, Nathan murmured, "I wonder that myself."

"So we decided to find me some other means of support," Amanda was saying.

"And did you?" Nat asked.

"No." She shifted uncomfortably in her chair. His casual slump behind the desk, along with the lazy cloud of cigar smoke he kept in the air between them hadn't changed an inch since she'd come in here this morning, and she got the impression he'd known the answers even before he asked the questions.

"Why not?"

She hadn't stopped to analyze it before now, so her answer, when it came, was simpler than she would have liked. "Nathan, that's why. He managed to cut short every interview for one reason or another. None of them seemed quite suitable in his opinion."

"And in your opinion?"

She just shrugged, not liking the feeling she was being led.

"What sort of employment were you seeking?" he asked.

"One for governess, and—"

"What happened there?"

"He said the man"—she blushed and looked down at the handful of green velvet skirt she'd been twisting—"wanted me for something other than a governess."

"I see. Go on."

Amanda looked up to see humor twitching at the corners of his mouth. "The second one was for a companion to an elderly lady. When I didn't answer one of her questions fast enough and she pinched my cheek, Nathan got angry and dragged me out of there." Nat was smiling outright now. "That's when I suggested we try the canneries."

His forehead pleated in surprise. "The canneries, eh? I'll wager he wasn't too happy about that."

"No . . . he wasn't. But how did you know?"

He blew a smoke ring. "Oh, just a hunch. I know my sons pretty well. Why didn't that work out?"

"The man, the boss, he got . . . well, fresh. Sort of."

"Mmmm. So have you changed your mind now?

Are you ready to concede that I know what's best for you?"

She sat up a little straighter. "No, sir. Actually, I came here today to ask you, to beg you one last time—please don't do this."

"But you've already proven there's no better alternative for you."

"Yes, there is. I've been thinking about it all night. You said you were going to join your sister and bring her back with you. Why don't I go with you and be her traveling companion on the trip back? Papa took me rowing sometimes. I never got sick, and I don't eat much, I wouldn't be a burden. I promise."

"No."

"Please."

He shook his head. "No."

"But why not?"

"Because you're marrying my son in the morning, that's why. Here." He handed her the piece of paper he'd been glancing at throughout the conversation. "Read this. I found it on my desk this morning."

She hesitated, then reached out to take it. *You win*, it read. *Tomorrow morning at ten in Judge Nessan's office.* It was signed simply, *N.*

Chapter 4

Amanda's shoulders slumped and she looked away. He had given in. Biting her lip to keep tears of frustration at bay, she looked across at her guardian.

"But, I'm sure your sister would appreciate a companion on the trip home. I'd be pleasant, I'd be invisible if that's what she wants."

His bark of laughter startled her. "Penelope has faced down hostile African natives all by herself and raced camels with bedouins. I doubt taking a sea voyage in a cabin alone would bother her overmuch. It certainly didn't on the way over."

"But what about for propriety's sake?"

"That's another thing my sister's never bothered herself with. No, I think it's better this way. I always have." With something close to a sigh of compassion he got up and came around to draw her to her feet. Holding her at arm's length, he said, "It'll all work out for the best, you'll see."

Amanda stared at her feet and nodded. What could she say? He had called her bluff, exposed her weaknesses, and vetoed all the alternatives. There was little to do now except concede defeat and leave. But even as she did so, another plan was formulating—a last resort, to be sure, but it had to work. It just had to. . . .

* * *

That night she lay on her bed fully clothed for what seemed like hours before the house grew still and Sophie and Joe finally settled into sleep.

Stealthily, barely daring to breathe, she got up and crossed the hall on stockinged feet to draw her father's old carpetbag from beneath the bed. Back in her own room, she began to fill it with clothing, combs, brushes, and the small miniatures of her parents, her movements ghostlike in their soundlessness.

During her ride home that day beside the silent-as-usual Joe, she had mapped out her every move. She knew she couldn't afford to miss a single detail. After packing, she would retrieve the small pouch of coins she'd been saving from the bottom of her all but empty jewel case. Then, she would sneak out to the barn and saddle up old Molly for the ride into town. In the morning, she would divide her money between stabling her pony, buying food, and purchasing a train ticket to the most distant point she could afford. She had to admit it wasn't much of a plan, but with her youth and willingness to work she was confident things would indeed "work out," as her guardian had predicted—even if it wasn't in the same context.

Careful to avoid the squeak of the top step, she tiptoed down the stairs. Her only moment of regret came as she was propping up her note to Sophie on the hall table. It said just that she was leaving, where to find Molly, and was signed "With love." They had already been told Nathan would find them work, and for some reason she didn't examine too closely, she trusted he still would.

Quietly, she felt her way to the front door and inched it open. She hadn't realized how stuffy the inside of the house was until she felt the cool night air brush her cheek. Backing out onto the porch, she

MATTERS OF THE HEART

closed the door with the smallest of clicks. All was quiet in the moonless night.

A split second before she identified it, a strange scent tickled her nose and a deep voice spoke from a few feet away.

"Going somewhere?"

She nearly fainted. Eyes dilated, she stared into the inky blackness as the red glow from a lighted cigar tip appeared, illuminated a man's features, then faded away. "Nathan?" she whispered through a constricted throat.

"Yes?" was the mild reply.

She sagged back against the door, her knees weak and rubbery. "My God!" she breathed. "You scared me half to death! What are you doing out here at this time of night?" She heard him move closer and she could just begin to make him out.

"I could ask you the same thing," he said, "but then I really don't have to. It's rather obvious."

She didn't care much for his tone. "So?"

He passed her and went to sit on the top step. "So come sit down." He patted the space beside him. "Let's talk."

After a moment of hesitation, she complied, setting the carpetbag down at her feet.

"Where you headed?"

She shrugged. "No place in particular—just as long as it's far away from here."

"And how were you going to pay for all this . . . travel of yours?"

Producing her pouch of coins, she answered, "With this."

He took it in one hand and weighed it thoughtfully. "Not much here."

Snatching it away, she dropped it back into her bag. "It'll do."

They were both quiet for a spell.

"I found out you'd been to see my father today. As a matter of fact, I saw you leave. You didn't look too happy." The cigar ash glowed again. "He still wouldn't change his mind, would he?"

"No."

"I didn't think so. That's why I came out here," he said, his voice husky in his effort to keep it low. "From the look on your face this afternoon I guessed you'd be planning something silly like this."

Looking at him now that her eyes had adjusted to the dark, she saw he was without a coat, his shirt open at the throat, the sleeves rolled up past his elbows, and she could smell the faint tang of sweat. He must've ridden hard once he'd guessed. "I wouldn't call it silly if I were you. It should get you your precious Rushton Enterprises, shouldn't it?"

He took a final drag on the slim cigar and flung it away, its red ash tracing a lazy arc into the night. When he spoke, the words came out in a long, sighing exhale. "Maybe, but I'm not so sure. He might sell the place for spite."

Inwardly, she groaned. Was there no way out of this mess?

"Besides," he went on, "do you think I could enjoy my victory knowing you were out in the world somewhere trying to earn your bread by stitching samplers in ancient Greek?"

"You'd get over it."

He snorted. "You flatter me . . . no, I don't think running away is the answer."

"Then what is?"

He sat hunched forward, elbows on knees, hands dangling down between. When he spoke this time, he did so to the space at his feet. "Look, Amanda—I'll be the first to admit you haven't had much of a choice

MATTERS OF THE HEART 85

this week. It's either working for a lecher or a witch, a trip to 'no place in particular,' or marriage to a jaded libertine. And you can call me a braggart if you will, but I don't think I'm exactly the worst of that lot." He held up a hand as if staving off argument. "Now I realize you don't want this marriage any more than I do, but looking at it logically, I'm beginning to think it's the best solution for both of us. I'll get Rushton Enterprises, and you'll get a home and whatever else you need for life." Taking a deep breath, he finally raised his head to look directly at her. "What I'm trying to say is I think maybe we ought to go ahead and get married—"

Amanda caught her lower lip in her teeth and waited, her pulse suddenly erratic.

"—strictly as a matter of convenience for us both."

She let out her breath. The other shoe had dropped. Bitterly, she chided herself. Fool! Romantic, silly fool! She hadn't realized it until then, but somewhere deep inside her, somewhere well away from the harsh light of reality, she had nurtured a tiny tendril of hope that the real reason he'd vetoed all her chances to work, even the reason behind his stopping her now, was because somewhere, buried equally deep inside him was a part that truly wanted to marry her. She knew it now for the childish and foolish dream it was. Marrying her was simply good business.

"Well, what do you say, Irish? Is it a deal?"

Say? She wanted to laugh and say *Sure! Why not?* but the tears had brimmed too thickly and fast to risk it. What could she say, after all? *I love you and I don't want a marriage of convenience? I want a real marriage, one where you share all the joys and sorrows of life? One with love and laughter and children and—and* . . . No, she couldn't say any of that. But the most hateful thing of all was knowing she would accept the meager crumb he offered. And she could rationalize all she wanted about the very real advantages for herself and those dependent upon her, but deep in her heart she knew the real reason was because a small, unquenchable part of her still had hope.

"You'll be well provided for," he coaxed. "You'll want for nothing. I even promise not to beat you." He suddenly grinned. "Too often, that is."

She tried to smile in return, but instead the hated tears spilled over her lashes. She dashed them away. "Aren't you being a little hasty? Wh—what if one day one of us should fall in love with somebody else?" she asked, thinking of the string of females he was about to disappoint.

"Don't worry," he said, misunderstanding. "If you should wake one morning to find you've 'fallen in love' with someone, you'll not only have my sympathies—" the sneer in his voice was loud, "but your freedom as well. You have my word on it."

"Freedom? You mean we . . . we'd get a divorce?" She couldn't think of a worse social stigma.

"No, more like an annulment, since you and I won't be—"

She waved him quiet, her cheeks flushing hotly in the darkness. "I understand." She felt the hurt all over again. He really didn't want her, not in any way. "What about you?" she pressed, refusing to let the hurt show. "What if you should fall in love with someone?"

He laughed. "In that unlikely event, I will most probably 'jump into the harbor and be done with it.' No," he said, sobering, "the rules will be the same for both of us. It'll be a live and let live proposition with each of us free to come and go as we please. Well?" he prompted.

"What? Oh. Yes." She nodded, feeling dazed by the magnitude of the whole thing. "Yes, I'll marry you."

For perhaps half a minute there was no sound, no movement, then he heaved so lusty a sigh it stirred the very hair at her temples. Reaching over, he lifted her hand from her lap and gave it a squeeze. It was silly, but she'd wanted something more intimate, even if it was only a kiss on the cheek.

"But on one condition," she suddenly added.

He reared back in surprise. "What? Again? You and your condi—oh, hey! That reminds me. Here."

"What's this?" she asked, taking the thick envelope he pulled out of his shirt and handed her.

"Fifty dollars in severance pay," he explained, leaning back on his elbows and stretching his legs down the steps in front of him, "along with two train tickets to York, Pennsylvania, for Sophie and Joe."

"Pennsylvania?"

"Well, you said find them work, and I did. There's a family by the name of Sperry on a farm outside of York who'll be glad to take them on. There are plenty of noses for Sophie to wipe and plenty of harness for Joe to mend. Light duties, just as you requested."

Amanda felt her world slipping away. "Can't they come with me?"

He shrugged. "That's up to them. I don't know what they'd do, but I'm sure we can find something. It seems there's always more than enough work to go around—but what's this condition of yours?"

He had rushed it all by her so fast she could hardly absorb it. Now all she could think about was what a tizzy Sophie would fly into over the insane lack of notice. "What? Oh, I just . . . I just want us to be friends, Nathan. Can we?"

His grin flashed in the darkness. "Sure, I don't see

why not. Even we jaded libertines need friends, you know."

Tired of having that phrase flung repeatedly in her face, she opened her mouth to retort, but it turned into a yawn; and yawns being what they are, Nathan followed suit.

"Hmmm. I agree." He sighed and rubbed a hand across his chest. "It's late and we both need to get some sleep. Since my father and I will be closeted with lawyers all morning, transferring titles and things, I'll send someone to pick you up and take you to the courthouse." Stiffly, he got to his feet, then put a hand under her elbow and helped her up. "Tomorrow at ten, then?"

Still dazed—was she really getting married in the morning?—she could only nod as she accepted his help. Dumbly, she turned to go back inside, but halfway across the porch stopped and whirled around. "What about Molly?"

"Who's Molly?" He sounded exasperated.

"My pony," she answered meekly.

He tossed her the carpetbag, and she saw the flash of his grin again. "I think my stables can hold another pony. Now, good night, Madam."

"Good night. . . . Nathan?"

"What?"

"Where's your horse?"

"In your barn."

"Oh. Good night then."

"Good night."

Having found sleep only in fitful dozes, Amanda was up like a shot at the first sound of Sophie stirring below. The old woman was still in her orange-flowered wrapper, her hair up in rags when Amanda burst into the kitchen and began to pour out everything in one long, excited sentence. With each word, the woman's dark face puckered up more and more, like that of an old bulldog's, all bug-eyed and jowly. When Amanda finished, Sophie sank heavily into the cane-bottomed rocker that sat in the corner of the kitchen.

"Lordy, child! First you are, then you ain't, now you are again"—her frown sharpened—"and you fibbed to me. You said his daddy was gonna think about takin' you with him."

Amanda blushed at her own lie. Sinking to her knees in front of the only mother she could remember, she squeezed the dry, weathered hands between her own softly fleshed ones. "I'm sorry. I didn't know what else to do. But Nathan's right. It's better this way, better for all of us."

The woman gazed tenderly down into Amanda's upturned face. "You love him, dontcha, girl?"

Nodding, she laid her cheek against the woman's knee. "But he doesn't love me," she whispered.

"Give him time, honey, give him time."

"But I'm so afraid, Sophie. Afraid he'll end up hating me. He's so angry inside."

A brown hand stroked the fiery hair. "You got lots to learn about love, child. There ain't but a mite of space 'tween loving and hating, and sometimes a man's anger is like a big ol' storm. All you can do is grab a hold of something and hang on tight 'til it's over. Trust me, baby. It'll all work out."

"Everyone keeps saying that. I hope they're right." Suddenly she sat back. "But what about you? You're not going to Pennsylvania, are you? You'll come with me, won't you?"

"Naw, I ain't going to no Pennsylvania—" she met the girl's eyes, "but neither am I going with you."

Amanda's fingers tightened convulsively on the

woman's arm. "What do you mean? Where will you go?"

"Well, I didn't want to say anything 'til I knew what you was planning, but Joe, he got hisself a sister down in Virginny, and that's where him and me'll be heading. Besides," she added, tweaking the girl's nose, "I already took care of the most important nose there is."

"But, Sophie, you've got to come with me. What will I do without you?"

A sigh which threatened the seams of the wrapper lifted her chest. "A lot of growing up, I expect."

"But—"

"Ain't no *buts* about it. Now girl, I got lots to do, so get outa my way and let me at 'em." With that, she smacked both palms on the arms of her rocker and was up and muttering, "Don't give a body no notice! What's that man think I am? A regular whirligig? How am I supposed to get us all ready by ten o'clock?"

For the next few hours the Alton household moved with a speed never before seen. After a hasty and burned breakfast, there were clothes to be aired, water to be heated, and baths to be taken. Even Joe was pressed into service filling and draining the tub, as well as dragging a trunk down from the attic when Sophie discovered how little Amanda had packed for herself. Snorting indignantly at the carpetbag's meager contents, she began to stuff it and the trunk to overflowing with everything from winter woolies to corset laces, even adding the porcelain figurines, hat pins, and powder boxes that had belonged to Amanda's mother.

When this fever of packing had died down, Joe was sent to sit with the luggage out on the front porch. As he passed Amanda in the hall, his chest looking more concave than usual in the Sunday finery, his yellowed eyes met hers and he shook his head. "Women and weddins," he muttered.

Minutes later, Amanda was stepping into the old tin tub in the kitchen. She had hoped to steep away some of her growing jitters in the steaming water, but time only permitted a quick scrubbing as Sophie stood over her and lathered up her hair with a cake of homemade soap cut from the big pan by the back door. Afterward, bundled in Sophie's wrapper and a blanket, she was hurried out to the porch to comb her hair dry in the early morning breeze. Joe looked up only once from the stick he was whittling, reaching over to pat her knee. She smiled nervously.

Her squirrel gray twill with its black braid trim had been laid out, aired, and brushed, and now while Sophie was busy pinning her curls into a heavy mass on top of her head, Amanda was repairing a small rent in the seam of the bodice, a split that attested to the fact that the dress was now on the snug side of three years old. It was the best warm-weather outfit she owned, however, and it would have to do.

Amazingly enough, everything and everyone was ready and out on the front porch when the telltale puff of dust announced the approach of a vehicle. Both women watched, hypnotized, as the cloud drew closer, gradually revealing a high-spirited, high-stepping mare and a sleek black buggy with bright red wheels—a rig built for speed and style, but no more than two occupants.

They waited without comment while the vehicle bounced steadily nearer and finally drew to a halt in the yard. With a nervous swish of skirts, Amanda stepped off the porch just as the driver, a severely dressed man of middle age, climbed down.

Gravely introducing himself as William Wellborn,

butler to Nathan Rushton, he doffed his large bowler to reveal a pink and balding pate.

"How do you do?" she returned, wondering at her own urge to curtsy. Surely such a social *faux pas* would not go unnoticed by a man whose collar was as stiffly starched as his. "We've been expecting you," she said, then pointed at the buggy, "but I can't believe we're all expected to travel in that."

William raised his eyebrows the barest fraction of an inch. "My only instructions were to deliver you and your personal effects to the courthouse, Miss Alton."

"Yes, I understand that, but what about Sophie and Joe?"

The bland expression did not change. "I couldn't say, Miss. Mr. Rushton made no mention of them."

"No mention!" *Nathan Rushton, you mean, thoughtless*— "Well," she said with a brittle smile, "we'll just have to follow in the wagon, that's all." She spun away, but Sophie blocked her path.

Her own eyes were sad. "Child, don't you think if Mr. Nathan wanted us there he'd've said so? Or sent a bigger buggy?"

"But it's my wedding, too, and I want you there!"

"Well, we don't always get what we want. 'Sides," she added with a shrug that was supposed to be offhand, "I gots me a million things to do around here before Joe and me leave."

"But—"

"If you'll just show me where your baggage is, Miss, I'll load it into the carriage."

Amanda suddenly wanted to whirl around and pummel the man's bowler to pulp. Instead, she just thrust her small chin toward the trunk and carpetbag on the corner of the porch, and turned back to Sophie with desperation in her eyes. "Sophie? Please?"

The woman gripped the girl's trembling hands. "Now, baby, don't take on so."

"It's time we were going, Miss."

"Not yet!" Amanda snapped. Real panic seized her now as she clutched Sophie's arm, tears threatening to spill. In a matter of minutes all that was familiar to her would be gone and she'd be swept into a world of strangers. She glanced over at Joe on the steps, but he was busy whittling the stick into nothingness and wouldn't look up. "I'll miss you. I'll miss you both."

Sophie patted the pale cheeks and smiled through her own tears. "Aw, baby, now don't you start or you'll get me to blubbering," she pretended to scold, chucking the girl under the chin. "Now smile pretty for me . . . that's a girl."

"Miss. . . ."

Sophie glared over Amanda's shoulder at the butler, silencing him. "You better git going," she told the girl in a loud whisper, "before that prissy little man messes himself. 'Sides," she fussed, "I raised you better'n to be late for your own wedding." When Amanda didn't move, she turned her forcibly around and gave her a small shove. "Now go on! Git!"

Her feet finally set in motion, Amanda followed the butler over to the carriage and numbly allowed him to help her up into the seat. It seemed impossible to believe she was on her way to get married.

As they wheeled out of the yard, there were repeated calls of "Good-bye" and "Good luck," and even Joe looked up once to raise his hand in farewell. The two women, however, waved continuously until they were separated from each other's sight by the line of trees along the roadfront.

Biting her lip, Amanda's hand gradually stilled. A part of her life was over forever now. Tears blurred the bright blue day, and she ducked her head back inside the carriage. *Just beginning,* she corrected, reaching for her handkerchief.

They bumped along in silence, the dirt road ahead of them a curling ribbon of hot brown between the cool green of young, new fields. Sunlight sparkled off the leaves and winked off the horse's jingling harness.

"Bright today, isn't it?" she asked with a sniff, refolding the daintily edged linen.

"A bit, yes."

"Warm, too."

Light gray eyes flicked briefly in her direction, then back to the road. Either by nature or by what he considered proper, the good butler was obviously disinclined to conversation. While she would have welcomed the distraction, pride kept her from trying again.

It was a long ride.

Their pace had not been especially fast, but when they reached the city limits they were reduced to a comparative crawl as they came up against great throngs of people marching in the streets.

She touched William's arm. "What is it? What's going on?"

"I'm afraid most of the streets will be similarly congested, Miss. All the trade unions are parading today," he told her, his tone indicating how plebian he considered such activities. "It's Labor Day."

Labor Day! Good heavens, she thought, today was May 1,* then! Some bride she was. She hadn't even taken note of her own wedding date!

But her own claim on the day gradually faded from

---

*Until June of 1894, when Congress declared the first Monday in September national Labor Day, Baltimore traditionally celebrated Artisans' Day on September 1 and Labor Day (the day its trade unions paraded) on May 1.

MATTERS OF THE HEART 95

her mind as she watched the colorful, noisy procession, enthralled as any child. While William concentrated on squeezing them past this cheering, singing flow of humanity, she was busy identifying the groups of glass blowers and meatcutters (cleavers carried as solemnly over each shoulder as a musket) and box makers and cigar makers and on and on. Perched high on the carriage seat, she saw and loved it all, including the bricklayers' union—a roiling, boiling sea of black and white faces that chanted lustily as they surged past, jostling the carriage wheels and making their horse prance and flick its ears nervously.

That was the worst of it. The groups that followed were smaller and quieter. Even the spectators were fewer, as most of them tagged along after the larger, rowdier, and more politically powerful guilds.

As the cacophony of too many brass bands faded behind them and their speed picked up again, Amanda spotted and watched with interest one of the last, straggling groups to file past. They were the sewing girls, the seamstresses, the piece workers. The Unknown Assembly they called themselves. Knowing how easily she might have ended up in their ranks, she looked curiously into their faces. With their backs ramrod straight and looking neither right nor left, as if daring anyone to challenge their right to be there, Amanda found something curiously intimidating in their dauntless expressions. Beyond gender, she felt no affinity with these crusading women and realized she was not cut out to be one of them. Perhaps fate, if not Nathan, had realized this, too.

The streets now seemed deserted in the wake of all the parades, normal life having a somnambulant feel to it in comparison. Even the usually raucous cries from the street vendors were no harsher on the ears than bird calls.

As William pulled their rig next to the curb across from the courthouse (a building with a most serious and imposing facade, complete with a set of antique stocks in front), he pulled out his timepiece. They were fifteen minutes early, he informed her, and asked if she would care to wait inside where it was cooler.

She thanked him but declined, not bothering to add that she already felt like ice from a sudden, renewed attack of the jitters. To distract herself, she tried taking an interest in the things around her, watching more attentively than the act required while William drew water for the horse from a nearby trough.

When an open-topped landau passed, she glanced up to see its occupant, a very fashionably dressed woman with a veritable garden of pink and yellow flowers on her head.

Flowers! Amanda looked down at her empty hands, suddenly aware she carried no bouquet of any sort. She hadn't thought about it, else she would have gathered some blooms from her own garden. As a bride still in mourning, the idea of wedding finery had been dismissed; on the other hand, she was not willing to forgo every symbol of the occasion, especially such a small one. She had already given up so much—loved ones, love itself. . . .

Remembering a flower vendor a block or so back, she felt in her reticule for the little pouch of coins. She hadn't a moment to lose. Leaping down to the cobbles, she called, "I'll be right back, Mr. Wellborn." Holding onto her straw hat with one hand, she lifted her skirts with the other and began to run.

William straightened up from placing the water bucket in front of the mare, and his mouth sagged open at the sight of her speeding away. "Miss Alton!" he called. "Miss! Come back!"

She turned and ran backwards a few steps, her chest

already heaving with exertion inside the tight bodice. "Flowers!" was all she could get out before disappearing into the crowd along the sidewalk.

The butler's mouth closed and his face returned to its usual passivity, but his eyes seemed drawn to the pair of stocks across the street. Removing his hat, he wiped a suddenly moist forehead.

Amanda moved quickly, begging hasty pardons as she weaved in and out among her fellow pedestrians, but when she caught sight of the vendor's cart, it was on the opposite side of the street from what she remembered. With a small hiss of frustration, she dashed into the street and right into the path of a team of horses. She froze. Mesmerized by the churning hooves coming right for her, she didn't hear the warning shout until she was suddenly seized and thrown across to the curb, where she and her rescuer went down in a tangled heap of arms and legs.

After a stunned moment of immobility, they began to disentangle themselves, and Amanda sat back to stare up at the person who had saved her. He was fastidiously brushing off his golden brown trousers and coat as he got to his feet. Expecting to be rebuked for her carelessness, she was surprised when he smiled and lent a hand to help her up.

"You aren't hurt, are you?"

"No . . . no, I don't think so. Thank you," she added with a look of chagrin, "for saving me from a rather shabby death."

He laughed. "I thought all forms of death were rather shabby."

He was a bit older than she, and handsome in an easy sort of way. "I suppose you're right, but thank you anyway."

"You're very welcome. Now tell me," he said, settling the tobacco-colored derby at a more precise angle, "what was it on this side of the street worth risking life and limb for?"

She nodded her head toward the flower cart beside them, the vendor for which was ignoring them now that the promise of bloodshed had gone unfulfilled.

"Flowers!" His tone spoke volumes on feminine frivolity.

"For my wedding," she explained defensively.

He threw up his hands in mock despair. "What is it in this town? It must be spring fever. Everyone I know is taking a wife lately. If I don't hurry, all the beautiful ones will be snapped up."

Amanda smiled shyly, but looked away. In daydreams flirting was easy, but in reality it called for a boldness she didn't yet have.

He retrieved her gaze by making a small bow and looking up into her face. "Might I at least have the honor of buying a bride's bouquet for her?"

She started to refuse, should have refused, but this very special, very romantic day had lacked even the barest flavor of that romance. Smiling, she accepted.

He pretended to scrutinize her with a critical blue eye. "Hmmm, let's see . . . you look as fair as a rose to me. How about roses?"

She shook her head. "Daisies, please."

He looked disappointed. "No roses?"

"Daisies."

So daisies it was. However, just as she accepted the bouquet from him, he reached over, plucked a single rosebud out of another bucket on the cart, and poked it down into the middle of her daisies.

A thorn pricked her, and she squeaked, sticking her finger into her mouth. When he asked to see it, she felt silly at the attention, but obligingly held out her hand. In horror, she watched him lift the finger to his lips and place a kiss on its tip. Flushing painfully

MATTERS OF THE HEART 99

scarlet, she jerked her hand behind her back, half expecting him to reach for it again. He only smiled.

"Good-bye, Daisy. I have to be going."

"So must I . . . Sir Galahad!" she dubbed him with a giggle.

His smile became a disturbingly crooked grin as he bowed in courtly acceptance of the honor. "Be careful the next time you cross the street," he cautioned her with a wink, then tipping his hat, threaded his way back into the crowd.

"I will," she promised with a lift of her hand, watching until he disappeared from sight. She hadn't even thought to ask his name.

When William finally spotted Amanda coming toward him, he stopped his pacing and sighed. She was expected in the judge's chambers this very minute, so without a word, he waved her ahead of him up the stone steps, and steered her through the maze of echoing corridors to Judge Nessan's door.

Amanda recoiled from the wall of cigar smoke that hit her in the face, but before she could beg for the door to be left open, Nat spotted her and came over to pull her arm through his and lead her over to the others.

"Ah, here's our bride now! Come," he beamed, "there're some people I want you to meet."

Squinting through the thick, blue haze, her mind registered the book-lined walls, the dark paneling and red leather chairs, but it was Nathan, all in black, on the other side of the room who drew her eye. Aloof from the others, he stood by one of the long, velvet-draped windows, smoking. He looked around at her entrance, but made no move toward her. Instead, his eyes dropped to the flowers she clutched. The dark brows arched.

Stupid flowers! I knew I shouldn't have gotten them!

Nat's tug on her arm brought her attention back and she acknowledged the greeting of Judge Nessan. A rotund little man, he looked better suited to playing Santa Claus at children's Christmas parties than to deciding the fates of the criminal element. Beside him, a tall woman in black bombazine, her dull brittle hair piled haphazardly on her head, was introduced as his wife.

"Ach, poor thing!" she exclaimed in understanding of Amanda's watering eyes, and went over to open the windows wider and fan the air around with her hands. "I know just what you mean."

Amanda had to turn slightly for the next introduction, and when she glanced up, her polite smile faltered. It was the man who had bought her the flowers!

"Amanda," said Nat, "I don't believe you've ever met my younger son, Teddy."

Teddy! Good grief! She'd been chatting with Nathan's brother and hadn't even realized it, though how she could have missed the resemblance she would never know. His hair and eyes were lighter, but their features were strikingly similar. Managing to mumble something resembling a greeting, she mechanically extended her hand.

Teddy bowed over it solemnly, but as he straightened up, his eyes shown merrily. "Those are lovely flowers you have there. They suit you perfectly," he said, "especially the rose."

"Th—thank you. They were a—a gift from someone very thoughtful."

"And obviously someone of excellent taste."

Her composure, already strained beyond normal limits, cracked completely at this and she laughed aloud, drawing a curious glance from Nathan as well as a scowl from her guardian, who was frowning suspiciously at this exchange.

"Shall we get started?" It was the judge.

"Yes, yes," Nat harumphed and went over to clap a fatherly hand to Nathan's shoulder. "Well, son?"

Nathan nodded and flung his cigar out the window with an energy that revealed the tension hidden behind his calm exterior. She held her breath as he came to take his place at her side, but all he said was, "Ready, Irish?"

Her teeth clamped off the sudden quiver in her lip and she nodded.

There was a lot of pushing and pulling as the Nessans arranged Amanda and the Rushtons to their liking; then with a great clearing of throats and taking of deep breaths, the wedding began.

It was nothing like Amanda imagined it would be, nothing like her girlish dreams had painted it. There was no puff-chested, blarney-spewing father, no weeping Sophie, no distant-eyed Joe, no friends, no air of celebration to mark the occasion. But as she listened, stealing little glimpses of the man beside her, she was suddenly filled with the rightness of it all, and she could well believe those solemnly spoken words were tinged with magic. Regardless of how it had come to be, she belonged here by Nathan's side, and as she spoke her vows, she knew with aching clarity she meant them. There was no memory of any deal struck to put the lie to her "I do."

As it came time for Nathan to repeat after the judge, Amanda watched the strong profile out of the corner of her eye and wondered what he was thinking as he, too, spoke the required words.

She was still watching when they came to the part

about the ring, and could hardly believe it when his face flushed and he shifted his weight from one foot to the other.

"I . . . I didn't get a ring," he confessed.

Chapter 5

Nathan's jaw muscles ached. Damn! He hated this, hated all of it. He could feel the tiny tremble in Amanda's hand, and couldn't force himself to look at her, to face the hurt he knew was in her eyes. Damn them, damn them all for forcing this.

Judge Nessan looked quickly from one face to another, each one staring into his with a different expression. "Well, we have to have a ring," he insisted.

It was Nat, looking like a thundercloud, who saved the day by removing a heavy gold signet ring from his own finger and handing it to his son. "Here, use this," he growled.

The judge was the only one in the room who looked relieved.

Repeating the proper words, Nathan slid the already warmed ring onto her stiffened finger, and curled her hand closed to keep it from falling off. When they were finally declared man and wife, and he was told he could kiss the bride, he found her staring straight ahead, obviously prepared for his refusal. It took surprisingly stubborn pressure from the knuckle he put under her chin to bring her face around toward his—and she still wouldn't look at him. The kiss he placed on her mouth was brief, soft, and flavored with more apology than he'd intended, but the expression in her eyes remained hidden behind a tangle of autumn lashes. He sighed. Well, it was done now.

The moment suddenly dissolved into one of handshaking, congratulations, and all the well wishing that went with such an occasion, and if anyone noticed the lack of smiles on the wedding couple's faces, they said nothing. Several times the groom's eyes were seen to collide with the bride's, but then both would look away. He maintained a lot of eye contact with other people, she did a lot of nose burying in her flowers.

Nathan shook the judge's hand. *She looks sad and uncertain, like she's about to cry.*

Amanda accepted the kiss from Mrs. Nessan. *He looks angry. So much for being friends.*

She's probably sorry she agreed to this.

No doubt he's regretting his bargain by now.

"Son . . ."

His attention turned by the hand on his arm, Nathan followed his father over to the corner.

"I believe these are yours now," Nat said, producing a thick envelope from an inner coat pocket and holding it out. "Believe me, son, you did the right thing." He held out a hand.

Nathan stared at the packet of deeds, titles, licenses, and permits for a prolonged moment, able to feel his brother's sudden, avid interest from across the room. Meeting his father's eyes levelly, he took the papers, put them in his pocket, and walked away without shaking hands. He knew it was a petty thing to do, but there had been so few vents for his frustration this morning that he couldn't pass one up. Behind him lay several hours of hearing his father say "my clients" and "my accounts," "my" this and "my" that, even as he was signing away his freedom in order to make them *his* clients and *his* accounts. Ahead lay several more hours of playing husband to a nervous bride, a

MATTERS OF THE HEART 105

role that would drive the thorns of his defeat even deeper.

Leaning a shoulder against a glassed and framed map of the city, the kind with out-of-scale trees and landmarks, he struck a lucifer off the heel of his boot and lit up another one of his dark, slim cigars. Through the veil of smoke he nodded at his brother's thumbs up sign, watched him kiss Amanda's cheek and leave. He'd obviously gotten what he'd come for.

Amanda was busy signing something for the judge. When she was through she walked over to his father and held out the ring. Narrow-eyed, he saw the old man chuckle, then kiss her, whispering something that made her smile and bury her nose in those damned daisies again. He decided to join them.

". . . and remember now," his father was saying, "lots of beauty and charm, and everything will work out fine. Who knows? Maybe by the time I get back you'll be able to tell me I'm to be a grandfather."

Nathan's cigar followed the other one out the window. "You've managed everything else up until this point," he said. "Maybe you'd like to stay and take care of that as well."

Nat's head snapped around, the veins in his eyes as red as Amanda's stricken face. "You're not too old to be taught some manners, boy!"

"How about now?" Nathan shot back. "Seems like a good time to me."

"Out in the hall!" Nat shouldered past him and threw open the door, sending it crashing into the wall.

Right on his heels, Nathan caught it on the rebound, elbowing it into the panels once again.

The sound still booming down the shadowed marble hallway, Nat pivoted with a stabbing finger already raised. "Who the hell do you think you are?" His voice shook. "You've behaved like a surly street

A-rab all morning—" the arm and the finger were flung toward the door—"and she deserves better than that!"

"You should've thought about that before you pushed things this far." Nathan's own face felt red-hot. "I can't believe it, I can't believe you actually did this! But the company's mine now." He smacked a fist against his breast pocket and the overpriced papers. "And you've played your last ace. There's nothing more you can use to hold over my head, ever. So don't go filling her head with ideas about babies because there's not going to be any. I married the brat, but that's the end of it!"

He loves me, he loves me not, he loves me, he. . . . The daisies were quivering so much Amanda was finding it hard to concentrate, and now they were beginning to blur as well. She'd been trying very hard not to listen to the sharp, echoing words out in the hall, but the sheer volume overruled her best efforts. Nathan's last words had even put an end to the Nessans' attempts to cover the angry voices with their own polite small talk. There was complete silence in the room now as the quiet rumble of Nat's reply was heard.

"Then you're not nearly as smart as I thought you were. . . ."

The rest of his sentence grew indistinct, and a moment later Nathan stalked back into the room. He reached for Amanda's arm, but the judge stopped him with, "I need you to sign here, Mr. Rushton."

Amanda avoided meeting anyone's eyes as Nathan snatched up the marriage certificate. The nib scratched loudly, then he threw down the pen and grabbed her wrist. "Come on."

"I'll have my clerk make a copy and send—"

MATTERS OF THE HEART 107

"Fine!" Nathan growled over his shoulder as she quickened her steps to keep up.

Out of breath and patience by the time they reached the carriage, she jerked her arm free. In no mood to brook an argument, however, he encircled her waist with both hands and lifted her bodily into the carriage seat.

"Where's Mr. Wellborn?" It wasn't what she really wanted to ask, but it was the safest question on the safest subject she could think of.

"My father," he gritted, "commandeered him to help him with his luggage, luggage that's already been seen to. The man will probably beat us home."

"Oh." She watched the lines on either side of his mouth deepen as he climbed in beside her. Nothing like a little engineering to help 'beauty and charm' along, she thought, remembering her guardian's recent advice. "Shouldn't we see your father off?"

A sideways glower was all the answer she received.

The ride out of the city was as quiet as the ride in, albeit with a different driver. She had no idea if he was calming down or still simmering, but she was getting a headache from all the suppressed temper, and was at the point of preferring open warfare.

"Why," she demanded, firing the first shot, "couldn't Sophie and Joe come?"

He looked at her with blank surprise. "Who said they couldn't?"

"You did, in effect, when you sent this silly little thing out to collect us."

"Silly li—!" His brows snapped back into position over the bridge of his nose. "I thought you'd enjoy riding in style. Why couldn't Sophie and Joe follow in something else?"

"I wanted them to, but Sophie said it was obvious you didn't want them."

"Well, I'm"—the word fought its way past the stubborn set of his mouth—"sorry. You shouldn't be so attached to servants, anyway. It's unnatural."

"Unnatural! They're more friends than servants, more family than servants, and since you don't seem to have a friend or a family member you care about—"

"All right, Amanda."

"—I wouldn't go around calling other people's attachments 'unnatural' if I were you, so—"

"All right! Enough!"

"But they're all the family I have!"

"Good grief! I haven't been married an hour and already I'm being nagged."

Amanda sucked the rest of her words back into her mouth, locked her fingers tightly around her bouquet, and jammed her hands between her knees. *I won't be a shrew. I won't be a shrew.* But hot tears welled, and even the carriage wheels seemed to mimic her silent complaint with each turn. *Un . . . fair. Un . . . fair.*

Irritation twitched along Nathan's nerve endings. Unfair, that's what it was. The whole thing was unfair. *He precipitates it, then traipses off to Europe and leaves me with the mess. If she wanted those damned servants along, why didn't she just say so, instead of letting it go by and then bawling like a baby?* He slanted a look in her direction to confirm his suspicions and saw a single tear tracing the curve of her cheek. He didn't mean to hurt her feelings, but he'd be damned if he'd apologize again. It seemed that was all he'd been doing lately. Frowning, he hunched a shoulder against the cooling wall between them even as the motion of the carriage brought hot thigh against hot thigh, soft shoulder against hard. Damn. . . .

For miles and miles they traveled through uncultivated countryside, the fresh green and unkempt tangle of feathery new leaves giving everything the soft, fuzzy look of a watercolor. Gradually, though, things began to take on the look of human care once again in the form of neatly plowed fields and well-tended fencing. When the mare picked up speed, her ears pricking forward, Amanda sensed with a mixture of relief and apprehension that they were finally nearing their destination. After they turned down a long private road, the occasional flash of sun on a slate roof teased her through the trees ahead, but the house itself remained hidden from view even as they came to an open gateway. Tall stone pillars in heavy mantles of honeysuckle vine guarded either side of the driveway like proud old sentries. As they trotted between them, Amanda unconsciously leaned forward, anxious for her first look at Nathan's home. Her home.

The road opened into a complete circle of well-worn earth. Facing each other from opposite sides of it were a huge house and barn built entirely of gray fieldstone, with all the trim, deeply silled windows, and doors painted a gleaming white. A dark green carriage house made a triangle of the larger structures, while a series of smaller ones meandered off behind the barn. The buildings rested in a majestic copse of tall oaks, their limbs spread with the promise of deep shade come summer, while the land surrounding them all was open and rolling.

Peace and *dignity*. The words seemed to emanate from somewhere outside herself as she exhaled slowly. "If ever a place deserved to be called home," she murmured, "this is it."

The trace of a smile lightened Nathan's expression as he wheeled them around to the flagstone path by the front door. "I've always felt the same thing. My mother's father built it. She grew up here. After my grandparents died, she closed it. Since it was left to me, I decided to open it up again when I came home from the army. My father lives just a few miles from here, but I couldn't go back there.''

Amanda absorbed this with an odd feeling in the pit of her stomach. Hearing about other people, some of whom she didn't even know about, gave her a sense of having married a stranger for the first time. Come to think of it, how much did either one of them know about the other?

"Amanda?"

She looked around to find him already at her side of the carriage offering one hand to her, while holding her carpetbag in the other.

"Having second thoughts?" he asked.

The accuracy of the question made her frown defensively. "Don't be silly. I've made my bed. . . ."

His fingers closed too tightly around the hand she held out. "And now you intend to lie in it? How noble."

She blushed, extricating her hand as soon as her feet touched ground. "That's not how I meant it—shall we go in?"

His free hand at her back, he guided her up the path and through the heavy front door without another word.

If Nathan's house was grand on the outside, it was even more so on the inside. From a gleaming-floored foyer bigger than any room in the Alton house, a wide central staircase led up to a second floor gallery where there were more doors leading to more rooms than Amanda could count in one glance. And one glance was all she had, for at the bottom of the staircase was a handful of servants hastily assembling themselves in a line to greet her.

Nathan seemed as surprised as Amanda, but recovered quickly enough to introduce them. First there was Mrs. Brown, a plump woman with good humor showing in her blue eyes and a little brown knot of hair on her head. Next was the dark-eyed cook, Mary, who had obviously been a beauty in her day. When an older man with a wrinkled red face and gray side whiskers was introduced as Donald Diggs, the gardener, Amanda had to squash the nervous impulse to laugh. He squinted at her and produced a dirt-clumped spade from behind his back.

"Sorry," he mumbled with a shrug, indicating a pair of tall, graceful plants standing at odd angles in urns on either side of the stairway. "Meant to have them palms done before you got here."

Nathan looked from them to him a bit blankly. "I thought something looked different. . . . And this one here is—I'm sorry. I've forgotten your name."

The little round-eyed blond bobbed a self-conscious curtsy. "I'm Rose, sir."

"Wait! Wait for me!" a young voice called from somewhere in the back of the house. Pounding feet were heard just seconds after a door banged, and a little tow-headed boy came skidding into the room. Unable to brake fast enough, he ran smack into Rose at the end of the line, causing a chain reaction of both bodies and laughter. Embarrassed under Nathan's scowl but recovering quickly, the boy fixed big brown eyes on Amanda and bowed himself nearly in half. "Welcome, ma'am. I'm Georgie, an' if there's anything I can do for you, anything at all," he emphasized, "you just let me know."

His offer was made so solemnly she could only respond in kind. Offering him her hand, which he took after wiping his own down the side of a dust-lightened trouser leg, she thanked him with a smile that caused him to blush.

"Who do you belong to?" she asked.

"Oh, Rosie here is my sister. Walt Heiler's our dad

He takes care of the horses. We got great horses." The brown eyes wavered slightly. "I mean, Mr. Nathan does."

She smiled and glanced back at Nathan, but he was looking impatient with all the warmth her arrival had generated. She decided to ignore him. "I see," she said, turning back to the boy, "and where do you—"

The front door opened behind them, and a huge hulk of a man came through with Amanda's small trunk hoisted on a shoulder. Spotting her bag by the door where Nathan had set it, he stooped to grab that, too, before heading up the stairs.

"Hi, Bob!" Georgie called. "He helps my dad," he told her.

Bob's upper body swiveled enough for him to nod down at her, his feet continuing the ascent. "Howdy, ma'am." He had just reached the upper landing and was turning right when Nathan's voice halted him midstep.

"Not that way, Bob. The lady will be taking the back bedroom on the left," he said, causing six pairs of eyes to widen, go from Nathan to Amanda, then down to the floor.

Mortified in the silence that followed, Amanda lamely attempted to make light of the moment. "Really, Nathan," she laughed, a false and brittle sound even to her own ears. "Shame on you. Didn't you tell them this was just a marriage of convenience? It's sort of a . . . business arrangement," she told the room at large. Her brilliant smile felt pasted to her face, and she knew she'd made it worse than it already was when everyone shifted uncomfortably. Nathan's sigh was loud, and she didn't have to look to know the black scowl on his face.

Suddenly, Mrs. Brown stepped forward and took Amanda's cold hands in both her warm ones. "You

MATTERS OF THE HEART 113

must be exhausted, my dear. Why don't you come with me and freshen up while I unpack your things?"

Grateful for the compassionate rescue, she nodded weakly. And, as if that were the signal, the rest of the staff scurried off to attend to their own duties.

Daring a brief glance at Nathan as soon as the housekeeper turned her back, she was surprised at the uncertainty in his face. Then his gaze dropped to the bouquet she still clutched and one eyelid drooped.

"Weren't you supposed to throw that thing?"

Glaring daggers, she slapped the flowers as hard as she could into his midsection, and wished she could do it several more times when she heard his slight *woof*. "Consider them thrown," she muttered, liking the mental image of him left helplessly holding the wilted things as she marched, posture-perfect, up the steps behind the housekeeper to her room. The back one on the left.

The room was done in blues and greens and graceful curves of polished cherry. It boasted everything from a lace-canopied bed to a Grecian fireside sofa and a dressing table not unlike her mother's. But Amanda was in no mood to be appreciative. There had been too many emotions in too few hours. Tired and dejected, she stood in the middle of the room and pivoted wearily to keep the ever-moving housekeeper in sight as she bustled about, cheerfully pointing out its many features of comfort like a tinker touting the merits of his wares.

"Yes, it's lovely, Mrs. Brown, but—"

"It actually has a better view of the garden than the master bedroom, and please, call me Emma. Everybody does."

"Thank you. I shall, but right now I'd—"

"And right through here . . . what is it, dear?"

"I'm sorry. Truly. It is a beautiful room, but I'm so

very tired and all of this is so—so. . . ." She shrugged her shoulders helplessly as tears of sheer exhaustion rushed behind her eyes.

Emma flapped her plain white apron in agitation and made an impatient face. "Of course, of course. How stupid of me. Here I am, chattering away like a magpie, and there you are, poor thing, about ready to drop in your tracks." Taking charge of her new mistress, she propelled her over to the bed, sat her down, and began wielding a button hook down the side of Amanda's boots with the speed and precision of a surgeon.

Grateful for the understanding attention at last, Amanda allowed herself to be undressed and tucked beneath the blue floral coverlet. "Thank you," she murmured, watching the woman draw the drapes across the French doors leading to her small balcony, then gather up her discarded clothing. It wasn't Sophie's motherly cluckings, but she was a married woman now, and Sophie was right. She had to do some growing up.

"Don't worry yourself about anything now," the woman said. "You just rest, and I'll be back later with these things all pressed again." The door closed softly behind her.

In the quiet she left behind, Amanda stared moodily at the lace overhead. Nothing was happening the way she had pictured it. At home, with her own people, her own surroundings, the goal of winning Nathan's love seemed possible. But here . . . so many walls, so many people . . . and he could use them all to keep as much distance between them as he liked. Sadly, it came to her that in a place this size, a marriage like theirs could quickly become a very sterile thing. It chilled her to think of all the detached small talk, the polite inquiries of health that could pass across the long dining table she'd glimpsed downstairs. A bored society matron . . . it was not how she'd envisioned her life at all.

She looked around the pretty but impersonal room, searching for something of hers, something to make her feel she belonged in these new surroundings, but there was nothing. It made her regret using the flowers to show her temper. She would have liked looking at them. Should've put them in water, she thought sleepily. Or at least pressed one. Perhaps the rose. . . .

Downstairs, Emma paused on her way through the kitchen to fill her lungs with the wonderful smell of dinner cooking. Her mouth watered. A roast of beef! Rarely did Mary consider an occasion grand enough to warrant such a treat, she thought. Maybe now there was a missus, things would be different.

Taking the two steps down into the servants' living room, all cozy with warm colors and a scrubbed pine floor, she looked about for William. She'd seen him arrive when she was at the window upstairs. Of course, if he was there, she knew he'd be in the biggest, most overstuffed chair facing the huge, open hearth. That his taste in chairs matched his personality did not escape her.

"Ah, there you are," she said, sitting down next to him in her own wooden rocker.

For a few moments, there was silence while he continued to peruse the headlines of the *Gazette* with interest, and Emma stared thoughtfully at the cold, sooty back wall of the fireplace.

"She's a pretty young thing, ain't she?"

"Hmmm," he allowed as he turned a page with precision.

"Too bad about their marriage." She shook her tightly bunned head. "Business arrangement, indeed.

Give some folks money and they get all kinds of queer ideas."

He seemed to consider this, his eyes lifting from the page. "Yes, well. . . . Are you staying or have you decided to take that position over at the Pellings?" he asked.

"I don't know now. I was thinking I might just stick around for a while, see if things get any better."

"Two dollars says it won't last a year," William offered without malice.

Emma pursed her lips, not in shocked disapproval, but in serious consideration. "He leaves or she leaves?"

"She does."

"You're on."

He turned another page. "And two bits says he gets into his cups before morning."

She hesitated longer this time. Here was a much riskier proposition. "All right, two bits."

William never looked up from his reading, he just held out a hand. "Then pay up. He's been locked in his study ever since you two went upstairs."

During the past year, the entire staff had learned that the only work their employer ever did when he closed himself behind his study door was to pop a cork and bend an elbow. Sometimes the long hours would stretch into days and wear on everyone's nerves. They all took care of their duties on tiptoe—and woe to the one finally elected by the others to brave the man's wrath long enough to check on him.

With the grimace of one who's been had, Emma dug in the side seam of her skirt for her coin purse. Perhaps she should reconsider. Life at the Pellings might be less dramatic, but at least she wouldn't end up hustled out of her pay every week.

William's moist palm closed around the money, and

he pocketed it with a smile. "Bring me a small pot of tea on your next trip through the kitchen, would you? That ride out here on horseback was taxing beyond measure."

Emma pushed herself to her feet with a hiss of exasperation. "You better hope you win this bet. Otherwise, you might end up working for a living like the rest of us."

The rattle of the paper was her only answer.

Amanda opened her eyes and was surprised to find the room in lamplight. She would have sworn she'd just closed her eyes.

"Ah, good. You're awake," came Emma's voice from across the room.

Stretching and propping herself on an elbow, Amanda blinked the sleep out of her eyes as Emma folded away the last of her things. It was the sight of daisies, daisies with a single yellow rose in the center, sitting on her dressing table in a ceramic vase, that made her come fully awake. "Where did they come from?" she asked cautiously, wondering if Nathan had put them there.

"Can you believe it? Found 'em downstairs in the umbrella stand, of all places. Lord knows who put 'em there."

"Lord knows," Amanda murmured, careful not to let the woman see her hurt as she slid out of bed to go wash. Advertising the status of their marriage was one thing, but showing the pain Nathan's resentment caused was quite another. It would never do to let on she was any less equable to the situation than he. Pride alone demanded she not appear as some rejected, lovelorn wife anxious for the slightest bit of husbandly regard.

"Dinner'll be served at half past," Emma said,

"and I've laid out your black taffeta skirt and white muslin waist."

"Thank you. That's what I'd planned on wearing." It was true, but she felt awkward at the pretentious wording. She only had four or five outfits to her name, yet they were both acting like the choice had been made from among dozens. Being clean and neat had always been the standard at home, but fashion—well, fashion was a word that rarely saw much usage there. She hadn't even become aware of just how little she owned until recently. Until Nathan.

"Will you be needing anything else?"

"No, I can manage. Thank you."

When the door closed, Amanda glanced at the gilt clock on the mantle. It was nearly seven. Suddenly, it hit her that in less than an hour she would be dining alone with Nathan for the first time. What should she talk about? What would he talk about? She had no idea how or even where he had spent the day. Again she thought of the oddness of two strangers finding themselves married. Another glance at the clock, however, told her this was not the time to worry about it.

Jamming her feet into stockings and then into her shoes, she began to throw her clothes on. She had just finished a vigorous brushing of her hair and was at the point of wondering what to do with it all, when there was a knock at the door.

"Yes?"

Rose's face peeped around into view. "Emma said you might be needin' my help, ma'am."

Amanda silently blessed the woman's thoughtfulness.

So it was Rose who quickly twisted Amanda's long, auburn curls into a soft knot on the top of her head, and it was Rose who buttoned the buttons and tied the sashes when Amanda's fingers shook so badly they made even the small task of dabbing lavender water here and there all but impossible. It was even Rose who finally had to pin the small cameo at her mistress's throat.

Criticizing her finished reflection in the framed glass, her great green eyes wide with anxiety, Amanda pinched her cheeks and bit her lips so hard it brought tears to her eyes.

"There," she breathed. "How do I look? No, never mind. It'll have to do in any case." With another, almost fearful glance at the clock, she made a move toward the door, then dashed back to pluck several daisies from their little vase and pin them, crownlike, into her hair.

Nathan sat in the drawing room below, drinking deeply from the wine glass he held and staring moodily out the French doors at the moonlit terrace. A discreet knock an hour ago by William had reminded him it was time to shave and change for dinner. So here he was. Now where was she, he wondered irritably.

His afternoon had not gone well. He had worked for hours and yet his progress could be measured in minutes. Each time he had tried to concentrate on work that badly needed his attention, the memory of green eyes slanted at him from behind a handful of daisies would return to tease him, and all he could end up thinking about was the fact that he was married. Married, for God's sake! He drained his glass in one swallow. If someone had predicted such a thing as late as last week, he would have called him either a fool or a lunatic.

He had already drunk half a bottle of the wine that was to be served with dinner, and as he leaned over to pour himself another glassful, he grimaced at the memory of William's timid knock on his door earlier. Owing to his past record, no doubt everyone had thought him skunk drunk by then. He let out a long breath. What he really needed to do was get his house back in order. Somewhere along the way, things had begun to slip badly out of control. And who could say? Maybe a wife to take care of the place was the answer.

His thoughts had come full circle. He could put as many labels or conditions of convenience on it as he liked, but the fact of the matter remained that he was really, actually, and legally married to the girl. Hell! All he had to do to make it more of a reality was to march up those steps and . . . Frowning, he emptied his glass again. Whoa, boy! he cautioned himself. It was precisely that kind of thinking that would make his father's victory complete and lead to more trouble than he had already. At least this way there were no ties, no attachments outside of a piece of paper and a few mumbled words to bind him. And that, he assured himself, was just the way things would stay.

"Nathan?"

He looked around to see Amanda framed in the doorway, and for several seconds he just stared. The basic colors and simple styling did more to enhance her own dramatic coloring than all the fancy accessories in the world could do. She seemed all hair and eyes and lips. For some reason, this only agitated him further.

"You're late," he snapped, coming to his feet.

Her smile of greeting faded. "I—I'm sorry. It's just that I—"

"Never mind." He cut her off with an impatient gesture. "Let's eat. I'm starved."

As wedding night dinners go, it was not a success. Nathan remained silent and morose despite Amanda's many attempts to draw him out. She tried subject after subject, but the poor lame things died quickly without his support, and when another carcass joined the pile on the table between them, she admitted defeat, lapsing into silence herself.

Good grief! she thought, stabbing irritably at her meat. What's wrong with him? For all his professed starvation, she noticed he barely touched his food, seeming to find the dark, swirling liquid in his glass more to his liking. As for herself and what should have been her own ravenous appetite, she could hardly force anything past the lump of tension in her throat. Gamely, she tried another taste of the wine he found so irresistible, but finding nothing in the sour taste to recommend it, renewed her attack on the roast beef.

"You certainly looked happy when you arrived at the judge's today."

Her fork stilled and her insides gave a sickening lurch. Had he somehow guessed? She looked up to find him staring balefully down the length of the table at her, his fingers absently stroking the stem of his glass. The flickering candlelight made his eyes mere needles of light. She lifted her chin. "We'd already made our bargain. I saw no reason to moan and groan about it, or cry my eyes out. Would you rather I had?"

He grimaced. "No."

"Perhaps I should've just followed your lead," she suggested sweetly, "and been sullen and disagreeable?"

The barest ghost of a smile flitted across his face and tucked itself into one corner of his mouth. "Hardly that."

"Then what? What is it? What's wrong with you?"

He frowned into his wine. "I don't know. Nothing. Everything!" Suddenly, he slammed down his glass, uncaring of the wine that sloshed. "I still can't believe he really made me go through with this!"

The hand in her lap clenched convulsively. What

was she supposed to do? Commiserate with him on the terrible fate that had stuck him with the likes of her? Tired of pushing her food from one side of her plate to the other, she put down her fork. "Well, if you'll excuse me," she said, rising, "it's been a long day."

He rose as she did but said nothing, so it surprised her when he reached out and caught her arm as she tried to pass.

"Amanda. . . ."

He searched her face, his own clouded by something she couldn't read. His eyes seemed to penetrate her very soul, and she felt naked, unable to look away. Could he see how much she cared for him? His eyes dropped to her mouth, and for the space of a single heartbeat, she thought he might kiss her. But no, his eyes and his hand went to her hair. Lightly, he touched the flowers entwined there, then tenderly he reached down to bring her hand to his lips.

"Good night, Irish. Sleep well."

With her eyes locked into his, it took several moments to realize he had released her and she was free to go. Swallowing hard, she nodded, hastily gathered up her skirts—along with what remained of her composure—and fled past him out of the room.

Nathan watched her go, her slender back held regally erect as she mounted the staircase. When the sound of her closing door reached him, he sighed as if released, then looked down to find himself twirling the stem of a small white daisy. With a muttered curse, he flung it across the table.

Lifting what was left of the wine from the cooler by his chair, he crossed the hall to his study with calm deliberation. It was going to be a long night.

Her heart pounding as if she had just run a foot race, Amanda leaned weakly against her closed door. How long could she keep this up? How long could she pretend she didn't love the man she was married to? She must have been mad to think she could pull it off in the first place. He had only to look at her to set her insides to trembling; sooner or later, he was bound to know and despise her because of it—or worse, taunt her with it. She cringed. The road she had seen earlier as narrow, now seemed little more than a tightrope. She rubbed her arm over the path his hand had taken, and shivered. How could she hope to keep her balance when even his touch made her feel all queer inside, carrying with it a heat that lingered long after it should have been forgotten?

Trying to draw needed breath through lungs too tense to cooperate, she pushed herself away from the door and struggled out of her clothes. She left them where they fell. Was this what life was going to be like, she wondered. Living in constant dread of discovery, while at the same time trying desperately to accommodate a man whose moods did an about-face every ten seconds?

At her dressing table, she undid her hair and laid the now wilted blossoms in a sad little heap. She had just begun to brush the dark, loosened tresses when there was a knock at her door. She froze, her wide-eyed reflection staring back at her.

"Y—yes? Who is it?" she asked, aware of the tremor in her voice.

"It's me, ma'am," answered Rose. "I've come to help you undress."

Amanda expelled a breath she didn't know she'd held. "There's no need. I managed quite well by myself," she called, kicking her discarded clothing out of sight as she went to the door. She stuck her head out and smiled at the maid. "But thank you, anyway."

Rose bobbed a curtsy and left, leaving Amanda still wondering at her own reaction as she closed the door again. She wasn't sure if she was relieved or disappointed it hadn't been Nathan.

Thoughtfully, she bent to blow out her lamps and crawl between the covers. After sleeping all afternoon, she fully expected to lie awake for hours, yet within minutes she was sound asleep again.

Nathan had his head thrown back over the edge of his leather chair, ankles crossed on the edge of his desk, a small glass cradled against his midsection. Using pressure from his feet, he pushed himself in the swivel chair as far as he could to the right, then as far as he could to the left, slowly. The dying fire behind him cast interesting patterns of orange on the ceiling, patterns he wasn't even aware of watching.

He had graduated from wine to brandy, but didn't yet feel the effects of any of it. He was disappointed. It would be hell, indeed, if he'd built up a tolerance to his one escape, he thought. It seemed no matter how much he drank, no matter what else he had tried thinking about, the word *wife* kept whispering itself in his ear. *You have a wife,* the voice said. A wife upstairs in a bed, alone. A wife with deep, inviting eyes—and they had been inviting; he had seen that across twelve feet of dining table—hips that moved her skirts, and a mouth that needed kissing. He had wanted to kiss her badly, to kiss, to touch, to press when she had left the table. Not to had taken more willpower than he thought he possessed.

The chair swiveled right, then left again, the glass forgotten as he contemplated how she must look, lying above him. Flannel, he decided. She wore pink or blue flannel with ruffles at her wrists and chin. Her long hair was brushed across the pillows. No cap or braids for that one. He felt the texture of it in the palm of one hand and scratched it absently with the other. Her breasts would be small and round, but fluidly moldable and satiny.

He ground the heel of one hand across his crotch, dropped his feet to the floor, and sat up. "Damn . . ." *Time to quit torturing yourself. Time to get some sleep.* Setting the half-empty glass aside with a clunk, he got to his feet. All this wanting, not wanting—it could make a man insane. It seemed there had been no pureness in anything he'd felt since that night in her father's study. Every emotion was tinged with something else, a whiff of contradiction. He wanted her, he didn't want her. He wanted away from her, he was drawn to her. He didn't want to marry her, he wanted to provide for her, take care of her. Not wanting, wanting. . . .

His hip hit the corner of his desk as he left the room, but he hardly noticed. The male need to seek an easing, a temporary end to the hunger, drew him without thought through the quiet house and up the stairs.

Chapter 6

Amanda opened her eyes, blinked and looked around, disoriented. When she saw the dimly outlined figure in her doorway, she instinctively pulled the covers higher as she struggled onto an elbow.

"It's all right. It's just me."

"Nathan?" She put a hand up, palm out, and squinted, trying to close out the light from downstairs so she could see his face.

"I've been thinking about you." He shut the door, closing the darkness in around them.

The female animal can sense the stalk, feel its movements even in the dark, and smell the scent of his intentions from the first throaty growl of the male. It's no different in humans. Suddenly, Amanda was wide awake, quivering with alertness. "Is something—" she bit her lip. "Are you all right?"

"Won't ever be all right again," he muttered, then swore softly when he misjudged the distance and hit the edge of the bed mid-thigh.

She felt the mattress sink in the same instant the smell of brandy enveloped her.

"Oh, here," she cried, "let me light the lamp—"

Somehow his hand caught hers in the dark and diverted its purpose. Opening her palm with both hands, he laid it against his chest just above where his heart was pounding as hard as hers. And just as a physical touch can still the resonance of a bell, so can it still the alarm in a human heart—Amanda wasn't afraid anymore.

The pads of her fingers felt the weave of warm and slightly damp linen mold itself to the muscled breast, her palm tickled by the distended bud of his nipple. Her hand moved to the bone-hard ridges below and felt the quick push of indrawn breath. Pleasure tilted her lips into a smile. Encouraged, her other hand joined in a pair of winglike sweeps across the hard rib cage and down the narrow waist. But her exploration ceased suddenly when he leaned down, crushing but not crushing, to put his mouth to hers. His tongue tasted like burned fruit, bittersweet and hot, its velvety roughness stroking the sensitive lining of her lips, the roof of her mouth, her own tongue.

He left her then for one empty moment while he shifted, bringing his entire length to hers, and she knew for the first time that full-weight feel of a man. She was still marveling at that gloriously solid yet supportable heaviness when he hooked a foot behind her ankle and separated her legs. A sweet ache, all liquidy and hot, streaked up the inside of her thighs, an arc so electric she couldn't find breath. Her hands seemed caught, frozen at his shoulders while his fingers worked at the throat of her nightgown. The air rushing in behind each opened button was hot—no, cold, she thought, her impressions fragmenting, colliding.

"I knew you'd taste good here," he murmured, his head dipping to a tightened, pulsing nipple. "I knew you'd be sweet and soft. . . ."

From then on it was hard to tell which words came from Nathan and which from her own thoughts. *I knew you'd feel good here, taste good here . . . and here . . . and here. . . .*

Their limbs were tangled, their breaths mixed when

he rolled heavily to one side, a hand stroking slowly down over her belly and thigh, then up under the hem of her gown and . . .

Amanda sucked air, trembling at the exquisitely torturous passage, biting her lip, waiting, waiting. When his hand slid off and was still, her thoughts took up the panicked rhythm of a trip-hammer. *Why is he waiting? Is it me? Am I supposed to do something? But what? Oh, God! I wish he'd say something! Sophie, your Woman's Duty lecture wasn't very complete, you know. There've already been things you didn't tell me about, things that 'hitch up your gown and let 'im do what he wants' didn't cover—* She swallowed hard, deciding to hide her ignorance behind some purple-smoked truth.

"Nathan, I thought you said we . . . we weren't going to—" She chanced a look at him from beneath her lashes, and found him staring down at her, a shadow that didn't move.

"Oh . . . God. . . ." he groaned, rocked slightly, then rolled heavily onto his back, away from her.

Brushing her hair out of her face, she dug an elbow into the pillows and peered down into his face. He didn't move. The heavy hand she picked up and let fall landed limply, and the smell of brandy reregistered itself. "Well, I'll be damned!" she muttered softly. "He's . . ." *passed out! I didn't think a man could pass out at a time like this—could he?* A loud snore was her only answer. Disgustedly, she flopped onto her back again and grumbled, "If this is a Woman's Duty, I'd say it's much ado about nothing!"

"I trust you didn't stub your toe on the way out of my room this morning—what with it still being dark and all," she added sweetly, her fork gripped more like she wanted to stab the man across from her than the scrambled eggs on her plate.

Nathan met her eyes for the first time over the rim of his coffee cup. "I'm sorry I disturbed you. I thought you were asleep."

"Who could sleep?" she grumbled, chasing a piece of brittle bacon onto the tablecloth. "You snore."

"I'm sorry."

"Quit saying that!"

"Now I've made you angry."

"You didn't make me angry!" *You made me furious, you made me feel cheated, you made me—jealous. At least you slept.*

"It won't happen again."

Her head snapped up. He was staring into his coffee much like he'd stared into his wine the night before. He was dressed impeccably, not a strand of glossy dark hair out of place, his shirt crisp and white. It was as if those few minutes of tenderness and heat between them had never happened. "Which won't happen again?" she asked him carefully. "Making me angry . . . or snoring in my bed?"

The question dangled blatantly before he answered simply, "Neither."

And now you make me hurt. Suddenly, earnestly, she leaned forward. "Why, Nathan? Why come to me drunk?"

He looked up from his plate and met her eyes with a sardonic smile. "Because drunks aren't responsible for what they do, don't you know that?"

The cynical honesty of that galled her. "Then why *be* a drunk? Why drink at all?"

"Simple." He made a negligent gesture with one hand. "It's the one thing I seem to be able to do on my own. I don't have control over anything else."

"Well, get control, take control!" she nearly

screamed, shoving her plate away. But the utter coolness of his heavy-lidded stare mocked the very intensity of hers, and the defeat she felt was a sharp sting in her throat. Grabbing up her coffee cup, she stared blindly through the lace curtains at the sun-washed lawn.

Watching him sneak out of her room that morning through slitted eyes had made her want to kick and scream and have a real tantrum. But she hadn't. Instead, she'd forced herself to lie there, waiting until the sounds of breakfast being set released her, gave her the excuse to jump up, yank on some clothes, and sweep down the stairs to see if he would look her in the eye. He hadn't.

"Shall we start over?"

She looked around, surprised, having almost succeeded in forgetting his presence. "Start over how?"

"Well, we could begin by going into town to buy you some new clothes, maybe a few trinkets or two."

The coffee cup clattered back into its saucer. She wasn't a child to be cajoled by a few trinkets. "There's no need."

"I beg to differ. Since I can see the tiny pink bow on the edge of your unmentionable there"—he sighted carefully down the length of a pointed finger as her hand sprang to cover the place he was describing—"I would say there definitely is a need." The charm and the crooked grin had returned. "Please?" he coaxed.

That had been an hour ago. Now she sat in the carriage beside him, the cool spring breeze and pleasant rhythm of the wheels clicking over the hard-packed road doing what the promise of trinkets was supposed to do—cajoling her into a better mood. That Nathan remained at his charming best didn't hurt, either.

Perhaps I *can* be bribed, she thought with a smile and not much regret.

"You find it amusing that Lord Baltimore gave away what's now Delaware out of sheer ignorance of knowing what he had?"

"No—or rather yes, I do, as a matter of fact. But please, go on," she urged with a small touch on his arm. Assuming she, like all natives, knew little about the area they lived in, Nathan had been giving her a history lesson as they rode along. He spoke with the enthusiasm of one who truly loved his mother state and felt himself to be one of her more productive sons. She tried to be attentive to the contributions of the Carroll family, but her attention kept straying to his hands on the reins, strong and sinewy with a sprinkling of dark hair along the backs. He didn't use his hands to talk with like her father did. Or she would find herself studying the healthy grain of bronzed skin along his jawline. He was made so cleanly, she thought; not a wrong line, a disproportionate feature anywhere—anywhere she'd seen, that is. But even the places she had only felt . . . She thought of where she had explored the night before, and wondered what he would do if she reached over right then—a shocking heat suddenly pooled between her legs and she jerked her face away.

"You aren't even listening," he accused.

She plumped the embroidered cloth reticule and bounced it nervously on her green velvet knee. "Of course I'm listening. You were saying something about London." She faced him with a bright expression and nodded for him to continue.

"Yes. Well. As I was saying," he went on, the bemused quirk in his brows more pronounced than ever, "Charles Street here has often been compared to the famous Bond Street in London."

She didn't need to know anything of this Bond Street to be impressed by the one now glittering ahead of her like a twin string of crystals in the sunlight. Shoulder-to-shoulder shops lined the street—Nathan pointed to each one as if he owned it—every window polished and filled with a display designed to outdo its neighbor's. It was the sort of place Miss Crittendon and the Millses probably shopped, she thought, listening to the genteel quiet, a quiet broken only by the clatter of well-tended wheels, the overheard word or two from well-heeled pedestrians.

By the time they pulled to the curb and a boy came running to take their rig around back, where all the merchants kept private stables for their patrons, curiosity had finally taken over. "Where are we going?" she asked when he set her on her feet.

He tossed a coin to the lad. "To see a man named Isaac about getting some jewelry for you."

"Jewelry? For me?" She thought of her empty ring finger with hope.

"It's expected of a man to buy his bride baubles and things, isn't it?" he commented, guiding her in the right direction by means of a hand at her back.

"Oh. I suppose so." He certainly knew how to deflate one's ego.

Isaac's shop was a little one, neat and clean on the outside but dark and cluttered and smelling of cooking odors on the inside. Dust motes in the air caught the light and hung, suspended in front of the one window like a tiny universe.

A little bell over the door tinkled at their entrance. From a curtained doorway in the back shuffled a middle-aged man with thin threads of bright red hair and deep-set eyes that looked as if they'd seen the miseries of the world. Recognizing Nathan immediately, he came forward to clasp both his hands in a

MATTERS OF THE HEART 133

warm greeting, but when Amanda was introduced, she was treated to an unctuous bit of inquiry as to her health and general disposition toward the weather, pronounced "a lovely, lovely girl," then promptly forgotten.

This surprised her until the two of them moved off to a table in the corner and she realized it was Nathan, the one with the money, who was viewed as the important one. A few minutes more and she realized even Nathan had no intention of consulting her. He sat on a wooden stool and carefully examined the pieces Isaac produced from a stack of flat wooden cases with the total absorption of a business man about to make an investment. Left standing at loose ends in the middle of the room, virtually ignored, she listened with a jaundiced ear as the two began to comment and haggle over relative qualities and value. Only men could reduce the romance of jewelry to something as dry as this, she thought.

Idly, not thinking much of anything, she strolled about, fingering the small oval "fancy boxes" bedecked with ribbons and lace that were strewn carelessly along the counter. When she came to a carved wooden jewel case and lifted the lid, she smiled to hear the tinkling strains of a waltz from somewhere within its blue velvet interior.

Circling back, she stopped to peep over Nathan's shoulder, curious to see his taste in ladies "baubles." On a square of green velvet by his elbow lay a gold locket set with a cabochon emerald, a French enameled brooch, a dog collar of garnets and gold filigree, a pretty swirled aigrette for her hair, along with an entire parure of jet pieces. Not overly impressed with the popular jewelry of her times, her eye wandered longingly to some lengths of creamy pearls all handsomely knotted on pale silk

"Oh," she breathed, "how lovely."

With a bit of annoyance at being disturbed, Nathan glanced over at the small choker-sized strand she was fingering, then up at her. "The lady has very good taste," he observed wryly, then returned his attention to the items he'd been examining.

Amanda blushed and backed away. She hadn't meant to sound like she was asking for anything.

Looking around her again, this time she wandered over to a tray of rings that gleamed in the light under the window. With a quick glance over her shoulder to make sure Nathan wasn't watching, she stopped to pore over the gold circlets with a small sigh. Elbow on counter and chin in hand, she ran a wistful fingertip over the precious metals, wondering if he wouldn't yet buy her one of these.

The stool scraped on the floor and she moved away from such a revealing bit of daydreaming to the other side of the room. Nathan had made his selections and was standing, stretching his legs, when another bell jingled from somewhere in the back.

Isaac hastily excused himself, and as he went through the curtain it flapped behind him and caught on the back of a nearby chair. From where she stood, Amanda was left with a perfect view of the jeweler as he conducted business with quite another kind of clientele. Silhouetted in front of the opened rear door, he carefully examined the object handed him by the other man, haggled briefly, his glass held firmly in his eye, then paid him from one pocket as he put the item away in the other. Amused, Amanda wondered what Nathan would think if he knew of the jeweler's other, "back door" business.

The delicate notes of a waltz suddenly distracted her from the interesting goings-on in the back room, and she looked over to see Nathan leaning indolently against the counter by the box she had admired. He was smiling at her.

"Do you like it?" he asked, pointing.

"It is pretty," she admitted cautiously, wanting to avoid her earlier fall from grace.

"It's yours then."

She smiled her thanks, and for the moment each seemed content just to look at the other without saying anything.

With the ankle of one long leg crossed over the other, a thumb hooked in his vest pocket, and his hat at that jaunty angle, he was once again the Nathan she had first known. Suddenly, the picture of him buying jewelry for some other woman came unbidden to mind. After all, it was obvious Isaac had done business with him before. An unreasonable wave of jealousy washed over her.

"Is there anything else you'd like?" he asked.

She cocked her head to one side, debating. Holding out her left hand, fingers spread, she eyed her empty ring finger. "What about a wedding band? I'm sure people will expect that as well."

His gaze slid straight over to the tray of rings under the window and she could feel herself turn painfully red. Pursing his lips, he dropped his head to stare at the floor a moment before shaking his head. When he looked back up his face was serious.

"Call me old-fashioned if you'd like, but I've always thought a ring should mean something, be a symbol of love in a marriage. This charade of ours is bad enough, let's not make it a total mockery." He shook his head again. "Besides, my father won the war. No need to hand over all the little victories, is there?"

Amanda hoped whatever expression was frozen on her face gave away none of the pain she was feeling.

When would she learn? When would this situation of theirs become real to her? No matter how much she cared for this man, to him she was just a means to an end, an end already accomplished. She couldn't afford the luxury of acting like a real wife and letting him suspect how she really felt. He would loathe her. No, the only safe thing was to put away the yearning part of her heart and play the part assigned to her.

"You're right. I agree," she heard herself whisper. Thankfully, Isaac chose that moment to reappear and she no longer had to stand there impaled on that dark blue gaze.

After the arrangements were made to have everything delivered, Nathan suddenly reached over and plucked a ring from a tray on the counter. "And here. Add this to the bill." Without even showing it to her first he took her right hand, straightened her fingers, and slid the ring into place. It was set with an emerald, a costly one judging by the size of it, but the ornate cigar band styling of the gold surrounding it didn't hold much appeal for Amanda.

"Like it?" he asked, still holding her hand.

So that she wouldn't be lying, she thought about how good his touch felt instead of the ring. "I like it very much." As far as the ring was concerned, she couldn't wait to get home and take the thing off. It would either be a wedding band or nothing, she promised herself.

The sun was still bright when they left Isaac's shop, but Amanda's pleasure in the day had dimmed. Even Nathan's spirits seemed more subdued than before, and they walked along in silence.

A block later her steps faltered and she stared. A few feet ahead of them was a shop, the like of which Amanda had never seen before. From doorway to curb ran a bright purple carpet, and stretching overhead was an awning of the same hue. Fancy gold script on the single arched window declared the place to be the establishment of one *Madame Daru: Fashions de Paris.* On display below this were several dresses in silk and lace that made Amanda's eyes widen with interest.

Nathan grinned at her expression. "Well? What do you think?"

"Think?"

"About your wardrobe? Shall we get it here?"

"Wardrobe?" she repeated stupidly. "Here?" She was willing to bet this place didn't even have a back door.

"Why not? I don't know much about women's clothing, but I've heard this place is the best. And judging from the way you're drooling," he said with a playful tap on her nose, "I think it will do just fine."

"I don't drool."

He rolled his eyes and made her giggle as he put out a finger to wipe an imaginary spot of dribble from the edge of her bottom lip. "No, of course not."

She sucked in the lip and ran her tongue over the place he'd touched. My passion for new clothes could easily be replaced, she thought.

"Come on, then. What are you waiting for?"

She shrugged, eyeing doubtfully the purple cloth overhead, its scalloped edges rippling in the breeze. "Nothing. It's just that it looks . . . terribly expensive, that's all." She didn't want to be accused of being after his money again.

When the lines bracketing his mouth deepened she braced herself for the cutting remark, but apparently he changed his mind. Smiling, he pulled her arm through his and said, "Don't worry. I know the owner."

Somehow this didn't surprise her, but she didn't give it any more thought as they entered the posh place and a heavily accented voice trilled from behind a curtained doorway in the back, "Be with you in a moment, *mon petit chouchou!*"

There was little time to appreciate the peach-and-cream grandeur designed to pamper the rich matrons of the city, nor to identify the faint smell of perfume flowering the air before that promise was kept and a small woman with huge leg-o'-mutton sleeves swept aside the curtain.

Bright-eyed as a bird and dressed in a tropical shade of turquoise, she stirred a bit of envy in Amanda's breast as she came to greet them. But her professional flutter ceased as abruptly as a bay breeze at dawn, only her skirts continuing to sway forward, when she saw who it was.

"Nathan!" she breathed, her finely drawn brows arching.

He nodded. "Bernice."

"This is a pleasant surprise," she continued in unaccented English. "It's been a long time."

Amanda saw the faint smile curve his lips. "Yes, it has."

After a brief look in her direction and a moment of hesitation, the dressmaker finally threw her hands up. "Oh, what the devil! I'm sure your friend here won't mind," she said, and with that, stepped up to Nathan with outstretched arms.

Amanda watched in horrified fascination. Instead of presenting his cheek, he met the woman's lips with his own, and the flush of pleasure brightening Bernice's cheeks as she stepped back made Amanda grind her teeth. Harlot! she thought, shocking herself with how quickly the word came to mind.

With an instinct she didn't even question, the hated ring made a quick change of residence from her right hand to her left behind her back.

At last, she herself came under the full attention of

the woman's lively brown eyes. "The others were pretty, Nathan, but this one . . ." She tilted her neatly coiffed head, the dark hair glinting with red highlights. "There's something special about this one."

Amanda forced a polite smile, hating the smoothness with which Nathan finally turned to her. *You'd think I'd been invisible these few minutes,* she thought nastily.

"Amanda, I'd like you to meet Bernice Daru. Bernice, my wife, Amanda." The words were toneless, polished, without emotion.

"Your—!" The woman's eyes grew rounder. "No wonder she looks different than the others. It's love I see in her eyes."

Oh no! Amanda cringed, her face flaming. Then, watching the woman's smile falter, Amanda knew the expression of coolness Bernice was seeing on Nathan's face, an expression that denied the feeling on his part as loudly as spoken words. Her stomach twisted with anguish. *Why did we have to come here, of all places?* And then she knew. It was Nathan who had steered her here. He must have known how it would turn out. He must have.

Whatever hope, however faint, there had been of the two women getting along, it died in that instant, and only fury propelled Amanda through the next awkward minutes without a misstep.

"How do you do?" she said crisply, nodding toward the table heaped with fabrics in the center of the room. "We're here today for a new wardrobe for me. It'll be quite a large order." She never glanced at Nathan as she went to finger the corner of some cream-colored lace. "I do hope you have the staff and materials to handle it."

Bernice Daru's professional demeanor shimmered

back to the surface. "But of course," she answered smoothly. The accent had not been resurrected.

The next hour was war.

Expecting him to feel ill at ease in surroundings so totally feminine, Amanda was surprised and irritated when Nathan not only didn't find a corner in which to become inconspicuous, but followed her around, approving or rejecting her choices out of hand. The fact that "Madame" herself would approve each time, the two of them discussing her as if she were no more than one of the headless mannequins that stood about the place, only dug the spurs of jealousy deeper. When yet another piece, a lovely mint green voile was vetoed, she turned on him with a hiss. "What's wrong with it, for heaven's sake?"

"It's too coarse."

"I thought you said you didn't know anything about women's clothing."

He shrugged. "I know what I like."

The mere fact that he could seem so unconcerned when she was ready to do battle over something much more precious to her than clothing made her want to rail at him and shriek like a fishwife.

"Here," he offered, holding out an edge of the disputed fabric. "Feel for yourself."

Very primly, with the air of an expert, she reached over and ran her fingers over the cloth. He was right. It felt scratchy, but she refused to give him the satisfaction of admitting it. She waved it away. "It doesn't matter. I've changed my mind about the color. I don't like it."

Tongue in cheek, he nodded. "Mmm-hmm."

When it was all over, she couldn't help but be grudgingly impressed by the array of silks, laces, muslins, and linens that had been put aside for her. There was pale yellow, turquoise (a shade much lovelier than Bernice's, she decided with catty satisfaction), emerald green, some ecru, and a length of sensuous white silk shot with gold. There was even a pale mint green, but this time in a sheer and soft muslin.

The urge to make him pay through his purse had dwindled in the face of his generosity, but the need to be in control hadn't. When it came time to select the styles, Amanda was determined to have her say, and she triumphantly intercepted the stack of sketches Mme. Daru was just about to hand to Nathan. Perched on the edge of a plump-cushioned chaise, it didn't take her long to pick out the ones she liked. After laying these aside, she handed the rest back, pleased by her own air of finality.

Nathan had been standing by her shoulder, absently playing with his derby. Without a word, he leaned over to look at her choices and made a face. Taking up her rejected stack, he went through them with a critical eye and chose nearly a dozen, which he handed across to Bernice, his look at Amanda daring her to argue.

She counted to ten and then to twenty while the woman sifted through the drawings, nodding her approval.

"How's your father?" the dressmaker asked.

She hadn't looked up and neither did Nathan as he answered, "The same."

"How unfortunate."

This bit of intimacy was too much for Amanda and she all but snatched the plates out of the woman's hands. With outward calm, she glanced through the ones he'd picked. "These are very nice, of course, but they have no bustles," she said, her smile sweet.

"I don't like bustles."

"You won't be the one wearing them," she said, still smiling.

"Neither will you."

Before Amanda could decide which form of violence to take, Bernice stepped into the breach. "I'm afraid he's right, my dear. These long flowing lines are all the latest rage in Europe." She plucked sadly at one of her own sleeves. "Alas, even these will be out of fashion soon."

This time it was Nathan's smile that was sweet.

Overruled once again, Amanda felt hot tears of frustration spurt, and she flapped the other two out of her path as she shot to her feet and dashed toward a bit of privacy at the back of the shop.

Behind her Bernice laid a hand on Nathan's arm when he would have followed. "Leave her alone. She'll get over it when she sees the results of today's work." She studied his face carefully for a second, then smiled and shook her head. "You've really been bitten hard, haven't you, my friend?"

Leaving Nathan to frown after her, she went up to Amanda, put a motherly arm around her stiffened shoulders, and led her behind a folding screen painted with vignettes of European aristocracy lolling about on lawns of watery green. As they stepped out of sight, Bernice looked back over her shoulder at him and pointed to a delicate Hepplewhite chair next to the screen. "We have to take some measurements now. You," she directed with a note of sternness, "may sit there."

Stripped to her threadbare chemise and stockings while she was measured with knotted cord, Amanda found it hard to return to her chin-up attitude of earlier. Near nakedness was hardly a position of advantage, she thought, absently twisting the ring on her finger.

Responding to the dressmaker's nudge, she turned slightly and found herself studying the two of them framed together in the long mirror. She was taller than the couturiere and her coloring was warmer, more autumn hued, but the figure flaws she looked for in the other woman were depressingly absent. If anything, she held a slight advantage with her air of fully achieved womanhood, which Amanda didn't yet have.

"That's a lovely ring," Bernice mumbled around the pencil she held in her teeth. "I've always wanted an emerald."

Amanda spread her fingers, tilting her hand this way and that so the stone could catch the lamplight. Perhaps it wasn't as ugly as she'd first thought. "Thank you," she said.

"From Nathan?"

"Of course."

Their eyes locked in the mirror, and slowly, Bernice shook her head.

"You needn't worry—there's nothing between us. Nathan and I have been friends for years." Dropping the cord around her neck, she pulled some pins from her cuff and began taking up the slack in Amanda's worn waistband. "As a matter of fact, he's the one who set me up in this business."

Amanda felt the curl in her own lip. "For services rendered or—*ouch!*"

"Sorry. Pin slipped."

Amanda bit her tongue before she could say something that would cause the woman's scissors to slip as well. "Worry," indeed! she thought. He was *her* husband, wasn't he?

Beyond the screen, Nathan had given up trying to overhear the women's conversation, but his ears picked up at Amanda's tiny yelp, then slid back into his own thoughts without even being aware of the transitions. He couldn't get Bernice's earlier observation of out of his mind. *It's love I see in her eyes . . . love in her eyes . . . love. . . .* Damn! The child was falling in love with him! Why hadn't he seen it himself? *Didn't you?* an inner voice asked. *Isn't that why you brought her here?* Nathan chewed the inside of his cheek as he glanced around the shop. Bernice was good, he hadn't been lying about that, but there were certainly other dressmakers who were just as good. Yes, he supposed it was why he had brought Amanda here. He only hoped Bernice didn't get the wrong idea and think he was trying to start things up between the two of them again.

Bernice had been a pretty thing to tweak his father with once upon a time, but it hadn't taken him long to discover that beneath that pretty exterior beat a heart that could give a man frostbite. And as far as her comment about him being the one smitten, well, that was downright laughable. Women, silly creatures that they were, seemed to go through life seeing romance around every corner, wherever they wanted to see it, in fact. Of course, if he seemed smitten to Bernice, he'd have to be extra careful around Amanda.

He frowned, shifting uncomfortably in the little chair. Episodes like last night's loins-and-liquor thinking would have to stop. He hadn't meant it to happen in the first place, and he'd have to watch the drinking if it was going to produce a weakness like that. The last thing he wanted was to hurt the child by encouraging her, especially when he had absolutely no intention, no interest even in—in . . .

It was at this precise moment that Mme. Daru had discovered she didn't have with her the little book in which she kept all her customer's measurements, and had darted out to retrieve it. In her haste, she left the panel open behind her—and Nathan with an unrestricted view of Amanda in a very appealing state of dishabille.

She stood with her back to him, totally unaware she

MATTERS OF THE HEART 145

had an audience. Her weight on one leg put her hips at a saucy cant, and the wide ruffle around the bottom of her underbreeches pointed up the long, slender curve of her legs. One thin strap of her camisole dangled provocatively off her shoulder as she lifted a hand to smooth some fallen wisps of hair from the shadowed nape of her neck. With her fingers still in her hair, she tilted her head, glanced around, and found herself looking directly into Nathan's blue stare.

Caught off guard, he was unaccountably annoyed. "Good God, woman! Have you no sense at all?" he growled, and leaned out of his chair to slam the panel shut.

Chapter 7

Rose shifted the tray from one hand to the other, balancing it on her hip as she knocked on Amanda's door. "I've brought you up a bite to eat, ma'am," she called.

"Thank you, Rose, but I'm not hungry."

Even through the closed door she could hear the mistress sigh. "You really should eat something, ma'am. It's been hours since breakfast. There's cold chicken here, stewed tomatoes, fresh bread, and even a bit of pie," she urged.

"No," came the answer again. "Thank you."

Rose shrugged and headed back downstairs. She may not have succeeded in whetting the missus's appetite, but she certainly had her own and could see no reason to let all that food go to waste.

Amanda listened to the maid's retreating footsteps and lifted the damp cloth from her forehead. She hadn't been able to sleep, but at least her headache was gone.

She had been lying there for nearly an hour, her curtains closed against the light, trying to figure out exactly how and why the afternoon with Nathan had gone sour. Ever since he had slammed that dressing screen shut, his mood had deteriorated rapidly. He had become terse and distant, retreating behind that impenetrable wall of his, and nothing she could do seemed to make much difference. During the ride home, she had tried everything she could think of to coax him into a better humor, but his scowl deepened steadily until finally, inside the front door, he turned on her, snapping that he had "played the doting husband long enough" before stalking off to his study.

She sat up, swung her stockinged legs over the side of the bed, and began to pace thoughtfully, hugging her arms close to her body as her toes dug into the ice blue carpet. *He wants me. I know he does. I saw it in his eyes just before he shut that screen.* She stroked a hand over her shoulder, feeling the heat of his gaze once again.

Last night had produced a curiosity, a need to know. Today, the desire itself had crystallized, and from Nathan's eyes she had learned of an answering desire, a power *she* held over *him;* a power that made her shiver—and play dangerous games.

Perhaps that was what was wrong with him. Perhaps in wanting to see that look again, she'd overplayed her hand, pushed too far. During the ride home, she had sat the barest fraction closer than necessary so that contact had been unavoidable, and she never failed to lay a hand on his sleeve whenever she wished to emphasize something. Knowing the differences in their ages and experience, it was a risky game to play, but the goal had been as compelling as it was elusive. If he was affected by any of it, if he felt the same stomach-twisting rush of electricity, he didn't let it show.

She paused by the open box lying on the sofa. Perhaps this is to blame, too, she thought, lifting the dress of creamy muslin out of its nest of tissue paper. Where she had gotten the boldness she would never know. Just as they were leaving Mme. Daru's, her eye had lighted on this gorgeous bit of froth, and by reminding him that her first fittings were at least a week away, she had overcome his reluctance to purchase something ready-made (even one that required no bustle), and had persuaded him to buy it for her.

It was a pretty dress, with its yards and yards of fluid material and tiny pearlized buttons, but the greater issue had been the measure of her influence over a man who was, thus far, proving intractable to all but his own will. That she had won out over Bernice's objections as well only sweetened the pot.

Bernice. She wrinkled her nose. She couldn't even think the name without doing that. Ber*nice*, Ber*nice* . . . no, it was quite impossible to keep the nose from wrinkling.

Still clutching the dress, and prompted by the mental image of Sophie shaking her head, Amanda leaned over to peer into the mirror. Sure enough, peering back at her from behind a curtain of dark hair, there was a pair of "monster" green eyes. She grinned at herself, nodded, and winked. "Eat 'em up," she said. "As for you, Nathan, my man . . ."

Shedding her blouse and skirt, she slipped the dress over her head. She wanted another look at this peculiar no-bustle style he seemed to like so much, but as she stood before the mirror, it was the neckline that caught her attention. It was low, too low for anything before five. Then again, she reminded herself, it all depended on what one had in mind before five. "Okay, Mr. Iron Will. Let's see if you can ignore this," she said, plumping the sides of her breasts and smiling when they swelled becomingly over the edge of her bodice. Then she sighed, letting herself flow back into natural shape. "Providing you ever come out of that old study of yours. Until then . . ." *I guess I'll just have to amuse myself.*

After a brief, bored look around her room, she plopped down on the sofa and began buttoning herself back into her shoes. Now was as good a time as any to take that tour of the house she had promised herself earlier.

The decision to begin with the portraits was an easy one—they were hung all around the walls of the upper hall. She passed the older, darker ones of serious-looking men quickly, moving to the family portrait of a young woman in old-fashioned dress, her proud husband, and the overdressed baby between them. The next was a smaller one, a girl, aged five or so, in a starched white pinafore. The little fingers she held out to the puppy by her side seemed more a gesture of fear than affection, and Amanda felt sorry for the child. The last portrait, the largest, in a baroque gilt frame, was of the same girl about a dozen years later. Her rose-colored gown brought some life to the pale skin, but her brown eyes held a sad, won't-somebody-love-me expression. Amanda stared at it a long time, fingers knitted behind her back. Something about the nose and mouth . . . Nathan's mother! He'd said this was her home, and now she understood the young couple, too. They were his grandparents.

She smiled, nodding at the pictures. "How do you do . . ." Absently, she patted the cracked gilt frame, then continued on with her exploration of the house, feeling an odd sense of accomplishment. Nathan's family. . . .

Moving further along the gallery, she began trying doors, opening cupboards, and poking her head around corners—curious, but like a child exploring a relative's house, fearful of being caught snooping. It never occurred to her that as mistress of the house what she was doing could hardly be considered snooping. Indeed, to her way of thinking, she was no more the real mistress of Nathan's house than she was a real wife to the man himself.

The rooms in front of hers, as well as the ones on Nathan's side of the house, weren't in use and apparently hadn't been for some time. Cracked and yellowed shades cast an eerie light over the groupings of sheet-covered furniture, and so long had the rooms been closed off that she left stark tracks, like ghost prints, wherever she walked on the dusty floors.

Peeking curiously under the dust covers and seeing the lovely turned legs and crystal drawer pulls, she wanted to open all the windows and uncover everything, restoring the rooms as they deserved.

It was the last door before heading downstairs that stopped her, her hand on the knob. Nathan's room. She had seen from her little balcony that it extended off the back of the house, its private porch forming a roof over the terrace entrance below. He wasn't there, she knew that, but still her pulse was jumping as she turned the handle and pushed the door open.

Done in muted tones of blue and brown, the large room was furnished with masculine-looking pieces free of ornamentation, yet far from Spartan in their concession to comfort. Believing a room revealed much about its occupant, she was pleased to find no evidence here of the severely impersonal man Nathan tried hard to appear. She smiled. It was the old wooden rocker in front of the fireplace that gave him away. It spoke of a love for things domestic and of—well, a certain tenderness he seemed bent on denying in himself.

With a guilty start, she remembered the need for stealth and quickly closed the door without entering.

At the bottom of the steps, she took note of the still closed study door with a sigh of relief, then paused to listen to the only sound that met her ears. Clocks, at least half a dozen, were ticking away the minutes. She decided she liked the sound; it was the only one that gave the house any feeling of life.

As she strolled through the blue-on-blue drawing room to look out across the terrace and garden beyond, she was thinking that even though it was a beautiful house, something seemed to be missing. Despite the stamp of wealth from imported furnishings and crystal chandeliers, there was an air of neglect about the place. Not from uncleanliness or clutter, certainly, but rather as if it languished, as if it hadn't held happiness within its walls in a very long time. *I wonder what his mother—*

Suddenly, the sound of female laughter coming from the kitchen broke her reverie and drew her to explore this last unseen area of the house. Timidly, almost as if she expected to be shooed out of the place, Amanda stepped into Mary's domain.

An uneven brick floor that gritted under her feet, the steam of boiling soup, open shelves, gleaming copper pots dangling overhead, and a huge iron stove—the impressions hit her all at once, but the chatter stopped abruptly.

Emma and Mary, both in white aprons and mob caps with damp strands of hair clinging to their heat-reddened cheeks, were peeling potatoes around a big worktable in the center of the room. At Amanda's entrance they had looked up expectantly.

"Yes, ma'am?" Mary wiped her hands on the front of her apron. "What can I get you?"

"Oh, nothing. Please—" She quickly waved them back to what they were doing, and was relieved when they hesitated only briefly before getting back in stride with both knife and tongue.

Listening to the gay chitchat, which consisted mostly of local gossip, she wandered about the large kitchen, surreptitiously lifting lids and opening cupboards—something strictly forbidden in Sophie's kitchen. A few minutes later, Rose drifted in to join the debate as to whether or not one Hank Mayfield had knowingly sold sick cows to his neighbor, Mr. Pickett.

Amanda leaned on her elbows, not really a part of the conversation, but not feeling left out of it, either. She marveled at the way all three tongues seemed to be moving at once, and smiled as the volume and pitch soon reached that of a flock of magpies. She was enjoying herself immensely.

Home had always been quiet, with very few people around. Now suddenly, her life seemed filled with them, and she couldn't have been happier. Sophie and Joe had done their best, but it hadn't been enough to satisfy her craving for other people. Her years of growing up, she realized, had been lonely ones.

At last it was settled. Mr. Mayfield *had* known about his cows' poor health since, according to a friend of Rose's cousin—who had it straight from a neighbor—he'd had their conditions confirmed by a veterinarian before he sold them. With that triumph neatly under her belt, Rose sailed off for parts unknown and left the other two to their potatoes.

Before things had a chance to settle down from that, Amanda, unheeded and unobserved, left quietly through the terrace door.

Making a complete circle of the place, she officially ended her tour on the front steps and stood for a moment to admire the way the late afternoon sun slanted through the trees, their shadows stretching thinly across the drive. A small sigh of total serenity escaped her, a sigh that suddenly reversed itself into a gasp of surprise.

Driving through the front gate at that moment was Bob, and beside him, the seat listing dangerously in her favor, was Sophie! Joe, his legs dangling like a child's, was in the rear of the wagon with what looked like the entire Alton household furnishings. Behind it all plodded Molly, the final note to this odd little caravan.

"Sophie! Joe!" With a cry of delight, Amanda ran across the drive, her arms spread wide as if she might embrace the whole lot of them at once. "What are you doing here? I thought you'd be in Virginia by now!" Breathlessly, she ran beside the wagon until it was finally drawn to a stop, and there she waited impatiently for both men to help Sophie down from her perch before she could be wrapped in that big bear hug.

Sophie snuffled and wiped at her eyes as she held the girl close even as she protested, "You'd think we ain't seen each other in years. Now lemme look at you, child. Jes' lemme look at you. I jes' can't hardly believe my baby's married, but she sure. . . . Lordy, girl! What're you wearin'?" The old face layered into a frown.

Amanda's cheeks pinkened and her hands fluttered self-consciously at her bare throat as she launched into the story of Mme. Daru's, her new clothes, and Nathan's eccentric taste in styles, a tale made bizarre by its very condensation. She ended this rather circuitous explanation by presenting her backside for Sophie's opinion. "Frankly, I don't know what he sees in it," she confessed with a laugh.

Sophie tipped her massive head to one side, her lower lip thrust out suspiciously as she studied the way the pale fabric clung to the curve of the girl's hips, gently suggested the rounded bottom, then swept softly away to the ground. The frown deepened. "Hmph! Well, I does—and it ain't decent, if you ask me!"

Amanda hardly heard her as she spun back around and grasped the woman by the arms. "Now tell me why you're here!"

"Didn't he tell you?"

"Who?"

"Why, your Mr. Nathan, that's who. He came out home after you two was married. Said he'd be honored—that was the word he used, too—said he'd be honored if we'd change our minds and come out here to live with you all." The whole time she was talking, she was fussing with Amanda's hair, tugging on the bodice of her dress, trying to make it cover more than it did.

Nathan, Nathan. . . . Amanda smiled to herself, absently waving aside the woman's ministrations.

"He said we could do as much or as little as we liked," Sophie continued. "We was to think of it as our ree-tirement. Don't that beat all?"

Amanda nodded, her eyes now on the wagon that was still being unloaded. Her first impression of the entire Alton household being piled between the high, slatted sides wasn't far off. Not only were there a dozen boxes and bundles, but Sophie's rocker was there, along with the needlepoint rocker from her parent's room . . . and her mother's dressing table . . . and her cheval glass . . . and . . . !

"Dear God!" she breathed in sudden horror. "Sophie, you didn't!"

The brown stare turned truculent. "I most certainly did. That was your mama's, and I can't see leavin' it even if it don't matter none to you."

"Sophie, it's not that it doesn't matter," she moaned in protest, "but what on earth am I to do with a *piano?*" Helplessly, she watched as both men lowered the huge instrument to the ground, their knees wobbling dangerously.

Sophie folded her arms. She had nothing more to say.

With a quick and fearful glance at the house, Amanda wanted only to get everything settled and out of sight before Nathan appeared, angrily demanding an explanation—and rightly so, she thought with a sigh. Hastily, she started assigning destinations for as many things as she could, grateful that Bob worked with the speed and strength of three men. The cheval glass and rocker would go to her room, Sophie's rocker to the kitchen (she'd let Sophie and Mary come to their own terms about that), the dressing table and most of the boxes could go into the empty room in front of hers, and the piano . . . she stared at the thing in dismay. The piano would have to go in the drawing room, and since there was no way Nathan could fail to notice the thing, she only hoped he wouldn't mind. Too much.

A little over half an hour later, Amanda again stood alone on the front steps. Everything had miraculously found a place, and neither Nathan nor any of the servants had made a fuss. Nathan, for that matter, hadn't even put in an appearance. Sophie had gone to rest in the room given her and Joe downstairs, while Joe had disappeared along with Bob, the wagon, and Molly—all presumably to the barn.

She heaved a great sigh. Her world was complete now, filled with those most dear to her. Exuberantly, she hugged herself, her feet doing a remembered jig of sheer joy.

In his study, Nathan pushed himself away from his desk in a long stretch. After double- and even triple-checking Teddy's revisions, he was satisfied they were correct.

The kid had a good mind when he chose to use it. Maybe the military would be good for him, give him the grit to use it more often, he thought. Still, he had to wonder if his brother was really serious. There'd been that threat about the French Foreign Legion, too.

In any case, he'd missed saying goodbye to him after

the wedding—and could only guess if he and the old man had exchanged farewells. He doubted it, though. Those two seemed to be on speaking terms less and less lately.

As he shook his head, his eye lighted on the liquor table under the window, and he swallowed to test the dryness of his throat. Glancing back at the stack of papers he'd just spent several hours checking, he decided a wet reward was definitely in order.

The heavy cut crystal clinked pleasantly against the lip of the glass as he poured himself a generous amount of the amber liquid. Downing that, he poured another. With one arm braced against the window frame, he had the glass halfway to his lips again when he spied Amanda out on the front steps just as she did her queer little dance.

He frowned. Now there's a puzzle, he thought. Figuring out what sort of creature this was that had been virtually thrust upon him was like trying to capture a handful of morning mist. Every time he thought her one thing, she turned into another. When he became convinced she was just another victim of his father's tyranny, she turned into the provocative tease—as she had today during the ride home.

The trouble with today was that he'd seen her ploy from the start and he still had been powerless to stop himself from responding. The heat in the pit of his belly, that prickly sweat under his collar every time she'd lay one of those small hands on his arm or look at him with those wickedly innocent green eyes of hers, they all told him he was not as indifferent to her as he would like to be. She had been obvious as only a novice flirt can be, but still, it was like watching a doctor test your reflexes with that little hammer. You knew your knee was going to jerk, and there was nothing you could do about it. Had it merely been what

MATTERS OF THE HEART 157

Bernice had said, that she was falling for him, or was it something else?

Lots of beauty and charm and everything will work out fine. He knew his father expected him to fall for the girl, counting on love to justify his dictatorial ways—and he'd be damned if he would; he'd jumped through his last hoop for that man—but had he somehow led Amanda to expect the same thing? His father could be a very persuasive talker. . . . Memory whitened his lips. Never again, he vowed, never again.

Putting his glass down, he stared out the window at the slender figure for a long moment. Leaning over, he threw open the window.

"Are you ill, madam?"

Amanda gasped and whirled around.

His coat was gone, his shirt sleeves were rolled up past well-muscled forearms, and his hair had been finger-combed several times. It looked like he had been working—and disturbed, judging by the frown on his face. Then she caught the glint of amusement in his dark blue eyes, and relaxed.

In sudden devilment, she advanced on him, fingers wiggling menacingly as one might demonstrate the attack of a bogeyman to a wide-eyed child. "Look out!" she warned. "It might be contagious!" Here, her attempt at an eerie wail dissolved into a fit of giggles.

"Let us hope not," he replied, smiling in return. "But why such high spirits?"

She stopped, her skirts swaying softly around her ankles, and smiled up at him. "Sophie and Joe are here."

"I see. That must've been all the racket I heard a while ago."

Thinking of the piano, she bit her lip. "Thank you."

"You're welcome, and now that you have your beloved pony—Molly, wasn't it?—and since you're obviously feeling so fit, perhaps you'll consider taking a ride with me? I had intended to try to get some more work done, but the day seems better suited to being out of doors. Wouldn't you agree?"

"Indeed, it does," she agreed, "and I would be most delighted, kind sir." She smiled and swept into a deep curtsy, unaware of the swell of her bosom as she did so. When she straightened up, she found his dark eyes regarding her intently, and for a fraction of a second, she saw that look again. You do want me! she cried in silent triumph.

His eyes were still on hers. "Shouldn't you change into something more suitable?"

Oh no, she thought. You're not getting off that easy. "No, I think I'll stay as I am—we're not leaving your property, are we?"

He shook his head, then with surprising quickness, he swung his legs over the sill and dropped lightly to the ground beside her.

He laughed. "I can see by the look on your face you never sneaked out of the house at night when you were little," he observed, taking her arm as they walked toward the barn.

"I can't think where I would've gone if I had."

"To a twelve-year-old boy," he said, making a sweeping gesture with his other arm, "the night holds a multitude of wonders."

"Didn't you ever get caught?"

"Only when Teddy ratted on me."

"Then what happened?"

"To me or Teddy?"

She laughed. "Your poor mother."

He slanted her a look. "My mother?"

"Yes, I was looking at her portrait today—that is hers next to my room, isn't it?" At his nod, she continued. "I was thinking she looked sort of sad and wistful—and no wonder, with the two of you to raise."

"That was done just before she and my father were married, but I always thought she seemed sad myself. My father was away a lot, and when he started taking me to work with him, she was really alone." He tucked the ends of his fingers into his trouser pockets and scuffed at the dirt in the driveway. "I remember sitting in the buggy beside my father in the mornings, waving good-bye to her. I used to wish I could leave someone in my place to keep her company."

"What about Teddy?"

"She died when he was born."

Amanda let go of his arm and laced her fingers in front of her. "Oh. I didn't know. I'm sorry."

"That's okay."

"Who raised him?"

"Who? Teddy? The servants mostly."

His answers were getting shorter, and she could sense he was tired of the conversation, but she couldn't help it. She had this need to know all she could about him. Maybe then, she would understand him. "What about you?"

He frowned. "I told you. I was at work with my father."

"Didn't you go to school?"

"What is this? An inquisition? My father hired a tutor—said public education was for the lower classes—and gave us an hour a day in the corner of a store room." He pulled the barn door open and gave it a shove. "Anything else?"

Amanda shook her head, deciding it best not to say anything more as she stepped into the dusky light of the barn—and straight into a shower of golden hay as little Georgie dropped out of the loft to the ground in front of her.

"Hi!" he said with a happy grin. Like one hypnotized, the youngster gazed at her as if she were Spring personified, and so enrapt was he that Nathan had to speak twice to gain his attention. Charged with readying Amanda's mount for her, the boy hurried to the task with all the earnestness of a questing knight.

Nathan stared after him and shook his head in amused wonder. The look he threw Amanda as he went to saddle his own mount was less easy to read. What now, she wondered.

Finding herself alone in the middle of the barn with nothing to do but wait, she looked from man to boy, and decided the child would probably make for easier company. The moody undercurrents she sensed in Nathan disturbed her.

"Nice pony ya got here. Had her long?" the boy asked as she walked up to the stall.

"Very long," she answered. "My papa . . . my papa gave her to me when I was just about your age." The lump of grief that rose in her throat took her by surprise. A lot had changed, and many new things occupied her thoughts, but there still had been precious little of that potent healer, time.

She stroked the velvet nose that had thrust itself into her hand in search of a treat. "Sorry, my pretty," she murmured. "No apples today."

"I guess she is kinda pretty . . . for a pony," the boy allowed. "But for a *real* horse, you'll never find one more beautiful than Striker."

"Striker?" she repeated, willingly distracted.

The blond head inclined toward the big bay stallion Nathan was saddling in the stall at the other end of the barn. "Brought him home with him after the army," Georgie explained, tugging his full weight on a cinch. "Named him after a sergeant he had. Said they both had the same wild look in their eyes."

She laughed aloud at that, delighted by such a droll bit of trivia, and drew a curious glance from Nathan.

Satisfied that every cinch was snug, Georgie led Molly from her stall, and Amanda, in stepping out of the way, backed squarely into Nathan as he was leading the bay. She apologized and would have retreated into the now vacant stall to let him pass, except he made the same move at the same time and they collided once again. She started to laugh, but swallowed the sound as he stepped firmly to one side and motioned for her to precede him.

Adopting a more serious demeanor, she followed the boy and her pony outside into the late afternoon sun. She was determined not to antagonize him. Still, his preoccupied scowl as he boosted her into the saddle made her uneasy, and she almost wished she hadn't agreed to this ride. It was a wish she would remember later.

Giving the pony's rump a slap, he started her off, then seconds later, cantered past on the big stallion to take up a position several yards ahead.

Behind them, Georgie called out, "Get Mr. Rushton to show you my pond!"

Too far away to answer, Amanda just raised a backward hand. She was trying to catch up to Nathan, but he seemed almost determined to forget her presence as he continued to maintain the distance between them.

They rode like this for some time, together yet not together, and while she tried to take an interest in the land around her, that ramrod straight back in front of her kept drawing her eyes like a magnet.

They crossed through several fields, each bright with new spring growth, and now they were following a tree-lined stream that zigzagged its way along for a good mile before it finally opened out into nearly an acre of water—Georgie's pond.

She thought it a beautifully peaceful place, with its steep grassy banks and glassy smooth surface. On the opposite side, a path had been worn down to a picturesque but crudely built pier. A tiny boat, badly in need of paint, was moored there.

Seeing Nathan look around him, she saw the tension ease visibly from his shoulders. Maybe now he'll be better, she thought; but as soon as he swung out of the saddle and came to help her down, she saw that nothing had changed.

Without a word, he went to squat on his heels at the edge of the bank, where he began flinging pebbles into the water with an inordinate amount of energy.

Settling herself quietly at what she considered to be a safe distance, she hugged her knees as the missiles broke and churned the surface into a froth. When the bombardment finally ceased, she looked over to see him staring into the distance, his profile silhouetted against the red sky of sunset.

"Why does Georgie call this his pond?" she asked, more to see if she could get him to talk than anything else.

He shrugged. "I bring him here and row him around every once in a while. Since it never had a name, I told him we could name it after him, if he'd like." His fingers began searching the grass for more stones.

"You like children, don't you?"

The monosyllabic reply was noncommittal.

Oh dear, she thought, hurling a small pebble of her own down into the dark green water.

Her heavy sigh drew his attention, and he stared at her, narrow-eyed, for a long, speculative moment before he suddenly patted the ground beside him. "Why are you sitting way over there? Come here," he commanded softly.

She chewed the inside of her lip. As soon as the sun

goes down, he changes as radically as the fabled werewolf. "It's getting late," she said, all at once feeling an apprehension she didn't understand.

"Come here."

The low, throaty growl in his voice streaked along the nerves in her spine, thickening her pulse into a dull throb, but she did as he bid her, hugging her knees even closer as she settled next to him. Watching the water turn from green to black as the sky above them darkened, she shivered with a sudden chill when she felt his warm breath on her neck—and caught the smell of whiskey that came with it.

"Sh—shouldn't we be getting back?"

"Mmm-hmm," he murmured.

Her breath caught in her throat as his lips began burning a fiery trail down the side of her neck to nibble at the pulse hammering there. "What are you doing?"

"I'm kissing you, silly."

"I—I know that . . . but why?"

"I'm married to you, aren't I?"

Her head felt too heavy for her neck and his kisses sent tremors all the way to the pit of the stomach.

"Besides," he murmured against her skin, "it's what you've wanted, isn't it?"

Blinking like one just awakened, she twisted around to face him. "What?"

He shrugged and smiled lazily down into her face as he lightly traced the curve of her cheek with one finger. "Today. All the smiles, the little touches . . ." His fingers brushed across her collar bone, then stroked their way down to the shadowed valley between her breasts. "This dress."

"I don't know what you're talking about!" she cried, knocking his hand away and scrambling to her feet. "I was merely trying to be a—a pleasant and—an agreeable companion, that's all!"

"Really?" He came to his feet beside her.

She stamped a foot, but before she could retort, he suddenly pulled her to him, covering her mouth with his own in a deeply intimate kiss. Even as an inner voice screamed for her to stay angry, she heard her own small moan and felt her arms twine themselves around his neck to hold him even closer.

He was surprised as he felt the willing press of her body, her lips parting beneath his own. He knew nothing beyond the feel and taste of her—until the ghost of his father loomed over his shoulder, taunting him . . . rescuing him. Abruptly, he dragged her arms from around his neck and thrust her away, the effort it cost him sharpening his features into a mask of twisted emotions. "Damn you! I suppose you call that being 'agreeable,' too? What did my father offer you? A bonus if you were with child by the time he returned?"

His words hit her like a slap, robbing her of breath as well as balance. One arm flailed the air weakly for some sort of support as she shrank away from him. "You were the one who . . . Oh . . . *oh!*" She fled for the horses, hot tears of humiliation nearly blinding her. Shaking all over, she was struggling to get her foot up into the stirrup when Nathan was suddenly beside her.

"Leave me alone! Don't you dare touch me!"

Ducking the swipe she took at him, he picked her up and dumped her unceremoniously into the saddle, guiding her knee around the pommel with a bruising grip.

She snatched the reins from his hand, planted a foot in the middle of his chest, and shoved. Wheeling Molly around she took off at a pace that startled the old pony. "And I hate it when you drink too much!" she flung over her shoulder for good measure.

A moment later, she heard the thundering of his

horse behind her, but it wasn't until they were within sight of the house that he rode up alongside.

Reaching out, he grabbed Molly's halter and slowed both animals to a more sedate pace.

"Let's not give the servants anything to gossip about, shall we?"

"Oh, that's right. Public opinion is the most important thing, isn't it?" Nonetheless, she wiped her eyes hastily. There was no sense alarming little Georgie, and drawing one of those blunt questions only children can ask.

Inside the house, the silence was heavy as both of them declined dinner, a bit of news that made Mary throw up her hands and return to the kitchen muttering grim prophecies for "certain people" if they didn't start eating right. Then they each went their separate ways, he to his study and she to her room.

Slamming her bedroom door shut, she pressed her forehead against the cool wood, fighting the urge to be sick. Why did he always have to be so cruel? She'd told his father it wouldn't work, but no, he wouldn't listen, would he? Still, it was her own fault for being here, and she knew it. Arrogance, that's what it was. It was nothing but arrogance that had let her think that somewhere, deep inside that man, there could ever be a love for her. For her! A bitter laugh turned suddenly to tears. She dragged the back of one hand across her eyes and began to tear herself wildly out of the dress, as if that were the sole cause of her pain.

Standing before her mirror, she brushed out her hair with more vigor than care, the muscles of her slender neck straining with the force of each stroke. He had accused her of flirting with him, and she burned with shame, knowing how obvious she must've been. But the idea that his father was somehow behind it was insulting and ridiculous. It made no sense. She threw the brush across the room. Nothing that man did made any sense! Couldn't he see her desire? That she wanted him—enough to make a fool of herself?

Suddenly, her face crumpled and she threw herself across the bed. She cried until she could cry no more, then wearily wiped her swollen eyes as she curled onto her side with a wet little hiccup. On the dressing table, the lone yellow rose caught her eye. She stared at it for a long, long time. Where were the heroes when you really needed them?

Hours later, Nathan stood on his darkened balcony, listening to the quiet of the night as he had one last smoke and a whiskey before going to bed. Without a shirt, the damp coolness of the spring night lay against his skin like a woman's touch, and the stars looked down on him with a thousand diamond-hard eyes. The moon was a silver disk against the black sky, washing the fields and trees in a white glow that made the light spilling from Amanda's window seem dim in comparison.

As his eyes rested briefly on that square of yellow light across the way, the lace parted and she stepped out onto her balcony. It was the first he'd seen her since their confrontation at the pond.

He watched her shoulders lift and fall in a sigh, the shape of her limbs dimly outlined through the demure nightdress.

How could one lone female wreak such havoc in a sane man's life? Little more than a week ago, she had been in the past tense to him, hardly more than a name. Now, she permeated his every thought. He had more than fulfilled any responsibility thrust upon him. That should have been the end of it. Instead, here he was, unable to see beyond bright hair and green eyes. He heaved an agitated sigh. Well, not only was she a

MATTERS OF THE HEART 167

whim he couldn't afford to indulge, but this was the one area of his life he refused to let his father control.

The damnable trouble was, he *was* attracted to her. Not that he was in any danger of falling before that monstrous ax, love, but from the moment he'd pulled her into his arms and felt the way she molded herself to him, he'd known she was his for the taking. That plus his own temptation had made him brutal. He wasn't proud of it—that wounded look in her eyes still haunted him—but maybe now she would keep her distance. He wanted no conquest, especially of her. She was probably more right than wrong when she called him a jaded libertine, but as far as he was concerned, he wasn't jaded nearly enough for comfort in this case.

Shifting his weight from one foot to the other, he took his last swallow, then stared into his glass, lips twisting wryly. She was probably right about one other thing, too. Perhaps he did drink too much. What started out as an escape had turned into a habit. *But one problem at a time, Nathan, my boy. Let's make sure one is handled before we tackle another.*

A movement from the other balcony made him lift his head. She was going back inside.

"Goodnight, Nathan. Sleep well."

Her words, soft and sweet, came to him without reproach, yet shamed him still for his silence.

Early the next morning, he sat in the dining room hunched over some paperwork and drinking a cup of black coffee the only thing his head and stomach could tolerate—when there was a knock at the door. He groaned, and only the fear that his raw nerves might have to endure another such attack kept him from waiting for someone else to answer it. Making his way gingerly across the hall, he was just about there when Amanda came daintily down the steps, dressed in a simple white shirt and rust-colored skirt.

She smiled pleasantly. *He looks awful.* "Good morning," she said, maliciously speaking louder than necessary.

He winced, but returned her greeting with a brief nod, then yanked open the door, only to stand and stare stupidly at the person on the threshold.

The tip of an ebony cane poked him in the ribs. "Close your mouth there, big brother. You're catching flies."

Chapter 8

The man on the doorstep was a fashion plate of stylish gray flannel and starched white linen.

"Teddy."

"In the flesh." The youngest Rushton grinned. "You look like hell," he observed bluntly. "What's the matter? Doesn't married life agree with you?"

Nathan frowned. "What are you doing here? I thought you were going to enlist."

"Well, I was going to, of course," his brother answered, stepping into the tiled foyer, "but then I began to think about some of the things you said the other day, about my buckling down to work and all that."

Nathan waited for the end of this surprising revelation, but none came. "So?" he prompted irritably.

Teddy shrugged. "So you're probably right. I'm turning over a whole new leaf, as they say. Thought I'd really make an effort this time, really do my share of the work, you know."

Nathan tugged on an ear as he mulled over this unexpected event. "Well, I can certainly use the help. And if you're really serious about it," he added pointedly, "I know someone else who'll be pleased to hear it."

"Oh, I'm serious, all right—but I think I'll leave the

pleasing to you. You've always been so much better at it."

Over his brother's shoulder, Teddy caught sight of Amanda standing at the bottom of the stairway, a shy smile lighting her face, and his own split into a grin. "Well, if it isn't my little Daisy!" he exclaimed. Shoving his hat and stick at his brother, he went over and scooped her up to swing her around in a complete circle.

"I never did get to kiss the bride, you know," he scolded with mock severity as he set her back on her feet, and without so much as asking leave, leaned over and planted a kiss squarely on her mouth.

Feeling her face redden, Amanda darted a quick look at Nathan to see his reaction to this affectionate display, but he seemed more concerned about what to do with the items he suddenly found himself holding. Miffed, she returned her attention to her new brother-in-law with a dazzling smile.

"We were just going in to breakfast. Won't you join us? I'm sure your brother would welcome the addition of some male company." She looked to Nathan for the expected confirmation of her invitation. "Wouldn't you, my dear?"

Handing over his brother's things to William, who had finally appeared, he merely nodded and waved them ahead of him into the dining room.

Failing to get even a small rise, not even the usual lift of an eyebrow, she deliberately turned her back on him and linked her arm through Teddy's. That's when she noticed that one end of the table was cluttered with dirty dishes and strewn with papers. "Well, well . . . it appears your brother has started without us, but you're still welcome to join me. I'm starved."

"As a matter of fact, so am I," Teddy confessed. "And," he added after sniffing the air appreciatively, "if those are apple muffins I smell, you couldn't drag me away."

Three eggs, five muffins, several sausage links, and a pot of coffee later, he threw down his napkin and leaned back in his chair with a groan. "Delicious. Absolutely delicious. Are you sure you won't trade Mary for old Burris? I swear I don't remember that old man making more than a dozen decent meals in my entire life."

The remark had been addressed to Nathan, but since his brother had become engrossed in his work once more and didn't look up, Teddy turned to Amanda with a wink she didn't understand.

"I spent the day yesterday at the office," he said, apparently to her, but she noticed that the intent scribbling at the other end of the table ceased abruptly and Nathan's head came up.

Teddy crowed with laughter. "See? Look at him! He's as protective of that place as an old mother hen! Well, don't worry, big brother. All I did was clean up the place a bit as you ordered. Besides," he added, "my presence seemed to give the hired help that extra bit of incentive they needed to work a little harder."

"From what I've seen," Nathan returned equably, "it's never been the hired help who've needed the incentive to do a full day's work."

Amanda saw the flush creep up from Teddy's collar, and felt sympathy for him as well as a touch of relief for herself. At least Nathan's abrasiveness wasn't reserved exclusively for her.

The smile Teddy turned on her was rueful. "See how he is? Be glad you've not been around long enough to feel the bite this man's words can deliver."

Her eyes locked with Nathan's across the table, and she imitated perfectly the superior arch of his brow. "Oh, I think I've felt it a time or two."

Teddy fell back in feigned horror. "What! So soon?" He turned to Nathan. "You cad, you!"

The muscle in Nathan's jaw worked furiously for a second, but he made no comment as he went back to his paperwork.

The silence that fell then was broken only by another groan from Teddy. "Oh, I'm stuffed," he said, apparently unaware of the strain in the air.

"I'm not surprised," she said impishly.

Pointedly, he leaned forward, chin in hand, to watch as she buttered her fourth muffin. "Talk about me. You're not actually going to eat that, are you?"

"Of course I am. Why shouldn't I?"

"Because," he wagged his head solemnly, "you might explode and ruin the wallpaper."

Pretending outrage, she made as if to stab him with her fork, a move he deftly avoided, but in doing so, nearly tipped himself over backwards in his chair. Her mouth full of buttered muffin, she laughed, sprayed the tablecloth with crumbs, then clapped a hand to her mouth in embarrassment, leaving Teddy to slap his knee in gleeful laughter.

The harsh clearing of a throat coupled with an agitated tapping sound made them both look up to find themselves under Nathan's malevolent stare, his pen drumming the table. Exchanging glances with each other as he went back to scowling over a column of figures, they sobered quickly and smothered any remaining smiles behind their hands like two school children caught clowning in class.

Seconds later, Teddy brightened. "Hey! I have an idea. Let's all go on a picnic."

Amanda stared at him in disbelief. "How can you even think of food after a breakfast like this?"

He waved away her question good-naturedly. "By

the time we fix it and get to wherever we're going, I predict that even you will be hungry again."

"I don't know," she said doubtfully. "What do you think, Nathan?"

Nathan's head came up again, the fierce frown of concentration still on his face. "A what? A picnic?"

She nodded, watching him come to his feet with a great explosive sigh.

"No, I think not—but you two go ahead. As for me," he said, shuffling his papers into a single pile. "I'm going into the office, where there's work to be done." His glare, an oblique reminder to his brother, was apparently lost on the younger Rushton. "Frankly, *I* don't have any more time to waste."

The protest she was about to offer against his working on a Sunday died on her lips. So now she was a waste of his time, was she? Well, he certainly hummed a different tune when his precious Rushton Enterprises was in the balance! Watching him roll his papers into an untidy sheaf and stuff them under one arm, she thought, Good! But her relief was grayed with misery as soon as the door fell shut behind him. Why did she have to love a man who obviously cared so little for her?

As if reading her thoughts, Teddy reached over and gave her hand a squeeze. "Don't mind him. Once a dull boy, always a dull boy. All he knows is work, work, work. As a matter of fact," he confided with crooked smile, "how he ever had time to develop a reputation with the ladies, I'll never know."

If her answering smile was forced, he didn't notice as he rubbed his hands together with enthusiasm. "Well, you heard the man. . . . Shall we get started?"

Trailing her fingers in the cool water, Amanda lounged in the stern of the little boat and listened to the oars chunk agreeably in their locks while Teddy rowed them in lazy circles on Georgie's Pond. He had promised her a pleasant afternoon and, so far, it had been just that.

After charming Mary into packing them a lunch fit for royalty, he had handed Amanda and the basket up into his little yellow and black tandem for what he called a "spin" about the place. As it turned out, this was little more than a mad dash over hills and fields at breakneck speed, and even though they were in constant danger of being upset, she had enjoyed the wild ride in spite of herself. Clutching the basket with one hand and hanging onto her seat for dear life with the other, she had squealed with laughter as he raced them over the countryside with all the abandon of a kid taking a dare.

When they had topped the ridge behind the pond, Teddy had stopped, suggesting they go for a paddle, and laughed when she eyed the dilapidated boat with distrust. He assured her it was sounder than it looked, and although it had taken some doing, she had finally been persuaded.

Gliding about on the smooth surface of the water, they had continued to laugh and talk, but gradually conversation had mellowed into a comfortable kind of silence that only a comment now and then broke.

She tilted her head back some more and let the pink ruffled parasol she'd been twirling drop back farther over her shoulder. She had never carried a parasol in her life, but Sophie had dug this one up from somewhere and insisted she take it. Married ladies, she'd been told cryptically, have to watch out for the sun. Well, it felt good right now, warm and soothing on her face, but she opened one eye the barest slit and surreptitiously studied her new relative.

He had left his coat back with the picnic basket, and

his white shirt, almost blinding in its brightness, rippled with the light, grass-scented breeze. He rowed leisurely, looking somewhat formal in his dark bow tie and starched collar and cuffs. He was very much like Nathan in many ways, she decided, yet feature by feature, it was difficult for her to find any specific resemblance. His hair and complexion were lighter than Nathan's, and even though his eyes were blue, they were a lighter and less intense shade. He was shorter by the barest inch but slenderer, too, exaggerating their difference in size. It was as if Teddy were a smaller and slightly bleached out version of his older brother.

His crooked grin, however, was enough like Nathan's to give her a start whenever it flashed, and make her wonder again what Nathan was doing at that particular moment. She couldn't help hoping his day was as proportionately miserable as hers was pleasant. It would serve him right for the way he'd treated her.

"What are you smiling at?" Teddy suddenly asked.

"Oh, nothing." She shrugged, pushing herself into a straighter sitting position. "Just enjoying the day, that's all."

"Good. I knew you would."

She squinted at him through one green eye. "Tell me something," she commanded idly. "What was Nathan like as a boy?"

"Oh, I don't know. Like any other, I suppose."

"Weren't the two of you close?"

"Does being related automatically make people close?"

"I'm sorry, I—"

"Never mind," he sighed, relenting. "We were close when I was little—he was Teacher and Protector—but by the time I was nine, he was too busy being groomed to take over the family business to have much time for me anymore."

She cocked her head to one side. "Oh? What were you groomed for?"

"Ah!" he snorted, and with a sudden movement, swung the little vessel around to pull vigorously in the opposite direction. "That certainly is the question, isn't it?"

The words sizzled with bitterness, but before she could even react, he disarmed her with a grin. "Okay. I've answered your questions. Now it's my turn."

She gave him a playful salute, glad that a dark, Rushton mood had been avoided. "Aye, aye, sir! What is it the captain wants to know?"

He accepted the salute with a grave nod. "Firstly, I want to know all about you, my pretty sister-in-law. Secondly, when do we eat?"

She laughed. "The answer to your second question is easy. Whenever you'd like. The answer to your first is, I'm afraid, very boring."

"I refuse to believe that anyone with hair the color of yours could possibly be the product of a mundane background. Now tell on," he commanded.

As they moored the boat and made their way back up the steep bank under a sky quietly darkening overhead, she gave him the brief outline of her life.

"There!" she said, handing him one corner of the red and white checked cloth from the picnic basket. "I told you it wasn't very interesting."

"Oh, but you left something out," he accused with a sly smile.

"What's that?"

"You left out what it's like being married to my brother."

Her expression was prim as she handed him his plate of cold chicken and fruit, then settled back with her own. "That's rather personal, don't you think?"

He shrugged away the fact that his manners were in

question. "I'm just curious. Knowing how my father pushed this situation on you, I was wondering how you and Nathan managed to work things out so quickly. Did you fall in love at first sight, or something?"

Amanda felt the heat in her cheeks as her eyes strayed to the spot, only a few feet away, where she and Nathan had been the night before. *I'm kissing you, silly.* "Hardly. Ours is strictly a . . . business arrangement, so to speak."

Teddy sank white teeth into a golden chicken breast. "Really?"

"You sound surprised."

"I guess I am a bit," he confessed, chewing thoughtfully. "You see, Nathan has a way of always turning everything to his advantage. As a matter of fact, I was beginning to think him possessed of some power no one—no female, that is—could resist. I'd fully expected you to be wooed into his camp by now."

It's what you've wanted, isn't it? What did my father offer you? She tossed her mane of russet-hued hair. "I have no intention of being 'wooed' into anyone's camp, thank you."

"Good."

"Why do you say that?"

"Because it's good to know we ordinary mortals still have a chance with him around."

Amanda shook her head. "Well, I can assure you," she said, smiling sadly, "Nathan Rushton can hardly be said to have squeezed you 'ordinary mortals' out of the race."

He nodded, apparently satisfied with that curious answer, and they both returned to the business of eating, still unaware of the storm clouds gathering over their heads.

After a time of nervously shredding the meat off her

chicken leg, she set her plate aside and hugged her knees to her chest. "You've mentioned Nathan and a lot of women, but was there ever a special one? One he really loved?" She tried to ask it as casually as if she were asking if he'd like more cake, but as she waited for his answer she hardly dared to breathe.

He nodded, swallowing. "One. Her name was Suzanne DuBell. They were engaged to be married."

DuBell . . . DuBell . . . The name snagged in her memory. Ah, yes. "The Social Match of the Season" the papers had called it. Maybe that was who she had seen him with once when she was in town. They'd been riding in an open carriage, oblivious to all but each other. Nathan's dark good looks had been the perfect foil for the girl's pale blondeness. "What happened?"

He gave a bored shrug. "I don't know. She left him, that's all I remember."

"Did you ever meet her?"

"Once or twice."

She stared at the pointed toes of her brown kid boots. "What was she like?"

He set his plate aside and stretched out full length, arms under his head as he thought for a moment. "Oh . . . charming, witty, vivacious . . ." As he spoke, he watched her from beneath lowered lids, a barely controlled smile twitching at his lips.

She wrinkled her nose. "You liked her then?"

He rolled over onto his side and propped his head on a fist. The suppressed smile made his eyes dance mischievously as he nodded. "But then . . . she paled in comparison to a certain flame-haired beauty I know."

She smiled in spite of herself. He'd been paying her the most outrageous compliments all day, apparently willing to go to any lengths to make her blush.

"There!" He grinned. "At least I got you to smile again, and since I—hey!" He suddenly jerked upright with a frown.

Wondering what was wrong, she stared. Then she, too, jumped as a large drop of rain splatted noisily onto the back of her hand. Both of them stared up at a sky gone black and rumbly with thunder.

"Come on!" he yelled "It's a cloudburst!"

Scrambling to their feet, they began stuffing everything into the basket and laughing at their own clumsiness as plates and chicken bones went flying.

"Good evening, sir."

Nathan handed over his hat and coat. " 'Evening, William."

"Your brother and Mrs. Rushton are in the drawing room, sir."

Nathan cocked his head as the sound of bad singing and worse piano playing reached out into the hallway. He smiled his understanding at William, who looked more pained than usual. "Yes, I hear them. Thank you, William. That'll be all for tonight."

"Thank *you*, sir.

Wincing at a particularly discordant note, Nathan strolled into his study and poured himself a generous shot of whiskey. Then, as a burst of laughter came from the next room, he decided to see for himself what all the merriment was about.

With his presence still undetected, he leaned a shoulder in the doorway and watched as Amanda and Teddy, seated side by side on the piano bench with their heads close together, tried to pick out the melody to "Turkey in the Straw." Teddy was giving the instructions and she was doing her best to follow them, but the end result was so halting and unrecognizable they both kept collapsing in laughter.

In the last few weeks, he had come home often to find the two of them either around the piano like this, or absorbed in one kind of game or another. His brother had proven to be little help at work—indeed, he rarely bothered to show up—but still, he was performing a valuable service in keeping Amanda amused and occupied. It left him free to go about his business without feeling guilty that she was alone.

He smiled and took another swig. Too bad his father couldn't see the two of them together like this, he thought. Even he would have to agree it was they who seemed the better suited pair. They were both so young and lighthearted. He stopped. Yes, he liked that. They were the ones, Teddy and Amanda, not Nathan and Amanda. It was a thought he would take out often in the next few weeks, a thought that would continue to grow.

Another attempt to get her part right failed, and Amanda rose to her feet, laughing and fanning herself with both hands. Giggling, she went over to open the terrace doors, the silk of her fawn-colored dress shimmering in the lamplight. "Believe me, Teddy, I don't think we'll have to worry about anyone clamoring for our talents any time soon."

Nathan swirled the whiskey in his glass. "I'm afraid I'll have to agree with you there."

She spun around with a gasp. "Nathan! It's so late . . . we were beginning to worry. Is everything all right?"

Teddy twisted around on the bench. "She," he said, pointing a finger in Amanda's direction, "was beginning to worry, not I."

Nathan smiled lazily at the two of them, and lifted a shoulder in a shrug. "I've been busy."

Amanda started to move toward him, but stopped herself. The look he gave her over the rim of his glass made her feel like a disease for which he'd finally found a cure. It was a smug, I-dare-you-to-matter-to-me kind of look that made her ache with frustration. "So how—" she swallowed and waved a hand in a self-conscious gesture, "how are things going? At work, I mean?"

"All right, I suppose."

"Are you hungry?"

He shook his head. "I ate in town."

"Oh." It was the fourth time this week.

Looking from one of them to the other, Teddy suddenly smacked both palms on his thighs. "Well, you're right about one thing. It is getting late, and I should be going." After closing the keyboard, he went over and dropped a kiss on the top of Amanda's head. "See you later, love. Keep practicing," he instructed with a grin.

Her face flushed and she hurried past Nathan to get Teddy's hat and coat. She had grown quite fond of Teddy, but sometimes his affectionate attentions made her feel awkward—and irritated her when Nathan never seemed to mind.

Strolling along in her wake, Teddy stopped and thumped his brother's chest with a knuckle. "Shame on you for leaving your new bride alone so much," he admonished in a gruff whisper.

Nathan regarded him mildly. "She's been with you, hasn't she? I'd hardly call that being alone."

Teddy's eyes flicked speculatively over his brother's missing collar and rolled up sleeves. "No, I guess I wouldn't either."

When Teddy didn't move on, Nathan prompted him with the arch of one brow and, "Was there something else?"

"Well, yes. There is," Teddy said, scratching the side of his neck. "I know you said you needed time to get things settled before we talked about my share of the company, but it's been . . . well, it's been almost a month, and you haven't said another word about it."

"I know. I'll get to you. There's a thousand little details I need to be on top of before we can start dividing it all up."

"So what are we talking about?" Teddy persisted. "A fifty-fifty split? What?"

"Of the work—or the business?"

Teddy's eyes narrowed. "What's that supposed to mean?"

Nathan grimaced on his last swallow, meeting his brother's stare directly. "I guess it means when you show me what percentage of the work you're willing to do, I'll be willing to discuss your share."

Amanda was waiting by the door with his things, but after a glance in her direction, Teddy turned back to his brother, the red creeping higher and higher off his collar. "I can do anything you can—and just as well," he ground out between clenched teeth.

Nathan shrugged. "Then prove it."

"You're not my father. I don't have to prove anything. Not to you."

Nathan sighed, looked around for a place to set his glass, but there wasn't any, so he held on to it. "I'm a business man, Teddy. I want to be fair about this, but I'm not stupid. If you devoted as much time to work as you've devoted to entertaining my wife, we wouldn't be having this discussion, now would we?"

"If you took better care of her, maybe I wouldn't have to. Not that it's a chore, but maybe then I'd have more time for work. Now do I get my share of Rushton Enterprises or not?" he hissed.

"You heard my conditions."

"Well, I wouldn't kowtow to him, and I won't to

you." The effort to keep his voice low was given up. "You and your conditions can go straight to hell!"

Amanda heard the low rumblings of conversation without much interest, but Teddy's last words made her start in surprise. As he stalked toward her with a black look on his face, she automatically held up his jacket, and he rammed his arms into the sleeves. She searched his face for some clue to the problem, but the sight of Nathan already heading up the steps diverted her curiosity. Absently, she accepted another kiss good night, then closed the door on him with some degree of relief. She was looking forward to time alone with Nathan.

Ever since that episode by the pond, the distance between them had widened steadily. She had been trying everything she could think of to bridge the gap, but it had reached the point now where she was convinced he would do almost anything to avoid her. In fact, if she hadn't known better, she could almost think he was afraid to be near her. When she tried to join him for breakfast, he hurried off without eating, pleading an extra heavy schedule that day. When she had offered to help him out at work, he reminded her of her dismal failure at such tasks and told her point-blank she would only be in the way. It was clear he wanted nothing to do with her, so now, watching him escape once again, she felt close to desperation.

"Nathan?"

He paused on the fourth step, but kept his back to her. "Yes?"

"Are you sure I can't get you something to eat?"

He sighed heavily. "Haven't you been domestic enough for one evening?"

"What?"

"Nothing. Forget it. I'm tired. I'm going to bed now."

Her own helplessness to stop him as he continued up the steps suddenly ignited her temper. "No wonder Suzanne left you!" she spat. Turning on her heel, she hadn't gotten three feet before he was behind her, grabbing her arm, and spinning her around.

"Who told you about Suzanne?"

"Let me go!" She tried to twist away, but his fingers dug through the silk sleeve and into the soft flesh of her arm.

"Who!"

"Your brother!" she flung at him, trying to pry his fingers loose.

"Well, I don't know what he told you," he sneered, "but the reason she left was because my father told her he'd disinherit me if we married. She took my ring one week, and a powder the next!"

Her struggles ceased. "Oh . . . Nathan!" No wonder he was the way he was. "How could she?"

The unexpected compassion stunned him and his grip loosened abruptly. "Apparently, she didn't find it that difficult," he said gruffly, letting go of her arm altogether. "It was a long time ago."

"Are you . . . still in love with her?" she whispered.

He blinked, his brows snapping back into place over his nose, but he didn't answer. Instead, he spun on his heel and headed back up the stairs. By the time she had regathered her wits, he was gone. Ensconced behind yet another door, he had left her staring up at an empty gallery. Alone again.

Damn your eyes, Nat Rushton! You break his heart and leave me with the pieces!

Damn you! Damn you!

Teddy's thoughts were much the same as he wheeled off his brother's property and onto the open road.

Heedless of the danger on such a dark night, he urged the skittish mare even faster. "Why is it always Nathan?" he demanded of his absent father. "You give him everything—Amanda, the company—and he doesn't deserve any of it. 'Prove it!' Who the hell does he think he is?" He snorted and snapped the reins again, feeling a certain satisfaction at his animal's response. "You did your job well, old man. He's just like you . . . just like you."

Nathan groaned and dug at the ache behind his eyeballs until black turned to red. Laying across his bed, fully clothed, he had been staring at the ceiling for nearly an hour, ever since he had come upstairs. Steeped in the fire's red glow, the room was as shadowed as his thoughts.

You taught me well, Dad. Too well. I can't let go. I can't. Why didn't you just give Teddy a piece of the company in the first place, and leave me free to run the rest of it? You must have known what would happen, the position I'd be in. Why couldn't you leave me alone—leave us alone?

A pretty, smiling face peeked out from behind his father's image, and his heart twisted.

Suzanne. . . . Blond hair, sky blue eyes, a voice as sweet as birdsong. His nostrils distended with the remembered smell of crushed flowers when he held her. Still loved her? Of course he loved her. And hated her. Damn Teddy for bringing her up, for telling Amanda about her—but damn his father most of all.

Damn you, damn you. . . .

Chapter 9

Amanda was just finishing her morning toilette when Rose tapped at her door.

"Mr. Rushton's brother is here to see you, ma'am."

Twisting the last end of a yellow ribbon through her auburn hair, a ribbon that matched her new dress, Amanda smiled at her reflection and pronounced herself satisfied. "Tell him I'll be right down."

Since it was Teddy's usual habit to make himself at home in the drawing room, she was surprised to find him still in the foyer when she descended. With several long rolls of paper tucked under one arm, he was leaning close to the mirror over the credenza, adjusting his tie and collar tips, his dark suit picking up a hint of iridescence from the sunlight streaming through the front windows.

Catching sight of her in the glass, he turned around with a smile. "Hullo, Daisy. Miss me?"

"Hullo, yourself," she smiled back, "and yes, of course, I did."

"Ah, so good to know," he murmured, kissing her cheek.

Amanda accepted the kiss, and looked up into eyes that showed red rims more often than not lately. He never drank around her, but she was beginning to suspect he indulged quite heavily at other times—like Nathan, she thought with a flash of irritation. Was the entire Rushton family doomed to look for life's solutions in the bottom of a bottle?

"Teddy, is there anything wrong? Anything you want to talk about?"

"Not a thing," he assured her. "I've been busy, that's all. Working for that slave driver of a brother is no easy task, you know. As a matter of fact," he said, tapping the rolls of paper he still held, "I have to run these drawings out to him today, and I thought you might like to come along."

"To the construction site?"

A small, bemused smile pulled up one corner of his mouth at her sudden enthusiasm. "That's the place."

In the carriage, Amanda was aware of appearing anxious, but there was no disguising her eagerness at the prospect of seeing Nathan, perhaps even talking to him. It had been ages since they'd done more than exchange polite greetings, and she had to fight the impulse to urge Teddy faster.

"How much farther?" she asked, grabbing her hat against a sudden gust of wind, and trying vainly to see past yet another of the warehouses that dotted this area known as Sparrows Point.

"About a mile less than the last time you asked."

She slumped back in her seat. "I'm sorry. I'm being a pest."

"I'd say you were many things, my love, but a pest isn't one of them." His brows crept upward much like Nathan's as he gave her a shrewdly appraising look. "I take it my brother hasn't been around much lately."

It was put as a question, but Amanda suspected he already knew the answer. "He's had a lot of work to do." She shrugged, defending her husband without quite knowing why. "He's been busy."

"He's been a fool. If you were mine, I couldn't stand being away from you so much."

Looking into eyes regarding her with unusual seriousness, she caught her lower lip in her teeth, but was saved the awkwardness of reply as they approached the steel mill.

A jungle of ugly brick buildings housing blast furnaces, rail and bloom mills, and a coke plant, with miles and miles of internal railroad snaking through it all—the Maryland Steel Company was one of the nation's largest. It had invested over ten million dollars in this eleven-hundred acre site so far—Teddy had told her that—and its newest concept of housing its own labor force, this "company town" Nathan was building for them, would cost them only a pittance in comparison.

As they lurched over tracks in the narrow roadways, Amanda didn't know what to hold first—her nose or her ears. All the hissing and clanging and noxious fumes made it seem like they were driving through the digestive system of some huge, metal beast. Loaded wagons and heavily garbed men crisscrossed the road, hustling in and out of places. When a pair of workmen paused to follow her passage with blatant speculation in their dark eyes, she blushed and looked away.

Beside her, Teddy chuckled, the ends of his tie fluttering in the wind whistling around them. "You shouldn't look so appealing."

"They shouldn't be so rude."

"I guess we men aren't the subtlest of creatures, are we?"

Again there was that look in his eyes that made her tongue-tied. Perhaps coming with him hadn't been such a good idea after all.

As they left behind the mill proper, the buildings

became scattered, and the noise faded steadily until the unmistakable sound of hammering could be heard.

"Listen!" she cried. "Is that them? Are we here?"

The shadow of a frown crossed Teddy's features and he sighed. "Indeed, we are."

They drove into an open, treeless area, rutted and bumpy, and still laced with several sets of railroad tracks. She could see Nathan's crew working about a quarter of a mile away, the curious antirhythm of hammering and sawing echoing and reechoing across the open expanse. The smell of new wood and creosote came and went with every gust of wind.

She looked for a familiar figure among those dotting the spidery, raw-looking skeletons of wood like gnawing little bugs. As they drew closer and finally halted, the "bugs" took on human form, with black pools of shadow for eyes, their flesh bronzed and gleaming in the bright sun.

She shaded her eyes with her hand. There he was! Most of the men wore only suspendered trousers, so Nathan's white-shirted figure, sleeves rolled to the elbows, was easy to distinguish. He was talking with a small group of men about fifty yards ahead.

Gathering up the drawings, Teddy told her he'd be right back.

She nodded, still intent on Nathan. The breeze ruffled his dark hair as he stabbed the air with a forefinger, giving instructions. When Teddy hailed him, he turned to gesture impatiently to hurry up. Quickly, he unrolled one of the drawings and squatted down on his heels to smooth it open on the ground. One by one, the men left the group as he gave orders, then he handed the rerolled paper back to Teddy and gestured toward a little shed Amanda assumed was their office.

Teddy headed away, and she watched in horrified fascination as Nathan strode over and scaled up the side of a half-completed structure with the ease of a monkey. Her heart was in her mouth at the way he walked around with little more care than if he'd been on solid earth. Power. That's what he exuded. His confidence, his air of command, all added up to an element of power so basic Amanda felt the instinctive female need to surrender to it, to be conquered by it.

Drawn, she stepped down from the buggy and walked toward the building, shielding her eyes as she stared up at him so dangerously near the edge of the scaffolding. The wind molded his clothing to him, outlining his thighs, his muscle-hard torso—and the sight made Amanda's mouth go dry. He was speaking to one of the workmen, then stopped, seeming to stare down in her direction. She smiled and waved, but decided she must have been mistaken when he gave no answering response. After a quick look around to see what else might have his attention, she glanced back just in time to see him turn away and move out of sight altogether.

Disappointed, she smoothed a curl blown loose from beneath the brim of her saucy straw hat and watched the activity around her, determined to put him out of her mind.

It was strange to see an entire town, from houses to stores, all rise from the ground at the same time, she thought. She tried to guess which buildings would be what, but she was sure only that the long rows of boxlike structures would be the homes for the mill's immigrant workers and their families.

In the lattice-work shade of one half-finished building, she paused to watch the gray slush of cement being mixed, but the harsh, grating sound made chills run up and down her back, and she moved on.

Suddenly, there was a shout from above and

someone seized her, yanking her backwards as more shouts and a loud crash filled the air.

"Amanda!"

She was spun around and crushed against a hard male chest. It was Nathan's voice and heart thundering just under her ear. The sweat-and-open-air smell of him filled her nose, and she closed her eyes. It felt so good to be held.

"Are you all right?" He pushed her away and held her at arm's length.

She couldn't answer. She was too busy staring. Where she'd been standing barely a second ago, there lay a twisted, splintered heap of lumber that had blown off the scaffolding. She could have been . . . Her knees began to tremble and she was grateful her arm was still in Nathan's iron grip.

"Amanda?"

She could only nod.

"You little fool!" he suddenly growled, giving her a small shake. "You could have been killed!"

By this time the workmen had all crowded around, asking if she was hurt and trying, all at once, to find out what happened. With one hand still on her arm, Nathan was starting to answer them when Teddy pushed his way through to her side.

"My God, Amanda! What happened? Are you all right?"

Before she could even answer, Nathan spun with lightning speed and a left hook that caught Teddy full in the mouth, laying him backward in the dust.

Instantly, the circle of men fell silent and dropped back a pace. This was a family affair—and strictly the boss's.

Amanda simply stood, a hand pressed to her mouth in wide-eyed shock, but Nathan ignored them all as he glared down at his brother. "I don't know what the hell you think you're doing," he ground out in a tone she had never heard before, "but if you intend to spend your days squiring my wife around, then you'd better have enough sense to keep her out of danger!"

Teddy made no attempt to rise, but sat, his face pale with anger as he wiped the blood from his lip.

"And *you*," Nathan barked, turning on her with the same fury, "if you don't have any more sense than he does, *stay home!*" Stalking off, he cleaved the circle of sweaty faces and effectively scattered the men back to work.

Even before she knew she was doing it, Amanda was stomping recklessly in Nathan's wake, the adrenaline in her veins making her feel larger than life, invincible. Just who did he think he was?

When he slapped open the door of the little office and slammed it shut, she slapped it open again. The impressions of raw wood and tin filed themselves without her noticing. She was too intent on the man who was shoving aside chairs and crates to get to the whiskey bottle and glass that sat on a shelf beneath the one window.

"Have you gone absolutely crazy?" she demanded.

He swung around, the cork still in his teeth. He spit it out. "What the hell are you doing in here?"

"I came to talk some sense into you!" She flung out a finger, bow sprung from the shoulder. "Providing I can get to you before you dive in there."

His mouth pinched in defiance, he slammed the glass down on the cluttered worktable and poured it full. Dropping himself into one of the chairs, he swung both feet onto the table and leaned back with exaggerated insouciance. "Then you'd better start talking." The liquor splashed over the rim and down his fingers when he grabbed up the glass, but he just changed hands and shook the drops off as he took a big swallow—all without flinching from her steady stare. "Well?"

She leaned down, shaking fingers spread on the table. "Why did you hit Teddy?"

He looked away. "Because he deserved it."

"Why?"

"You could have been killed."

"Would you care?"

"Of course I'd care."

Their voices hit the metal roof and bounced back, ringing strangely.

"Do you love me?"

He frowned, the lines on either side of his mouth deepening. "Just because I don't want you dead doesn't mean I love you."

"Don't look away when you say that! Look me in the eye and say it!"

Accepting the challenge, he rose to his feet, put down the still full glass, and leaned squarely across the table.

She lifted her chin. Someone else, someone far braver than she had taken over her vocal chords. "You do love me, don't you?" *God in heaven, why am I pressing this?*

The sound of hammers and saws and steam cranes doubled the silence in the little shed.

"No."

Amanda didn't flinch. All she did was bite her lip and swallow. She wouldn't cry, she wouldn't. "You're never home anymore," she whispered. "I miss you."

He straightened abruptly, kicking aside a box labeled *Nails*. With his back to her, he opened the door on the little stove and threw a piece of wood into its cold belly. "Look! It was because of a woman I almost lost this place before. I'm not going to risk that again. It has nothing to do with you personally, but I just don't have the time to play calf-eyed husband with you."

"You're a liar!" she spat at his back. When he froze, every nerve in her body screamed for her to turn and run, but some streak of perversity made her stand her ground.

He turned around, his eyes blazing. "What did you say?" he demanded hoarsely.

"I said—" she tried to prevent the nervous swallow but couldn't. "I said you were a liar," she repeated with a lot less venom.

Deliberately, he walked up so close she was forced to give ground until her back was firmly against the wall. She could feel splinters of wood digging through her dress and into her shoulder blades. The yellow feather in her hat dangled ludicrously between them, and when he swatted it aside, she did flinch this time, thinking he was going to hit her.

"Just what is it that makes me a liar?" he asked in a voice controlled and level.

Amanda tried to take a deep breath, felt her whole face quiver, and had to force the words out. "You're afraid of me, afraid if you stay around me too much you'll end up loving me."

He had leaned his hands on the wall on either side of her head, much like he had that night in her father's study, only this time she prayed he would crush her in his arms and kiss her. Her whole body was beginning to tremble. *Please, Nathan. . . .*

His eyes narrowed until she could barely see them at all behind their dark, tangled lashes. One eyebrow arched upward, and she detected the slight shake of his head—as if she had only confirmed some sort of suspicion. "You'd like that, wouldn't you?" The words were soft, but the fingers he closed around her upper arm were hard and cruel.

MATTERS OF THE HEART 195

Later, she would say she didn't know what made her do it, but right then she knew it was desperation curling her free arm around his neck and pulling him down to meet her kiss. The heat coursed from his lips to hers and all the way down to her toes; she heard a moan, but which one of them it came from she would never know. When she opened her eyes, his face was white and still. "Finished?" he asked.

Her arm slid limply back to her side. Her mouth formed the word *yes*, but no sound came out—and he didn't wait for any. Turning her around, he opened the door and shoved her out. The door banged behind her.

She sagged back against it, knees shaking so badly they wouldn't support her. She started to crumple, then steeled herself. She wouldn't give him the satisfaction. Not now. It was a gamble and she had lost.

Blinking, her mind and eyes gradually focused on her surroundings, and she began to walk, woodenly at first, then with more purpose, as she headed for the carriage and Teddy.

His own body pressed up against the door, Nathan heard her steps fade away, and his head sagged forward. He was breathing hard. He had let his guard down only that once on their wedding night, made just one mistake, and he'd been paying for it ever since. He pushed himself away from the door and shook his head, the dark strands of hair brushing his brow. He shouldn't have been surprised. Let a man, any man, show the first sign of weakness and some woman was sure to pounce on it for all she was worth.

Dropping wearily into his chair, he picked up the whiskey bottle and stared at it for a long, long time.

Teddy was on his feet, still brushing himself off, when Amanda came up beside him.

"Oh, Teddy!" she cried, dabbing her handkerchief

gently at his still bleeding mouth. "Are you all right? Does it hurt badly?"

He pulled his head away from her ministrations, wiping his own hand across his mouth, his face darkening with anger at the blood smear on his knuckles.

"It's all my fault," she moaned when he swore under his breath. "Are you angry with me? I wouldn't blame you if you were but—oh, Teddy, I'm so sorry."

"I'm not angry with you," he said shortly, "and it's not your fault either, so quit apologizing." He began to brush at himself again with a sneer so disdainful it was obvious he was trying to rid himself of more than just the dust that chalked his clothes.

"But if it hadn't been for me and my carelessness," she insisted, "he would never have hit you."

He shook his head grimly and steered her toward the buggy. "It's not the first time," he muttered, handing her up into the seat.

The sudden, explosive sound of glass breaking made them both look back toward the shed, but beyond an exchange of glances, neither commented, and Teddy hauled himself into the seat beside her.

Amanda stared at his forbidding profile as he wheeled them sharply around and away from the construction site. "What do you mean—not the first time? Do you two fight like this often?"

The bumpy road and railroad tracks behind, he touched his whip to the horse's rump and the carriage leaped forward. "Not like this, no, but in case you haven't noticed it yet, we don't get along. Of course, our beloved father deserves the credit for that. He's always pitted the two of us against each other in everything, but Nathan always won with such a splash it didn't look like I was in the running.

"Take this business for example," he went on,

suddenly needing to tell it all, "even though Nathan drank himself blind for a year, and rarely set foot in the place, *I* wasn't considered good enough to inherit. Yet I"—he thumped his chest in sudden emphasis—"I was the one who ran it for that year! But Nathan's the fair-haired boy, the one who could do no wrong. Me, well, I could never do anything right!"

Hearing the years of hurt behind his words, Amanda laid a comforting hand on his arm. "I'm sure that can't be true."

"No? If you believe my father, it is."

"Well, I wouldn't and I don't."

His rancor spent, he glanced at her with a smile. "If someone as sweet as you will take my side, maybe it isn't true after all."

Amanda smiled back, glad to see the old Teddy returning.

They drove for a while in silence, but when the city was about a mile behind them, he spotted a small, low-banked stream, and pulled off the road into the shade of some nearby trees.

"It's hot and I've been driving the old girl pretty hard," he said by way of explanation as he stepped down and unhitched the mare. Leading the horse down to the edge of the water, he gave the dusty brown coat a perfunctory pat, then strode back to Amanda's side of the carriage.

He seemed content just to stand and gaze at her, but uncomfortable under such regard, she finally prompted him to say something with an inquiring look.

"Lucky, lucky Nathan," he murmured. "He got the family business and a bride who's worth it all—and both without so much as lifting a finger."

She knew better. Perhaps he'd gotten her without lifting a finger, but she'd spent too many lonely hours to believe the latter. Nathan worked hard

Bracing an arm on the edge of her seat, he leaned forward to speak into her ear. "If it had been me," he told her softly, "I'd've taken you and let the business go to the devil."

She felt his warm breath and her heart thumped. This was a Teddy with whom she wasn't quite sure how to deal. She cleared her throat. "Sophie will be expecting me. We . . . we really should be getting back."

He sighed. "I suppose so."

The ride home was quiet. Teddy seemed unusually lost in thought, while Amanda was busy trying to sort out her jumbled pile of emotions. The scene in Nathan's office played itself over and over in her mind until she felt queasy with humiliation. What devil, what demon had possessed her to be so bold? She squeezed her eyes shut, but nothing could obliterate the memory of Nathan's face after she had kissed him. He had looked so . . . cold.

"Cold?"

She jumped. "What?"

"I saw you shiver just now. Shall I put my arm around you?" he asked with a slightly bawdy grin.

"No, of course not. I'm fine."

"Sure?"

Mutely, she nodded, but here was something else that disturbed her—this thing, this attraction for Teddy. Something had changed in their relationship, but she could pinpoint neither what nor when it had happened.

"Well, here we are." Pulling them to a stop by the front door, he slung the reins carelessly around the brake handle and settled back in the seat, his arm thrown across the back. He looked around him with a jaundiced eye. "Nathan's home, Nathan's business, Nathan's wife, and one day," he looked at her pointedly, "Nathan's children—the clincher to everything my father ever wanted, and all from his favorite son.

Sometimes I wonder why he even bothered to have a second one."

Averting her face, she climbed down. "Would you like to come in and let Sophie take a look at that cut?"

"I don't think so."

She nodded in understanding, started to turn away, then changed her mind. "Teddy . . ." she began, trying to choose her words carefully, "things may not always be what they seem, so don't give up," she finished cryptically.

His mild gaze sharpened. "What are you saying?"

"You might as well know that there aren't going to be any children." She shrugged. "At least not from this marriage."

"Surely you can't know that already. You and Nathan have only been married—"

"I tell you there won't be any children. Not now, not ever!" She had said it more heatedly than intended, but she wanted to make her point and drop the subject before the whole mess of worms came to light.

He stared at her, finally shaking his head. "I don't understand," he confessed. "Why not?"

"Because!" Oh, dear. Why had she ever begun this? "When I said our marriage was strictly a business arrangement, that's exactly what I meant."

"Good God!" he whispered, her meaning gradually dawning. "You mean . . . you and Nathan haven't—"

"No! I mean, yes! That's what I mean."

His bruised lips formed a silent whistle. "Well, I'll be damned. Who's idea was this?"

"His."

"You're kidding."

"You don't believe me?"

"It's not that. It's just that I would've sworn he. . . ."

She waited for him to finish his sentence, but he had apparently drifted off into thought. "You thought what?" she prompted, realizing all at once what an improper conversation this was.

"Oh, I don't know," he said with a vague wave. "Just that he's either blind or he's got more willpower than any man I've ever known."

Or he doesn't love me, she thought, pretending interest in the tufting of the leather seat.

He leaned over suddenly and covered her hand with his own. "Look, don't worry about it. It doesn't matter." One finger tipped her chin up. "Okay?"

Feeling curiously vulnerable, she nodded and smiled. "Okay."

He sat up. "Good," he said, unwinding the reins and flicking them lightly. "See you soon."

Amanda watched him tool smoothly out of the drive, hearing what sounded suspiciously like a whistle, albeit breathy and none too clear, float out behind him.

Amanda sat in the drawing room and listlessly pushed her needle in and out of a sampler begun months earlier, trying to convince herself she cared about it. When more than an hour had gone by after breakfast, and she was still scuffing around the house, she'd finally decided it was either the sampler or boredom—one and the same at the moment.

She hadn't seen Teddy in three days, nor Nathan in twice that long—not since that disaster at the construction site. She made a face. Hardly a sustaining memory.

Even with the diversion Teddy offered, time still weighed heavily on her hands. In this alien world of Nathan's, where she was neither wife nor servant nor guest, she found little to fill her days. Only when she pleaded with Emma or Mary was she allowed some small chore to do, and whatever wifely duties might have been open to her, William accomplished with the proprietary air that warned her such pleading would be useless with him.

"You stick that bottom lip out any more, girl, and you gonna fall right over on your face!"

Amanda looked up to see Sophie eyeing her closely from the doorway, her hands on her aproned hips.

"What's the matter, honey?" the woman asked her gently. "I ain't seen you smile in days. You too young for the blues."

The embroidery hoop sagged and was finally, carelessly, tossed to one side. "Am I?"

"Aw, honey, don't take on so. It'll all—"

"Don't! Don't tell me again how 'everything is going to work out just fine!' I don't want to hear it anymore. It would take a miracle at this point, and frankly, I'm too old to believe in miracles."

To Sophie's uncomplicated way of thinking, this sounded suspiciously like blasphemy, and her face puckered forbiddingly. "Here now, let's not have any of that kind of talk. Ain't it a miracle you got yourself such pretty clothes to wear? And this here fancy house to live in?"

"Ha! That's no miracle, Sophie. It's the way of nature." Angrily, she swiped a hand against the side of her skirt, stirring countless yards of apple green muslin, and demanded, "Haven't you ever seen a brightly feathered parrot stuck in a gilded cage before?"

Before the woman could decide how to deal with this new mood of Amanda's, there was the sound of someone rapping on glass, and they both looked around to see Teddy, his face pressed comically against one of the panes in the terrace door. He grinned at them and let himself in.

"Good morning, ladies. Hope you don't mind my coming this way, but it was too early in the day to face someone as stuffy and sour as William." His blue seersucker jacket hung on a crooked finger over his shoulder, and his matching trousers broke cleanly over the tops of darker blue spats. As usual, he was the epitome of style.

Amanda smiled. "Good morning to you, too—and no, I don't mind in the least." It was as far as etiquette would let her go in agreeing with him on the subject of the venerable butler. She only regretted she couldn't avoid the man as easily.

As Teddy dropped his coat, straddled the piano bench, and leaned his hands and chin on the inevitable stick of ebony, she asked, "Now what can I do for you, sir? I'm afraid you've missed Nathan. He left hours ago."

He made a face, and she noticed his lip was no longer swollen and discolored. "Good," he said. "Why contemplate his dark and forbidding visage when there's a much sweeter one around to behold?"

She laughed and shook her head. It was part of an exchange that had become so standard as to be almost ritual by now. "Then I repeat, what can I do for you?"

"Well, I came by to ask if you would—"

Abruptly, she waved him to silence as Sophie began her pillow-plumping routine. It was obvious the woman planned to stay and keep a watchful eye on this, "the honey-tongued Rushton," as she persisted in calling Teddy. Amanda was sorry to thwart her well-meant intentions, but she was equally determined not to be spied upon like a child. Suggesting to Teddy that they go for a stroll out of doors, she ignored the woman's indignant frown.

Arm in arm, she and Teddy crossed the terrace together.

"What's that woman got against me, anyway?" he muttered. "Every time I come here, she watches me like a hawk."

Bending to pull up a small daisy that grew alongside the terrace, Amanda answered with a shrug. "Don't take it personally. I guess it's just that she's watched over me all my life and doesn't know how to stop. Sometimes, I don't think she even realizes I'm grown."

"Then she must be blind as a bat."

After admonishing him with a playful swat, she linked her arm back through his, and they walked down a narrow, flagged path to where an ancient willow grew at the farthest corner of the lawn. Beneath one of its massive boughs hung an old, inviting bench swing with only a ghost of its whitewash remaining. It had become her favorite retreat.

He held the swing steady for her to sit down, then stood back with his shoulder braced against the tree where he could gaze at her freely.

It was ironic, he thought, but he'd come here that first day more to gloat over his brother's capitulation than anything else, yet he had been coming back ever since for a far different reason. She was quite simply a beauty, this woman who was his brother's wife. With an earthy blush in her cheeks and the coolness of deep woods in her eyes, she sat before him now a creature of that wood, a nymph, dressed in the lace of dappled sunlight. Looking at her like this, it was hard to understand his brother's neglect. But then, he and Nathan seldom understood each other, not anymore. Once, but not anymore. And if this was how his brother wanted things to stand, who was he to object? It just seemed a shame that a lovely woman like this would remain virtually unclaimed.

Feeling his eyes on her and finding such close

scrutiny uncomfortable, Amanda pretended to be absorbed in the symmetry of her flower, her fingers plucking studiously at a petal now and then. Such silence from Teddy was unusual. Rarely did he go this long without at least one attempt to make her laugh.

"God, but you're lovely," he suddenly breathed. "Did you know that?"

The mutilated blossom fell to the ground, forgotten, as she met his adoring stare in stunned silence. He was so serious she couldn't think of anything to say. She knew she couldn't scold him. It was his laughter when Nathan only frowned, his company when she was lonely, and his compliments when no one else noticed that made her feel alive. He was the only one. No, she couldn't scold him, but the way his eyes touched her made her nervous, and she looked away. All at once, she was acutely aware of how alone they were, curtained from view by a green waterfall of willow fronds that nearly swept the ground.

"I—I believe you wanted to ask me something?"

He straightened up and away from the tree like one recovering from a trance. "Oh, that's right, I did. Have you decided yet about the summer festival tonight?"

She sighed. She had successfully distracted him from one uncomfortable subject only to divert him to another. "I'm sorry, Teddy. I haven't had a chance to ask Nathan yet. You'd better go without me."

He was suddenly annoyed. "Why? Why do you keep putting me off? I've asked you to dozens of places, and each time you turn me down with the same excuse: 'I haven't asked Nathan.' I don't understand it. Why ask him, anyway? Does he ask you before he"—one hand gestured vaguely, as if searching the air for the right words—"before he squires half the women in town around?"

A giant hand squeezed the breath from her lungs. Everything—the breeze, the insects, all movement of life—seemed to come to a screeching halt around her. "What did you say?" It was barely more than a whisper.

He looked surprised at her reaction, then suddenly was down on one knee, taking her hands in his. "I'm sorry. I thought you knew. I thought it was all a part of this 'business arrangement' of yours."

It'll be a live and let live proposition . . . each of us free. . . . She pulled her hands free. "Yes. Yes, of course it is. It's just that you caught me a little off guard, that's all."

Searching her face with a frown, he finally shrugged and tried to make light of the whole thing. "Well, it's not like it's an uncommon thing in these arranged marriages, you know."

"No. No, I guess not."

"After all," he added, "Nathan's only doing what you're doing"—there was the barest pause—"with me."

She got to her feet with a jerk. She hadn't been aware that she had been 'doing' anything with Teddy, but if what he said was true—and she was terribly afraid it was—then she was sure Nathan's 'doings' were not nearly so innocent.

Unable to stand still any longer for fear she would start screaming in utter rage, she turned and flung herself back up the path. So! She wasn't good enough for him, was that it? He thought he could make a laughingstock of her, did he? Well, two could play at that game! Up until now, she had always refused any offer of Teddy's that would have taken them into the glare of public speculation. She had done so not only because it had been Nathan's company she craved, but also because she had wanted to protect their marriage from any sort of scandal. Nathan, it appeared, felt bound by no such rules of decency. Well, if it was scandal he wanted, she thought with narrow-eyed determination, then it was scandal he'd get!

The delicate nostrils flared as she came to an abrupt halt and spun to face Teddy, who was right on her heels. "Do you still want me to go with you tonight?"

His face brightened. "Will you?"

She gave him a single, emphatic nod before resuming her brisk pace.

He matched his stride to hers. "I'll come for you around six o'clock, and we'll make a night of it!" he told her. "We'll have a grand time, you'll see."

Enthusiastically, he went on to describe all the things that would color this evening of theirs, but Amanda hardly heard him. All she could see in her mind's eye was Nathan, looking down at the person on his arm, laughing and talking, like that day he had taken her shopping. Only the woman she envisioned wasn't herself anymore. It was some stranger, someone like Bernice—maybe it *was* Bernice feeling the touch of those dark blue eyes, the strength of those tanned fingers as they steered her protectively through crowded streets . . . or held her close. Pain gnawed at her insides, and she stumbled over the edge of the terrace.

Teddy caught her elbow, but if he noticed her misery, he didn't say anything as he gave her a quick kiss on the cheek. "See you in a few hours," he said.

Left alone in the middle of the terrace as his cheerful whistle faded around the corner of the house, she looked down to find her hands clenched into fists, the knuckles white.

Clifton Park, all of its nearly seven acres, including the lake, was alive with people. The men in striped coats and straw hats or bare-chested in rowdy contest, the women in swirling ruffles and ribbons, the squealing, sticky-faced children, the hawkers and the vendors, all strung together on the bright brass notes of a Sousa march, were everywhere. Where movement seemed impossible, there was constant movement. And noise—laughing, shrieking, talking, shouting. And enough food to feed the entire city. For the children young and old there were cotton candy and peanuts, taffy straight from buttered hands, and pickles right from the barrel. There were dainty cakes, and huge slabs of beef smoking the air, pretty loaves of bread, and chicken parts that had been fried, boiled, spitted, or steeped in everything but sin. Ice cream was cranked out by the gallon, beer was ladled from tubs, tea was poured from crocks, and after everybody had had his fill and more, there were greased pigs to catch, ropes to climb, poles to shinny, darts to throw, kisses to buy and steal, raffles to win or lose. The dancing, which would last until well after midnight, had not even started yet.

It was all there, every kind of licit entertainment ever devised by man, and Teddy, Amanda soon discovered, wasn't content until he'd tasted it all, tried it all, or at least cheered others on in his stead.

Intimidated at first by the sheer size of the whole thing, Amanda clung tenaciously to the fringes of the melee for a while until finally, at Teddy's constant urging, she plunged in with an abandon that rivaled his own. At last, when it seemed there was little left they hadn't tried, she gave in to sheer exhaustion and pushed her way through the crowds to drop, panting, at the base of a tree.

He found her there a few minutes later and folded himself into a loose-jointed heap beside her.

Leaning their backs against the tree, they smiled at one another out of the corners of their eyes as they both waited to catch their breaths, there in the relative quiet of their little oasis.

"Are you . . . having fun?" he was able to ask at last.

She closed her eyes and nodded her head weakly. "Oh, yes—yes."

"I knew you would. I just . . . knew it."

She nodded again, but it was more in agreement with her own statement. She was having fun, and it was something she hadn't expected.

After Teddy had left, she'd spent hours readying herself with the same exactness one would use in preparing a sacrifice for heathen gods. That was how she saw herself at the time: a sacrifice to the heathen state of her own marriage.

She had been unusually quiet while she dressed. Sophie, on the other hand, seemed proportionately talkative. Fretting the entire time, she begged Amanda to reconsider, or at least to wait and give Nathan a chance to deny or explain his brother's charges. When she was nearly badgered to the point of doing just that, Mary had suddenly poked her head through the door to ask if the missus would be wanting her usual cold supper that night, since the mister had already left word he would not be dining at home. That had done it. All the hurt, all the anger of betrayal, and all the resolve for revenge crystallized, sharp and brittle, in that one moment. Even Sophie knew her cause was lost. She hadn't said another word, not even as she handed Amanda her shawl when Teddy's carriage pulled up in front of the house.

Knowingly resplendent in lilac cotton and white lace, Amanda had walked out to meet him.

"I swear," he had said to her, "you're lovelier each time I see you."

She opened her eyes and looked down at herself now

as she half sat, half sprawled beneath the tree. The front of her bodice had a small spot, her cuffs were soiled, and grass stains streaked the hem of her skirt. But she didn't care. She was having fun.

Teddy suddenly reached over and squeezed her hand, bringing the back of it against his chest.

"I'm glad you changed your mind and came with me."

"Me, too," she answered honestly. She started to extract her hand and get to her feet when he sat forward, gripping her hand tighter.

"Hey! It's almost dark. They'll be starting the dance soon." Scrambling to his feet, he pulled her the rest of the way to hers. "Come on! We'll have to hurry or we'll never get a place inside the pavilion."

The pavilion was nothing more than a huge roof and a painted floor separated by tall pillars of stone. It had been built from donations by the city's wealthy to house the summer concerts, the speech makers, the camp meetings, and the dances, now that the young people had taken up the slightly shocking practice of socializing without chaperons.

On this particular night, in honor of the festival, bright paper lanterns hung between the massive pillars. Scores of volunteers climbed ladders to light them, just as dark gathered the night in closer.

A hush descended on the crowd as the mood shifted from the high-spirited exuberance of the day to the mellow and contented mood of an early summer's evening. Old ladies and children were trundled home or settled in some comfortable spot to nod off while the rest of the night was left to lovers.

Stray curls were patted into place and the toes of shoes were given a quick polish on the backs of trouser legs as everyone who was squeezed in under the pavilion roof waited for the band, its brass buttons winking at the crowd, to settle itself and begin.

At last they were obliged, and as the silver sounds began to move their feet, and the swirling, twirling couples in the center required more room, those on the outer edges good-naturedly spilled out under the stars without missing a step.

It was among these Amanda and Teddy found themselves, and there on the grass, they turned and moved in the crush of a hundred other couples until Teddy's energetic version of the waltz carried them to the outermost edges of the crowd.

When she pleaded exhaustion, he picked her up, held her with her feet dangling inches from the ground, and continued dancing. "Madam," he said, "you're so light on your feet!"

She didn't know what she was enjoying more—his constant antics, which kept her laughing until her sides hurt and she would beg for mercy, or the mere fact that she was here, dancing out in the night under the moon and the stars.

As they spun, slower and slower, to the music of one more waltz, she tilted her head back to gaze up at the black velvet sky. With a sudden pang, she thought of Nathan, and wondered what he was doing right then . . . and with whom. She swallowed the sudden, bitter taste in her mouth. She should have been here with him. He should have been the one to make her laugh and hold her close as they danced. It should be his body heat warming her as the chill of the night settled dew on the grass. It should be his muscles she felt beneath her fingers, his breath on her cheek, his lips seeking hers. . . .

Amanda's eyes flew open. With a strangled cry that was half shock and half protest, she struggled out of Teddy's embrace.

He shrugged, and she saw the brief flash of his grin. "Don't get so upset. It was just a brotherly kiss." When she said nothing, only continued to stand and stare at him, he raked a hand through his hair and sighed. "All right. So it wasn't so brotherly. What do you want me to say? Should I tell you I'm—"

"No! Don't!" she cried, afraid to hear any more. "Just . . . just take me home. I'm tired."

Wearily, she closed the front door behind her and leaned against it while she worked up the energy to tackle the stairs. There seemed more than the usual number tonight. From her feet up, everything hurt, and she decided she was past exhaustion and somewhere closer to dead. It had been all she could do to keep from falling asleep during the ride home. The awkward silence hadn't helped, either. That . . . kiss would definitely require some thinking about, but it would have to be done on the morrow. Right now, only the thought of sleep held any meaning for her.

With great effort, she pushed herself away from the door and went to blow out the lamp that somebody, probably Sophie, had left burning for her on the hall credenza. Why she wandered first over to Nathan's study door, she would never know—except perhaps that it was rarely left standing open like it was now.

She frowned into the darkness of the room and was about to turn away when she recognized the dim shape of someone at the desk. Carefully, one step at a time, she approached until she was close enough to touch the person. It was Nathan. He was sound asleep, head on his folded arms, his deep, even breathing loud in the quiet room. Her mouth twisted wryly. Asleep, ha! Drunk's more like it, she judged, spying the half-empty bottle by his elbow. Nearby, a glass lay on its side, and as she leaned over to set it upright, she dipped her head a bit lower and sniffed. Instead of liquor, the faint scent of bay rum wafted up. His collar stood away from the shadowed nape of his neck, and beckoned her closer and closer until she could feel the heat emanating from his skin. Unable to resist, she let the tip of her nose brush lightly against the hair just behind his ear. It was crisp and soft all at the same time. He stirred, murmuring in his sleep, and she drew back. But as she straightened up, her hand hesitated over the dark head. So great was the urge to touch him again that her whole body felt the denial when her fingers clenched themselves and pulled away.

She turned to go, but paused at the door to look back at the sleeping form of her husband. Could it possibly be that he'd been trying to wait up for her? She gave herself a small shake. Fool! her brain scolded. The time for that kind of wishful thinking was long past.

Slowly then, too tired to move any faster, she blew out the lamp and headed for bed.

Hours later, an explosive crash of thunder brought her bolt upright in bed, wide-eyed, her heart pounding. Stupidly, she stared at the sunlight streaming in through her lace curtains before something made her look around to find Nathan standing in her doorway.

"Where the hell have you been?"

Chapter 10

Amanda struggled to sit up. "What's wrong?" she mumbled, her tongue thick with sleep.

"You tell me! Was there some natural disaster I didn't hear about? Some fire or flood, perhaps, that called you away? Am I to suppose you were rolling bandages and tending the injured all night?"

Her thoughts still sluggish, she eyed him with an uncomprehending squint. His blue shirt was wrinkled, and his hair was mussed and matted to one side of his head. "What are you talking about? Are you drunk?"

His face whitened and he took a menacing step closer. "No, Madam, I am not drunk. Not because I wouldn't like to be, but because I spent most of last night trying to discover your whereabouts—without success, I might add. Now where the hell have you been?"

Resentment burned its way through her sleep-fogged brain, leaving her wide awake and as ready for battle as he. "How dare you ask me that!" she hissed, crouching forward and setting the crocheted ruffles at her breast to trembling. "Do I ask you where you've been?" She answered her own question with a shake that sent auburn curls flying. "No! I don't ask you, you don't ask me, remember? 'Live and let live' was the way you put it, I believe."

Implacably, their eyes locked, and she watched in

satisfaction as some of his ire deflated on the prick of his own words.

When he spun on his heel and left, she sank back on her haunches, her flaming burst of fury settling like cold ashes. His leaving had sucked away the strength of her righteous indignation and left her feeling bereft of any victory. She listened to his receding footsteps with a sinking heart.

"Nathan?" The footsteps continued down the stairs. "Nathan, wait!" she called, leaning as far out of the bed as she dared, her arm outstretched as if she might physically reach out and hold him back. But he continued to ignore her plea, and the front door slammed. Her arm dropped.

How had they come to this? She had wanted to fight, to scream and vent her hurt, but more than that, she'd wanted to rip that wall between them into shreds, to break through in the end to a warmth she knew was there, prayed was there. But the coldness in his eyes, the same coldness growing steadily within her own breast, frightened her. If only she could turn things back in time to the days of their friendship and try again. Or maybe if she could just bridge the gap where he couldn't.

With a sudden sense of urgency, and no thought at all about the way she was dressed, she flung back the covers and raced out along the gallery, praying she could catch him in time.

The sun was already bright, but the early morning chill quickly penetrated the thin muslin of her gown, and the stone path was cold beneath her bare feet. Even the dust of the driveway sifted through her toes like cool silk as she sped toward the barn door.

Sunlight poured in ahead of her, gilding the dust motes, while the smell of hay, horses, and manure jolted her early morning senses. It took a second for her eyes to adjust to the dimness beyond the door, but then she saw him in one of the stalls. He was readying his big stallion for bridle and saddle, his back to her.

"Nathan?"

He looked around with a frown. "What do you want?"

"I just wanted to—to say I'm sorry."

"For what?"

"For worrying you."

He returned to what he was doing with a small shrug. "Then next time you might consider letting someone know where you'll be."

"But I did. I told Sophie," she protested without thinking.

He spun on that like a striking snake. "Then if you want her to stay on here, you'd better think twice before getting her to protect you again!"

She stamped a bare foot on the straw-covered ground. "I didn't have her protect me! I didn't think it would matter!"

He yanked on a cinch so hard Striker gave an indignant snort. "It matters," he growled, not looking at her. "When a man comes home expecting to find his wife and doesn't—and can't get a straight answer as to where she is—it matters, all right."

Amanda's breath left so fast it felt as if her chest had caved in. She couldn't believe this! "If it mattered all that much," she spat, eyes blazing, "you'd come home more often instead of—of squiring half the women in town around!"

His dark brows were at a dangerous slant as he dropped an arm across the saddled back of his horse, but as his eye began to follow the silhouetted curve of her hip through the thin nightdress, he almost forgot she'd spoken. Her hair, aflame in the morning sun and curling riotously down her shoulders, made him want to reach out and pull the silken tresses through his fingers. Only the glare on the face below the curls cooled the sudden heat in his loins. Reluctantly, he snapped himself back on track. "Who told you that?" he asked with a sigh.

"Never mind who! Do you deny it?" She watched him return to readying his mount, and waited, her insides twisting with suspense and the need to know. "Well? Do you?"

To her surprise, he looked around with a mild grin. "You mean to tell me you'd expect a jaded libertine to deny such a charge—then believe it if he did?"

"Oh, Nathan, stop it!" she cried, refusing to be distracted by that tired old herring. She moved closer, willing him with every ounce of her being to do his part in salvaging their last chance to have anything good between them. "I'd believe it. I'd believe you."

Looking down into the earnestness of that clear green gaze, he felt the hard edge of his resolve soften and begin to crumble. With effort, he kept his voice light, giving no clue to the war raging just below the surface. "Then I'm sorry to disappoint you, madam, but I have no intention of denying anything."

Like sand beneath the surf, she felt the bottom of her heart wash away. "I see," she murmured, and his face suddenly blurred.

"Do you? I wonder." He saw the flood of tears gather before she looked away, a shiver wracking her whole body—and the war escalated. Jamming his hands deep into his pockets, he had to take a hasty step backward in order to hold his ground. "You're cold," he said gruffly. "You'd better go back to the house before you catch a chill."

"No," she sneered, "I certainly wouldn't want to get sick and die and make things that easy for you, would I?"

"Amanda, I—"

"No, don't. Don't bother. At least I know Teddy was telling me the truth now." Something flickered across his face, but was gone before she could put a name to it.

"That's who you were with last night?"

"Yes. We went to the summer festival at Clifton Park. And we had a lot of fun," she added, lifting her chin a notch.

"I'm glad."

"Yes, I imagine you are. Should I let your happiness be my guide in the future?"

His gaze hardened. "If it pleases you."

Suddenly, it hit her why he was never jealous of Teddy. He was grateful to him for taking her off his hands. The whole thing was planned! Instead of wreaking revenge, all she'd done was go along with the program! How stupid could she be? How stupid and blind!

Stonily, they stared at each other, then with a small nod, she turned and left, her feet making a mere whisper of sound over the straw.

Nathan watched her go, more sad than angry. It was a cruel fate that had brought two such different souls as theirs together, he thought. But then, it wasn't surprising. Not when fate wore the mask of his father.

The summer of '94 warmed quickly into scorching, steel-skied days and sticky nights that made cool breezes as valuable as gold. It was a time of picnics in the shade, outdoor concerts, ice cream socials, and nickel street car rides for a bit of air. Whatever the city offered, Teddy presented it to Amanda with all the charm and flare of a born courtier.

In the weeks following her confrontation with Nathan, she rarely turned down an invitation from

Teddy, but if he wondered at the sudden change, he never asked. He seemed content just being the one to show her off.

For her part, she was going after the good times now with a vengeance. She wanted to go and see and do until there was nothing left of the day. That way she could fall into bed and immediately into sleep without the time to wonder or think or care about anything. Or anybody.

When she was home, she stayed to herself, ignoring the rest of the house and keeping mostly to her room. It wasn't until Sophie came barreling upstairs one morning with a bit of news that Amanda emerged, fuming with indignity. The hobbled skirt of her cream-colored dress hampered her angry strides, but her heels clicked with purpose as she stormed down the steps.

Her humiliating status in this household was bad enough without this, but this was positively the last straw, she fumed, causing the tiny, gauzy pleats across her bosom to rise and fall sharply. She rapped on the study door, realizing it was the third morning in a row Nathan had stayed past the breakfast hour to work at home. Getting no answer, she rapped again and entered.

Nathan was standing behind his desk shuffling papers with a frown of concentration as brown as the vested suit he wore. In the moment before he acknowledged her presence, she looked around at all the clutter and dust and wrinkled her nose.

The desk, the sill behind heavy gold drapes, the carved-front bookcases, even the mantle over the fireplace and the green, winged leather chair in front of it were strewn with books and papers. It was a wonder he could ever find anything, she thought.

Without looking up, he asked, "Did you have fun last night?"

"Why, yes I did," she replied sweetly, not missing a beat. "Did you?"

"Is there something I can do for you?"

She folded her arms. "I need to have a word with you. It's important."

He scooped papers into an untidy stack, creased them in half, and jammed them into his coat. The gold watch was pulled out, opened, and shoved back. "I was just leaving. Will it take long?"

"No, it shouldn't take long to inform you that your servants find it great sport to make wagers on our every activity, including what we say and wear."

She had his attention now. "What in the world makes you think that?"

"I don't think it, I know it. Sophie's overheard them doing it, and more than once, I've discovered."

He considered this as he tucked one last paper into his coat and came around in front of the desk. "And you want me to do something about it?"

"Of course I want you to do something about it! I want you to put a stop to it. After all," she pointed out, "they're your servants and—"

"They're not my servants, Amanda, they're our servants," he corrected irritably. "And if you didn't spend so much time romping all over the countryside with my brother, perhaps—just perhaps, mind you—you might find time to run this household so the servants don't have so many idle hours on their hands."

"Oh, so now it's my fault?"

"It is."

"Are you telling me not to see Teddy anymore?"

The answer came a shade too late to be automatic. "No."

In an unexpected movement that lifted her own hand in reflex, he reached out to touch the pearls around her neck.

They had been a surprise, a gift tucked in with the other jewelry he'd had sent to the house weeks ago. She had meant to thank him at the time, but he wasn't home. After that, it just slipped her mind.

"Pretty . . . very pretty." He fingered the creamy nuggets near the tender hollow of her throat, smiled slightly, and swallowed.

She nodded, smiled slightly . . . and swallowed.

His hand dropped, and he spoke tiredly. "I'm not telling you how to spend your time, Amanda, but I had hoped you'd be able to run things here so I could be free to devote my time to work. It was one of the reasons I married you."

She didn't know what to say. She'd come in here on a tide of righteous indignation, and now he was making her feel she was the one remiss in his duties. "I thought you married me to get Rushton Enterprises."

He made a face and looked away. "It was one of the reasons—but very well," he said, "I'll see to the matter."

The wind was definitely gone from her sails as he escorted her to the door.

"William!" he barked, making her jump.

Immediately, William's somber figure appeared in the archway of the drawing room next door. "Yes, sir?"

Nathan beckoned. "Come in, and close the door. I'd like to discuss something with you."

"Very good, sir."

William didn't glance her way as he passed, and Amanda wondered if he'd been eavesdropping. Not wanting the same wondered of herself, she quickly moved across the hall just as the door closed behind the two men.

In the study, Nathan sat down behind the desk, and laced his fingers in front of him. "I'll come straight to the point, William. I've been hearing rumors that the staff has taken so much interest in the affairs of Mrs. Rushton and myself that they've begun to bet on the outcome of those affairs."

The butler stood before his employer, a veritable paragon of virtue. "Indeed, sir? Most distressing."

Nathan stroked his chin and eyed the man silently for a second. "Indeed, William, most distressing—to Mrs. Rushton and therefore to me. Now I don't know exactly who's involved in this—you wouldn't know, would you? No, I thought not. Well, as I said, I don't know who's involved, but pass this on for me: If I ever hear of it again," he leaned forward, "I *will* discover the party's identity, and he or she will be promptly sacked. Do I make myself clear?"

The man swallowed. "Indeed, sir . . . uh, most assuredly."

Nathan's smile was tight as he came to his feet. "I'm glad to hear it."

The study door opened, and Amanda turned from the vase of orange tiger lilies she'd been rearranging. Again, William passed her without a glance, but this time his bald pate was a bit pinker than usual.

Right behind him, Nathan stopped beside her to adjust his collar in the mirror.

"Well?" she prompted.

"He didn't know anything about it." He shrugged, heading for the front door. "I'm afraid you'll have to handle it from here."

Her jaw dropped, but before any words came out, he was gone. That was "seeing to the matter"? With a squeal of frustration, she stomped back up the stairs, glared at the portrait of Nathan's mother, and vented her rage with an inarticulate, "*Ooooh*, your son . . . !" Then she threw her door closed with a slam heard all the way down in the kitchen.

For the next few days, the Rushton household was a camp divided. Amanda avoided the staff as much as she could, and when that wasn't possible, endured their cool *Yes, ma'am*s with gritted teeth. Sophie, meanwhile, took a more direct approach by snubbing them with a loud sniff whenever she passed one of them. The only person who failed to notice the tension was Nathan—who wasn't around long enough to notice if they'd all grown extra heads, Amanda observed sourly.

It was that kind of sour mood, coupled with a momentarily unguarded tongue, that eventually gave her the chance to solve what was becoming an unbearable situation.

For the sheer satisfaction of beating William to the task, Amanda snatched up Nathan's brown felt derby and handed it to him as he left the house one day. All her thoughts were centered triumphantly on the butler hovering closely behind her, so at Nathan's look of curious surprise over this unusual service, she gave him a somewhat absent smile. It wasn't until her eye focused on his retreating back that a terrible pang of longing struck her. She'd thought that emotion effectively squelched by now, yet here she was again wondering when he would return. "Two bits says he's home by dinner," she muttered. It was totally aimless sarcasm, but behind her William answered without thinking.

"You're on," he said.

Realizing what she'd just heard, she turned around to find him staring fixedly ahead, his Adam's apple bobbing convulsively. After a long moment of silence, in which it was apparent neither had anything further to say, the staid butler bowed and excused himself.

For the next few hours, Amanda tried to amuse herself with her usual pastimes, but her thoughts were never far from William. What should she do? She had him. Caught him red-handed, as it were. She could go to Nathan, but then the entire household would ultimately suffer. Yet, if she didn't deal with it in some way, the whole staff would hold her in contempt. She was in a quandary.

That evening, as she sat eating dinner—alone—she knew she had to make a decision. If only some good could come of all this, she thought. If only . . . She clinked the silver fork on the edge of her rose-patterned plate.

A glimmer of hope made her pause, then come to her feet and dash upstairs in a flurry of turquoise silk. Fumbling in her reticule, she retrieved her small coin purse, and with purpose squaring her shoulders, headed down to the kitchen.

The usual sounds of feminine chatter stopped as soon as she pushed open the swinging, paneled door. Silence and the smell of that evening's chicken were her only greeting. Mary lifted soapy hands out of the zinc-lined sink to pump more water. Emma sat on a stool beside her, sharp knees poking out the front of her gray skirt, as she dried dishes with undue concentration. But it was she who broke the silence. Biting her lip, her eyes never quite finding Amanda's, she asked, "Yes, ma'am?"

Amanda was hurt. She'd thought Emma was her friend. But one thing at a time, she cautioned herself. One thing at a time. "I'd like to speak to William. Where is he?"

Mary and Emma exchanged a quick glance before the latter pointed a finger toward the living room. "He's in there."

"Thank you."

Stepping down into the long, cozily lighted room, she looked around, but saw no one. "Mr. Wellborn?"

When the butler's tall figure unfolded from a chair by the empty fireplace, she was immediately struck by the man's rumpled appearance. It wasn't his clothing—his black cutaway and striped four-in-hand were as impeccable as ever—but much of the starch was gone from the venerable servant. For the first time, she realized he had to be somewhere close to sixty years old. Funny, but she'd never noticed before. It made her wonder if she had the maturity to handle this after all.

"Yes, madam?"

"William, I'd like to have a word with you . . . alone," she added, feeling the others in the doorway behind her. "If you don't mind."

"Certainly, madam." A nod from him, and the presences behind her scurried into retreat. He waited, posture erect, hands clasped behind his back—ever the professional, she thought, feeling her first spark of admiration for the man.

For a second they stared at each other, then she opened her little purse, extracted some coins and held them out.

"It appears you've won our little wager."

Gray eyes stared at the money as if it would bite. "Madam, I don't think—"

"Oh, but I insist," she said. Stepping closer, she lifted his arm and put the money into his palm. "I always pay my debts, William. Quickly . . . and quietly," she stressed, hoping her intention not to tell Nathan was clear.

As his fingers closed slowly over the coins, his expression warmed almost, but not quite, into a smile. "Thank you, ma'am."

The tension in Amanda drained away. "Good night, William."

"Good night, ma'am. Oh, and . . . ma'am?"

"Yes?"

"I'm sorry you didn't win."

She shook her head. "I'm not. Not this time."

Going back through the kitchen, she bid the staring ladies a pleasant evening. "By the way, Mary, the chicken tonight was excellent, but next time, you might use a bit less tarragon."

Startled, the woman nodded. "Yes, ma'am."

Amanda smiled. She was feeling better than she had in a long time.

In the following days, it became clear the Rushton household had finally gained a mistress. Determination tempered with a natural sweetness earned Amanda all the cooperation she needed to learn how to run a large house. And learn she did.

She took stock of the pantries and went over menus with Mary; with Emma, she inventoried everything from linens to cleaning supplies. Everyone's responsibilities underwent her scrutiny until she felt confident enough to make a few suggestions, a few changes here and there.

No one balked at what could have been viewed as interference. Instead, they seemed relieved that someone was finally willing to take charge.

One morning she was bent over the sideboard in the dining room taking stock of the china and crystal, when a voice behind her said, "Well, well . . . who do we have here? Cinderella?"

She started, nearly losing the stack of plates she held. "Teddy!"

"Well, that's encouraging," he said, pulling out one of the lyre-back chairs and straddling it. "At least you still recognize me."

"What's that supposed to mean?"

He shrugged, a don't-mind-me look on his face as he pushed his sporty straw boater to the back of his head. Its red, white, and blue band picked up the blue of his eyes as well as the stripe in his seersucker trousers. "For the last week I've been trying to get into to see you, but some bald-headed fellow keeps telling me you're 'unavailable.' "

She laughed and set the dishes down on one end of the table. "I'm sorry, but I really have been busy lately."

"Oh? Doing what?"

"Learning to be the lady of the house."

"Keeper of the keys, eh? I take it Nathan's been giving you the old 'better earn your keep' speech he keeps giving me."

"But it obviously hasn't worked in your case," she replied without thinking. She bit her lip. It was the first criticism she'd ever offered, and it gave her a stab of guilt. Trying to cover her own embarrassment, she stepped back, put her hands on her hips to survey all the plates, bowls, stemware, and other pieces she had sorted out along the length of the table. "Will you look at this hodgepodge? There must be fifty pieces here, and not more than half a dozen of them belong to any one set."

Chin in hand, Teddy eyed her, not the dishes. He was trying to pinpoint the changes he saw. She was dressed in a skirt of some brown, functional material and a green shirt that could have been a man's. Her hair was twisted into a fuzzy knot on top of her head, but stray wisps fell everywhere, painting her cheeks and collar with coppery streaks. She looked disheveled . . . and exciting. But there was something else, something more elusive.

"He won't notice, you know," he said quietly.

She sighed. "No, I suppose you're right. Men rarely notice what's right under their noses."

"No, I mean he won't notice all . . ." he made a vague gesture that included everything from the dish-laden table to the large, dusty cloth pinned about her waist, "this domestic business."

Amanda frowned over the list she was making, added something, chewed her pencil, and added something else. What did he expect her to say? How could she explain she was doing this as much for herself as for Nathan? She'd never talked about what it was like to live with no purpose to her days, and some instinct, only vague and half-formed, told her Teddy, free-and-easy Teddy, wouldn't understand.

"I've missed you." He had leaned over, and was peering up into her face.

"I've missed you, too," she admitted with a smile.

He slapped his thighs. "Good. Then you'll come for a drive with me?"

Brows knitted, she eyed the job she had started, and shook her head. "I really can't. I still have this to do. But you could stay and help if you've nothing else to do."

He reared back, palms out. "No, thank you! The speeches didn't work on me, remember?"

"I'm sorry, I shouldn't have said that. It was uncalled for."

"Maybe, maybe not. In either case, I've never let it bother me." He gave her a slyly hopeful look. "But if you think you need to make it up to me, you can always agree to ride with me, if not today, at least on Saturday?"

"Put that way, how can I refuse?"

He wiggled his eyebrows in playful menace. "Exactly as I planned, m'dear. Exactly as I planned."

She laughed. "All right. On Saturday." She went back to counting plates.

"You love him, don't you?"

Her hand hesitated only slightly as she reached for

some wine glasses. "What?" she asked, gathering the slender stems with care.

"You heard me. You love him, don't you?"

The accusing tone made her look at him sharply. "What if I do?"

"I don't believe this! His charm works even when he's not trying!" he snorted. "Well, don't worry. Your secret is safe with me, puss, because you can be sure he'll never notice. I've told you before he only notices one thing, and that has his name emblazoned across its front in big gold letters."

Amanda felt her insides shrivel, and this time, she could only make a pretense of sorting the items before her.

Unstraddling the chair, he stood up and leaned down to kiss her cheek. "Never mind. I appreciate you. Don't forget Saturday."

"I won't."

"Good. 'Bye."

" 'Bye."

She watched him leave the room, his jaunty, swinging stride making her smile slightly until her eye settled on the door to Nathan's study.

He'll notice. I'll make him notice.

And Nathan did, too. He couldn't quite put his finger on it, but he found himself wanting to stay home more. He began to do most of his paperwork in the mornings in a study that had been mysteriously aired, dusted, and straightened. He told himself it was quieter than the construction site, or even the office. It had nothing to do with Amanda's presence, nothing at all. He was cured of that affliction. Still, he kept an ear constantly tuned for the quick tattoo of her step, or the little, slightly off-key tunes she hummed as she took to the role of mistress of the house with enthusiasm.

Gradually, he became the object of that enthusiasm.

He had risen early and, with only a cup of coffee, had shut himself into his study. An hour later, his door was unceremoniously thrown open, and Amanda entered with a large tray in her hands.

"What's this?" he demanded.

"Breakfast," she answered blithely, setting the tray on his desk. "I know it's been a while since you last took the meal, but surely you still recognize it." She lifted the lids with a flourish. "We have eggs here and sausage and—"

"If I'd wanted to eat, I'd've done so earlier," he groused. "Now take this stuff away."

Fists on her hips, she admonished him with a wag of her head. "You're going to ruin your health if you don't "

He came to his feet, and she unconsciously took a step backwards.

"I'll eat when I damned well choose—now get the hell out of here, and take this stuff with you!"

Snatching up the tray, she did an offended about-face. "And a pleasant good morning to you, too!" she huffed.

Watching her sail out of the room, white muslin skirts billowing, his scowl faded, until he found himself scratching one corner of his mouth where a smile was beginning to twitch. He wouldn't have admitted it at the time, but when he settled back to work, he did so in a much better frame of mind.

It took Amanda all of twenty-four hours to work up the courage to beard the lion again.

She was going down the stairs as William was coming up with a stack of Nathan's shirts in his arms, the starched collars and cuffs curled neatly on top. She bid him good morning as they passed, then paused. This chore was usually done much earlier in the day.

"William?"

The butler turned back. "Ma'am?"

"Is Nathan—Mr. Rushton, I mean—still upstairs?"

"Yes, ma'am. Shaving, I believe."

She eyed the shirts, lips twisting in thought. "I'll take those up for you, William."

The man hesitated for the barest fraction of a second, then turned them over. Her authority, it appeared, was firmly established.

Heading back up the steps to Nathan's room, she took a deep breath, rapped once, and entered.

Nathan stood at his washstand, dressed only in dark trousers, with a white towel slung over his tanned shoulder. His face was distorted as he scraped the blade along his jawline, and his mumbled "Good morning, William" sounded funny.

She giggled. "It's not William."

He jerked his head around so abruptly his razor left a thin red line along his chin. "Ouch! Damn! What are you doing here?" he demanded, trying to stem the sudden river that flowed.

"Bringing you your shirts," she answered serenely.

He left off his ministrations long enough to glare at her. "Where's William?"

"Attending to other things." She was delighted to realize that the oh-so-sure-of-himself Nathan was actually embarrassed by her presence.

"What 'other things'?"

Her eyes widened innocently. "You did say you wanted me to run the household, didn't you? And the servants as well?" she pressed.

"Hmmm . . . I think I've created a monster," he muttered, eyeing her narrowly in the mirror.

"I beg your pardon?"

"Nothing. Just put those in there," he said, pointing

a finger at the armoire. He went back to shaving, but followed her movements in the framed oval glass.

Refusing to make the hasty exit she knew he expected, Amanda ignored her sweating palms and, in an effort to keep her eyes off his lean, muscular back, wandered around, obliquely satisfying her curiosity about the man by studying his room.

The rocker drew her, but when she looked up from thoughtfully stroking its worn, satiny arm it was to find Nathan glaring defensively at her, daring her to comment. Impishly, she just grinned and began scanning the titles of the books on his night stand. Her finger paused in surprise as it came upon the familiar spine of a Greek lexicon. It seemed she still had much to learn of this man who was her husband. With a start, she looked up, realizing he'd spoken. "Excuse me?"

"I asked if there was something else you wanted," he repeated. Wiping his face with the towel, he tossed it behind the basin and stood with hands on his hips, awaiting her reply.

She shook her head slightly. "No. Well, actually. . . ." She stopped and ran the tip of her tongue over her lips. She was having a difficult time keeping her eyes off the broad chest with its heavy mat of dark hairs that tapered gradually down to . . . She jerked her eyes back up to his face.

One eyebrow quirked impatiently.

"I . . . I just wanted to thank you for the mare you gave me, that's all."

His expression softened slightly. "You're welcome. I thought she'd please you."

"Oh, she does! She's beautiful." She couldn't help smiling as she remembered going out on the morning of her birthday to take a ride and finding the lovely dapple-gray in the stall where Molly usually was. A note attached to the animal's halter said simply,

> Molly told me she'd been carrying you around for years, and was ready to retire to the pasture. She hoped you'd find this lady a worthy replacement.
>
> –N.

"She's fit for a princess," Amanda added happily.

Nathan smiled. Looking at her animated face, her skin dewy in the morning light, and her hair wound crownlike around her head, he found he couldn't agree more.

The silence deepened, and they stood there, lost somewhere in the depths of each other's eyes, until Amanda broke the spell. Swallowing nervously, she tried to make her move toward the window look nonchalant. "I have to admit," she said over her shoulder, "I was surprised you remembered."

"Madam!" he exclaimed in mock horror. "I assure you I have a mind like a steel trap. I forget nothing, Miss . . . uh, Miss . . . What did you say your name was?"

She laughed, turned back around, and was startled to find him right behind her. She could see the tiny pores in his chin, the faint blue shadow below his bottom lip, and one tiny whisker stubble his razor had missed near the corner of his mouth. He smelled of bay rum again.

"What did you name her?"

The movement of his lips mesmerized her. "I . . . I named her Sam."

"Sam!"

"It's short for Samantha," she lied, unwilling to admit she had badgered poor little Georgie into wracking his brains until he could come up with

Nathan's old sergeant's first name—which turned out to be Sam, of all things.

He scratched his head. "Well, it's better than Pidgie, I suppose."

"Anything is better than Pidgie." She grinned, and he laughed, a warm, rich sound that rippled pleasantly over her nerves, a sound she had missed.

The curls of glossy dark hair at the base of his throat moved slightly with each breath he drew. She couldn't drag her eyes away. She didn't know what he was looking at, but the spot just below the cameo at her breast burned curiously. Abruptly, she swung to lean against the window sill and draw a full breath.

Perhaps if he had been a bit faster, or she a bit slower, things would have worked out differently. But in the same instant Nathan reached for her, she spotted a lone rider topping the ridge across the lane and recognized Teddy. With a gasp, she remembered her promise not to be late for their ride this time, and whirled, just missing Nathan's hastily withdrawn hand. Flinging an excuse over her shoulder, she ran from the room in a froth of eyelet-trimmed petticoats, leaving him to stare after her with a bemused smile.

He was still smiling a few minutes later as he stood by the window, fastening the cuffs of his shirt. At the clatter of hooves, he looked out to see a bright-headed rider moving swiftly through the front gates and across the open field. Another figure, one he knew equally well, emerged from the trees to meet her. Slowly, Nathan's smile froze and fell away, his face once more becoming a mask of unmoving stone. He had almost forgotten.

As Amanda sped up the grassy slope to where Teddy waited, she gloried in the graceful stride of the sleek animal beneath her. First the pearls, and now Sam, she thought. She prayed she wasn't being foolish, but she felt that here, embodied in this slender-legged creature, was evidence her campaign to break through Nathan's hard, protective shell was finally succeeding.

"Hullo!" she called, waving to the coatless figure on the hill.

Teddy urged his chestnut-colored mount forward to meet her. "Hullo, yourself." He moved to help her down, but with an exuberance that seemed ill advised on such a hot day, she jumped to the ground before he could reach her. "I was beginning to think you weren't coming," he said.

Breathlessly, she brushed back a loose strand of hair from her face. "Don't be silly. I was busy, that's all."

His smile turned slightly cynical as he came to stand in front of her, reins dangling loosely from one hand. "What was it this time? Were you polishing his boots?"

Her smile faltered. She could tell he had been drinking because it always made him waspish. "Are you all right?" she asked, touching his arm.

"As right as rain," he assured her easily, "now that you're here. It's been days, you know."

She sighed. It was beginning to be a familiar complaint. "I know."

"I miss the old days when we went places together." He leaned close. "When you always had time for poor old Teddy."

Looking up to see his best woebegone face, she couldn't help laughing, although she suspected he was far more serious than he pretended. "I'm sorry. I've tried to explain to you—"

"Yes, and I've tried to explain to you that you're working yourself ragged for nothing. Nathan doesn't care about you and he never will."

In a self-protective gesture she wasn't even aware of

making, Amanda reached back to stroke the warm, silky mane that was the color of smoke. "He cares," she said quietly. "I know he does."

"Why? Because he gives you a piece of horseflesh? Something that fits nicely into his plans to get a good bloodline going for his stables?"

More and more their times together were beginning to take on this tone of argument and counterargument, and she was growing tired of it. She missed their more lighthearted times. She tried to turn away, but Teddy took hold of her shoulders and forced her to look at him.

"Listen to me, Amanda. I'm not saying any of this to hurt you. I'm saying it because, well, because I do care. I care very much."

"I know you do."

He gave her a small, emphatic shake. "Then stop fighting for something you can't win. Stop fighting yourself. Look at me!" He forced her chin up. "I'm the one you ought to be with, and you know it. All three of us know it."

"Don't! Please don't. You frighten me when you talk like that."

"You shouldn't be afraid of the truth."

"But I don't know what the truth is!" she declared, fists balled at her sides. She didn't add the word *yet*, but the word slyly added itself in her head, and she hated it.

His blue eyed gaze, so like Nathan's yet not Nathan's, caressed her face and hair, a faint smile touching the corners of his mouth. "You will. Sooner or later, and then . . . then you'll come to me."

"Please. . . ." Her hand fluttered weakly in the air between them, the emerald in the ugly gold ring mocking her. "Can't we speak of something else?"

He dropped his hands from her shoulders. "If you'd

like—but it's too hot to stand here. Besides, there's something I want to show you. Shall we ride for a while and see if we can scare up a breeze or two?"

Pressing her cheek into the satiny coat of her mare, Amanda nodded. "I'd like that."

"Then so be it." Holding out his cupped hands to receive her booted foot, he smiled at her crookedly. "The lady's wish is my command."

Amanda shielded her eyes as she obediently looked up at the three-storied house on the corner of Sharp and Montgomery streets. She had no idea why they were here, but Teddy had insisted on it. After leaving the horses at his place, he'd driven her here in his carriage, answering all her questions with "Wait and see."

It was built of rosy pink brick. Its shutters, door, and railing down white marble steps gleamed blackly, while the richness of brass trim winked at her here and there. The house was the end one of a group of three, but it clearly reigned supreme under the shade of a single, massive oak.

"It's beautiful," she breathed. "Who lives in it?"

"No one. It's been empty since the day it was built. The owner refuses to sell."

She swung a brief, puzzled look at him before returning her attention to the house. "Who's the owner?"

"Nathan. He built and furnished it for Suzanne."

Amanda's heart squeezed, and slowly, very slowly, the hand shielding her eyes fell away.

She paced her bedroom that night, silently fuming under the oppressive heat that hadn't diminished with nightfall. The water-dampened handkerchief she pressed frequently to her temples and throat did nothing to cool her heat-prickled skin.

It was nearly midnight. The ticking of the clock on her mantle and her own muffled tread were the only sounds that broke the stillness in the house. The rest of the word had long since retired to a motionless state of waiting, silently counting off the seconds between each puff of air that brought relief.

For the hundredth time since she had come home, she went over everything that was said and done. Teddy was beginning to frighten her. Only now did she think of all the things she should have said but didn't.

He was wrong about Nathan! He had to be. Yet even as she insisted this, she was aware of a black rodent of doubt scuttling near the bottom of her certainty.

And why did he show her that house? What was he trying to tell her? That Nathan still loved Suzanne? No. She didn't want to believe that. Then why was he keeping it? Was that where he 'squired half the women in town' to? She didn't want to believe that, either.

She knew what she wanted from him. She wanted him to demand her surrender, to ignite the heat his nearness always stirred, to do unspeakable, unnameable things to her body with his own, with his hands, his lips. Oh, if only he felt what she felt! If only he could reach past all those stumbling blocks of his long enough to give her some encouragement, some reason to hang on . . . some reason to deny Teddy.

In the corner of the room, she pivoted again. But was Teddy right? Did that mean she only lusted for Nathan . . . and loved him? It wasn't a question she could answer.

Irritably, she brushed aside the motionless lace at her window, her eyes going automatically to Nathan's darkened ones. She'd heard a rider coming through the front gate an hour ago, but a door had never opened.

She tossed the ineffective cloth away and pulled open

the balcony door. The air was hot and heavy out there, too—nothing to soothe the restlessness in her soul. She had felt like this once before—that night after Nathan had come to her father's study. She hadn't known what she wanted then, but she knew now. She wanted Nathan. Nathan! Her pulse seemed to quicken and beat with the rhythm of his name. Nathan . . . Nathan . . . Nathan!

Suddenly, her feet were moving, each step quicker than the one before. She sped around the gallery, down the steps, and out into the black closeness of the night, instinct guiding her toward the barn and the one person who could put to rest this all-consuming fire.

She slipped silently through the doors. The sweet scent of fresh hay hung pungent in the still air; and there in the back, just as she knew he would be, was Nathan. His starkly white shirt lay open across the dark furring of his chest, his sleeves rolled up along forearms gleaming with exertion. He was spreading a fresh bedding of straw, working the rake with a slow, steady ebb and flow of movement her eyes followed hypnotically as she drew closer.

"Nathan. . . ."

His head jerked around, his eyes darkening with concern at the urgency in her voice. "What is it?"

"Kiss me."

Chapter 11

Frowning slightly, Nathan searched her face, brushing the backs of his knuckles along her cheek as if checking for fever.

She shivered under his touch. "Kiss me," she repeated in a husky whisper.

His heart began to thud as he looked down into her eyes and saw the raw desire there. His mouth went dry, and the rake clattered, unheard, to one side. Ever so slowly, as if succumbing to a will stronger than his own, he reached out, cupped her face in both hands, and lowered his mouth degree by slow degree to hers.

The shock of melding lips made them both tremble, yet when she would have clung to him, he stepped back.

"There," he said in a voice not quite under control. "You've had your kiss. Now get out."

She swayed, eyes closed. It wasn't enough. It would never be enough. Moaning his name, she reached out. "Nathan, no, don't. Don't do this to us, don't—"

He grabbed her arm, fully intending to spin her around and send her on her way, but something happened inside him, some floodgate opened at the feel of her again, and he pulled her closer. Wild with need, his mouth opened over hers.

The force of their hunger arched them together until, bending a knee, he took them down onto the bed of sweet-smelling hay and rolled her beneath him. His fingers tangled in the long silk of her hair as he drank heated kisses from her lips. It wasn't enough. Cradling her head with one arm, he stroked her hip as he pulled her close against him, and her keening moan of compliance tightened his loins. He kissed her mouth, her chin, her throat, then her mouth again, his hunger renewed.

Pulled out of herself with each kiss, with each caress of those strong hands, Amanda's soul cried, *Yes! Yes! This is what I want, this is what I need!*

Sliding his hand beneath the freed edge of her shirtwaist, he stroked higher and higher along the narrow, sweat-slicked valley of her spine, then around, fingers splaying over satiny ribs, his thumb brushing the tender underside of her breast.

Her mouth left his in a gasp for breath. Wind, not blood, was tearing through her veins, and she felt herself spiraling upward. When his hand withdrew, her tightened nipple felt abandoned, deprived. "Nathan. . . ." She moaned in protest, but already his fingers had returned, pulling her buttons free, undoing the tiny ribbons of her camisole. Then his head dipped, and she whimpered, feeling the suckle in places his hot, wet mouth hadn't touched. Everything was magnified—the silk strands of his hair on her breast, the coarse material between her thighs where his knee had thrust under her skirt. "Yes, oh yes! Love me, Nathan, love me . . . !"

Love me . . . love me. . . . The words dropped on his ear and fell into the waters of his heart. *Yes!* came the answering echo.

By now her fingers were fluttering at the opening of his shirt, even as he trembled, fumbling with her skirt-band. Frustration increased the ache in his blood as the secret of its fastener eluded him.

"Nathan. . . ." she whispered. Slim fingers were now tracing his bare ribs, her breath feathering through the hairs on his chest, tickling him.

His lower lip clamped between his teeth, he abandoned the fastener, his hand stroking greedily under her skirt, along her thigh to whisper-soft muslin.

As greedy as he, she shifted, lifting her hips, willing him to find the source of her heat.

The hay rustled and crackled beneath them, digging sharp little points into tender spots, but they hardly noticed. Nathan distractedly pushed it away, brushing it free from dampened skin time and again until it finally surfaced in his mind as a problem. Agitated, drugged with passion, he raised his head to look around him.

He groaned. They were in the barn. He was about to make love to his wife for the first time in a damned barn. Arms shuddering with the effort, he rolled away. Breathing raggedly, as if through tortured lungs, he came to his feet, reached down, and pulled her to hers. They both swayed as he closed the edges of her camisole together. "Not here. Not now. Let's—"

Amanda heard the words, felt the blow of another rejection, and never let him finish. "No!" She spun away, stumbled and nearly fell.

"Amanda!"

"*No!* For God's sake, don't say any more! I don't want to hear it!" With a sob deep in her throat, she scrambled for balance and ran—back to the darkened house, back to the empty silence of her room.

Behind her, Nathan took two steps—

Go after her, you fool!

Do and you hand him his victory!

—and stopped. His personal perdition. He sagged against a stall, weak-limbed and weary. Why? *When?* When would he be free of the ghosts? He raised bleak eyes toward the doorway. When would he no longer want her?

When you're dead, my boy, when you're dead. . . .

He dropped his head again and stared at his hanging shirttails, the wedge of his own chest. His skin glittered under a fine film of perspiration, cooling.

Slowly, brick by brick, he reconstructed the wall of his defenses, a wall almost breached by his own need . . . and a siren's call.

Upstairs, Amanda sank into a boneless heap on her bed. She lay there for a long time with dry, aching eyes and a heart that refused to stop beating. Even the comfort of tears was denied her now.

Not until dawn tinged the sky with gold did she finally loosen her numbing grip on the pain and allow herself to drift, exhausted, into sleep.

She awoke, feeling empty and detached—and grateful. Anything was better than that crushing, stomach-wrenching anguish of the night before.

She realized now that, no matter what she did, no matter how hard she tried, Nathan's iron will would always be the final victor. But there would be no more battles—no more losing, no more wanting what she knew she could never have. It was over. If he had wanted her, he would have come after her.

Steeling herself with a vow never to think about it again, she dressed with mechanical precision and drifted down toward the dining room. She had no appetite, but eating was a mindless activity guaranteed to take up at least part of her day.

As she reached the hallway, her steps faltered at the distinct sound of a curse coming from Nathan's study. The door was open. Swallowing hard, she forced herself to walk the dozen or so steps over to it, and ooked in. If she could make it through the first meeting, she'd be fine.

Nathan, clean shaven and impeccably dressed once more, was seated behind his desk, frowning at a piece of paper he held. He glanced up, and they stared at one another in the safety of silence for a second.

"Good morning," he finally said.

"Good morning."

"Did you, ah, sleep well?"

"Not really. It was too hot."

He nodded, his attention returning to the paper in his hand.

She started to turn away, then changed her mind. "Is something wrong?" He was silent for so long, she thought he wasn't going to answer. Then the paper sagged, and he leaned back in his chair with a heavy sigh.

"It's all in how you look at it, I suppose. My father is coming home. He'll be here day after tomorrow." He stared into space at something only he could see, his fingers curling, crushing the letter until his knuckles whitened under their tan.

Watching him locked in the throes of a struggle she could neither see nor understand, Amanda knew her presence had been totally forgotten.

So Nat Rushton, once her guardian, now her father-in-law, was coming home. The news shouldn't have affected her, yet, as she walked away, she felt a chill start somewhere around her heart and spread outward to numb her fingers. She sensed a turning point in all their lives. Would it be the beginning of something . . . or the end?

When Nathan received the expected summons from his father, he ignored it. He decided he was too busy to stop and give someone an accounting of recent events. That had been four days ago. It wasn't until his foreman hesitantly approached him about his snapping and snarling at everyone for little apparent reason that he realized he was only putting off the inevitable.

So here he was, standing on his father's front step, hat in hand, the dutiful son. Apparently, he was still fighting the inevitable to some degree, though. He'd been standing there for several minutes already, and hadn't yet lifted the knocker. Staring at the lion with the big brass ring in its mouth, he wondered why even the prospect of a confrontation with his father always caused his stomach to tie itself into knots and make him feel like a wet-nosed boy again. He hated that. He was a grown man, for God's sake—and his own man, at last. He should relish the opportunity to recount his accomplishments since taking over. He reached for the ring again, and like a dispassionate observer, one portion of his brain noted his hand was as steady as a surgeon's.

The door opened almost immediately.

"Why, Master Nathan! It's been ages."

Nathan smiled and pumped the old servant's hand affectionately. "Hello, Chester." With his gray hair and wrinkled turkey neck, the man had seemed old to him as a boy, but he seemed positively ancient to Nathan now. "How've you been?"

The old face split into a grin. "Oh, you know me. I've got my share of aches and pains, but I expect I'll outlive you all."

Nathan laughed and shook his head. "I wouldn't be a bit surprised."

The man beamed at the boy he'd helped to raise. "It sure is good to see you. Come to see your daddy? Thought so. Come on, and I'll take you to him. He's in the study. You know, it sure seems strange having him home during the day after all these years—and what with your brother being back home now, too, this old place is getting right crowded again."

Both of them knew that Nathan could make his own way with no trouble, but each one respected the other too much to break with tradition. So as Nathan followed Chester's knobby back through the huge house, he looked around at the once familiar surroundings with the eyes of a stranger. It had, indeed, been a long time.

When he entered the study, his father rose from behind a desk stacked with correspondence. "Son! It's good to see you." As expected, he didn't mention the four-day delay, but reached out to shake Nathan's hand vigorously. "Sit down, sit down," he said, pushing a leather-bound humidor to the edge of the desk. "Have a cigar. I'll be with you in a moment. I just need a second to finish this up. So much has piled up since I've been gone, you know."

Nathan nodded, and in an effort to cut through their usual parryings, he took the seat and the proffered cigar at the same time. He used the time it took lighting up to study the change he saw in his father. The air of vitality was still there, but as he watched the liver-spotted hands move a pile of letters to one side, he realized with a small jolt of surprise that the man was getting older. Funny, but he'd never noticed it before. Maybe he was mortal, after all.

Leaning back in his chair, he rolled the smoke appreciatively over his tongue and looked around him. This room, more than any other, had always seemed to embody the very essence of his father's power. The cases of ponderous-looking books, stolid portraits upon the walls, along with a pair of crossed cavalry swords above the mantle, made it an impressive place—and were designed to do just that. Impress, and therefore, intimidate. Suddenly, the falseness of it all became clear. He'd never so much as seen his father crack a book, and knowing most of his antecedents had been poor, he had little confidence that those solemn faces looking down at him were any relation. He also knew that neither his father nor his grandfathers had served in the cavalry, so God alone knew who the sabers belonged to. It was odd how many things could remain the same, and yet be so different.

He looked back to find his father regarding him thoughtfully. The diamond-hard stare was as brilliant and piercing as ever, though, and Nathan was curious to see where today's confrontation would lead.

"So how have you been?" he was asked.

"Fine, sir. And you?"

"Fine, just fine."

"You're looking well rested."

"Eh? Well, I'm feeling good. Fit as a fiddle, in fact."

"I'm glad to hear it. How was Europe?"

"Decadent. Decadent and dirty," he said, dismissing the entire continent with a wave of the ever present cigar. "What they need over there is a good clean dose of American thinking. That would straighten them out."

Nathan smiled at the characteristic response. "I'm sure they must've gotten plenty of that from Aunt Pen."

Nat chuckled. "They did that."

"How is my favorite aunt these days?"

"Feistier than ever, I'm afraid." Nat shook his head and sniffed. "Gad! but that woman has a sharp tongue in her head."

Nathan grinned as he thought of his irascible relative. "Always has had, as I remember. In fact, I wouldn't know her any other way."

"She'd really like it if you went over to see her sometime."

Nathan nodded. "I'd already planned on it."

"Good, good. She'll love seeing you."

Nathan watched his father idly fiddle with his watch fob, turning the small gold acorn over and over between his fingers. He'd never seen him fidget before.

"So tell me," Nat commanded conversationally. "How have things been going since I've been away? I'm afraid I've been a little out of touch."

Knowing the man's network of friends and business acquaintances, if not outright spies, Nathan doubted the truth of that statement, but obliged him anyway. He was about midway through the details on how the company had landed a lucrative city contract when he realized his father was only half listening. The man obviously had something else on his mind, and he'd come to the wrong conclusion for the reason behind the summons.

"And last but not least," he finished, quickly abbreviating the recounting, "the MacGruder project is back on schedule."

Nat's attention picked up. "Oh? That must've taken some doing. Your brother much help?"

"When I've asked."

"Perhaps it would've been better if you'd done more than 'ask.' "

"He's a grown man. What would you have me do? Chain him to the cornerstone?"

"Not a bad idea," his father grumbled. He scowled blackly into space for a moment, then snapped back abruptly. "You and this MacGruder thing—don't you think you might be pushing too hard? Considering the initial problems, I'm sure Mac has already reconciled himself to at least a short delay."

Nathan's eyebrows shot upward. This hardly seemed

like the same man who'd preached the work ethic and its virtues all his life. "I thought you'd be pleased."

There was some harrumphing and the cigar stub was waved about again. "I am, of course, I am—and our other clients will certainly be pleased, but—"

"*My* clients."

"Eh? What was that?"

"I said 'my clients' will be pleased."

"That's what I said. They'll be pleased, but my point is that there are other things in life, you know."

"Oh? Like what?"

"Like home and family."

"Mmmm," Nathan replied, feeling the real subject getting closer.

The gold acorn tumbled faster. "Uh, speaking of home and family . . . how's Amanda doing?"

Ah, warmer and warmer. "She's fine."

"How're things going between the two of you?"

Nathan's jaws suddenly ached. "About as well as can be expected."

The cigar stub received a fierce gnawing. "What's that supposed to mean?"

"It means considering the way we were forced on each other, we're doing 'about as well as can be expected.' Contrary to the way you planned it, I did not fall head over heels in love with this girl simply because you decreed it." He felt like he'd been holding his breath for months and just now let it out. He'd been waiting so long to fling that information in his father's face, he expected to feel triumphant; instead he only felt sad—sad and suddenly very dejected.

Nat sat grim and tight-lipped, and when he finally spoke, he sounded as tired as his son felt. "I had hoped you'd fall in love because it was right for you—not me. I'd hoped the two of you would be able to work things out."

"I suppose you could say we have. In a way."

Suddenly, Nat banged a fist down on the desk and leaned forward. "How? By letting your brother make a fool of you by publicly stealing your wife? That's what's happening, in case you didn't know!"

Ah-ha! They were finally to the crux of the matter. "I know."

"You know? *You know!* Well, what are you going to do about it?"

"Nothing."

Nat's face turned beet red. "Nothing! She's your wife, damn it!"

"Exactly. And my wife, along with her . . . activities . . . is my business."

"Not anymore. The whole town's talking about it. It seems that's all I've heard about since I've gotten back."

Nathan shrugged. "People always talk," he answered in a bored, flat voice. "If not about one thing, then about another. I've learned not to let it bother me."

"This time it had better bother you, and you'd better do something about it or else!"

"Or else what?" he challenged softly. Watching the man across from him vibrate with rage, he felt a strange sort of calm steal over him. "If I'm not mistaken, you've played your last ace."

"Now see here! You—"

Nathan stood up. "I think we've said all we have to say to one another. Thanks for the cigar." He closed the door quietly behind him.

It was a Wednesday morning when Aunt Pen came to call.

Amanda was out in the garden gathering flowers when William appeared on the terrace to announce the arrival of one Mrs. Penelope Rushton Albaugh, who now awaited her in the drawing room.

Her first impulse was to disappear and leave William to make her excuses, then she felt a flash of irritation at what surely must be an inspection visit. With that thought in mind, she screwed up her courage and charged past William, slapping the flowers into his hands. The best defense was an offense, she decided, sweeping into the house. She refused to be cowed by another Rushton.

Prepared to face a female version of her erstwhile guardian, she was momentarily taken aback by the frail little woman who leaned too much of her weight upon the handle of her parasol. Dressed in black bombazine, with a matching clump of grosgrain and tulle pinned to her snowy crown, she looked like everybody's grandmother. The eyes, however, were Nat's completely—bright blue and riveting.

A foot or two inside the room Amanda stopped and inclined her head in a brief, cool nod. "How do you do, Aunt Pen? I'm Amanda."

"Well, of course you are! Despite the dirt on your hands, I certainly didn't mistake you for the gardener."

Flushing to the roots of her hair, it was all Amanda could do to keep from wiping her stained hands down the sides of her lilac cotton skirt like a scolded child. Instead, she clasped them firmly in front of her and raised her chin a notch. "I'm afraid you came all this way for nothing. Nathan isn't here."

"On the contrary, I came to see you and you very well know it," came the warbling reply.

It took a second, but Amanda finally regained some of her composure and motioned to the settee. "Then, please . . . won't you sit down?"

With a crisp nod of acceptance, she marched, rather than moved, over and sat down. Keeping her back ramrod straight, she folded her hands precisely atop the handle of her parasol and fixed Amanda with an expectant stare.

Warily, Amanda perched herself on the edge of the adjacent chair. "Would you care for tea?"

The woman made a rude noise. "I've had enough of that beastly British brew to last me a lifetime. No, some good, strong American coffee is what I'd like."

"Of . . . course." She rang the porcelain bell at her elbow, and they waited in total silence until Rose appeared, received her instructions, and left. Enviously, Amanda watched her go before turning back to her guest, only to find herself the object of close scrutiny. She lifted an eyebrow in what she hoped was a disdainful attitude, but it had absolutely no effect. The woman continued her inspection unperturbed.

"So!" she said at last. "You're what my brother picked out for Nathan. I told him what a perfect numskull he was, but Natty always has been a bull in a china shop." She broke off long enough to wag her head. "Considering what a muddle he made of his own life, I'm frankly surprised he had the nerve to try and do up other people's for them. Of course, don't misunderstand—I didn't care one bit for that little blond piece of fluff Nathan had picked out for himself, either. She was a complete nincompoop." She stopped and peered closely at Amanda. "You're not a nincompoop, are you?"

Amanda blinked. "I . . . I wouldn't rightly know."

"Well, of course you know! You either are or you aren't. Which is it?"

"Well, I . . . no. No, I'm not!"

"Ah, that's better. A definite answer to a definite question. It's a sign of character, you know."

Thankfully, the coffee was brought in and served then, giving Amanda a chance to try to regather some of her wits—if such a thing were possible around Penelope Rushton Albaugh.

After a few sips and an appreciative sigh, the wrinkled face tipped to one side, and Amanda was regarded from this new angle for a moment. "You do look a lot like your mother, but there's a lot of your father's Irish about you, too . . . especially around the eyes."

"Y—you knew my parents?"

"Of course, child. We all grew up together, and Natty, well, he was head over heels in love with your mother. We all thought they'd marry, but then Emily, in typically fluffy-headed fashion, up and married Freddie—who was equally fluffy headed, I might add."

Amanda's cup clattered back into its saucer. "I beg your pardon, but you're speaking of my parents!"

She was pooh-poohed with a wave. "Oh, come now. Don't take offense, my dear. Everyone knows your father had a heart of gold, but when it came to brains, well, the man had absolute straw, I'm afraid."

Amanda could only stare. She didn't know what to say at this point. In the few minutes the woman had been there, every rule of polite conversation she'd ever known had been trampled past recognition. She stared blindly into her coffee cup for a moment until she could think of a more acceptable, less personal direction in which to steer the conversation. "When . . . when Nathan was telling me about you, he said you'd been in Europe for a long time. Did you enjoy it?"

"Heavens, no. It was just one of those goals one sets for one's life. I did it, and I'm glad, but thank God I don't ever have to do it again. I couldn't wait for Natty to come and get me." The expression in the blue eyes sharpened slightly. "But you said Nathan told you about me. Exactly what did he tell you?"

Taking a deep breath, Amanda decided it was time

to take the bull by the horns, and deal with this lady on her own terms. Carefully, she laid her cup aside—she wanted no telltale rattling—and folded her hands in her lap. "He told me you were his favorite relative, but that . . . well, that you could be an interfering old lady at times, and that I was to watch out for you." The blood pounded in her ears at her own audacity. She steeled herself for the blast.

The blue gaze never wavered. "Oh, he did, did he?"

She swallowed and forced herself to nod. "Yes, ma'am. I'm afraid he did."

There was a moment of horrible silence, and just when she was about to break down and beg for forgiveness, the black bombazine shoulders began to vibrate and then to shake. Oh God! she thought, here it comes.

"Well, good for him!" the woman wheezed. "And good for you, too!"

It was several seconds before Amanda realized the sound she was hearing—like someone flicking a fingernail against a sheet of paper—was not the gurgling of anger, but of laughter. She was laughing! Suddenly, her own icy insides turned to water, and she started to laugh in sheer relief.

Like a pair of schoolgirls, the two of them rocked back and forth, clutching their sides in mirth until they were both gasping for air, their eyes streaming—friends at last.

"Oh, dear!" Pen breathed, wiping her eyes. "Dear me, but that felt wonderful! I like you," she smiled. "You've got spunk. Just what my nephew needs to keep him from becoming an old stick-in-the-mud like his father," she pronounced, fanning herself with a bit of lace she'd pulled from a sleeve. "I'm afraid he's right, though," she added, "about the interfering, I mean. It's what happens to those of us who never have children of our own. We just can't resist giving our advice liberally and often to anyone who'll listen. My dear Stephen was always sickly, and died soon after we were married. He left me a fortune, but no one to spend it on.'' She wagged her head. ''Just be thankful Nathan has his health and you'll be spared the same sort of fate.''

At the mention of children who would never be, Amanda sobered instantly, looking away with a sudden, heart-wrenching sense of loss.

The movement didn't go unnoticed. ''What is it, dear? Are things not going well between you and Nathan?'' It was not an unkind question.

She gave a small shrug. ''Oh, no. Things are fine, I suppose. Really.''

The old woman's lips, bleached and chiseled by time, pursed in consideration. ''I'm too old to fool, you know, and that answer just won't wash, won't wash at all. Now tell me the truth. How are things working out between the two of you?''

Amanda stared into the old face, a face that seemed kinder now than it had at first, and without warning, she felt the unexpected prick of tears. Her answer was full of misery. ''You won't like it.''

''I expect not, but I want to hear, anyway.''

With a shaky sigh and fingers knotted whitely together, the story began to pour out of her, slowly at first, then with gathering momentum as the months of confusion, frustration, longing, and need came into focus. She spared nothing and no one, all the way from Nathan's offer of an annulment when he proposed, to her times with Teddy, up to and including the townhouse. Like lancing a festering wound, it felt good to relieve some of the pressure and get out the hurtful poison she'd carried inside for so long. When the words finally ceased and the room was quiet except for the ticking of the clock, she sat back, drained and exhausted.

"Oh dear," Pen breathed at last. "This is worse than I thought. It looks like Natty really made pea soup of this one, doesn't it? Something must be done, of course, but I'll need some time to think first. In the meantime," she advised, leaning over to give Amanda's knee a reassuring squeeze, "don't give up. I know my nephew, and he may be stubborn, but he's no fool—and only a fool would give away someone who loves them, as you so obviously do."

She sniffed. "Even if they don't want to be loved?"

"Poppycock! Everyone wants to be loved." The parasol thumped the floor emphatically. "Fight for him, girl! You're a redheaded Irish with a temper to match, I'll warrant, so use it. Fight for him, show him how you feel!"

The night she had gone to him in the barn returned to her in painful memory. "I already have. It didn't work."

"Hmmm. Just remember that nothing worth having comes easily—and Lord knows the Rushton species of male is more obstinate than most. Now don't look like that! Everything will work out fine. I'm never wrong about these things." Her manner had become brisk once again, and she consulted the tiny watch pinned to her bodice. "Well, child, I really must be going."

Rising with her guest, Amanda walked with her as she hurried out into the hall. Although she made several attempts, she failed to inject a single word into the final, steady stream of dictums.

"I made this visit at Natty's insistence," she was told. "His conscience has been nagging him—as well it should—ever since he saw Nathan last week. I imagine he's feeling a bit like the man who fires the starting gun at a race and can only sit by and wait for the outcome." She pulled on her gloves without missing a beat. "As I said, I came for Natty, but I'm glad for myself now that I've met you. You're better than I'd hoped. You're a lovely young woman, and don't let this go to your head and spoil you, but you're just what I would have picked for Nathan myself. Of course, I shan't tell Natty that. The only thing he'll hear from my lips is what a complete and utter numskull he's been." A hand, now encased in black lace, fluttered and came to rest against the small, shrunken bosom. "Oh, I nearly forgot. Next Saturday evening, Natty will be giving a small party at his house. It'll be a splendid opportunity for me to introduce you to some people, so you and Nathan come early, won't you? Oh, dear me! Look at the time. Well, I'm off. Good-bye, dear."

She blew out the front door as abruptly as she'd blown in, leaving Amanda to stand in the open doorway with a hand to her cheek, where a quick, dry kiss had been unexpectedly placed.

Much like one who's survived a hurricane and is vaguely surprised to find life and limb still intact, she closed the door and returned to the drawing room.

Absently, she picked up her needlework. It was all well and good to counsel fighting for what you wanted, she thought, but when you've fought and lost so often, you begin to wonder if you're not beating your head against a wall. If Nathan wanted her, he'd have to be the one to do the fighting from now on. She was just too tired.

It could have been several minutes or several hours later when she became aware of another's presence, and looked up. Her eyes widened.

"Hello, Irish. Did I startle you?" Nathan's arm was

braced in the doorway, his coat slung carelessly over a shoulder.

"Yes—I mean, no . . . I mean, I didn't expect to see you home so early."

"I have a lot of paperwork to do." He shrugged. "I thought I'd do it here where it's quieter." He glanced around the room with apparent interest.

As if he didn't recognize the place, she thought dryly. "Your Aunt Pen was just here. I like her. She's a real firecracker."

He smiled. "She can be."

Still under the attention of those dark blue eyes, she concentrated on making her next few stitches with extreme care. "She says there's a party at your father's next Saturday." When he didn't answer, she looked up to find the same clouded expression he always wore at mention of his father. "Shall I send our regrets?"

He made a face and sighed. "No. We'll go." Shifting his weight, he jammed both hands in his pockets. Ever since the victory over his father, he'd been left with an emptiness he couldn't explain and couldn't fill. Instinct was beginning to tell him Amanda was behind much of it, but he found himself fumbling in the dark. "Did you, ah, have anything planned for this afternoon?" Her green eyes turned on him oddly, and he felt like a schoolboy instead of a man ten years her senior.

Amanda heard the strange note in his voice, but couldn't account for it. "No. Why?"

It irritated him to realize he'd been holding his breath waiting for her answer. Now he shrugged. "No reason. I just thought it might be nice to know where my wife was for a change."

The hope that had flared at his question died abruptly. She would *not* be piece of property to be kept track of. Her lip curled and her voice dripped sweet poison. "Oh, I'm sorry. I'd forgotten. I'm supposed to lunch in town," she lied baldly. "With Teddy."

Not a flicker of expression crossed either face, but as their eyes locked, the temperature in the room dropped palpably.

Inclining his head, he stretched his lips into a tight, polite smile. "Then I'll leave you to your pleasures, madam."

Amanda stabbed her needle into the cloth, then hurled the whole thing across the room when the door to his study slammed. Why did she continue to hope he would ask, would demand she not go? Was she destined to stay a fool? Teddy was right. Nathan didn't love her, and he never would. He just wanted to control her.

Penelope Rushton Albaugh, the senior by a mere year and a half but very definitely the 'older' sibling, opened the door to her brother's study and poked her head in. "What are you doing in here, Natty? Your guests will be arriving soon."

He was sitting, dressed in black silk evening clothes, on the edge of the cordovan leather couch, hands dangling and gray head bent. He glanced up when she closed the door, but didn't say anything.

"What's the matter with you? Chester says you've been moping around ever since you got back—and I can well believe it, remembering what little company you were on the trip home. Here, let me look at you," she commanded, reaching for his hand and pulling him to his feet. Tipping her head back, she searched her "baby" brother's face with a mixture of motherly concern and sisterly irritation. "You look awful. What have you been doing to yourself—and who dressed you? A blind elephant could've done a better job with that tie. If it's guilt that's bothering you, you have good cause, Nathan Rushton," she scolded, pulling the jacket this way and that over his thinning shoulders. "I went to see Amanda, and the situation is worse than we'd thought. That son of yours, Teddy, is going to start trouble if you don't do something to prevent it. I always said you should've remarried after Meg died. That child needed love, still does, and I'm afraid for all of them if you don't do something soon." He tried to interrupt, but she waved him still and began tugging on his sleeves. "That girl is confused. Between those two sons of yours, she's being torn to pieces—and all because of this mess you made by forcing that marriage. I still don't understand what you were thinking. Why was it so important? And why now? And why Amanda?" She broke off, responding to the grip he had on her elbows. "What is it, Natty?"

"Penny, I . . . because I'm dying, Penny. I'm dying."

For a stunned moment, Pen didn't move, didn't breathe. "Dying! What on earth are you talking about? You've lost a little weight—probably all that foreign food—but you'll gain it back. You're fit as a fiddle . . . aren't you?"

He shook his head. "They say it's some sort of cancer. They say it's only a matter of months."

"They say! They say! Who's *they*?"

"The doctors here and—"

"Quacks! We'll get another opinion! We'll—"

"I did, Penny." Nat squeezed his sister's shoulders, his eyes willing her to accept the truth. "That's why I went to Europe. The doctors there told me the same thing."

Pen blinked as a flood of childhood memories poured through her head . . . the two of them stealing apples, then sharing the whipping . . . her reading to him when he had that awful fever . . . him punching that cheat,

Wesley, in the mouth, and sneaking her back into the house so no one would know she'd tried to elope. Her brother.

With a small flinch, she freed her arms. "Here, let me fix this awful tie of yours. I swear, here you are a grown man, and I'm still dressing you. You do it like this . . . and then this. . . . Oh, dear. This light—it must be this light. I can hardly see. . . ."

Nat brought his handkerchief up and gently blotted the cheeks of his pretty, ebony-haired, belle-of-every-ball sister.

She snatched it from him and pressed it to her own eyes. "Damned pollen!" she sniffed. "It gets worse and worse every year. Now come on," she said huskily, stuffing the handkerchief back into his pocket and linking her arm tightly through his. "People are starting to arrive. I can hear Chester out there making a fool of himself by trying to be charming."

Amanda gave her reflection one last critical look before going downstairs. Mme. Daru had done her job well. The jacquard emerald silk with its tiny puffed sleeves and skirt that molded itself to her hips and thighs was the most beautiful dress she had ever seen. The color, which deepened the hue of her eyes, made her skin translucent cream and gave her hair the burnished gleam of autumn. All these things her eye noted, but her heart took no joy in her carefully constructed beauty.

Nathan had commissioned the dress for tonight's party without consulting her; and just as his horses were now being groomed to take them to his father's house in style, so she had been groomed as a personal ornament to dangle from his arm.

She turned her head slightly from side to side. Even the emerald studs she wore in her ears, ordinarily a gift to delight any woman, had simply been placed on her dressing table where she would find them that evening. Adornments for the adornment.

With a heavy sigh, she gathered up her lace fan and shawl. They were already late, and she had no wish to make Nathan angry by dawdling. Even anger was attention of sorts, and she wanted nothing unsettling to intrude upon the protected little niche she found herself in these days. As the distance between her and Nathan widened, time had begun to pass with a comfortable sort of drone she was loathe to have disturbed.

At the bottom of the stairs, Nathan waited, tall and powerful, to take her hand. He seemed in good spirits despite the fact that he hadn't wanted to go tonight and had agreed, she knew, only from a sense of duty.

Looking into his eyes, eyes the color of a winter sky at midnight, she recognized the admiration and warmth in his regard, but no warmth touched her. Carefully, coolly, she resisted his efforts to bring her fingers to his lips. Her heart, chilly and remote, was protected at last from the shattering effect of this man—and she wanted no kiss from the prince to awaken desires finally and mercifully put to rest. She would be at his side tonight and any other time her wifely duties should require it, but she would never again allow her hopes to be as cheaply robbed as they had in the past. Her heart, she told herself, was once again her own.

He allowed her to withdraw her hand from his, and the warm look in his eyes tempered slightly. "Hello, Irish," he murmured with the barest ghost of a smile.

His voice ran over her nerves like warm sand, but her mind quickly counteracted its passage by the cynical observation that their relationship had finally deteriorated to the greetings of casual acquaintances. Her answering smile was as wry as her thoughts. "Hello, Nathan. How are you these days?"

He didn't move an inch, but she could feel his withdrawal, and watched his expression shutter, his face close to the chill in her response.

Silently, he offered his arm, she took it, and they left.

Nat's house was large, even larger than Nathan's. A giant music box set against the black backdrop of night, it let sweet stringed music and soft yellow light spill from the tall windows onto lawns silver and black in the moonlight. The curved drive was ringed with a long train of empty carriages, and as Nathan halted them opposite the gracefully fanlighted door, attendants sprang to their assistance.

As she descended to the ground with the help of one of these silent professionals, Amanda's heart began to pound. His aunt had said a "small" party. Suddenly, her safe cocoon of lethargy was penetrated by an icy stab of anxiety, and she was grateful for the long white gloves that concealed her perspiring palms.

With what almost seemed like a reassuring squeeze, Nathan tucked her hand into the crook of his arm, and before she could prevent it, they were inside the gaslit, marble-floored entrance hall.

Swept into one round of introductions after another, it wasn't long before they became separated by the oh-you-must-meet-so-and-so's, and the last image she had of him, as she was carried in the opposite direction by a tide of women, was the smiling, bent-head attention he was giving some blond.

Chapter 12

The fat woman in red popped another morsel of cake into her mouth and laughed along with the others. Amanda, her attention caught by the trail of crumbs disappearing down the woman's cavernous cleavage, missed the remark that had caused all the mirth. Hoping to cover her straying attention, she smiled brightly at the elderly gentleman beside her, and as unobtrusively as possible, began to fade from the edge of the group.

Her escape successful, she looked around for a place where she could hide from the crush of this "small" party of Nat's. Fanning herself vigorously, she picked up her skirts and squeezed her way past perfumed, jewel-encrusted matrons and the pearl-studded paunches of their escorts to a hopefully vacant corner she thought she'd spotted. Her face ached after an hour of smiling, and she was feeling more than a little out of place here in this room full of success stories, where money gleamed and flashed from every appendage. She had, indeed, married "above her station," as Sophie would have so bluntly put it.

She finally made it to the corner, but her sigh of relief was cut short by the sight of another good dame already ensconced on one end of the red velvet sofa. Another vapid conversation just wasn't in her, but when she turned away, a querulous voice stopped her.

"Aren't you going to sit down?"

Amanda looked again and wondered how she could have failed to recognize the small, queenly figure of Aunt Pen. The bombazine had given way to silk, but it was still black, and the only other concession to the occasion was the jet dangling from each withered, papery earlobe.

She sank down beside her. "Hello, Aunt Pen."

"Hello, dear. You're looking lovely tonight."

"Thank you." Silently, she gave thanks that the woman hadn't remarked on how well the color of her dress matched her eyes. It seemed to be the standard comment so far.

"I like that color on you. It brings out your eyes," Pen continued. "But what are you doing tucked away in here with all us old fogies? You should be over there having fun dancing with the rest of the youngsters."

Amanda looked past the crowd there in the library, past the people milling about in the hall, and beyond to the ones dancing in the dining room, where all the furniture had been pushed against the walls to accommodate them. She smiled at the colorful scene, but when Nathan's tall figure—along with the small blond in his arms—revolved into view, the smile vanished abruptly. "I don't like to dance—and you're not a bunch of 'old fogies,' either."

"Oh, of course we are. It's just that we have so much money," she confided in a loud whisper, "everyone pretends not to notice. Besides," she added, tucking her chin in with fierce disapproval, "I'm tired of seeing that little blond person twirl by over there on Nathan's arm."

Amanda swallowed hard. So she wasn't the only one with good eyesight.

"You'll never get his attention by letting him spend

so much time with other women," she was told. "Go cut in or something."

Stubbornly, Amanda shook her head, deciding not to explain that nobody "let" Nathan do anything, he just "did." "It's a lovely party," she pronounced breezily, changing the subject. "I just wish I could remember names better."

A blue-veined hand waved away her concern. "I shouldn't worry about it. Now that everyone has satisfied their curiosity about Nathan's new wife and realized their little plain-Janes never had a chance, they won't bother with you anymore."

Such frankness made Amanda stare for a second before the humor of it struck her. "Lucky me," she began to giggle. "I suppose I should be grateful."

Pen's nod was serious. "You should. Believe me, some of these old biddies have paring knives for tongues, and you're better off being ignored."

Amanda thought that was a bit like the pot calling the kettle black, but refrained from saying so, expressing interest instead. "Oh? And which ones are they?" She frowned. Beginning a question with *and* was one of Nathan's bad habits, and she found it annoying that she'd picked it up. With a bitten lip of effort, she pulled her thoughts back from the well-worn path and focused on Aunt Pen again.

". . . and Etta Kefauver," Pen was saying, "as well as that awful Louise Abell."

Amanda shook her head. "Sorry. I can't place them."

"Oh, you know who I mean. Etta's the one with all the feathers in her hair. Suits her perfectly, too. What a birdbrain. And Louise walked by just a minute ago—the one with the dress so heavily beaded she clicked when she walked?"

Nodding, Amanda barely got her fan up in time to

hide her grin at this typical Aunt Pen-ism. For the next few minutes, she was treated to a brief but equally assassinating description of several others who fit into the general category of "vipers to avoid." Obviously, the woman was in her forte. Pinning labels on people with the point of her own knife-sharp tongue did for her what croquet and whist did for others.

"Well, well. So this is where my favorite aunt and sister-in-law are hiding."

Both women looked up to see Teddy, his slender figure draped rather casually in evening clothes, hands shoved carelessly into his pockets.

"Teddy! You scoundrel!" his aunt exclaimed. "We're your *only* aunt and sister-in-law. Well, don't just stand there. Come give me a kiss. That's better. Now when are you going to come see me?"

"Soon, Auntie, soon. I promise."

"Hmph! That's what your brother keeps saying, too."

"In that case," he answered with a lazy grin, "I'll consider this my golden opportunity to outshine my older sibling for once." He winked in Amanda's direction. "Perhaps I'll even be the one to inherit all your millions in the bargain."

"Impertinent brat. Why don't you put yourself to good use and bring us some champagne?"

With a good-natured nod, he went off in search of a servant, but as soon as he disappeared from sight, Pen inclined her head conspiratorially. "He's a thoroughgoing rascal, that one. I love him dearly, of course, but he never had the mother's love and attention he needed, and Natty never knew quite how to deal with him. As a result, the boy's been a regular pot of trouble over the years. I'd watch myself around him if I were you."

Amanda felt the indignant stretch of her own neck.

MATTERS OF THE HEART 267

"Well, I'm not—" she began, but Teddy's return cut short her defense.

"Here we are," he announced. "Champagne for the two most beautiful women in the room."

"Flatterer," his aunt sniffed, taking a glass.

Teddy gave her a wounded look of reproach. "Auntie, you cut me to the quick. Now I suppose you're going to turn me down when I ask you to dance."

"Don't be a jackanapes. Of course I shan't dance with you."

Amanda's lips had barely touched the rim of her own glass when Teddy whisked it away again and set it on a table. "Then you force me to settle for Amanda here," he said, taking her hand and tugging her to her feet.

Amanda caught her breath and glanced at Pen, but the grande dame was obviously torn between wanting Amanda to be in there with Nathan and wanting her to beware of Teddy. Her indecisive frown was the last thing Amanda saw before Teddy pulled her out of the room.

"Well, what do you know about that?" he remarked, catching her eye. "That couldn't have worked out better if I'd planned it."

"You did plan it—and it wasn't a very smart thing to do."

"Why not? I plan to have you for myself one day, and the world might as well get used to it."

"Don't you think you're rushing things a bit?"

"No." When she looked away, he stepped in front of her, forcing her to look at him. "Come on, Mandy. Don't chide me. Would a fair maiden like you be so cruel as to harden her heart against such a true and lovesick suitor?" he asked dramatically, hand to his chest in mock despair.

"She might—if she were married, as I am."

"Ah, but you're not really married. You have a 'business arrangement,' remember? You told me so yourself. Now smile, please. If you do," he bribed teasingly, "I'll tell you how beautiful you are."

In spite of herself, she could feel the humor beginning to tug at the corners of her mouth. She could never stay angry at him for long. "All right," she conceded with a short laugh, "just as long as you don't tell me how well my dress matches my eyes."

"I promise. Now what's wrong? That's the first genuine smile I've seen in ages."

She made a face and shook her head. "Nothing. But I would like some more of that champagne, if you don't mind. I barely got more than a sip of the last one."

"*Voila!*" he said, scooping a glass off a passing waiter's tray. "No sooner said than done—but I'd watch that stuff if I were you. It can do strange things to your head if you're not used to it."

She took a sip, pleased by the flavorful fizz. "Hmmm, maybe that's what my head needs."

"What?"

"Nothing. Where've you been? We've been here for an hour already."

He shrugged. "Around. This sort of thing just isn't my cup of tea, you know."

Catching the faint smell of liquor that came with his words, she nodded. "No, I suppose it isn't."

He took the empty glass she handed him, put it on another waiter's tray, and indicated the room full of dancers. "Shall we have a turn now?"

"All right, but I warn you: I'm not very good at this."

"Oh, I don't know. As I recall, you did very well under the stars not so long ago."

MATTERS OF THE HEART 269

Her face colored, but he only laughed as he took her hand and threaded their way through the crush of dancers to an open spot on the floor.

So acutely was she aware that Nathan was somewhere among the other dancers, Amanda found it hard to relax, to let her feet move freely with the music. Resolutely, she kept her eyes on Teddy's face, but after a few minutes of facing the undisguised warmth in his eyes, even that became an uncomfortable choice. She'd finally opted to stare at the studs in his starched shirtfront when she felt him stiffen, and looked up to see him staring over her shoulder.

"May I?" came a voice behind her.

It was Nat, and judging from the frozen expression on Teddy's face, he was about to refuse and cause a scene. "Teddy. . . ."

He glanced down at her, then made a tight-lipped bow in his father's direction before stepping aside.

Except for a brief greeting earlier, she hadn't spoken to this man since the day of her wedding.

"Hello, my dear. We didn't get much of an opportunity to talk before, did we?"

Her smile was polite as she shook her head and moved into step with him. She had forgotten the sheer width, breadth, and height of this man, who blocked out all but himself from her view as he led her with expert ease.

"Marriage must agree with you," he said, tilting his head to look down at her, his blue eyes crinkling at the corners. "You're looking lovelier than ever."

She demurred the words with a tiny laugh, but something behind his smile made her uneasy. He had the look of a man about to apologize, and she didn't think she could stand having her whole life branded as a mistake, a useless, pointless mistake. "You're too kind. It's this dress, actually. Nathan picked it out. It brings out the color in my eyes, don't you think? Nathan's good at such things, but then he's good at anything he sets his mind to. Of course, me being his wife and you being his father, we're bound to be prejudiced, aren't we?" The words were rushing past her lips as fast as they came to mind. "Well, what do you know? There's Teddy. That was a quick turn, wasn't it?"

Concern plainly in his eyes now, Nat released her and stepped back to bow solemnly over her hand. "Thank you for indulging an old man, my dear. You do both my son and my family a credit with your unfailing charm."

The quiet dignity of his voice caught at her heart, and she felt a prick of conscience at having shut him out. But the painful doubt, the questions in his eyes panicked her. She had no answers—for either of them.

A terse nod was exchanged between father and son, then she was returned to the younger man.

Teddy's face was closed and stony as he took her back into step with the music, but little registered in Amanda's mind as she spotted Nathan.

He was off in a corner with that same little blond. Their heads were bent close together, and he was chuckling at something she was saying, patting the hand laying so possessively on his sleeve. Even at this distance, above the music and hum of conversation around them, Amanda imagined she could hear the warm, rich sound of his laughter.

Like a wind-up toy whose spring had run its course, her steps slowed to a stop.

Teddy's grip tightened. "What's wrong?"

Feigning dizziness, she put a hand to her forehead. "It—it must be the champagne. Can we please get out of here?"

* * *

Miriam Bloomfeld, the blond beside Nathan, was growing frustrated. Every time she thought she'd captured the undivided attention of this man—once considered the best catch in Baltimore, and rumor said he would be again—those compelling, jewel blue eyes of his would leave her face to scan the crowd. It told her she was little more than a momentary diversion, and it was a rank to which she was not accustomed. Time and time again, she'd used the ploy of laying one of her small, milk white hands on his arm to bring him back, but she knew it couldn't work indefinitely.

Nathan groaned inwardly, near petrified with boredom at the girl's string of witless witticisms. With the same polite smile he'd worn pasted to his face for hours, he let his gaze wander toward the dancers again. He scanned their faces quickly for the one he sought, the one with the tip-tilted nose and green eyes under a shimmering mass of russet hair—the one he'd been watching. He frowned when he found her. She was back with his brother. Where was his father, and why, he wondered irritably, didn't someone else cut in?

A hand on his arm yanked him to attention, and his smile widened automatically—but then Amanda swayed dizzily against his brother, and the two of them made a beeline for the terrace door.

His eyes narrowed and the smile vanished. "Excuse me," he said, and walked away, leaving Miss Bloomfeld's mouth in the small *O* of a half-formed word, her hand resting on air.

Outside in the cooler air, Amanda felt she could finally draw a full breath again.

"Better?" Teddy asked, their steps ringing faintly on the stone terrace.

"Mmm-hmm." Her arm linked through his and they walked slowly, the blue glow of the moon lighting the night with a strange brilliance, the muted sounds of the party the only proof they weren't alone in the world. "It's beautiful out tonight, isn't it? I wonder your father didn't think to have the party out here."

He snorted. "Out here, my father couldn't compete. He couldn't impress anyone with all his possessions."

"Oh, Teddy. Sometimes I don't think either of you ever give your father a chance. We're all human and—"

"Not him. In his case, it's rumor, pure rumor."

"I don't know. I think he's realized a lot of his mistakes, and regrets them. He seemed . . . different tonight, didn't you notice?"

He stepped in front of her and took her by the shoulders. "Look, I don't want to talk about my father. I'd rather talk about you. You're prettier. As a matter of fact," he said, pulling her close, "you're the most beautiful woman here tonight."

An ancient mimosa tree hung over the terrace wall, dappling them with sweet-scented shade. "Why, thank you, sir," she laughed lightly, aware of the sudden jump in her pulse.

His grip tightened. "No, I mean it . . . and I'm glad you came tonight. I was afraid you wouldn't."

"Why wouldn't I?"

"To avoid me."

"Oh, Teddy. . . ." Her words came out in a long sigh. "I haven't been avoiding you, truly I haven't. I've just needed some time to think."

His thumbs began to caress the bare flesh of her arms. "About what? Us?"

She nodded, feeling his warm breath on her face.

"Amanda. . . ."

She looked away, then railed at herself. *Coward! He wants to kiss you, so let him. How else will you know if what you feel for Nathan is real? Kiss him, stupid. Kiss him!* She tilted her face up.

MATTERS OF THE HEART 273

Gently, he framed her jaw with his fingers, and brushed his lips across hers once, twice, lightly. Then his hands slid over her back, and he pulled her to him, deepening the kiss.

On her tiptoes, she leaned into him, arms circling his waist beneath the coat. It felt good to be held, to be kissed. But something was wrong, something was missing . . . or was it some*one?* With a sinking feeling, she realized only Nathan's kiss could ever stir the fires in her. Nathan. The man who didn't, who wouldn't, love her.

"Oh, Mandy . . . Mandy," Teddy whispered against her mouth. "Kiss me back." He held her tighter, but lifted his head when she pulled away, shivering. "What's the matter? Don't tell me you're cold?"

She stepped back, hugging herself. "No, but . . . I am thirsty. Would you mind getting me some more champagne?"

"I thought you said it made you dizzy."

"It must've just been the heat in there. Please?"

He didn't seem happy about it, but agreed. "I'll be back."

She watched him go, feeling a little guilty, but sighing with relief. She didn't know what had come over her, but all of a sudden, she felt irritable and jumpy.

"It's always nice to see my father's guests enjoying themselves."

With a gasp that nearly strangled her, she whirled around just as a tall figure emerged from the shadows next to the house.

"Nathan! Wh—where did you come from?"

He gestured over his shoulder. "From the library there."

She stared past him at the shapes of people milling around beyond the curtained French doors. Good grief, the library! He'd been watching them. He'd seen them kiss.

He wiggled an unlit cigar where she could see it. "I came out for a smoke."

"Smoke, ha! Spying's more like it!"

"Spying?" She stood there, hair a reddened mass of midnight, eyes and lips places of inky mystery, and her breasts, pearled by moonlight, trembled above the edge of her bodice. "Now why would I spy?" he asked mildly.

"Maybe to see what a real man does with a woman!"

Nathan heard the hiss of his own breath. Flicking the cigar over the wall, he closed the distance between them. "Who the hell do you think you are? You stand out here kissing my brother where the whole world can see, and you *dare* to say that to me? If you want it that badly, go out to the barn with the rest of the animals, but don't stand here in my father's house, in front of my friends, and play your little games, because I won't have it!"

The narrowing of her eyes gave him just enough warning, and he caught her arm mid-swing. Their breaths puffed into each other's faces as she continued the struggle. His grip tightened. "A 'real' man, huh?"

The fingers he threaded through her hair were neither rough nor gentle, but commanding, bringing her close. Fiercely, his mouth slanted over hers, tongue probing past her resistance to thrust and explore in a rhythm as primal as the urge it imitated. He stroked and plunged, seeking a response—a response that sucked a deep growl from his throat when it came.

Amanda's senses reeled. The raw fury in his words had lacerated her ears, but this was something else altogether. Her face and lips were all he touched, yet she could feel the heat burst everywhere—behind her knees, at the points of her breasts, between her legs. What was he doing to her? She moaned and swayed, knees buckling, but he caught her to him, pressing her into the heat at the top of his thighs. Then slowly, like an ebbing tide, his lips left hers, and she drew a ragged breath.

"Just so—" he stopped to clear the huskiness out of his voice, "just so you know the difference."

She gripped his arms and steadied herself before prying open weighted lids. "Difference?" she mouthed. What was he talking about?

"Between a man and a boy."

Her spine stiffened, backing her abruptly out of his embrace, but before she could retort, Teddy reappeared.

The two brothers exchanged nods.

"Teddy."

"Nathan. What's going on here?"

"Nothing much. Amanda here," Nathan said smoothly, "was just saying how she'd changed her mind about the champagne."

"I said no such thing!" she snapped, and with a glare at Nathan she took the glass from Teddy's unresisting fingers, and downed its contents in three swallows.

Nathan's only comment was the arch of one brow before he walked away, his heels making little gritty noises on the flagstones.

"What happened?" Teddy took the empty glass and set it on the wall. "What did he say to you?"

"He didn't say anything, he—"

Nathan looked back, gave her a small salute, then went inside.

"Listen, I—I just remembered something." She gave Teddy an absent pat on the arm. "I'll be right back."

"But—"

"I'll be right back!"

Picking up her skirts, she hurried across the terrace and inside, nearly colliding with a pair of dancers whirling by. "Oh! I'm—excuse . . . Have you seen—"

"Looking for me?"

Her head snapped around. Leaning against the other glass-paned door was Nathan. His hands were in his pockets, his jacket was unbuttoned, and strands of hair had fallen over his forehead. He looked mussed and slightly fevered. Had she done that? "No, I am not looking for you!" she hissed, moving closer nonetheless. "Are you waiting for me?"

"Keep your voice down."

"Why the hell should I?"

"Curse again and I'll turn you over my knee—probably what I should have done when I found you out there with Teddy."

"You do and I'll scream the house down."

By now, heads were beginning to turn in their direction, and they both looked away, aware that in another instant they'd come to blows right there on the dance floor.

She folded her arms.

He folded his.

Damned, pig-headed bastard!

Damned, temperamental bitch!

Several minutes went by. One tune ended and another began. They glanced at each other, then away. She fiddled with a button on her glove. He rocked a heel on the floor.

"Amanda?"

"What?"

"Want to dance?"

"What's the matter?" she sniffed. "Wear out your little blond friend?"

He smiled and looked out across the bright sea of dancers. "Do I detect a note of jealousy, my love?"

"No, you certainly do not." Her voice was perfectly controlled—more than she could say for her racing pulse. What did he want from her? One minute he ignored her, the next he sought her out and provoked her. She didn't know what to think anymore. He riddled every gesture, every word with ambiguity and double meanings.

Without looking at her, he reached over and twined his work-roughened fingers with hers. "Come on, Amanda. Dance with me."

When he did look at her, she felt caught, disarmed by the unexpected gentleness in those blue depths. "I . . ."

He didn't wait for her to finish, but tugged her behind him as he threaded their way to an open spot on the floor, then twirled her into his arms.

The muscled flesh beneath the cloth of his coat was firm and hard, and the feel of his hand at her back brought with it a slight shock. It caused memories to come sizzling back, memories of other places and other times when those same arms had held her in a far different way. She dropped her gaze to the floor, pretending a beginner's concentration, but soon she felt compelled to look up again. He was staring at her, an oddly intent look on his face as his eyes swept over her face and hair.

"My brother's right," he murmured. "You are the most beautiful woman here tonight."

Stunned by the seriousness in his eyes, she didn't even care that he'd been eavesdropping on her and Teddy. It didn't seem important anymore. Instead, the music seemed suddenly sweeter, the lights more dazzling, the rainbow kaleidoscope of colors more pleasing. And just as suddenly, the ice she had so carefully constructed around her heart began to melt at an alarming rate. Experience after painful experience had taught her how closely hurt followed any show of warmth from this man, and she felt a growing sense of panic.

Mercifully, the music ended, and she turned abruptly out of his arms to join the others in polite applause.

His warm breath touched the wisps of hair on the nape of her neck. "Amanda, I—" he began, but she moved a step away and continued clapping. Finally, she was forced to stop when the leader of the small ensemble rose to his feet to announce that the following set was to be a ladies' choice.

Beside her, Nathan cleared his throat loudly, and she looked up to see him giving her the most expectantly hopeful look she had ever seen on anyone's face. She giggled. Her earlier trepidations disappeared, her urge to escape along with them, and she was just about to go through the motions of asking him for the next dance, when the forgotten blond suddenly bloomed at his side.

"There you are!" she exclaimed, latching onto his arm possessively with a trill of laughter that ran the scale.

Nathan's expression became carefully polite as he performed the necessary introductions, but Amanda saw only that he made no attempt to loosen himself from the girl's hold.

"Amanda, this is Miss Miriam Bloomfeld. Miriam, my wife, Amanda."

The girl nodded in her direction. "How do you do, dear?" she murmured and smiled, but her china blue eyes remained oddly untouched by the gesture that dimpled her cheek so prettily. "You have a wonderful husband here. Why his eyes alone are enough to make a woman swoon."

Amanda nodded, but couldn't bring herself to smile, or even speak beyond a hasty, "If you'll excuse me. . . ."

Without a glance at Nathan, she picked up her skirts and fled, urgently pushing her way past the other couples. No power on earth could make her stay and compete for her own husband's attention.

Out in the hall, her head pounded, and she felt as if she couldn't get enough air into her lungs. She made for the stairs; she had to lie down. Halfway up, a group of giggling, chattering women on the descent crowded her against the railing overlooking the atrium below.

Glancing down, she found herself directly over the heads of two women, and the feathered head of Etta Kefauver caught her attention as her companion's words came floating up.

". . . young Rushton's new wife? She's decent enough looking, I suppose, but then without *breeding*, looks don't mean very much, do they?"

"Exactly. From what I hear, she was little more than a simple farm girl, a peasant, before he was forced to marry her. For the life of me, I can't imagine what his father was thinking when he arranged such a thing."

"Nor can I, Etta, nor can I. Why, as I understand it, her father was practically a raving *lunatic*. Now don't misunderstand me, I can *appreciate* Rushton's wanting to rid himself of the obligation of being her guardian, but to marry her off to his own son—well! It's just *totally* beyond me."

The feathers tilted with impending confidence. "Of course, rumor has it young Rushton'll find a way out of it soon—and after being forced into such a tasteless marriage, who could blame him?"

"Who *indeed?* And have you *heard* about the way she's been carrying on with his brother? That's the trouble with the lower classes. They have no morals at all. None."

"Oh, I agree, I really do."

Amanda felt the floor tip, and the sounds of the party faded until all she could hear was the slow thud of her own heart and the hollow rush of air as the wind left her lungs. Unseeing, her gaze drifted out over the heads of the other people below until she found herself looking into the same dark eyes that had haunted her every moment since they first touched her. Nathan hadn't stayed with the blond! He'd come after her! Even now, he was trying to make his way toward her, trying to push his way past the group of gigglers and their waiting partners now thronging the bottom of the stairway. His eyes never left hers, and even though her fingers were numb from clutching the banister, she knew it was on the strength of that intangible bridge alone she leaned. She would fall unashamedly into his arms. He would deny all those words, take away the awful hurt that moaned inside her. Somehow, magically, all the wrong, the doubts, the longing would be over and together they would finally work things out.

On the landing above, Teddy's foot was in midair over the first step when he saw her. He watched her clutch the banister until her fingers whitened, but it was the naked look of yearning on her face that stopped him. His insides twisted. Drawn down one step at a time, he followed her gaze to the hallway—and his brother moving through the crowd. *No! She's mine!* he wanted to shout. *You didn't want her, not until I did!* Amanda leaned against the railing, trembling visibly. *Aw, Mandy, don't. He doesn't want you, he just doesn't want me to have you.*

Nathan had reached the bottom step, and Teddy knew if he didn't do something, it would all be over.

Nathan would win, he'd have the lion's share of everything—company, money, and Mandy, *his* Mandy. Teddy hurried.

"There you are!" he said, gripping her arms and turning her around. "Finished with the something or someone you remembered—or is he finished with you now?"

Amanda's gaze held no recognition for a second. "Wha—? Oh. Teddy." Nathan! She spun around, but the floor below was empty—empty of the one person who could fill it. Nathan had gone, he'd given up, left. The glitter of hope settled like heavy ash in her heart. The urgent message she'd thought she'd seen in his eyes, the one of a need finally shared, had only been her imagination after all. Dully, she turned back to Teddy. "Yes, I . . . suppose he is, at that."

He grinned. "Always said he was a fool, but then I shouldn't complain. His loss is my—hey, are you all right?"

"I'm fine, just a little tired. I thought I'd lie down for a while." Her own voice sounded far away.

"Oh, come on," he said, pulling her arm through his. "Doctor Teddy says what you need is fun, not rest."

Not having the will to resist, she let him draw her down the stairs. "Fun?"

"Yes, you remember—dancing, laughing—that sort of thing?"

"And champagne?" she asked without much interest.

"Twice an hour if you can take it."

She began to laugh, a harsh, brittle sound, and she hugged his arm to her. "Oh, Teddy, haven't you heard? We peasants can take anything!"

Nathan paced the floor of his father's study. He'd

told Teddy to meet him here—he pulled out his watch, frowned, and snapped it closed—twenty minutes ago. What was keeping him? The possible answers lengthened his stride.

A burst of party laughter from another room made him grind his teeth. It was probably Amanda again. It seemed she'd become the life of the party. She'd laughed and flirted and danced her way through half the men there. He hadn't been able to get near her. Everytime he'd tried, Teddy materialized to take her in another direction. This whole thing was becoming a circus. He hadn't been able to turn around tonight without hearing some whispered comment about one of the three of them. Apparently, he wasn't the only one who'd seen that damned kiss on the terrace.

Nathan's fists clenched. The image of Amanda, up on her toes, leaning into his brother's embrace, had burned itself into memory. He couldn't close his eyes without seeing it again—each time with a different ending—all of them violent, and all of them ending with Teddy flat on his back. That's what he should have done. He should've yanked Amanda out of his arms, punched Teddy for good measure, and taken her home then and there. Even on the steps later, that's what he should've done.

The watch came out once more, then was shut with enough force to threaten the delicate crystal within. Damn it! Where the hell was he?

Nathan was heading for the door when it opened, and Teddy came through, bringing the sounds of the party with him. His coat was undone, his tie loose, and as he leaned back, closing the door, he crowed with laughter.

"Oh, God! This is rich! Have you seen the way the old man glares at me every time I dance with Amanda? I swear!" he went on with a wheezy chuckle. "You ought to see the look on his face. *Me!* With the girl he—"

A handful of shirt, and Nathan slammed Teddy against the wall, sending an English hunt picture crashing to the floor. "You son of a bitch! Don't you dare brag about it! Stay the hell away from her, you hear me?"

Teddy struggled to get the fist away from his Adam's apple, his eyes flaming red. "Why? You don't want her. Hell, you've never even made love to her!"

It was acid in the wound, and Nathan roared with pain. He drove a fist into his brother's middle, then flung him away. He dove after him, and the two rolled across the Turkish carpet, knocking over tables and chairs, grappling for each other's throats.

"She belongs to me!"

"Not for long!"

Suddenly, the door crashed open.

"What the hell's going on in here?" Nat demanded.

Behind him a dozen guests crowded for a better view. He pushed them back and slammed the door in their faces. Stalking over, he kicked at the tangled legs, leaned down, collared a son in each fist, and pulled them forcibly apart, anger lending him strength. "What's gotten into you two, huh? Huh?" He shook them both like mongrel curs while they continued to glare at each other, panting and wiping their sweating faces. "Have you both lost your senses?"

Nathan jerked himself free, his eyes never leaving his brother's. "No, but he's lost his if he thinks he can just walk away with my wife!"

Teddy's lip curled. "What's the matter, big brother? Afraid you overlooked something good? Afraid I might come out on top for a change?"

Nathan lunged for him again and met the solid resistance of his father's arm.

"That's it! Stop it! You two have made complete asses of yourselves tonight. Have you forgotten there's a party going on? We have guests out there!"

"What's the matter, *Papa?*" Teddy's gaze flicked to his father's. "Afraid the Rushton name can't take it?"

"It sure as hell can't take you standing outside kissing my wife. *My wife!*" Nathan bellowed.

Nat shouldered between them again, gave Teddy another shake, then shoved him back. "You two have aired this whole dirty business in front of everybody, and I won't have it, not any more! You've got five minutes to settle this thing once and for all. Then pack your things, Teddy, and get out! And you, Nathan, get yourself under control, and take your wife home. If you'd done something when I first told you to, none of this would have ever happened. But settle it, settle it now, then get out—both of you. This is my house and those are my friends out there." With a last warning glare at each of them, he righted a small table and chair, then strode out of the room, closing the door behind him.

Nathan glared at his brother a second longer, then swung away. Behind the desk he sat, grabbed up pen and paper, and without looking up asked, "You wanted part of the company once—how much to leave Amanda alone and never see her again?" The pen was poised. "Ten per cent? Twenty? Thirty—what?"

Following to the edge of the desk, hands in his pockets, Teddy jingled his change and laughed. "Oh, it's hard to measure love. If I had to put a number to it, I guess I'd have to say I loved her at least . . . ninety . . . maybe even a hundred per cent."

Nathan's head snapped up. "You planned this all along, didn't you? You've been using her to get to me."

"Maybe. But then, using people is what we do best

in this family. You used me, didn't you? I was supposed to take an unwanted wife off your hands, but I wasn't supposed to get too attached, was I? You always managed to give her just enough to keep her pining after you—in case you ever wanted her back. Like now. Oh, I could see it coming, so yes, I guess I did decide to use her to get back some of my own."

"And how much is that?" The question was a deadly quiet one—and so was the answer.

"I want it all."

"No!"

"Ah, love. . . ." Teddy pursed his lips, and kicked idly at one leg of the desk. "The best things in life aren't always free, are they?"

Nathan came to his feet, his height advantage of one inch magnified. "I want you out of her life! I want you out of mine!"

"She may pine for you, big brother, but"—he pointed to himself—"she loves me and I'm going to have her."

"I'll see you dead first!"

Teddy just shrugged.

"All right, Goddamnit! Take it! Take it all." The pen scratched furiously across the page. "Here!" He flung it in his brother's face. "Now Amanda's mine!"

Teddy looked at the scrawled words, smiled, and tore the paper into shreds. "Well, what do you know? I guess you do love her—but you're the one who can be bought, remember? Not me." White confetti fell around his feet. "All I ever wanted from that stupid company was enough money to live on. Money, do you hear? I hate the grit, the dirt, the noise, the rubbing elbows with sweaty, smelly laborers all day. No, I don't want your precious company, what I want is Amanda."

"Teddy, I've made a lot of excuses for you over the

years—" Nathan had him by the shirtfront and halfway across the desk when the door opened again.

"Well, well, well. . . ." cooed Amanda. Graceful as a willow, she swayed unsteadily into the room, a half-filled glass in her hand. "What have we here? It looks like the Rushton boys are deep in discussion about something. Uh-oh . . . is that blood I see, Nathan?"

Nathan touched the corner of his mouth and scowled.

"Ah, poor things. You've been fighting. What could it be about, I wonder?" She stopped to trace a corner of Nat's desk with a slender fingertip. "Money? A woman? Me?" She batted her lashes, then jerked to regain her balance. "Well, which one of you won? Do I go home with you?" she asked Teddy, who was on his feet now, brushing at his lapels. "Or you, Nathan? Can't decide? Well, you could always draw straws." That struck her as exceedingly funny and she started to laugh, but hiccupped instead. "Oh, dear—that—"

"You're drunk!" Nathan's voice slashed across hers like a knife as he reached for her glass.

"Of course. Rushtons always get—drunk when things don't work—out. Don't they?" Seeing his intention, she tried to avoid him, but he was too fast. In the struggle, wine sloshed all down the front of her dress.

"Now look what you've done!" Spreading her skirts, she turned to Teddy. "Look what he's done! And such a pretty dress, too," she pretended to pout. "Nathan has such good taste, you know. Now me, I'm just a coarse peasant with—"

"Shut up and come on." Nathan grabbed her wrist, and started for the terrace doors at the other end of the room. "I'm taking you home."

"I don't want to go yet!"

"You're going anyway," he growled, pulling her when she resisted.

"No!" She cast an appealing glance back over her shoulder. "Teddy?"

"Come on, Nathan. Let her—"

"You stay out of this!" Nathan whirled and jabbed the air with a finger of his free hand. "And I meant what I said earlier."

He yanked open a door and pulled her behind him, across the terrace, and through the low hedge toward the drive. A small group of people out on the lawn stopped their conversation to turn and stare at the couple going by. He ignored them.

Amanda tried to pry his fingers loose from her wrist, but when that failed she held back, making him have to yank her every step of the way. By the time they reached the carriage, and he jerked her around in front of him, both their tempers had flamed to the point of combustion.

"How dare you embarrass me in front of all those people!"

"How dare you embarrass *me* by acting like a common little trollop!"

Her hand cracked against the side of his cheek so suddenly it surprised them both.

Shock left him slack-jawed. *Hit her back!* instinct raged.

"Go ahead!" she taunted, seeing the thought in his eyes. "Hit me!"

Chapter 13

Nathan stood with his fists clenched, panting for control. *Hit her.* Watching her chin jut forward in challenge, he wanted to—or maybe just shake her until she came to her senses. He sucked in a ragged breath. No. He wouldn't do that, either.

She cringed and threw up her hand as if fully expecting the blow when he grabbed a wrist and yanked her toward the carriage. "Don't say a word," he growled. "Not another word." Tossing her into the seat, he vaulted up beside her and roared to the horses, and they leaped forward.

Amanda had to grab onto her seat as they careened around the drive, their wheels spewing stones against the other carriages. The air rushing into her face helped to clear her head, but sharpened her fear, too. Nathan was cracking the whip over the horses' heads, driving them onto the winding, moonlit road at breakneck speed. What was he trying to do? Kill them?

"Nathan—"

"Shut up!"

She opened her mouth again, then closed it, clamping her lips between her teeth. *Please*, she began to pray, eyes squeezed closed, *just don't let him kill us . . . just don't let him kill us!* It was the swiftest eternity she'd ever spent, her heart thudding in her chest the whole time.

MATTERS OF THE HEART 289

The sight of home brought a sigh of relief, but even that was cut short as he hauled the lathered horses to a halt, jumped down, and pulled her along without ceremony.

Her wrist was still in his grip when William met them at the door. She held her head high, but kept her eyes on the floor. She had worked so hard to gain the butler's respect. To have Nathan humiliate her like this in front of him was a worse blow than if he'd actually hit her.

"That'll be all tonight, William," he said, brushing past the man and dragging her behind him. Throwing open the study door, he shoved her ahead of him into the room, which was lighted only by taut white bars of moonlight.

She stumbled, regained her balance against the desk, and turned just in time to see him lock the door and pocket the key. "Afraid I'll scream for help when you beat me, and the servants will come running?"

"I'm not going to beat you," he said, but the way he advanced on her wasn't reassuring, and she backed up. He stopped an arm's length away. "I *am*, however, going to make one thing clear to you."

She judged the distance between them with a careful eye, then regarded him with queenly disinterest. "Oh? What's that?"

"You're to stay away from Teddy."

She sniffed and tossed her head. She'd waited a long time to hear that, but she hadn't yet heard the words that gave him the right to say it. She hadn't yet heard "I love you." Now it was a matter of pride—hers or his. Besides, if he was going to divorce her anyway . . . "Why should I?"

"Because you're my wife and I say so."

"Really?" She let her mouth drop open in coy surprise, then pranced the length of the room, returning to hold up her left hand, fingers spread. "Funny, but I don't see any wedding ring here, do you?"

"Ring or no ring, I have a piece of paper that says—"

"Yes, and that's all you have! That's all either of us has."

"That may be, but that piece of paper makes you my wife, and until that's no longer true—"

So he was planning to divorce her!

"—it gives me the right to demand you not act the whore!"

"Whore!" Rage, white hot and primitive, scorched its way through her small frame. With a predator's screech, she flew at him.

He fended her off easily, pinning her arms behind her and crushing some of the fight from her by pulling her tightly against his chest. "Stop it!" he warned, but her struggle continued against this grotesque embrace, muscle pitted against muscle.

"Let go of me, you bastard!"

Transferring both her wrists to one hand, he grabbed a handful of her hair. "Stop it, Amanda!"

Looking down into those green, turbulent depths, he felt the strangest mixture of lust and wrath. He wanted to take those pale, parted lips so distorted by anger and make them soft and sweet again with the pressure of his own mouth. Only the searing fury in her face warded him off, taunting the frustrated, evicted Adam in him.

Suddenly, he flung her away from him with a strangled curse. "Get out of here! Get out of my sight!"

She staggered and nearly fell, but like a woman insane, flew at him again, screaming her hatred.

He grabbed for her arms again, but her struggling pulled him off balance, and they crashed to the floor. He twisted, trying to absorb the impact with his own body, but it all happened too fast, and he heard the air leave her with a small *whoof!* For a second, neither of them moved. Then he rolled off her, pulling himself to a sitting position. She lay beside him in a forlorn little heap, gasping for air, sobbing. Wearily, he leaned against the desk and pulled her to him, cradling her head against his chest.

Without the strength to resist, Amanda lay limply, tears streaming down her cheeks. "I . . . hate you," she whispered brokenly. "I hate you."

Eyes squeezed shut against his own tears, Nathan laid his cheek on her hair. "I know," he sighed. "I know."

Outside, a nightingale incongruously trilled her song of love.

The morning sun, pale and watery, filtered its way down through a lingering fog from off the harbor and onto streets just beginning to stir with life. Looking out of place among the aproned greengrocers and the hucksters in their patched coats, a man in black silk evening dress walked along, hands in his pockets, head bent in thought. Beyond a knowing smile or the shake of a head, his passing received little notice from the others. The industrious people of the city were long used to the all-night habits of the rich, yet had they known this was a man who'd walked the streets all night while they lay a-snoring, it wouldn't have made any difference. They lived in different worlds, their views of one another a matter of heritage.

As for the man in the open coat and dangling tie, he was so deep in thought he was unaware of any living creature he passed. His steps took him north along Howard Street, then up to the fashionable neighborhood of Bolton Hill, where sleepy-eyed serving girls gathering in the morning milk jugs paid him little more notice than the greengrocers had. The man neither paused nor looked up until he came to a huge corner place of red brick behind a black wrought iron gate. He stared up at the house for a long moment, seeming to debate deeply over something. He looked down at his shoes, then right, then left—not furtively, but more like he was considering where else he might go. Finally, with a sigh of resignation lifting his shoulders, he pushed open the gate and started up the well tended walk. With obvious reluctance, he lifted the brass knocker and let it fall.

A moment later, the door was opened by a man whose dignity made him taller than his five-foot-six-inch frame could achieve on its own. "May I help you?" he inquired, his tone implying the doubtfulness of such a possibility.

"I know it's very early," the other began, "but is my, uh, is Mrs. Albaugh up yet?"

"I believe so, sir, but as you say, it's much too early to be receiving—"

"Tillman!" a voice called from within. "Tillman, who is it?"

The man by that name disdainfully read from the card he'd been handed. "It's a Mr. Nathaniel J. Rushton, the third, Mum."

"Oh, Tillman, quit being a prig and let my nephew in. I'm in here, Nathan."

With the painfully bored look of a lizard, Tillman stepped aside to let Nathan enter, then walked away, leaving him to find his own way through the dark, Victorian hallways to his aunt. Using his memory of the place, Nathan found her in the dining room.

"Hello, dear. I apologize for Tillman," she told him from the red velvet chair at one end of the long table. "I picked him up in London. I really shouldn't have hired him, I suppose. He had no recommendations to speak of, but I just couldn't resist his dimples."

As Nathan approached her chair, he thought about the many butlers she'd hired over the years—all for similar reasons: smiles, dimples, or some other obvious qualification. "Wondrous, wavy hair" had been the last one, as he recalled.

She tilted her cheek up for his kiss, then indicated the silver servers on the table. "Will you join me for breakfast?"

"I'm not hungry."

Penelope regarded her nephew carefully over the rim of her coffee cup, her shrewd eyes taking note of the rumpled evening clothes as well as the bruised lip. "What is it, dear? Can I help?"

He made an irritable face. "I doubt it. I probably shouldn't even have come."

"Is it Amanda?"

Pain creased itself into the tired lines of his face, deepening them. Restlessly, he began to pace. "Yes . . . and me."

"I thought as much." There was silence for a moment as the nephew paced and the aunt watched. "Do you love her?" she asked at last.

He stopped to run a finger across crystal teardrops dangling from the rim of a lamp, his mind's eye seeing the redheaded woman-child who carried his name. He saw her again in all the ways, in all the settings he ever remembered. "I don't know. God knows, I don't want to."

"Oh? Is it so terrible then to fall in love with one's own wife?" she asked with just the hint of a smile. "It may be propaganda, of course, but I've heard it's the desirable thing in most cases."

"Well, not in this case."

"For heaven's sake, why not?"

"Because in this case, it isn't just an 'arranged marriage'—that would be bad enough—but it's some sort of a . . . contest of wills with my father." Leaving the crystals to tinkle against each other, he ran both hands through his already tousled hair and resumed his pacing. "If he wins, it'll turn this whole thing into a living, breathing 'I told you so.'"

"So?"

"So don't you see?"

"No, I do not see. As a matter of fact, I can hardly see anything at all with your pacing back and forth. You're making me dizzy." She gave the seat beside her such a whack with her cane a puff of dust rose from its tapestried surface. "Sit down!"

Nathan dropped wearily into the abused chair.

"Now let me see if I've gotten this whole thing straight," she began. "If you fall in love with Amanda . . . your wife . . . and have a happy, successful marriage, then . . . that means your father was 'right' . . . and he 'wins'? And if he 'wins' . . . you 'lose'? Is that it?"

Elbows on his knees, he continued to stare at the floor long after his aunt had finished speaking. Finally, he heaved himself to his feet and went over to stare, unseeing, out the bullion-fringed window.

"What's the matter? Did I get it wrong?"

"No. You got it right." His mouth twisted ruefully. "A man can be a real fool sometimes, can't he?"

The old eyes softened. "We all can, dear. Just be glad you're one of the lucky ones who discover their mistakes before it's too late."

"It's already too late. You see, she informed me last night—rather heatedly, in fact—that she hates me."

"Oh, nonsense! She doesn't hate you, she's hurt, that's all. Hurt and confused."

He looked back over his shoulder at her and shook

his head, smiling with self-mockery. "Oh, but that's not all. Right before that, Teddy told me, point blank, too"—he fingered his tender lip—"that he intended to take her away from me."

"Yes . . ." she sipped her coffee, "I think we all heard something of that last night. So short of beating your brother's brains out again, what are you going to do about it?"

"What can I do?"

"What can you—! Oh, for heaven's sake! Do you know what your trouble is, Nathan Rushton? You've spent so much of your life fighting against things, you've forgotten how to fight for something—even something you want! It's obvious to me that, like it or not, you're in love with the girl, and while you're busy playing these games with your father, Teddy's getting ready to take away the best thing that ever happened to you—and he's not playing!" Penelope glared at him much as she had his father on occasion. "Mark my words, young man. If you let that bounder of a brother get her, you'll regret it for the rest of your life—not the least of which will be because I shall never speak to you again!

"You know, it absolutely galls me the way you three—you, your father, and your brother—have treated that girl." She thumped her cane on the floor as she rose to her feet, black silk bosom trembling. "Frankly, I think she deserves better than the whole lot of you! Now, if you'll excuse me, I have better things to do than to sit here and listen to the brayings of another Rushton jackass! Percy! Percy Tillman, where are you? Why is that man never around when I need him?" she muttered, stumping her way out of the room without a backward glance.

Nathan stared after her as she disappeared in search of her beloved butler and his dimples, and slowly, like a creeping warmth, a smile began to spread itself across his haggard features. Soon it was an outright grin.

A cheery whistle on his lips, he went to let himself out, glanced in the horse-collar mirror, and stopped to tie his tie. "You look a wreck," he told his image, smoothing his shirtfront and running tongue-moistened fingers through his hair. "There. Much better," he pronounced, and the whistle resumed as a buoyant stride took him out the door.

Outside of town, though, a similar scene was ending quite differently as Nat, his face suffused with anger, brought his fist crashing down on his desk. "By God! I won't have it! She's your brother's wife, and you will stay away from her!"

"What's the matter?" his younger son sneered, dropping the stuffed valise at his feet. "Afraid you might be proven wrong for once? That you might be exposed for the ruthless, manipulative old fraud you are, instead of the great 'oracle of Baltimore' people think you are?"

Nat sat back, wary at the sudden venom he saw in the other's face. "I don't understand you . . . I don't understand you, at all."

"No, you never have, have you?" Teddy's hooded eyes glittered. "I don't expect you ever will."

Nat shook his head in bewilderment, and went on, half to himself. "It's not that I'm asking for gratitude, but after all I've done for you, after all I've given you, everything you ever wanted—"

"*Everything I ever wanted!* Ha! I've gotten only what you wanted me to have, so don't try and railroad me with that old gratitude bit." His father's implacable frown of warning went unheeded. Unleashed at last, all the years of pent-up resentments came spewing forth with such force neither man could have stopped it. Stiff-legged with emotion, Teddy faced the man from the middle of the study, his voice rising with each case he laid before him, his judge and jury, the accuser and accused. "*I* wanted to raise that stray goat I found as a boy, but *you* wanted me to have a damned thoroughbred instead. *I* wanted to study music, but what did you say?" He flung out both arms and did a sweeping imitation of Nat at his benevolent best. "*You* said music was for ladies, field hands, and Negroes! When you found me in the barn working with Roper, the old blacksmith, you took a strap to me on the spot, saying . . . saying—" Furiously, he cleared his throat for fear he would choke on his own bitterness. "You said no son of yours would disgrace your name, your years of work to put us at the top by doing menial labor." He thumped his chest with a clenched fist. "Well, it's my name, too! And when I wanted to learn the business along with Nathan, when I wanted you to be proud of me, to love me, too, you sent me off to that damned university instead. You never asked me what *I* wanted. You never cared! There was only room for one chip off the old block, and that was Nathan, always Nathan. I'm not good enough, I never have been. I don't measure up, isn't that right? Oh, I was always good enough to take over in a pinch, to hold things down when Nathan was too drunk to see straight, but not good enough to actually inherit anything, was I? That pittance you gave me was nothing compared to what you gave Nathan." His eyes narrowed. "Nathan's the only one who ever got what he wanted. Well, not this time. This time, I'm the one who's going to get what he wants." He pointed to himself with a look that dared his father to say otherwise.

"So," he said, his manner suddenly milder, "I'll tell you just what I told him: Not only am I going to continue to see Amanda, but pretty soon, very soon now, she's going to belong to me." A wolfish grin lighted his face strangely, and he began to stride about the room and gloat over his impending victory. "Can you imagine that?" he asked, laughing as he swaggered over to the door. "Me!" he crowed. "*Me!*"

Nat rose and shot out an accusing finger that shook with barely controlled fury. "You come back here. Come back here, I say! I don't care what I have to do, but you'll not have her! I'll see you dead first, but you won't have her! Do you hear me, Freddie? You won't have her!"

Teddy's body jerked and went rigid, then something seemed to snap, and he whirled savagely. "*My . . . name . . . is . . . Teddy! Teddy!* Do you hear me? My name is Theodore Rushton! I'm your son, remember?" His voice cracked, and he staggered over to grab his father by the lapels. "For God's sake, look at me! *Look* at me! I'm your son, too. Don't *I* count? Don't I matter?"

Repulsed by such an outburst, Nat pried the rage-stiffened fingers from his coat. "Of course you do, of course you do. What's wrong with you, boy? Get a hold of yourself."

Teddy's face cleared so suddenly it appeared to go blank. "You called me Freddie just now . . . why?"

Nat was stern. "I did no such thing."

"Yes, you did," he insisted softly, a softness emphasized by the echoes of rage still swirling around the room. "You said, 'You won't have her, Freddie.' Who's Freddie?" Teddy looked from one blue eye of his father to the other, and suddenly, his face blanched. "Freddie . . . Alton! Amanda's father!" His face crumpled in horror. "Oh, my God! Why, you . . . *sick,* disgusting . . . *vile* old man! You! You wanted her for yourself, didn't you? And since you couldn't have her, you gave her to Nathan, to a younger version of you." Suddenly, he threw back his head and laughed. "All that talk about her being the right one for him was just that, wasn't it? Talk! Well, what do you know about that?" He shuffled back toward the door, holding his sides in his mirth. When he stopped for his bag, he looked back over his shoulder. "What do you know about that? It looks like I'm the only one who's going to get what he wants this time, doesn't it . . . *father?*"

Nat sputtered in protest. "It's not what you're thinking, Teddy. Teddy, wait a minute. Son! Listen to me, you don't understand," he insisted, but he was only trying to convince a blank, empty doorway. Teddy was already gone. "I swear it," he called. "It wasn't Amanda, it was her mother. It was Emily I loved. Emily. . . ." Slowly, Nat sank into a chair and stared at the floor.

Amanda lay curled on her side, staring into space and remembering, over and over, every detail of the night before in painful clarity. She'd never felt so poisoned with her own misery. That party was the biggest disaster of her entire life, nothing but one humiliation after another. All she could do was pray she'd never have to see any of those people again. But it was the fight with Nathan afterward that haunted her the most. Every blow, every cruel word, the very look on his face with the brand "whore" on his lips remained vividly alive in her memory. Even the sound of her own voice as she had screamed her hatred at him kept coming back to make her cringe and cover her ears.

It was true. She hated him, she didn't think she could ever hate anyone the way she hated him, yet the odd thing, the thing that stuck out as if it were a piece from a different puzzle, was the way he hadn't retaliated with the fact of his own hatred. Why hadn't he told her then he was going to divorce her? Instead, he'd held her, even tried to soothe her while she cried out the bitter toxin of frustration. When she had cried all she could, he had lifted her up in his arms and carried her to bed. Maybe he'd acted out of guilt, or from one of those mysterious male senses of something-or-other the female of the species could never quite grasp, but whatever it was, it confused her, and left all her other judgments of him open to doubt. Trouble was, she was tired of the struggle, and she had the feeling that no matter how she put the pieces together they wouldn't add up to the total picture of the man she had married.

A noise intruded on her thoughts and she turned—gingerly at first to see if her head was better. She'd been awake for hours, staring and thinking, and one at a time, Sophie, Rose, Emma, and even Mary had come up to try and coax her into at least taking a tray in her room. She had refused each time until they had finally given up. Who could it be this time, she wondered. Georgie? The ever proper William? Diggs? Amusement flitted across her mind if not across her face as she sat up slowly. "Yes?" she called. There was no answer.

She frowned, heard the noise again, then realized it came from her balcony door, not the hall. She rose and went to part the lace just as something else *pinged* off the glass. Fully curious now, she opened the door and peered out down through the iron railing.

"What are you doing here?" she asked the figure standing below with a handful of pebbles.

"I have to talk to you," Teddy whispered hoarsely. He was still in evening clothes. "Now."

"What is it? What's wrong?"

MATTERS OF THE HEART 301

"I'll explain later. Now please, will you come down?"

"All right." She pointed down toward the drawing room below. "Go on in and I'll be right there."

"No." He shook his head vigorously. "I'd better not. Someone might hear. I'll wait for you to let me in."

"But—"

"Please, Mandy! Just do as I say!"

Realizing she wouldn't get any answers except on his terms, she sighed, went in, and threw on her peach wrapper, and hurried down the stairs.

"What is it?" she asked again, pulling open the door. "What's wrong?"

He stepped in and darted a quick look around. "Is he here?"

"Nathan?" Her features gave a weary shrug. "I don't know. I doubt it—why?"

Brushing past her, he tossed his tall hat and ebony stick on a chair. "Do you know what he did?"

"Who? Nathan?"

"My father. He kicked me out. Told me to pack my bags and leave. He wanted me gone last night, but then didn't want the guests asking any more questions, so he let me stay 'til this morning. Lucky me, huh?"

"Oh, Teddy!" He took the hug she gave him with the sigh of one who needs the comfort. "What will you do? Where will you stay?"

Letting her go, he shrugged. "I don't know. But that's not what I came here to talk to you about. You know Nathan and I got in a fight last night? About you?"

She flinched, then nodded.

"Nathan told me to stay away from you. He even tried to bribe me with the company—"

Her eyes widened.

"—but I wouldn't take it. I love you, Amanda, and I want you to go away with me. Today. Now. We'll go far away from Nathan, my father—everybody. I'll make you happy, I promise I will."

Amanda was aware of the look on her face, of her fingers twisting the sash at her waist. "Teddy, I—I don't know what to say, I . . ."

"Say 'yes,' that's all you have to say—yes."

I hate you! . . . I know, he'd said, *I know.* "But, I . . . he told me the same thing, too—that I couldn't see you anymore, either." It wasn't just the wrong answer, it was the worst answer, and the look on his face made her want to cry.

"I see. You're not ready. You think you still love him."

"Oh, Teddy, I don't know what I think anymore. I'm sorry, but—"

"No, no, it's all right. I can be patient. I can wait. Don't worry about it." He snorted, and swung away a few steps before facing her again. "But after you hear the real reason you're in this marriage, maybe you'll be able to make up your mind a little faster."

A thousand possibilities rushed to her mind and made her palms suddenly sticky with dread. "What do you mean?"

"Did you know," he inquired pleasantly, "that my father is in love with you?"

"What?"

"That's right. My father—he's in love with you, and that's why he married you off to Nathan. He knew he could never have you himself, so he gave you to the man most like him."

She started to giggle, then caught herself when she realized how in earnest Teddy was. "Oh, Teddy . . . no. You don't understand. I don't know where you heard this, but it's not me, it was my mother. He loved her—but that was before he married your mother. It's true. Aunt Pen told me."

Slowly, his expression changed from one of triumph to a haunted, hurt look, and he seemed to stare right through her.

"Teddy?"

"I . . . was just wondering if my mother ever knew."

"Ever knew what?"

"If she ever knew my father didn't love her."

"Oh, Teddy, don't!" She went over and picked up one of his hands that hung slack by his side, pressing it between her two small ones. "Don't do this to yourself."

It was as if she hadn't spoken. "I was always told she died having me. I thought that's why my father always hated me. I thought I killed her." His eyes went to hers with jolting sharpness. "But now I'm not so sure. Maybe she died from not being loved. A person can die from that, you know. Maybe she died from being treated the same way my father treats everyone he doesn't like."

She pressed the unresponding hand again, her heart aching for this family that never treasured one another, for all the hurt it spawned. "I'm sure he loved your mother, Teddy. Otherwise, he would never have married her, would he?"

His look was so pointed, the unspoken what-about-you-and-Nathan so loud, she flinched.

But all he said was, "Why not? He couldn't have your mother, remember?"

"Yes, but he must've loved her, too. It *is* possible to love two people at the same time, isn't it?"

"Is it?"

She bit her lip. She didn't have to be told that the

subject had suddenly shifted from their parents to them. "Yes . . . I think it is."

He reached up and touched her cheek with his free hand, the fingers of his other curling around hers. "Go out with me tonight."

It took her a second to absorb the change. It was as if none of the previous conversation had taken place. "What?"

"Go out with me tonight. Spend time with me. I think I'll go mad if I have to spend another hour alone."

"I don't know, Teddy, I—"

"Please. You know you're the only friend I have."

"Oh, I am not."

"You are!"

His sudden vehemence startled her and she instinctively backed up.

Changing his tactics, he smiled and reached out for her hand to draw her back again. "I'm sorry. Look, we'll do anything you want to do, we'll go any place you like. How about a day on the lake? If you bring a change of clothing, we can even dine afterward at a nice restaurant somewhere." He bestowed his most charming smile. "Come on, Daisy, what d'ya say?"

No, was what she wanted to say. She didn't want to go. She wanted to be alone. To think. To sort things out. In truth, she was tired of Teddy and all his charm—but he was right in one way. Friends owed friends, didn't they? "I suppose so," she said on a sigh. "Give me a few minutes to change. You need to change, too," she told him, pointing.

The corners of his eyes crinkled with pleasure as he brought her fingers to his lips. "You won't regret it."

But she already did.

* * *

"What do you mean, you don't know?" Nathan bellowed.

Rose flinched and nervously twisted the corner of her apron. "I mean she didn't tell nobody where she was going, sir. She wouldn't come out of her room all day. We kept trying to get her to eat something—honest, we did—but she kept refusing, so we finally give up. When I went up, about three o'clock, to see if she wanted to dress, she was gone. There wasn't no note or nothing—"

"Note!" The word brought a new and horrible possibility to mind. She'd left him! He'd pushed too hard last night and she'd left him!

He took the stairs two at a time, stiff-arming her half-open door out of his way, and swept the room with a glance. Nothing! There wasn't a slipper, a ribbon, a hairpin in sight. The blue floral coverlet on the bed was smoothly impersonal, the cool-colored room mocking him faintly. His heart sank another notch, then he smacked himself in the forehead. Rose would have picked up the room and made the bed!

The key resting in the lock of Amanda's wardrobe flew off and clattered into a corner as he threw open the doors. "Oh, God!" he whispered, dropping his head against the center brace. Dresses, hats, and shoes, a glorious mélange of colors, were all there. She was coming back.

His hand crushed the peach silk wrapper hanging on the door and brought it to his nose. Lavender. She still smelled of lavender. He rubbed his face in the cool folds. But where had she gone?

With Teddy.

The little clock on her mantle chimed, and he lifted his head. Five o'clock. He'd been home an hour already, bathed, shaved, and put on fresh clothing. He had just assumed she was home, just assumed she would be there when he was ready to talk, to start over. Now all he could do was wait, wait and hope he wasn't too late.

Amanda sat in the hot darkness of the enclosed carriage and stared out the one unshaded window. The afternoon and evening had proven long and tiring, and she was anxious to get home.

She knew it had been a mistake to go with Teddy. His moods had been typical Rushton ones, shifting so often and fast, it exhausted her trying to keep up. The air had been hot and still over the lake, the sun a painful, headache-producing glare off the water. By the time Teddy had started tipping a silver flask to his lips, she'd had enough. After makeshift ablutions and a quick change in the bathhouse with the help of a stranger, she'd demanded to be taken to Aunt Pen's. She and Teddy had argued, and there'd been a few unpleasant minutes followed by a sullen ride, but at last she was free of him. The Rushtons, she recalled thinking as he drove off in a steam, couldn't *always* get their way.

Amanda smiled, remembering Aunt Pen's peculiar lack of surprise at her visit. The woman acted as if she'd been expecting her, in fact. Tea had been laid, and conversation flowed—all with never a mention of Nathan or his brother. Then seeing that Amanda was dressed for it, Pen swept her off for an early supper before an evening at the theater. Afterward, Pen had refused to let her hire a hack, but insisted her own driver bring her home.

Now if they would only get there.

She shifted uncomfortably, lifting the sweat-dampened silk slightly away from her legs, hoping for a waft of cooler air. The first thing she would do when she got home was shed petticoats, pantalets, and dress—a dress whose restrictive bodice chafed her sensitive nipples. She didn't think she'd ever get used to Bernice's risqué sense of design that required neither stays nor camisoles under evening gowns.

Her eyes slid closed as she imagined herself in the middle of her room, naked, her loosened hair held up off her neck. It would feel so good.

With the tip of her tongue, she licked the salty moisture from her upper lip, then shivered when the innocent movement brought Nathan and the night she'd gone to him in the barn to mind. It had been hot that night, too, her camisole binding. Nathan had loosened each tie, his lips following the path his fingers made. It was . . . delicious torture, it was . . . the heat, she decided, pushing the images away. There must be something about hot, sticky nights. . . .

The carriage slowed, and the lights beyond the little window told her they'd arrived. She didn't wait for the driver's assistance, but scooped up her bundled day dress and opened the door as soon as the vehicle swayed to a halt.

"Thank you, Dan," she called, stepping down into the relative coolness outside. "Good night."

"Good night, ma'am."

As the carriage wheeled out through the front gate, Amanda took the flagstone path to the front door in a rustle of white-and-gold silk.

Inside, she closed the heavy oak door and sagged against it, eyes closed. For some reason, once conjured, the ghost of Nathan's kiss refused to leave her, and it brushed her lips yet again. She wet them with her tongue, then touched them with her fingertips. Oh, why did love have to be so complicated? Why couldn't a kiss be more than just a memory?

From the darkened doorway to the study, a pair of

brooding eyes marked the gesture with a scowl, and continued to watch as she went up the stairs.

At the sound of her bedroom door closing, Nathan's stare returned to the front door, where he saw again the telltale gesture. Once seen, a man never forgets the look of a woman who's been kissed, of a woman in love—and Amanda wore that look. A pain that was close to being physical constricted his chest. These hours of waiting had been pure hell, and there was nothing to say they were over now.

He leaned heavily in the doorway and looked back over his shoulder at the room where he'd spent most of the evening, indeed, most of his waking hours for over a year. It sickened and disgusted him. He had wasted a big part of his life, and maybe more than that. With a snort, he pushed away from the door frame, and without being conscious of doing so, made a decision, a vow, as he turned back into the gloomy interior of his study.

Upstairs, Amanda kicked off her shoes and stockings, then shed her pantalets and petticoats in a billowy heap on the floor. Standing beside the bed, she struggled with the tiny back buttons of her dress, but the feel of silk sliding against her bare hips increased her agitation and frustrated her efforts. Damn that Bernice! Why put the buttons in the back?

Her shoulders were beginning to ache with the strain when the door opened behind her. "Oh, Sophie," she sighed, arms dropping limply, "I'm so glad you waited up. There must be a hundred of these stupid buttons."

When Sophie neither answered nor came to her aid, she glanced around and froze, breath catching in her throat. In the doorway stood Nathan, a decanter in one hand, the stems of two wine glasses dangling from the fingers of the other.

Chapter 14

Woodenly, Amanda turned to face him. "What do you want?" she asked, guilt giving the words a sharpness she hadn't intended.

His only answer was to take a step into the room and close the door with the toe of his boot.

Instinctively, she backed up—and ran directly into the bedpost. She was racking her brain for something to say, some way to fill the silence. She hadn't thought he was home; indeed, she hadn't given his whereabouts any thought at all. His coat and vest were gone, and his once crisp shirt was halfway unbuttoned, the sleeves turned back several times to reveal browned and muscular forearms.

Why was he just staring at her with that one eyebrow raised as if waiting for her to challenge his intrusion? Was he drunk? No, his eyes were too clear and they lacked that sullen, belligerent expression she'd come to know so well. So why didn't he say something? She had defied him. Wasn't he going to say anything?

Nathan had stopped in his tracks at her sudden retreat, unwilling to frighten her into further flight. He watched the quick rise and fall of her breasts, wondering how they kept from spilling over. His gaze took in the slender waist, traveled over the softly draped hips, and down thighs molded in the gold-shot silk . . . all lovely, yet it was the one bare foot peeking from beneath the hem that stirred something deep in the pit of his stomach.

Setting the decanter and glasses on her bedside table, he went over to her. "Here," he said quietly, "let me help."

When she continued to stare at him, his eyebrows lifted in amusement, and he had to make a circling motion with one finger, as if signaling to a deaf-mute. "Turn around."

Stiffly, she turned around and lifted her hair, sending up a musky wave of lavender and woman from the shadowed nape of her neck. He swallowed, then started pushing the tiny silk-covered buttons through their loops, feeling her shiver when his fingers grazed her flesh. "There," he breathed.

Hugging the now-loosened dress to her, she turned around, her green eyes widening to find him still so close.

Bracing one hand on the post that rose behind her head, the other on his hip, he studied her face closely. For the first time since their marriage, he allowed himself the luxury of drinking in her beauty. Her eyes were a deep and cloudy emerald. Her skin, with just a hint of freckles across her nose, was smooth and fine-grained. Irresistibly, his gaze fell to her rose-colored mouth and the swollen lips that seemed to beg for the pressure of a kiss.

Breathing in the clean, male scent of him, Amanda was passive under his scrutiny until he began staring at her mouth. Was he seeing her on that terrace again, kissing Teddy? In a nervous, unconscious gesture, she bit her lips—and knew instantly by Nathan's narrowed eyes it was the wrong thing to do. When he suddenly raised a hand, she flinched. But all he did was lay hard fingers along her cheek and drag his thumb deliberately across her lips, erasing Teddy's brand. Then he bent his head and replaced it with his own.

It was a gentle, tender kiss with the flavor of claiming, like the sealing kiss of a vow solemnly made. Yet there was a hesitancy, as if he half expected her to pull away. The moment hung by a thread.

Her lips began to tremble beneath his. Too hungry, too needful of this elusive man, she leaned against him with a soft sigh—and the thread snapped. Nathan's hand came off the bedpost, and his other gripped the back of her head, crushing her to him for a kiss that was far too fevered to be gentle. As his mouth slanted hungrily across hers, a shock wave coursed through her body clear to her toes, and she clung fiercely to him. The ghosts between them were gone. The muscles of her belly tightened with a jerk, and her knees turned to butter when he pinned her back against the post with a bold thrust of his hips. Wave after wave of first hot, then cold, washed over her quivering flesh. Insistently, he explored her mouth with his tongue, sucking, thrusting. His hands caressed her from throat to shoulder to back, thumbs tracing the curve of her waist as he stroked down over the fullness of her hips to cup her bottom and lift her, forcing her legs to straddle his. The aching, exquisite torture made her gasp. When his mouth left hers to travel down her throat, her head sagged backward, her breathing no longer automatic, but regulated strictly by the passage of his lips. Now quick and light, now deep and slow.

As his lips burned a path from collar bone to breast, Nathan pushed the dress from her shoulders, lowered it to her feet, and let it fall between them. Then he pulled her to him again as if he could drink in her milky skin right through his own and quench the need that had burst so suddenly into flame. Each ragged breath he took was another blow to his reeling senses, pulling the scent of lavender and the taste of woman deeper and deeper. Another kiss, and he stepped back a pace. He wanted to look at her. His eyes confirmed what his mouth and hands had discovered. She was splendid, beautiful, her pale skin smooth and sleek. She was full-breasted with a flat belly and rounded hips that called him back to her.

Amanda leaned against the smooth column at her back, feeling no shame as his eyes burned paths over her in the soft, yellow lamplight. Was it love that made him look at her so intently, his eyes so heated and glowing? Or was it lust? She wasn't wise enough yet in the ways of men or love to know—and right then, she didn't care. He was here and he desired her. That was enough for now. Reaching up, she let her fingers trace lightly through the dark hair inside his shirt, her nails making white lines across his tan. Wasn't he ever going to undress? "Nathan—"

He frowned and laid the ends of his fingers along her lips. "No," he whispered huskily. "No words, not tonight." Words had always been his downfall with this woman, and he wanted nothing to turn this night away from his purpose.

She consented without question, watching with a lazy smile while he shucked his shirt, then trousers, undergarments, and boots all at once. The rest of him was made as finely and cleanly as the face she'd always loved. He was a masterpiece of design. His legs were heavily muscled and sturdy, his torso long and flat, tapering to paler, square hips and—she pulled her gaze back up to his face. She was curious, but didn't want to stare. Not yet, anyway.

As he came to her again, Nathan pushed away any visions of his brother embracing her as he was now. Instead, he concentrated on pulling the last of the pins from the mass of auburn curls atop her head, luxuriating in the silky feel as he combed the tresses out with his fingers. *Ahh....* He'd been wanting to do that for so long.

Amanda sighed and closed her eyes at the warmth of his bare skin against hers. His hot mouth came down on hers again, and he pressed her back onto the bed. As his hands stroked across her belly and down the insides of her thighs, separating them, she was dimly aware of the low moan that came from her own throat. His mouth and hands seemed to be everywhere, nipping, rubbing, probing, making her writhe and strain for something that had no name.

Nathan, too, was glorying in the sensations, the pleasures he'd long denied himself. A single throaty growl had become a near purr, a constant hum of satisfaction. God! but this woman was incredible, and he buried his face in the dark wine of her hair. Sliding a hand beneath her, he lifted her hips to meet his, and pressed deep.

With a small cry, she propelled herself away from him with such force she bumped into the headboard. Nathan's head snapped up and he stared into green eyes regarding him more with uncertainty than fright. He hadn't expected the resistance of virgin flesh. Without ever forming the actual words to himself, he believed Amanda and his brother had been lovers. He now had undeniable proof to the contrary. Suddenly, somewhere deep inside him there was the sensation of walls and defenses crumbling, falling away. Even though she'd been thrown into the path of temptation and given every cause to stray, for reasons he didn't yet comprehend, she had refused the comfort of another man's arms. She had remained faithful.

It was this knowledge that caused his hand to tremble slightly as he reached out to draw her back to him, her name falling from his lips in a whisper. With tender kisses and a gentle touch, he comforted and reassured, igniting the coals of desire again with ease. This time when he made her his, it was with a heart feeling the first delicately clinging tendrils of love.

After the first stab of pain gave way to that instinctual rhythm, Amanda felt a sense of rightness, of long-awaited homecoming. But even this faded as the all-consuming fire built within her. Her back rounded in the primitive rite as she learned to match his eager thrusts. She tasted the warm wetness of his mouth, gloried in the feel of his muscles moving powerfully beneath the skin of his shoulders and back. As she gave herself up to Nathan's intimate embrace, she was aware of climbing, climbing, until she suddenly catapulted into dark and airless space. Slowly, slowly then, by small, shuddering degrees, she drifted back through the moist, hazy atmosphere until she was once more in the warm circle of Nathan's arms.

Gradually, their savoring slowed, hands grew heavy, and with the sweet salts of passion spent, they slept.

In a stretch of muscles that ached deliciously, Amanda rolled over, felt the welcome touch of cool morning air, and smiled. *Ah, Nathan, Nathan, Nathan!* It was a song, a pulsebeat, a litany. She turned her head to feast loving eyes on his sleeping form, only to be disappointed. He was gone. The room was empty. There was nothing, no shoe, no sock, no trace of his ever having been there. Even the decanter of wine and unused glasses were gone. Damn, damn, damn! That was twice he'd slept with her, and twice he'd sneaked out without a word. If it hadn't been for the indentation on the pillow where his head had rested, and for the faint new awareness between her legs, she might have believed the whole of last night to be no more than the richly textured fantasy of a woman obsessed.

Rolling over, she flung her arms around his pillow, filling her lungs with the faint, manly smell that lingered. It was no fantasy, no dream. He had been there, and all of last night was real. Real! She sighed. It took too much effort to be angry.

Giving the unresponsive pillow another squeeze, she swung her legs over the side of the bed and stood up, back arched, arms flung wide in the lithe, graceful stretch of a young animal. Between small snatches of song, she washed, dressed, and hurried downstairs. Maybe he was waiting breakfast for her.

But Nathan wasn't there, either, and all anybody could tell her was that he'd gone already. No one knew where or for how long. Resigning herself to the situation, she ordered a big breakfast and attacked it ravenously. After all, she reasoned with a smile around a mouthful of eggs, he'd have to come home sometime.

After breakfast, she took a long, loping ride on Sam, the high flame of her spirits not even beginning to flicker. With Mary, she planned a special lunch, then dinner for two, choosing the dishes Nathan loved best. She took sugar to Molly, and stayed to watch Bob work the horses. Joe, perched on the fence beside her, reached over at one point and gave her shoulders a squeeze. She laughed and returned the hug. Joe had always known when things were going well.

Later, with childish exuberance, she waded back to the house through a field of ripening wheat, found little Georgie picking berries along the fence, and played an impromptu game of tag with him.

The September sun had reached its zenith when she wandered toward her shady swing retreat. Spreading her rose-embroidered skirts, she settled on the old swing and listened to the wind ruffle through the long, sweeping willow fronds. She swung gently, eyes closed, humming a small tune. Her world was falling into place at last, and she knew the buoyant peace only love returned can bring.

"Hi."

Her eyes flew open, but she wasn't really startled. She'd been halfway expecting this visit. "Hello, Teddy."

He was a fashion plate in cream-colored trousers and blue striped shirt, but he had the woebegone face of a little boy shamed, hands jammed deep in his pockets.

"I'm . . . sorry I got carried away last night. I shouldn't have drunk so much," he mumbled, then cast her a hopeful look. "You won't let it make a difference between us, will you?"

She shook her head. Maybe they could still be friends.

Teddy's face brightened instantly, and he sprawled on the other end of the swing in a thespian gesture of relief. "Am I totally forgiven then?"

"Totally." She laughed, her heart much too light to bear the weight of a grudge.

"Good!" he breathed, and with the distasteful chore of apology successfully behind him, he eyed her curiously. "Now are you going to tell me what's making you look like the cat who's just swallowed the canary?"

"I'm sure I don't know what you mean."

"No? Well, you look different somehow."

Funny, Amanda thought. She'd looked for a difference in her mirror that morning, and was disappointed not to find one. "I do?"

Watching her pluck at her skirt, all of Teddy's senses sharpened. She did look different today, he just couldn't put his finger on quite how. "What happened when you got home yesterday? Did Nathan say anything?"

She shook her head, her hair catching rays of afternoon light and her cheeks glowing with the same color.

Teddy's insides knotted with suspicion. "What did he do? Make love to you?"

Her color heightened. "Teddy, I don't think this is something we should be discussing."

Snorting disgustedly, he got to his feet and stalked a couple of steps away. "He did, didn't he? He made love to you!" He whirled. "Didn't he?"

"Teddy, I—"

"Oh, Amanda! Don't you see?"

"See what?"

"How convenient this sudden burst of love is? Doesn't it strike you as even a wee bit strange that he doesn't have anything to do with you until I want you? He probably knew we'd been together. Of course he'd do whatever he could to put his brand on you. Any man would—and any man can make love to a woman, but loving her is something else again!"

"That's a vile thing to say!" Flinging herself to her feet, she pushed past him, then spun back again. "You don't know what you're talking about because you weren't even—"

"There?" he supplied with a sneer.

His smugness tore at her pride and she pounded his chest with both fists. "That's right! *You . . . weren't . . . there!*"

Grabbing her wrists, he used her own stiff arms to pull her close to his face. "No, I wasn't here, Mandy, but I am now, and I love you. *I love you.* I've always loved you. I turned down a company for you, remember? You're all I need to complete my life." A lot of the fight left her, but something, some instinct prodded him on. "Did he tell you he loved you?"

No words, not tonight. She looked away.

"Did he? Or did he just use you because he knew you'd been with me?"

She felt her bones wilt. She was so very tired. "What do you want me to say, Teddy?"

"I want you to see last night for what it really was." He let go of her wrists. "An attempt to keep you tied to him for appearance's sake."

She twisted away when he attempted to pull her into his arms, and rubbed her throbbing temples with icy fingertips. "Go away, Teddy. Just go away. I need some time to myself. Everything is so . . . confused right now." She looked up, pleading with her eyes as well as her words. "I need some time."

He looked as miserable as she felt, emotions chasing themselves across his face. "All right. I'll go—but I'll be back, Mandy. I'm not giving up."

She waited behind her curtain of willow leaves until she was sure he was gone, then paced slowly back to the house. A short time before, the world had been a warm and wonderful place. Now she felt a chill that went clear through to her soul.

Common sense told her Teddy had every possible motive to be untruthful, yet where was the lie? It was all so plausible. It all fit. Nathan hadn't said 'I love you.' She had just assumed it, hoped it, believed it. Oh, why did Teddy have to show up today of all days? Why hadn't Nathan been there when she woke up? Why wasn't he here now to hold her and answer all her fears? The corners of her mouth twisted with mirthless humor. What a silly question! So far, they'd been able to argue, and finally be intimate, but never had they been able to talk, to tell each other how they felt. Maybe they never would.

What if Teddy was right? she wondered. If she quit seeing him, would Nathan lose interest and ignore her once again? She stumbled, sudden tears blurring her vision. She couldn't bear that, not after last night.

A small, frustrated whimper escaped her. She felt as if she were trying to see through a bucket of muddy water. If only she could get away somewhere and think. If only she could get away. . . .

Whistling a nameless tune born from the heart, Nathan bounded up the front walk, a small gold ring burning a hole in his pocket. With his hand on the knob, he paused to school his features. He didn't want to give himself away. He'd been rehearsing all day, looking for just the right way to finally tell Amanda what she meant to him, how much he loved her, needed her. It chafed him sorely when one problem after another kept cropping up to keep him chained at work and away from her.

He flung open the door. "Amanda? Amanda!" He tossed his hat with more enthusiasm than accuracy, hardly noticing when the gray felt derby careened off the edge of the credenza and landed in a potted palm. "Amanda!"

When he called her name for the third time and she still didn't appear, he decided a drink might help calm the sudden case of nerves that gripped him. In his study, he lifted the heavy decanter from its case, paused, and put it back. He wanted nothing to spoil that special moment before he put the ring on her finger.

Unbuttoning his gray alpaca jacket, he sat down behind the desk and propped his feet up with a satisfied sigh. A moment later, like a child with a prize, he dug the precious ring out of his watch pocket, and began to toss it up in the air. It was as if he spun the world itself on the ends of his fingers.

At the sound of her familiar step, he snatched the

flashing metal out of the air, jerked his feet down, and bent over the nearest stack of papers in an attempt to look busy.

"Nathan? I need to talk to you. May I come in?"

He raised his head, the light of suppressed pleasure in his eyes dying at the sight of her tear-swollen face. "Yes . . . of course. What is it?" He started to rise and go to her, but she stayed him with a small gesture before going to stand at the window. Slowly, he sank back to his seat and waited, the sour taste of dread in his mouth. "What is it?" he repeated.

The afternoon sun seemed to blind her, for she kept blinking as she stared into it, twisting a bit of ivory linen absently through her fingers. "I . . . I hope you'll try to understand this." Her glance at him lasted only long enough to make sure she had his attention. "I've come to ask your permission to leave. To go away."

He gripped the arms of his chair, and cleared his heart out of his throat. "May I ask why?"

"Time." Slender fingers, a delicate shell pink in the sunlight, spread in a vague gesture of helplessness. "I need some time to think things over. Everything has happened so fast. It's all so . . . blurry and confused." Her voice was hardly more than a whisper, a mere pulse of sound.

He wanted to jump up, rant and rave, and forbid her to go. He wanted to fall down, beg and plead, and beseech her not to leave. Why? Why did she want to leave him now? Last night had . . . he squeezed his eyes closed . . . last night had felt so right, so good. He could still feel her, the textures, the responses. He could still taste her on his tongue. Could it possibly have been one-sided? Could he really have been that blind, that selfish?

"Where will you go?"

"I . . . to a hotel, I suppose."

"That won't be necessary. I'll go." It was astonishing to hear such reasonable things come out of his mouth. "I have a place in town."

"The one you built for Suzanne?"

Suzanne. . . . Funny. He hadn't thought of her in months. It used to be the mere sound of her name stabbed at him, and now it did nothing. She meant nothing; her memory meant nothing. Strange time to realize it, but she had been little more than a fleeting fancy, a beautiful bauble snatched away before he'd had a chance to grow tired of her on his own. It had been his pride, not his heart, that was wounded. He knew the difference now—now that he was losing the one woman he truly loved. And he had no one to blame but himself.

"Yes," he said. "It's on Sharp Street. How did you know?"

"Teddy told me. He showed it to me one day."

His nostrils flared in sudden suspicion. "Does this . . . decision of yours have anything to do with him?"

"No. Not exactly."

His face whitened, and for the first time in his life, he understood what it meant to have a broken heart. While he sat there seeing, hearing, breathing, he could feel his insides crack and crumble into worthless pieces. He'd still been too late. She loved his brother after all, and this was the only way she could think of to end their marriage with some semblance of grace.

He wanted to answer her in a voice that revealed none of his misery, but his throat was too dry. He worked his tongue against the roof of his mouth convulsively, as if scraping ashes from its surface. He rose to his feet and nodded. The ring, unnoticed and unbestowed, slipped back into his pocket. "I'll pack and be gone by tonight."

"So soon?"

She had turned around, and was looking at him so anxiously, he took a half step toward her.

"There's no need to hurry," she said. "Tomorrow will be soon enough."

He sighed an old man's sigh, one filled with wonder at how life's functions could continue even when there was no longer any will for them to do so. He walked to the door, then stopped and looked back.

Amanda's bottom lip began to tremble, and she clamped it between her teeth. *Don't go. Stay. Take me upstairs and make love to me again. Tell me you love me, Nathan.*

Looking at her, he waited. *Tell me not to go, Amanda. Tell me you want me as badly as I want you. Tell me it's not too late. Tell me you don't love Teddy.*

"Will you be all right?" she asked.

"I'll be fine," he said.

The next morning, Nathan stood in the foyer, giving last minute instructions to William while Bob took his luggage out to the little tandem he'd be using.

"Oh, and here's where I'll be staying in case . . . well, just in case," he said, handing over the piece of paper he'd taken from his breast pocket.

William looked at it, then folded it carefully. "Sir, I just want you to know—"

"I do, William." He clapped the man lightly on the shoulder. "And thank you. Listen, I've already given Aman—Mrs. Rushton money, but there's more, if needed, in my bottom desk drawer. She knows it's there, but she might forget if she gets excited or something."

"Don't worry, sir. I'll take good care of her. We all will."

Nathan nodded as he pulled on his gray kid gloves. "I know you will." He pulled open the door, was

MATTERS OF THE HEART 323

halfway out, then stopped. "William?" He didn't look around.

"Sir?"

"My brother—don't let him in the house again. Don't let him anywhere near Amanda."

"Yes, sir."

Upstairs, Amanda heard the front door close and bowed her head, letting the tears flow. Earlier, he'd tapped on her door and shoved several hundred dollars into her hand. Spending money, he'd said. On either side of the threshold, they'd faced each other in awkward silence, then he'd leaned down, kissed her cheek, and left.

Pressing her hand now to the place he'd kissed, she dropped her face back into the pillow, and sobbed brokenly.

Beside her, her bulk putting a giant dip in the bed, Sophie rubbed Amanda's hot, shuddering back, her own eyes brimming. "There, there, honey. There, there. . . ."

"But I love him, Sophie! It's not Teddy, it never was. I know that now. It's Nathan I love!"

"He be back, honey. He be back."

Outside, Nathan took the reins from Bob and nodded his thanks. As he wheeled slowly out the drive, he searched the upper windows, but no face disturbed their blankness. He sighed. *It's not over, Amanda. Not by a long shot. I'll be back, and this time, I'll do it right.*

The next week was a long, boring one for Amanda. Mornings began with a light breakfast, then marketing with Mary, which was interesting only because the woman could outhaggle the most seasoned vendors. Her eyes searched every crowd for Nathan, but she was always disappointed. In the afternoons, she tended the flower beds with Diggs, willingly distracted with lessons on planting and grafting and mulching. Evenings were spent quietly in reading or in doing needlework again, anything to keep her mind off the man who wasn't there. Somehow life had slipped back in time to the same patterns as before her marriage. She waited just as she had waited for her father, and just like then, she waited in vain.

Despite his promises, Teddy hadn't shown up again, and for that she was secretly relieved. She missed his company, the friend she'd had when Nathan wasn't there, but she knew things could never be like that again. He'd said he loved her, but perhaps that was why he was staying away. He must've realized it would never work.

Besides that, the only things different from before Nathan had left was the number of nuisance callers—peddlers, she was told after the door was closed—and the sudden vigilance of the servants. Everywhere she turned, every window she looked out, there was someone doing something. Bob was now paddocking some horses across from the front gate, Diggs was trimming back the willow where her swing hung, windows were being washed almost daily, and the door was answered almost before the caller knocked.

That's why when Amanda found herself the only one in the foyer that morning just as the knocker fell, she was startled and a bit hesitant. She'd practically been run over the last time she'd attempted to answer the door. When the knocker fell again and no one else came, she smiled, rubbing her palms down the sides of her rust cord skirt. Maybe it was the man who sold sewing supplies. She needed some embroidery thread.

"Yes? May I help you?" she asked, opening the door.

There on the front step stood a huge potted palm on dark-clad legs.

She blinked, puzzled, but moved obligingly out of the way as the heavily breathing palm stepped into the foyer.

"Nathan!"

"Hi." He smiled as he set the plant down and brushed off his hands. "Diggs said you wanted this."

Her heart gave a leap. The bronzed skin contrasting sharply with his white shirt, the deep blue of his eyes, the crisp dark hair—she drank in the sight of him. He was more handsome than ever.

"Why?" he asked.

"Why what?"

"Why did you want the plant?"

"What? Oh." She stared at the thing, then at its two cousins on either side of the staircase. Why, indeed? "I . . . I wanted it for my bedroom."

"Your bedroom?"

"Sure. Why not?"

He shrugged. "It just seems . . . a little . . ." He let the sentence trail off. "You look wonderful. Did you do something different with your hair?"

Self-consciously she patted the pouf that ended in a small knot on top of her head. "I saw it in a ladies' magazine. Do you like it?"

He nodded, but he wasn't looking at her hair anymore. "Very much." He was staring at her mouth. "Very, very much."

"How . . . how are you getting on?" she asked, licking her lips.

"Fine." He raised his eyes. "Just fine. How are things here?"

She nodded. "Did you hire someone to take care of you?"

"There's a couple who come in during the day, but I'm not there much."

"Oh?"

"Work."

"Oh."

They stood, each one wrapped in the protective cloak of small talk, only their eyes speaking the truth of longing and doubt.

"Well," he said after a moment, "I'll be leaving you now."

The wording brought an instinctive protest to her lips. "Oh, but won't you stay—" she smiled, feeling awkward at inviting the man into his own house, "for tea, or something?"

"No"—but he smiled, too—"I'd better not."

When the door closed behind him, she reached out to stroke the feathery palm fronds absently, lovingly. *Thank you, Mr. Diggs.*

Two days later, he came again, this time bearing an armload of things that he transferred one by one into her hands.

"Here's the shawl Emma left at her sister's. Here's the jar of ground ginger Mary asked for, and here," he said, pulling a small yellow envelope out of his pocket, "are the herbal headache powders Sophie sent word she needed."

Smiling, but suspicious, she accepted each item he handed her. Apparently, there was a plot afoot to insure she and Nathan saw each other often. Or he was making all this up.

In the days that followed, there were more delicacies, more "discovered" items left somewhere, and more missions of mercy for Sophie. Each time, she asked him to stay, but each time he refused.

Then the day came when he arrived with nothing but a bouquet of deep red roses.

"Another order from Diggs?" she asked, burying her smile in the fragrant blossoms.

"No," he answered simply. "Me." And this time he stayed.

They sat in small wrought iron chairs on the terrace, and sipped sherry from tiny crystal glasses.

"How's the work for the steel company going?" she asked.

"If the weather holds, we should finish in another month."

They spoke of other things, too, inconsequential things. His voice was as warm as the autumn sun, with no veiled insults or prickly barbs, and she was so content, it was hard not to show her disappointment when he rose to leave.

At the door, she unthinkingly offered him her hand, but before she could take it back, his fingers closed around hers and held. His thumb rubbed first the emerald, then the backs of her knuckles, sending streaks of warmth up her arm.

"Amanda?" *Is it too soon? You seem to be over Teddy. Do I tell you how much I miss you yet? Can I tell you I love you now?*

"Yes?" *Oh, Nathan, it's been so long. Do you miss me like I miss you? Don't you know that I love you?*

He shook his head. *Not yet.* "Nothing. I'll see you again soon."

She nodded, and her hand was released. *Not yet.* "Soon."

It took every ounce of willpower Nathan had to turn around and walk out the door. Everything was coming along so nicely, he couldn't afford to spoil things by being too hasty. But soon he could make his move. Soon, soon, he chanted, as he climbed into his tandem and clicked to the horse.

With minor variations, he was still telling himself the same thing when he got to the townhouse and turned the rig over to the temporary groom he'd hired.

Whistling tunelessly, he scuffed his way up the brick walk and let himself in the back door.

The house was silent; it was the Pardoes' night off. The narrow hall that ran between the stairs on one side, dining room and parlor on the other, was usually shadowed until it reached the front door. But not tonight. Tonight, a square of light from the parlor fell out across the black and white tiles. Frowning, Nathan headed down the hall, his heels ringing hollowly in the confined space.

"Who's there?" he called, approaching the archway.

It was the green banker's lamp beside the gray velvet sofa that was lighted, and his eyes swept the large, high-ceilinged room from fireplace to piano, checking all the groupings of chairs in between.

"Hello, son. I have to talk to you."

Nat Rushton was sitting in one of the winged, yellow-brocaded chairs at the end of the sofa where the light was weakest. He'd lost so much weight, spare flesh hung in folds from the once square jowls, and his eyes were dull and ringed with dark circles. My God! Nathan thought, feeling his way into the opposite chair. It's only been a few weeks since I last saw him. What's happened to him?

"Wh—what is it?" he heard himself stammer.

Instead of answering, Nat folded his thick-knuckled hands atop his cane—a new item, Nathan noted—and looked around him. "First time I've been here." His voice was threadier, lighter. "You did a nice job, son."

Nathan blinked and forced himself into the small talk. "Thanks. It was a labor of love," he couldn't help adding.

His father's eyes swung back to his with their old sharpness. "You're never going to forgive me for that, are you?"

Forgive? Nathan shifted uncomfortably. Was he asking for forgiveness?

"You know the girl could have proven me wrong? She could've told me to go to hell, and married you anyway. Nothing said she had to—"

"All right! all right! Why are we going over all this again, anyway?"

"I just want you to understand, to admit—if just to yourself—that she wasn't good enough for you. She could've taken a chance on you, and didn't."

Nathan chewed the inside of his lip and waited.

Nat searched his son's face in silence for a second, then cleared his throat. "Your mother and I . . . ours wasn't a love match, either. And we didn't have the happiest of marriages, at least not in the beginning. I was just getting Rushton Enterprises started back then—and she was pretty lonely." One hand left the cane in a palsied gesture. "There was this young preacher, who—"

Nathan shot to his feet. "Is this what you wanted to talk to me about? You came all the way out here to tell me my mother was an adulteress? Well, I don't want to hear it, I tell you! I don't want to hear it!"

"Son, son . . . sit down. Please."

His insides a knot of jagged, cutting edges, Nathan stared at his father, then jammed his fingers into the back of his waistband, and began to pace. "Just say what you have to say. There was this preacher *and?*"

"And I used to come home to find him with your mother a lot. Oh, nothing to raise any eyebrows, just playing cards or drinking out of those fancy little teacups. At first I was grateful—at least she was happy—but then I became jealous. I told that little worm to stay the hell away from my wife."

"And did he?"

Nat nodded. "I never saw him again. After that,

Meg and I had some pretty good times together. But then I got distracted with business again, and . . . Well, when your mother told me she was pregnant with your brother, I got suspicious. We fought horribly. I accused her of . . . of being with the preacher. She swore it wasn't true, and God knows, I wanted to believe her, but . . . Anyway, things were never the same after that. But I still loved her, more than ever, I think."

"Did you ever tell her that?" Nathan asked, then bit his lip when he saw his father's figure dwindle even further in his clothes.

"No. No, I never got the chance. She died in childbirth, you know."

"I remember."

"Yes, that's right. You were old enough to remember, weren't you? I felt so cheated, son—and looking at your brother, I still could never be sure that—"

"Oh, for God's sake! Teddy looks just like me, and *I* look just like *you!*"

Something like a smile tugged at Nat's mouth. "That's what Pen always said, too."

Nathan sighed, dropped down on the sofa, and ground the heels of his hands into burning eyes. "Why are you telling me all this?"

"Life is short, son. Don't waste a precious moment of it. I made a terrible mistake with your mother, but I thought I had all the time in the world to fix it. Don't do what I did. Don't make the same mistake with Amanda."

"I'm not you."

"Maybe you are more than you think. Go back to her, son. Give it another chance."

Nathan lifted his head, letting his hands dangle between his knees. "Mind your own business."

MATTERS OF THE HEART 331

For an instant, there was a flash of the old Nat in the tightening of the jaw. "So how's business these days?" he asked, abruptly. "Mac stopped by to see me the other day, and said what a good job you'd done."

Maybe it was just the greenish glow from the lamp making him look sick, Nathan thought, seeing the same stubborn profile. "He *should* be happy. I went several thousand over budget and didn't charge him."

Nat's chuckle was dry. "Never let your customers take your guilt to the bank, son."

Nathan smiled. "I'll try and remember that."

"What kind of construction jobs you got coming up?"

"Oh, I got a couple of bids in on some city projects."

"Yeah? Whoever gets the one to build the Mount Royal Pumping Station will get a real feather in his cap—not to mention the hefty profit."

All of the old warning bells started going off in Nathan's head again. "Yeah, so I've heard." What was he pulling this time?

"You put in a bid?"

Nathan nodded.

"Of course, the winning bidder's already been selected, but it won't be announced until Monday."

Nathan nodded again, his jaw muscles beginning to jump.

"You do realize I still have some friends in high places, don't you? Some strings I can pull between now and then? It'll take some doing, of course, but I can get that contract for you."

"If?"

Nat let the silence hang for a second. "If you go back to Amanda."

"And if I don't?"

Thinning shoulders shrugged. "I'll let it ride, and you won't get it."

"Good God! I don't believe this, I don't believe you." He threw his arms over the back of the sofa and laughed. "You never give up, do you? You never know when to quit, when to let go. Well, you know what you can do with your 'influence,' because I"—he jabbed a thumb into his own chest for emphasis—"I am the one who already got that bid! They told me yesterday. Me, I got it all by myself, without your help."

Neither man said anything for a moment, and Nathan waited, jaw clenched, for the next push.

It never came.

Instead, Nat's eyes suddenly crinkled and a smile played over his lips. "It's about time."

His son just stared at him.

"Why didn't you ever sell this place?" Nat asked him abruptly. "Was it just to keep the company—me—from seeing a profit from what I'd done?"

Wearily, Nathan nodded. This was the strangest conversation he'd ever had in his life. Had that been the whole point of this visit? To see if he was finally his own man? To see if the transfer of power was complete?

When his father levered himself shakily out of the chair, Nathan instinctively tried to help, but was waved away.

"I'd've done the same thing myself," was all Nat said, moving slowly across the rug to the door.

Nathan's hand dropped, and he stared at the floor, listening to his father's slow shuffle. "Dad . . ."

Nat stopped, but only half turned his head.

"I'd already planned on going back."

Amanda leaned over her dressing table, pulled a few

curls forward around her face, then met Sophie's pouty stare in the mirror. "Oh, Sophie, don't look like that. You always said things were going to work out. Well, I'm just helping them along a little."

"Don't care what you call it, it's chasing after a man—and it ain't ladylike."

Straightening up, Amanda snugged the netting of her gloves down between her fingers, smoothed the front of her caramel-colored skirt, and readjusted the tilt of her ribbon-, rose-, and bird-bedecked hat. "Well, I don't care what *you* call it. I haven't seen Nathan in three days, and I can't stand it anymore. I love him, don't you understand?"

The woman sniffed, pushing her broad nose from one side to the other with the corner of a huge linen handkerchief. "Might as well save my breath. You ain't gonna listen to me nohow."

Amanda grinned, then looked around her as one who's sure she's forgotten something. "Have I got everything? Oh! The picnic basket! Has Mary—"

"It's already out in the carriage, but I'm telling you—it's too late in the year for sitting on the ground."

"Will you quit worrying? I'll be fine." She leaned over, kissed the dark cheek, then sailed out the door with a twiddle of her fingers.

Passing the painting of Nathan's mother, she patted the gilt frame and smiled. "Don't you worry. Everything's going to work out just fine."

Outside, Bob helped her into the seat, clicked at the horses, and they were off.

It was a perfect autumn day—bright azure sky, warm sun, and cool air. The leaves were just beginning to turn, and the shadows beneath the trees had that faint blue cast. The tang of the season's first woodsmoke hung in the air and steeped pleasantly on the back of Amanda's tongue.

When Bob started to whistle, she puckered up and added her one breathy note in time to the beat until Bob screwed up his face in pain. "All right," she said, laughing. "I'll just listen—but do 'Captain Jinks,' will you?"

So "Captain Jinks" it was, then "Daisy Bell," "The Mulligan Guard," and "Li'l Liza Jane" ". . . way down south in Baltimo." They clip-clopped along at a lively pace. Still, Amanda found it hard not to urge the man to drive faster. By the time they reached the city, she was leaning forward in the boot as if to help steer them through the crowded streets. She fussed and fumed at everything that impeded their progress, even to the point of waving back a pedestrian trying to cross in front of them while loudly assigning his thinking processes to an unlikely portion of his anatomy. Bob's fit of choking did nothing to deter her, but the final turn onto Sharp Street and sight of the pink brick house did. Clamping her bottom lip between her teeth, she sat back abruptly.

What if Nathan wasn't home? What if he didn't want to see her? What if that's why he hadn't come by for three days? What if—

"We're here, ma'am." Bob halted them opposite the white marble steps, and reached behind her to bring the picnic hamper forward.

Staring at that black front door, she found her palms were suddenly sticky and it was hard to take a deep breath. *Don't be a coward, Amanda. What's the worst that can happen?* Before she could answer with a dozen terrible possibilities, she stepped down onto the pavement. "Wish me luck, Bob."

Handing down the basket, he winked at her. "I don't think you'll need any of that, ma'am—but if it'll

MATTERS OF THE HEART 335

make you feel better, you have the wish. Shall I wait?"

She glanced at the door. "You'd better, I suppose—in case he doesn't let me in." Amanda thought she heard him chuckle, but she was already heading for the lion's den, and didn't look back.

Setting down the basket, she took another deep breath and let the brass ring collide with the door.

Nothing.

Again.

Nothing.

Her hand was in midair for a third try when the knob rattled and the door swung inward.

Chapter 15

"Amanda!"

Oh, God! He's home! He looks glad to see me! He's . . . gorgeous. His round-tip collar and cuffs were fastened neatly, his watch chain glittered across the front of his dark trousers, and the pointed tips of his boots gleamed. Her heart fell. *He looks ready to go out.* "Am . . . I disturbing you?"

Nathan felt his own childish joy flood his face at the sight of her. Standing on his doorstep in swirls of ribbon and lace, she looked good enough to eat, a confection in colors of caramel, cream, and chocolate. "What? No! No, come in." He reached for her hand, disappointed when he could only feel the coarse crocheting of her glove, and drew her across the threshold. Without releasing her, he closed the door, then captured her other hand.

The angular, lumpy-haired figure of the housekeeper came into the corner of his vision, but he couldn't take his eyes from Amanda's.

"Oh, sir, I'm sorry. Had my hands in the wash water and—"

"It's all right, Mrs. Pardoe." His thumbs found the skin above the gloves. "Everything's . . . fine."

Neither of them noticed the woman's tactful withdrawal. Amanda was aware of nothing but the hot circles being rubbed into her wrists. Nathan was aware of nothing but a pair of parted lips.

"I've missed you," he said.

"I've missed you, too. It's been—"

"Three days." He nodded, eyes clouding. "I know. I'm sorry. My father came to see me. . . ."

She squeezed his hands. "How is he?"

"Not good. I—I think he's dying, Amanda."

"I know," she said softly.

An understanding that took away the need for words showed in her eyes and settled in his heart. His grip tightened. "Do you . . ."

Amanda watched the rise and fall of his chest—it was as if he'd just remembered to breathe—and waited. "Do I what?"

"Hmmm?" He blinked. "Oh. Do you . . . want to see the house?"

It was her turn to blink. "Sure. Fine. Whatever you want."

She did her best to concentrate on the drawing room, the dining room, and kitchen below—"an idea peculiar to Baltimore," he said—but as they began mounting the three flights of banistered stairs to the floors above, only the impressions of lemon-and-gray elegance remained. Her senses were more attuned to the warmth of his hand holding hers, of the swish of their clothing when they brushed through the narrow doorways together.

On the second floor, there was a cozy brick- and book-lined study, a marble and mahogany water closet, and a private parlor to the master suite. In the bedroom itself, Amanda rocked her shoes in the deep, gray pile of the rug while she looked around. There was something feminine in the peach tones and fancy gold-and-white furniture. Then it hit her. This place had been built for a woman. Another woman.

"Nathan?"

He was standing slightly behind her, but still had his fingers laced with hers. He pulled her back in the doorway beside him. "What?" he asked, leaning an arm on the frame above her head.

She could see the tiny, blue-black stubbles on his chin, and when the crinkles around his eyes relaxed, there was paler skin in the creases. She found herself breathing deeply for the scent of bay rum. She shook her head. She didn't have the courage to say it. Not yet. She looked at the bed and swallowed.

"You shouldn't be so impatient," he said under the brim of her hat near her ear.

She jumped and yanked her gaze away. "What?"

"I was just leaving when you arrived."

Her spirits plummeted.

"I was coming out to see you. Maybe bring you back into town for luncheon or—" Her gasp cut him off.

"The hamper!"

"The hamper?"

"The hamper. I thought we'd have a picnic together, and Mary packed us a lunch, but I left it on the porch."

He laughed, and tugged her back when she would have rushed off. "I'll get it," he said, still smiling. "One look at me, and you forgot your stomach, eh?"

She gave him a playful swat on the arm, but the humor left her as she followed him down the stairs. It didn't matter about the house. It didn't matter about anything except the squeeze of her heart whenever she thought of this man. He let go of her hand at the bottom of the steps, and headed for the door.

"Nathan, I love you."

He stopped, mid-stride.

"It doesn't matter if you don't love me—" At the

sight of his rigid back, she dropped her attention to her mesh-encased fingers, and began picking at the knotted tips. "Not any more. It's just that I had to tell you, and if you come back home, I promise to be a good wife and—" She was suddenly in his arms, caught up in a whirling bear hug, and he was laughing.

"Nathan! My ribs!" She wasn't really complaining.

The circles slowed to a feather-light return to earth, but his arms stayed wrapped around her, his voice muffled against her neck. "I just said you were impatient. I've thought of and discarded a hundred ways to tell you the same thing ever since you walked in the door."

Tears stung her eyes and nose, and she kneaded the muscles of his shoulders more to assure herself it was all real, it was all happening. He loved her! He loved her!

Now he pushed her away, rubbing frankly tear-rushed eyes with the heels of his hands. "Oh, God, Amanda." He took her face between his hands. "I love you, too . . . I love you, too." His kiss was hard, sure, and full of relief. "I *love* you."

Heavy sighs left them both feeling weak and weightless, and they clung together for support. He laid his cheek on top of her hat. She buried her nose in the warm hollow of his throat.

He loves me.

She loves me.

It started with her giggle, followed by his chuckle, and suddenly they were both laughing and staggering, neither one willing to give up their hold on the other. Finally, he steered them over to the staircase, and they both sank heavily onto the bottom step.

"Ohhh!" he groaned, dropping an arm around her shoulders.

"Whew!" she breathed, taking out a handkerchief, dabbing at her eyes, then handing it to him.

He took it and wiped his own eyes. "Well, are you ready for lunch, yet?"

"I think so."

"Good. I'm starved."

They went to Federal Hill, strolled around the perimeter, and looked down at the crowded harbor ringed with fingers of red wooden warehouses. They sat on the cannons the last war with England had left behind, and Amanda listened dutifully while Nathan tried to decide which gun Butler had turned on City Hall—with the mayor inside—during the War Between the States. She looked and listened, and tried to decide why it was she loved him so much, but there was never a reason. She just did.

And did he really love her? The waiting and hoping had become such a part of her life, it was hard to let go of it for fear she was wrong. But he had said he did, and she found the added confirmation she needed in the smiling glances of the people they passed. It was all true; everything he'd said was there in his face for the world to see. Like a bird on the wing, her hopes for their future soared.

"What are you smiling about?"

Fingers locked with his, she was forced to stop when he did. "Nothing. I'm just happy, that's all."

His eyes held hers with an intensity that made her heart pound. "That's all that matters to me."

She could have stood under the spell of those eyes forever, but like a bolt out of the blue, the realization hit her. He was courting her. He'd *been* courting her ever since he'd left! How could she have missed it?

Suddenly, she laughed and danced away. "Hey!" he protested, but never having been properly wooed and won, Amanda was determined to savor every nuance, every look and gesture the chase brought. "Hay is for horses!" she called, and after that, whenever his gaze or his words turned too serious, she tweaked his nose and skipped away, confident he would follow. When he tried to draw her into his embrace, she would slip from his grasp, and as if understanding her need to play it through, he would let her go.

He chased her around the maypole, pushed her on the swings, and made her squeal on the seesaw, but finally he complained, "Woman, I'm hungry. Feed me."

Sophie was right. The ground was cool, and they were the only picnickers in the park, but that was fine with Amanda as she spread the red and white checked cloth on the ground and began setting out the food. Only once, when she was unpacking the chicken, did her mind stray to another picnic with another Rushton.

"I'll be dead of neglect at this rate," Nathan said over her shoulder, pulling things out of the basket himself.

After that, his attentions grew more and more insistent. Still, she found ways to put a pickle into an outstretched hand, or a forkful of cake into a seeking mouth. But when every last crumb was gone, and he was flat on his back, eyeing her over the carnage, she knew her game was nearly at an end.

Knees up, he drummed his stomach and groaned. "I'm stuffed."

"Me, too."

He drew out his watch, and tucked his chin down to look at it. "It's almost five. It'll be dark soon."

She nodded. Even now, the trees were casting long, cool shadows across the grass.

"Amanda?"

She looked over and found him staring at her, hand

stretched across the cloth, palm up. Tonight would be the start of something new for them, something special and long denied, but she was loathe to rush it. She got to her feet. "Better start packing up." She tried to move away, but found she couldn't. Nathan had a fistful of her hem and wouldn't let go.

"What are you doing?" he asked, only a wedge of bright blue showing amid a squint of dark lashes.

"Doing?"

"Yes, doing. You haven't let me kiss you; you've hardly let me touch you all afternoon. Why? Changed your mind about loving me?"

"No, of course not! I'm just playing hard . . . to . . ." she stopped, blushing hotly.

"Get?" he finished. Laughter rumbled in his chest. "You don't play hard to get after you tell a man you love him, goose! Because—" he smacked her behind the knees, caught her, and rolled her to the ground beneath him, "you're already caught!"

"My hat!" she squealed as the item hit the ground and rolled away.

"Forget it. It's ugly anyway. Can't stand a hat that looks back at me."

She laughed, but strained for it just the same, becoming a series of little points beneath him—nose, chin, shoulders, breasts—and Nathan dropped his head to plant a kiss on the exposed point of a collar bone. He growled when she struggled, her gasp pushing her harder against him.

"Nathan! People will see!"

He raised his head. "And what will they think?"

"Why, they'll . . . they'll think . . ."

He leaned down, nipped her ear, and whispered, "That we're making love?"

She shivered, and he rolled over, pulling her with

him until she was the one on top, knees straddling his hips, her skirts frothing all around them.

"Is that better? Wonder what they'll think now?"

She laughed and pushed at his chest. "That you're crazy, and I need rescuing."

"Over my dead body." But he let her up, and while she shook her skirts back into shape, he bundled everything back into the wicker hamper.

Night was bleeding violet hues into the sunset by the time it was all packed and she had her hat back.

Basket handles over his arm, he took her hand. "Shall we go have dessert?"

Her eyes widened. "Dessert?"

"I'm hungry." He wasn't talking about food.

"Me, too." And neither was she.

William heard the knock on the back door, but finished reading the "The Future of Horse Racing in Maryland" before closing the paper and getting up.

Going to the window, he peered through the glass, then opened the door. "Yes?" he inquired. "Who is it?"

"It's me," Bob snapped, "and you damned well know it. I caught this fellow " he snatched into the light the person whose collar he held firmly in one meaty fist, "skulking around out here."

"I wanna see Amanda," the captive slurred. "I wanna see Mrs. Rushton."

William eyed the unkempt, whiskey-reeking person being dangled on the doorstep, and arched a thin brow. "Hello, Mr. Rushton. Mrs. Rushton is not at home."

Teddy made an uncoordinated grab for William's lapel, but found himself yanked away like a marionette.

"Here now . . . sir," Bob cautioned uncomfortably.

"Let go of me! Let go!" The loose end of a cuff protruded from his jacket sleeve as he tried to slap away the hand that held him. "You people have been keeping me away from her for weeks, and I—I demand to see her. Mandy!" he bellowed desperately over the butler's shoulder. "Mandy . . . please!"

A small wave of pity for the heartsick youngster was all that kept William from telling Bob to find the nearest gutter in which to deposit their visitor. "It's the truth, Mr. Rushton. She's not here. She's in town with your brother." There. Maybe now he'll get the message, and stop torturing them along with himself, he thought.

Teddy's bleary eyes focused briefly. "She's gone . . . with him?"

"Yes, sir."

Tears filled the reddened rims of his eyes, but he didn't say anything else. *She's gone with him . . . she's gone with him. . . .*

Bob cleared his throat. "What should I do with him?"

"Put him in the buckboard and drive him home."

"Don't have a home," Teddy mumbled. "No home. Jus' an old hotel room."

Bob raised questioning eyebrows, and William nodded. "Take him wherever he's been staying, then."

Nathan pulled the carriage up to the curb in front of the townhouse and climbed down. As he handed her down beside him, his fingers tightened. "Amanda. . . ."

On the bottom step, she turned to find her face on a level with his, and all thought of being coy vanished as she came face to face with the honest desire in his eyes, desire she could no longer ignore. With the pink, trembling tip of her tongue, she reached out to moisten her upper lip.

Mesmerized by the sight, Nathan leaned toward her.

Their lips had no more than met when a man walking his dog rounded the corner, and they broke apart.

Smiling at the frustration on Nathan's face, she took his hand, and tugged him up the steps and inside.

The chill of the September night still clung to their clothes as he pushed the wrap from her shoulders and let it fall to the floor, concerned only with drawing her closer. Lacing his fingers in the silky hair at the nape of her neck, his thumbs traced her jawline as he tilted her face up to his.

Parched with need, she closed her eyes and stood gratefully under the rain of his kisses. He kissed her eyes, the prominent thrust of each cheekbone, across the bridge of her nose and down to the corner of her mouth, where the stroke of his tongue jolted her like a hot current of electricity.

"Mr. Rushton?"

He lifted his head with a groan. It was Mrs. Pardoe.

Pulling Amanda with him, he ducked out of the gaslit foyer into the darkened front room. There she turned to meet his kisses with an eagerness that matched his own, her body arched into his, and they became souls straining at the barriers of flesh, flesh at the barriers of clothing.

"Mr. Rushton?" Mrs. Pardoe's voice sounded hesitant as the doorway was brightened by the aura of an oil lamp.

He started to pull away, but Amanda's arms held him fast. "Yes?" he called. He tried to make his voice sound normal, but decided he hadn't succeeded when the woman came no closer.

"Is there anything else you need before I leave?"

Mouthing the word *me,* Amanda giggled, and he pulled her face into his shirtfront against the huff of his own laughter. "No—yes! I left the carriage out front.

Tell Pete to take care of it before he leaves for the night."

"Yes, sir. Good night, sir."

Amanda had found the ticklish spot on his ribs. "Ha—good night, Mrs. Pardoe."

As the light receded and the woman's steps faded toward the back, Nathan sighed and leaned them back against the wall.

"Don't you ever give those people a day off?" Amanda whispered.

"As a matter of fact, they have off tomorrow."

"Really?"

His lips brushed her forehead. "Really."

Smiling, she looped her arms around his neck. "Then how about if I come back, and we have dinner here tomorrow night?"

"Dinner, hell," he murmured against her lips. "Breakfast."

They stood together in front of the mirror. Nathan was buttoning his collar. Amanda was spearing a long amethyst-headed pin through the crown of her hat. She liked this shared domesticity of getting dressed in the morning together.

He caught her smile and winked at her. "Piglet," he accused.

"Piglet!" Glowing green eyes were at variance with the indignant pout on her lips. "Who are you calling a piglet?"

"You!" He scooped her up, and she giggled as he made little snorting noises up and down the side of her throat. "It was a greedy little piglet that kept me up all night."

"Ha! I think you've got that backward."

Snuggling her close against his chest, he was quickly serious. "Maybe you're right," he murmured, brushing parted lips across her mouth before crushing them in a kiss that stirred memories for both of them.

Caught in a shaft of sunlight, they were like lovers everywhere, curved in the tangled pose, the eternal symbol of man and woman.

With a gasp that hurt his chest, Nathan pulled his head back. If he didn't stop now, he wouldn't be able to. "I have to go," he said. "But are you sure you don't want me to drive you?"

She shook her head, feeling the letdown reality always brought with it. "No, I can get a hack to take me." She chewed her lip, watching him stretch his neck and do his tie. "You like your work, don't you, Nathan?"

"I like to build things, to start with nothing and end up with something."

Like this? Like us? "What about after they're built?"

The blue eyes left their task in the mirror to meet hers. "I don't know. I just enjoy them, I suppose. Why?"

She shrugged and picked up her gloves from the peach coverlet.

"Hey," he said, taking her by the shoulders. "I'm not going to lose interest, if that's what you're afraid of. I like my work, but I *love* you."

Reassured by his knowing what was in her thoughts, she relaxed, toying with a button on his shirt. "I know."

"Are you sure you don't want me to—"

"Yes, I'm sure. I'm just being a spoiled baby, that's all. Now you'd better go."

Taking her face between his hands, he kissed her again, slowly, lingeringly, until she sighed. "Tonight," he promised.

Her hand firmly in his, she obediently followed him out into the hall. The word *tonight* had a wonderful sound to it, but a sudden wave of impishness made her pull away. "How do you know I'll show up again?"

His answer, that of picking up her hand and straightening the fingers, puzzled her at first—until she saw the bright gold band he was sliding onto her finger. "This is how," he said.

She stared at the glimmering metal behind a sudden mist of tears. *"Oh . . . Nathan. . . ."* A wedding ring, a symbol of love, he'd called it. Raising her head, she could only stare at him in shocked silence.

Reaching out a finger, he caught a single tear drop just as it fell. "I swear to you, Amanda, that's the last tear you'll ever shed because of me." His voice shook, and she could see the emotions in his face warring for control.

She laid a hand against his chest, but as if her touch burned him, he snatched her fingers away and held them to his lips.

"Tonight," he stressed huskily. "Go home and pack whatever you need, and we'll have a few days of honeymoon here."

Watching him bound down the stairs and out the front door, she smiled, and shook her head. "Oh, you'll make me cry again, Nathan Rushton, I just know it." She glanced down at the band on her finger. It was such a little thing to want. "But I'll love you, anyway."

She was just closing the front door and turning around into the early morning sun when a hand shot through the black railing and grabbed a handful of her skirt.

"You had to go and do it, didn't you?"

"Teddy! My God! You scared—"

"You had to let him"—he struggled to his feet beside the steps—"have it all, didn't you? Now he's got everything—the business, the money, *you*." He let go of her skirt as if it was tainted.

She reached down to touch his unshaven cheek. "Teddy, what's happened? You look—"

He jerked his head away, but his fingers clamped hard on her wrist and pulled her down the steps to face him. "Awful? Terrible? Like I've spent the night out here in the street watching the two of you together up there?"

The whites of his eyes were laced with red, he looked and smelled as if he hadn't changed clothes in days, and the grip he had on her was frighteningly strong. "Watching us!"

"I loved you," he shouted, "and you betrayed me!"

The street was empty, and there wasn't a face at any of the windows. She tried to twist her wrist free. "I never betrayed you! There was nothing to betray. I love Nathan, don't you understand? If you don't stop doing this to yourself, to me, you'll destroy us all, Teddy, you'll destroy us all. Now let go!" To her surprise, he started to, his fingers sliding down to capture her hand. Then he felt the ring.

"Well, well, well," he sneered, holding her hand up, turning her finger to catch the sunlight. "So he decided to make it official, did he?" He twisted the band roughly. "I ought to kill him."

Fear lent her strength, and she yanked her hand free. "And I still won't love you! I'll still love Nathan and I'll hate you forever!"

Before he could do or say anything else, she was running, sobbing, her wooden heels striking the cobbles like stones. *Aunt Pen . . . Aunt Pen . . . I have to get to Aunt Pen!*

She didn't look back. She didn't see the pain on his face as he just stood there, looking after her.

* * *

"Child, child!" Pen thumped her cane on the drawing room carpet. "Stop that sniveling. I can't understand a word. Take another sip of brandy, and compose yourself."

After unballing her handkerchief and blowing her nose, Amanda obeyed, holding the miniature snifter in both trembling hands. She had run for blocks before flagging down a hack, barely managing to convince the driver she wasn't a raving lunatic. "I'm s—sorry."

"Pffft!" A hand waved away the apology. "Percy?" Twisting first one way, then the other in the red Napoleon chair, Pen looked for the butler who had been standing by with the brandy tray.

"Yes, mum?" He stepped from directly behind her.

"You can go now. I'll call if I need you."

The man nodded, then heel-and-toed it through the fringed archway.

As soon as he was gone, Pen turned her attention back to Amanda. "Are you better now?"

Amanda nodded and took a deep, shuddering breath. "What I said was Teddy was outside the townhouse all night—"

"Yes, yes. I heard all that. It's the part afterward."

Tears welled afresh, but Amanda brushed them away quickly. "Oh, he looked so d—dreadful, Aunt Pen. I mean he slept out in the street or on the sidewalk or something."

"So?"

"So? So I feel . . . responsible somehow."

"I see. You make the decisions on where he'll sleep then?"

"No, but—"

"But nothing. Teddy's a grown man, even if he isn't acting like one. When you get to be my age, you learn not to take on unnecessary guilt. The world is all too eager to give you more than your share as it is."

Amanda started to protest, but Pen waved her quiet. "Don't worry. I'll talk to his father about taking him back in. It's obvious he's not doing well on his own . . . but surely that isn't why you're so upset . . . is it?"

Amanda swallowed, the fear clawing its way back with remembered words. "He said he'd kill Nathan."

The old eyes didn't flicker. "Oh, Teddy wouldn't hurt a fly! He's just distraught—and, if I know my Rushtons, he had too much to drink besides."

Amanda looked down at the snifter she clutched in her lap, and gingerly set it away from her on the marble-topped table.

With a rustle of black taffeta, Pen leaned forward, poured herself a cup of coffee from the silver service, then sat back and peered at Amanda over the rim of her cup. "But speaking of someone who's been in the same clothing for days—you're all grass-stained and wrinkled. I take it you and Nathan spent the night at the townhouse?"

"I—we . . ." She nodded, feeling herself blush. "I took him a picnic lunch yesterday."

"That's a girl! That's the ticket—run 'em down, if you have to!" She shook a knobby fist in the air, and Amanda giggled. After another sip of coffee, she asked, "Are things better between the two of you now?"

"I think so." Taking a last swipe at her eyes, she held out her left hand. "See?"

Fumbling for the eyepiece that hung from her neck on a long black ribbon, Pen brought it up and peered dutifully at the gold band. "Lovely, child, lovely. I'm happy for you. I'll have to admit, though, when Natty told me Nathan had moved into town, I was beginning to have my doubts about how it was all going to turn out." Putting down her cup, she struggled unsteadily to her feet. "Can't sit still for too long. Arthritis makes these old bones stiffen up," she muttered. She stumped around her chair, then stopped to stare out the velvet-draped window for a second.

When the snowy head tilted in her direction again, Amanda was struck anew by the vitality in the woman's eyes.

"So where was Nathan during all of this?"

"He went to work. I'm supposed to go home and pack some clothes, and we're going to have a real honeymoon."

"Good, good." Pen nodded her approval, then sighed in vicarious fulfillment.

Amanda smiled, then dropped her attention to her handkerchief as a darker thought intruded. "Aunt Pen?"

"Hmmm?"

"Is . . . Nathan's father dying?"

Pen's bosom rose sharply, then fell. "Yes."

"That's what we thought. That's why he forced this marriage, isn't it?"

"Yes."

Amanda looked up. "Does Teddy know—about his father, I mean?"

"No."

"Too bad."

There was a moment of silent agreement, then after another glance out the window, Pen waved Amanda to her feet. "Well, go home, dear. Pack, bathe, primp for a few hours, then come back and start a new life, eh? Percy!" she called. "And don't worry about this morning. I'll take care of everything," she promised as the butler glided back through the fringe.

On impulse, Amanda hugged the frail body and kissed the dry cheek. "Thank you, Aunt Pen. I'm not sure why, but I do feel better somehow."

"Good. Now Percy will see you out—no, dear. Go the back way, will you? I'm having the front gate painted."

Puzzled, Amanda allowed herself to be waved toward the back of the house. She didn't remember any painters.

"When you're through there, Percy," she heard the woman add, "come back to me here."

Pen waited until their steps faded, then went to the rosewood secretary in the corner, dipped a pen in the pot of ink, and scribbled something on a small sheet of vellum. She was staring out the window, folding the paper absently, when Percy returned.

"Go ask the young man by the front gate to come in. If he won't"—without looking around, she held out the note—"give him this."

A moment later, she nudged the fringed edge of the curtain aside for a better view of the pantomime taking place. As expected, the young man gestured violently, shaking his head. She couldn't hear the words, but she could guess them. When the note was offered, he hesitated before taking it, then waited until Percy was halfway up the walk again before opening it.

She held her breath.

The paper trembled, a spot of blinding white in the sunlight. When he sank slowly to the sidewalk, cross-legged like a child, and rocked, his shoulders shaking visibly, Pen's eyes flooded. "I'm sorry, Teddy . . . I'm so sorry."

"Damn it, Penny!" Nat slammed the desk with an open palm. "You had no right to tell him!"

"Desperate times call for desperate measures. Nathan and Amanda needed protection, and Teddy needed to be forced to do some growing up. He's your son. He has a right to know how ill you are. Nathan's already guessed." Pen leaned across the desk and squeezed her brother's hand. "Give Teddy another chance, Natty."

Nat pulled his hand away. "I can't. Don't ask it of me."

Pen sighed, but before she could offer another argument, Chester knocked on the study door and entered.

He regarded them a bit uncertainly. "Pardon the interruption, but—"

The door was pushed out of his grasp. "But I'd like to come in."

Pen caught her breath. It was Teddy. He'd shaved and changed into a neat brown suit, and his hair was still damp and slicked down from a recent bath.

His eyes flicked over his father, then came back to her. "May I see my father . . . alone for a few minutes?"

She was on her feet, stopping him in his tracks with her cane on the middle of his chest. "Now see here, young man. If you've come here to cause trouble, I won't have it. I won't have you upsetting him any more."

"I promise I'm not here to cause trouble, Auntie." His eyes looked tired, older. "Please?"

She tried to gauge his intentions, but couldn't read anything in the steady gaze. "All right," she relented, "but I'll be right outside this door, and if I hear any shouting, I'll march back in here and toss you out on your ear."

"Yes, ma'am," he said meekly—but held open the door.

He waited for her and Chester to leave before looking at his father. The old man's expression was guarded and truculent. Nothing new there, he thought.

"I . . . I've come to say good-bye."

Surprise flickered across his father's face.

Teddy swallowed and scuffed at the gold patterns in the carpet. "I just can't stay around here and watch . . . watch her with him." Giving into the nervous tension, he paced over to the fireplace, fingered one of the sword hilts, then moved away again. "I know what you always thought—that I wanted Amanda just because she was Nathan's, but that wasn't it at all. I really did love her . . . do love her. That's why I can't stay here anymore."

"I understand."

"Do you? Oh, that's right. You had to watch Amanda's mother with Fred Alton, didn't you?" There'd been no attempt to soften the words, and now he met his father's eyes squarely. "You should have fought for her if you loved her that much."

Nat sighed tiredly. "Why? She loved him, not me."

Teddy looked away. "Yeah."

"Besides," Nat went on, "if I'd married Emily, I would have missed marrying your mother."

"Oh, right. And you loved her a lot, I'll bet."

"Yes, I did. Very much. Very, very much."

There was no doubting the honesty of those words, and Teddy felt some of his pain ebb. "Thanks," he whispered. "You know"—he blinked and cleared his throat—"I realized, more than anything else, I've always wanted your approval, your love. Isn't that funny?"

The silence stretched while the two men looked at each other. Finally, Nat's face folded into lines of pain.

"I'm sorry, son."

Feeling a curious kind of release, Teddy heaved a sigh and shook his head. "No, I'm the one who's sorry." He headed for the door.

"Son. . . ."

Teddy stopped and looked around. "Yes?"

"Here." Nat fumbled through some papers on his desk. "Let me give you some money."

"I don't want your money."

"But what will you live on?"

"I still have some of the other left. After that's gone . . ." He shrugged. "Who knows? I might try a novel approach, and earn my living. Hard to imagine, isn't it?" He waited, but nothing else was said. "Well. . . ." He held out a hand, his bottom lip tightened so hard, his chin showed little white dimples. "I guess this is good-bye. Take care of yourself . . . sir."

Nat gripped his son's hand hard, then coughed and looked away, leaving Teddy to openly run a sleeve across his eyes.

When the door closed, Nat slumped heavily in his chair. *I do love you, son.*

Pen had been pacing irritably in the hall, and when she saw Teddy, she stopped and leaned on her cane, waiting for him to come closer. "Well?" she prompted.

He shook his head. "I'm leaving, Aunt Pen. There's nothing for me here, and hasn't been for a long time. I realize that now. I can't stay around and watch them and I can't . . . stay and watch this, either."

"He'll need you now."

"He's got you."

The old blue gaze swept his face, probing for secrets. "Teddy Rushton," she muttered, handing him her cane, "you're the spitting image of your father when he was this age—and there are a lot worse things you could be, you know." She was dusting off his lapels and retying his tie. "There. Now you take care of yourself because . . . because I love you."

* * *

Amanda and Nathan lay drowsily entwined in the big bed, the room and their bodies bathed in the molten, golden light of the fire. Mingled with the hiss and sigh of the flames, there was the soft hum, the occasional murmur of sated lovers as they nuzzled tender earlobes and stroked newly discovered flesh with wonder in their fingertips.

"You know," he said, voice rumbling low and soft as he smoothed a long curl around the curve of her breast, "we've never talked about children. How many do you think we should have?"

She slid him a look. "I don't know. I suppose it'll depend on whether or not your father's still offering that bonus."

He groaned and dropped his head onto her breast. "I said some pretty despicable things, didn't I?" he mumbled against her skin.

"Despicable," she agreed.

"My only defense," he looked up, eyes glowing more with mischief than penitence, "is that it was my only defense. So what's my punishment to be? Bread and water? Breaking rocks? Flogging?"

She giggled as she pulled him up for her kiss. "Flogging. Definitely flogging. . . ."

It was later, when she lay watching him sleep, a burnished copper giant in the dying light, that she heard the knock. At first, she thought she was imagining it, but when it came again, she rolled over to get Nathan's watch from the nightstand.

One-fifteen? Who in the world . . . ?

A sixth sense supplied the answer and made her fingers shake as she belted the peach silk wrapper and sped down the darkened steps. Down in the foyer, she fumbled for a lucifer, wincing at every noise, every clink of glass and brass it took to light the lamp beside the door. There couldn't be a fight, there just couldn't. Not between brothers.

The area flared with light, and she yanked open the door. "Teddy, please don't do this!"

"Shhh," he said, laying a finger to his lips. "It's all right."

He wasn't drunk. He was neat and clean and dapper—if a little tired looking—once again. Her fear subsided a bit.

"I just came to say good-bye."

Her glance fell on the carpetbag in his hand. "Good-bye? Where are you going?"

"I don't know. There's a lot of country out there, a lot to see."

They were both whispering, and now she shivered with the brush of night air.

"I'm sorry if I hurt you, Amanda. I know I must've frightened you this morning. I'm sorry for a lot of things, including myself." The lamplight picked up little points in his eyes. "But I have to know—why him . . . and not me?"

"Oh, Teddy . . ." She hugged herself. "I don't know. We don't choose who we love. It just happens."

"No, I suppose we don't. If I had it to do over again, I wouldn't choose to fall in love with my brother's wife. But I did . . . and I do."

She shifted uncomfortably, and looked down at her toes curling against the cool tiles.

He made a face. "I'm sorry." There was a breath of laughter. "Again."

She smiled, then caught the expression in Teddy's eyes, and looked around. Nathan was barreling down the steps, buttoning trousers and shirt as he came.

"What the hell are you doing here?" he growled.

Amanda tried to put herself between them. "Nathan, please, he's just—"

MATTERS OF THE HEART 359

He pushed her aside, but came up against Teddy's hand in the middle of his chest.

"Whoa, slow down, big brother. I've come to say good-bye, that's all."

Jaw still hardened and ready for a fight, Nathan backed up until the hand fell. "Yeah? Where you going?" he asked suspiciously.

"West."

The two men stared eye to eye, and when Teddy finally extended his hand, it was left out there for a long moment before Nathan gripped it with his own.

"You take care of her—"

Amanda felt Nathan's fingers dig into her arm when Teddy leaned down to kiss her cheek.

"—or I'll come back and beat the hell out of you." He grinned crookedly at them, settled the derby more firmly on his head, then went down the steps.

Amanda sank back against Nathan's chest, and he wrapped his arms around her. Together they stood in the doorway, watching Teddy pass through a pool of lamplight, then into darkness.

She sighed and nestled closer into her husband's warmth. "Do you think he'll be all right?" she asked, feeling the heavy sigh as he rubbed his chin along the top of her head.

"Somehow I think he'll be just fine."

She glanced down. Propped against the doorsill, the ebony frog grinned up at them. "His cane! He forgot his cane."

"I don't think he needs it anymore. He's standing on his own two feet."

Her sight suddenly blurred behind a rush of tears, and Amanda turned into Nathan's embrace. "Oh, Nathan!" she whispered. "I love you!"

Understanding the fierceness in her words, he tightened his arms around her. They had come so close to losing each other, and now . . . now they had all the time in the world. "I love you, too. I always have."

Together they climbed the stairs, and with the silent, mutual consent of those who have come to know the fragile, tenuous thread called love, they held vigil over the remaining hours of night.

As the first light of dawn slanted through their room, they knew it was more than just the start of a new day. It was a new beginning. There was much to learn, much to forgive and forget, but as they sat and watched the sun come up, they held each other close, speaking of love and planning a better, brighter future together . . . always together.

MAYO LUCAS

The daughter of a Renaissance woman and an air force pilot, MAYO Marcella Cochran LUCAS spent her childhood "in the backseat of a '58 Ford," as her family moved around the country. Currently she lives in Baltimore with her husband, son, and her computer, which she counts as a member of the family even before her cat. Mayo started writing at an early age, doing terrible saga-length episodes of her favorite TV westerns. A goal-oriented person, Mayo is a happy woman who eats up life—and spits out the bones!

Attention Aspiring Writers!

AVON BOOKS
accepts all unsolicited manuscripts for consideration. Please send your work to:

**EDITORIAL DEPARTMENT
AVON BOOKS
105 Madison Ave.
New York, N.Y. 10016**

Avon Books cannot be responsible for materials sent to us. We will not return the material to you.

AVON BOOKS
The Hearst Corporation

Each month enjoy the best...

THE AVON ROMANCE

in exceptional authors and unforgettable novels!

HOSTAGE HEART　　Eileen Nauman
75420-7/$3.95US/$4.95 Can

RECKLESS SPLENDOR　　Maria Greene
75441-x/$3.95US/$4.95 Can

HEART OF THE HUNTER　　Linda P. Sandifer
75421-5/$3.95US/$4.95 Can

MIDSUMMER MOON　　Laura Kinsale
75398-7/$3.95US/$4.95 Can

STARFIRE　　Judith E. French
75241-7/$3.95US/$4.95 Can

BRIAR ROSE　　Susan Wiggs
75430-4/$3.95US/$4.95 Can

Buy these books at your local bookstore or use this coupon for ordering:

Avon Books, Dept BP, Box 767, Rte 2, Dresden, TN 38225
Please send me the book(s) I have checked above. I am enclosing $_____
(please add $1.00 to cover postage and handling for each book ordered to a maximum of three dollars). *Send check or money order*—no cash or C.O.D.'s please. Prices and numbers are subject to change without notice. Please allow six to eight weeks for delivery.

Name _____
Address _____
City _____ State/Zip _____

AvRomF 2/88

If you enjoyed this book, take advantage of this special offer. Subscribe now and...

GET A *FREE* HISTORICAL ROMANCE

NO OBLIGATION (a $3.95 value)

Each month the editors of True Value will select the four best historical romance novels from America's leading publishers. Preview them in your home Free for 10 days. And we'll send you a FREE book as our introductory gift. No obligation. If for any reason you decide not to keep them, just return them and owe nothing. But if you like them you'll pay *just* $3.50 each and save at least $.45 each off the cover price. (Your savings are a minimum of $1.80 a month.) There is no shipping and handling or other hidden charges. There are no minimum number of books to buy and you may cancel at any time.

send in the coupon below

Mail to:
True Value Home Subscription Services, Inc.
P.O. Box 5235
120 Brighton Road
Clifton, New Jersey 07015-5235

YES! I want to start previewing the very best historical romances being published today. Send me my FREE book along with the first month's selections. I understand that I may look them over FREE for 10 days. If I'm not absolutely delighted I may return them and owe nothing. Otherwise I will pay the low price of just $3.50 each; a total of $14.00 (at least a $15.80 value) and save at least $1.80. Then each month I will receive four brand new novels to preview as soon as they are published for the same low price. I can always return a shipment and I may cancel this subscription at any time with no obligation to buy even a single book. In any event the FREE book is mine to keep regardless.

Name _____

Address _____ Apt. _____

City _____ State _____ Zip _____

Signature _____
(if under 18 parent or guardian must sign)

Terms and prices subject to change.

75537-8A